One Vacant Chair

□ □ □

OTHER BOOKS BY JOE COOMER

One Vacant Chair

JOE COOMER

Graywolf Press
SAINT PAUL, MINNESOTA

Publication of this volume is made possible in part by a grant provided by the Minnesota State Arts Board, through an appropriation by the Minnesota State Legislature; a grant from the Wells Fargo Foundation Minnesota; and a grant from the National Endowment for the Arts, which believes that a great nation deserves great art. Significant support has also been provided by the Bush Foundation; Target; the McKnight Foundation; and other generous contributions from foundations, corporations, and individuals. To these organizations and individuals we offer our heartfelt thanks.

This book is made possible through a partnership with the College of Saint Benedict, and honors the legacy of S. Mariella Gable, a distinguished teacher at the College. Support has been provided by the Lee and Rose Warner Foundation as part of the Warner Reading Program.

Published by Graywolf Press
2402 University Avenue, Suite 203
Saint Paul, Minnesota 55114
All rights reserved.

www.graywolfpress.org

Published in the United States of America

Printed in Canada

ISBN 978-1-55597-514-2

2 4 6 8 9 7 5 3 1

Cloth Edition: ISBN 978-1-55597-385-8

Library of Congress Control Number: 2008928255

Cover design: Christa Schoenbrodt, Studio Haus

for Isa

Those painters who have best understood the art of producing a good effect, have adopted one principle that seems perfectly conformable to reason; that a part may be sacrificed for the good of the whole. Thus, whether the masses consist of light or shadow, it is necessary that they should be compact and of a pleasing shape; to this end, some parts may be made darker and some lighter, and reflexions stronger than nature would warrant. Paul Veronese took great liberties of this kind. It is said, that being once asked, why certain figures were painted in shade, as no cause was seen in the picture itself; he turned off the enquiry by answering, "una nuevola che passa," a cloud is passing which has overshadowed them.

□□□ Sir Joshua Reynolds,
Discourses on Art,
from Discourse VIII

Still Life
□ □ □

PERHAPS OUR LIVES ARE SUSTAINED by a suspense of dying. There are things I know and things I don't know and everything else is in between. Grandma Hutton called Aunt Edna to her deathbed and then decided to linger for twenty-two years. She measured her life with spoons, the brimming spoons of medicine or milk or soup that my aunt balanced with a painter's sure grip over her own cupped palm, her free hand mimicking in form and movement the dull spoon's bowl, her arm the narrow handle. My grandmother, for the last few years of her life, answered the telephone as if she were standing at the mouth of a dark cave, halooing for a lost soul. When someone answered she was always taken aback. That's how we talked to her at last, by phone, everyone but Aunt Edna. Then the family returned to Fort Worth for the funeral like separate drops of condensing water pooling in the bowl of a cold spoon, a last offering to an old dead woman none of us cared for. That's not true. Aunt Edna missed her.

We began by carrying the chairs out to the vacant lot next to the house. The old house was full of chairs, to the exclusion of almost all other furniture. This was my aunt Edna's collection.

"It's one thing men are good for," she said, shooing them away from the Saran-Wrapped food, "carrying chairs." She pulled a cane-seated, ladder-back chair away from the kitchen table, thrust it into my husband's arms, and said, "Out to the vacant lot. Everybody pick up a chair. I want evenly spaced rows with the chairs facing west so Brother Roberts is looking into the sun." Then she looked at me. "Sarah, you help me with Momma's chair. We'll put it up front next to the preacher and put her in it."

"You could leave it empty," my husband said. "It would be like one of those missing-pilot-formation flyovers."

It bothered me that I still thought Sam was funny. Someone you didn't respect shouldn't be able to make you smile.

Grandma's chair was overstuffed, rotund, a depression-era lounge chair covered in pale green mohair. It was some work to get it out of the bedroom, through the hallway and outside onto the porch, where we sat it back down to rest.

"Momma loved this old thing," Aunt Edna said.

"There's no good place to grab it," I huffed.

"It's got good lines."

"We should brush it off while it's outside. There's cat hair on the backside."

"It crossed Momma that her favorite chair was the cat's favorite chair, too. She'd hold her forearms up in the air after she sat down till I came and brushed the hair from the nap. I'd tell her the cat only sat in her chair because he loved her but the cat and I knew that was a lie."

"What happened to your cat, Aunt Edna?"

"Oh, I gave him up, gave him to a friend. He was a good kitty, too. He always sat in the light, just like a model should."

"Grandma made you give him up."

"Well, she was sneezing, sort of between sniffing and sneezing. She didn't make me."

"Was there ever any snot on her Kleenex, Aunt Edna?"

"No. The Kleenex just comforted her. Me getting rid of the cat comforted her, too."

"You can get that cat back now."

"Oh, that cat's long dead. This hair here's the last of him."

"Maybe we won't brush it off then," I said.

Chairs moved past us in my family's arms, more than twenty chairs from the living room alone: Windsors, Empire, Colonial, Victorian, Edwardian, Arts and Crafts, Art Deco, chairs from every period, none alike, no pairs, much less a full set. The dining-room table was surrounded by eight chairs that were separated by two hundred years in the making, not to mention the variety of style, seat covering, and finish. Whenever we sat down for a meal, everyone was at a different level, children likely to be as tall as their parents, full-grown men with their chins resting on their plates. There were chairs where end tables should have been, chairs where cabinets and hampers should have been, chairs sitting inside dark closets, chairs hanging upside down on the walls. The television sat on a chair, as well as the microwave, a room fan, and a fish bowl. They all left the house one by one and were set in rows in the Saint Augustine grass, so that the vacant lot came to resemble an outdoor theater crossed with a yard sale. Aunt Edna and I sat Grandma's chair next to a tall oak stool that was reserved not for Brother Roberts to sit on, but to stand behind and rest his book on.

"Should we have a pitcher of water for him?" I asked.

"Well, I hope the sun in his eyes will keep him from talking too long, but if he bears up to it he might need some water. I'll bring over a little chair to set the water on. Now, which of these chairs would accept a glass of water?" She turned to the growing audience of empty chairs, scanned them, and said, "You." Four rows back, on the groom's side, was a white wicker corner chair, low, with a rather unstable seat. It took her a full minute to balance the glass on the uneven reeds. "Now," she said, "if he stops in the middle of his speech for a drink he'll have to down it in one gulp. It will be too bothersome to set a half-full glass of water upright in this chair during a sermon. We don't want any of this talk awhile, take a sip, talk some more, have a sip, business."

"Are we in a hurry, Aunt Edna?"

"Doesn't that wicker make the water seem cool and inviting? Don't stomp on the ground as you pass by."

I followed her back into the house, which would now be her house, I supposed, and found it virtually empty. There were beds and dressers in the two bedrooms, and a table and sideboard in the dining room, but the remainder of the house seemed almost littered. Under the twelve-foot ceilings, lying on the oak floors, was everything that had been held in the chairs: books, clothing, toiletries, magazines, knick-knacks, dishes, photographs, and telephones. In my aunt's room all her paints and brushes were shoved into a corner and they, in turn, held pinned to the wall sheaves of watercolor papers and sketchbooks. Aunt Edna's favorite chair, a 1950s kitchen chair, chrome tubing supporting a thin red vinyl seat and back, was the only chair left in the house. No one was brave enough to remove the dozens of open medicine bottles stacked precariously on its seat. She swept them all into a box in one movement. The vinyl of the seat cushion had split, like a ripe tomato left in the sun too long. The back rest sported a gray Band-Aid of duct tape, as if a tomato could be repaired. Once she carried her chair outside, the house was empty of chairs, and yet still full of them.

Every chair we'd carried out was still there. Aunt Edna's chairs were simply her models. Every wall in the house was hung with sketches, watercolors, and paintings of chairs: simple pencil studies of foliate carvings on knees or stenciled crest rails, watercolors of single chairs in a meadow or parking lot, a flight of chairs winging through deep grass, an oil portrait of a stodgy banister-back paired with a low, bow-backed Windsor that had to have been influenced by Grant Wood's *American Gothic*. She'd continued to paint since I'd left Fort Worth twenty-six years earlier, since everyone had left, and she was still painting chairs and only chairs. It seems odd now to write it down, that she only painted chairs, but at the time no one in the family remarked upon it much. Aunt Edna liked to draw and paint chairs in the same way that my father liked to read books about the Civil War, or Aunt Margaret liked to play charades. I think it only seems eccentric now, now that her paintings have become important to people outside the family. Maybe we were wrong not to notice. The fact that her house was full of chairs was more interesting than it being full of chair paintings. The reviews use words like "compulsive" and "addicted" and "driven," but we only knew she loved chairs. Caring for Grandma and her job at the elementary school seemed the biggest part of her life. These people who now care about her art look at all of us in a dumbfounded way when we can't provide more details about her life, about her passion.

But we didn't return to Fort Worth often, after my parents and Aunt Margaret and her family, my cousins, my brother, after we all left home in the mid-seventies, a year or two before Grandpa died. We'd return for an occasional holiday, or stop by Refugio Street if we were driving through on a business trip. Aunt Edna was left behind to care for Grandma, and although we were fond of Edna, neither Dad nor Aunt Margaret could abide their mother, and so in refusing Grandma we lost Aunt Edna in the bargain. I was like everyone else in the family. I visited Grandma only twice in the twenty years after I graduated from college. She threw a fistful of pill bottles and a clock at me the first time, and on my second visit eight years later she was asleep. I spoke with Aunt Edna for a couple of hours that visit, invited her up to our house in St. Louis, and continued on to Austin to a crafts show. All the time I spent inside talking with Aunt Edna I was worrying about the glue melting on my Christmas ornaments in the back of the station wagon, that I'd have nothing to show in Austin. So I have nothing left of that conversation but my worry of glue.

But I do have the summer that was before us, the day of Grandma's funeral service. I lived with my spinster aunt that summer, back in the old house on Refugio where I'd played as a child. We were two fat women, eighteen years apart, a chair artist and a designer of Christmas ornaments, who only knew we had troubles and a hot summer to get through. I can tell you about that summer. I know that much.

When Brother Roberts arrived, Aunt Edna led him into the kitchen and put a tall glass of water in his hand. His hand shook with Parkinson's and the lip of the glass rattled against his dentures. Grandma and Grandpa were members of his church till the day Grandpa died, and although Brother Roberts was retired he still did services for members of his old congregation and sixty-five dollars. Nearing ninety, his coal black toupee fit his head like a single sock drying on a tin mailbox. My father and Aunt Margaret followed him into the kitchen and thanked him for coming, but all the kids cleared out of the house, afraid they were going to be baptized by Brother Roberts's second glass of water. Aunt Edna was pushing the water on him.

"God bless you," he said between sputtering gulps.

"Awful warm this time of May," Aunt Edna said.

"We missed you in church these last twenty years, Edna," he said.

It was all I could do not to reach up and twist his toupee ninety degrees. The way it hung over his ears made my own itch. How could he stand someone else's hair in his ears?

"Well, after Daddy died, Momma got sad," Aunt Edna said.

Brother Roberts spoke slowly and softly, almost biting down on each word to get it out. "She forgot that Jesus still loved her. But I miss your daddy, too. He was a good man."

"Another glass of water, Brother Roberts?" Aunt Edna asked.

"No, I'm full of fire and I don't want to put it out. Are we ready to begin? I'd like everybody seated before we go out." He reached up and put a finger in his ear, pushing a tuft of toupee farther into the canal. I kid you not, everybody in the room put a finger in their own ear and twisted and scratched. It was as if we'd all heard something we couldn't believe, which isn't a good crowd reaction for a preacher.

Brother Roberts had left his wife on the front porch. Daddy told me later he did this because the money was always paid inside the house, and Mrs. Roberts was known to refuse all payment if it occurred in her presence. "We won't profit on others' pain." So he'd left her on the porch, a tiny, aged woman, surrounded by eight or nine kids from Manuel Jara Elementary who'd come to the funeral for Aunt Edna's sake. Sister Roberts was handing each of them a single peppermint, holding her mouth wide as she did so, signaling to them to eat. "Sweet little birds," she rasped, in a voice as dry and light as the pages of a Bible. Brother Roberts and his wife were a package deal: he sermoned and she sang. She wore a pink pillbox hat and matching short gloves. Her stockings hadn't shrunk as much as her calves had. Her hose were so twisted from knee to ankle that it seemed she was screwed into her shoes.

There was a big crowd in the front yard. The family and guests stood in the grass and on the sidewalk, the men holding their hands over their crotches the way they do when they wear suits to funerals and weddings, the women with their fingers pressed to their lips as if they'd just been told the deceased died, the kids moving around like dogs and cats, sniffing their own and everyone else's unfamiliar facial expressions. I looked over at the vacant lot, already broiling in the morning sun, the shadows of Aunt Edna's chairs crawling and stumbling over one another, stretching out beyond the stool pulpit and climbing up into the two big pomegranate trees near the alley. With its rows of individual chairs, short and tall, plain and adorned, the vacant lot now looked like a 200-year-old cemetery, the varied tombstones of the inhabitants of a small town.

Aunt Margaret, my father's older sister, waved the crowd toward the empty chairs as if she were conducting an orchestra, using both arms fluidly, her head snapping toward the vacant lot at each cre-scendo. She was five years older than my father, and another five years older than Aunt Edna, and four hundred years older than everyone else on the planet now that Grandma was dead. She slipped behind the mass of the crowd, and using her two joined and cupped hands gently scooped everyone toward the funeral. Both gestures were ones of control. She was an expert in the body language of authority. Tiny inflections of her pelvis, the capitulation of her chin, the affected drop of her eyelid were all designed to manipulate. She would never say she wanted her way, only pose for it. Any suggestion that Aunt Margaret pointed her cheek toward was doomed. Men buckled at the collapse of her thumb. If she gazed off into the distance, everyone in the room stopped speaking. To my great delight this language was only human, and therefore dogs and cats treated her with the same benign intolerance they showed a couch they didn't like. I have seen three different animals pee on her ankle. Even then she wouldn't utter, "Bad dog," but only intimate the animal should be executed with dull forks by responding to your apologies and questions with a protracted examination of her fingernails. Sam said the animals were just marking her to warn away others of their kind. He thought one of us should pee on her foot, too, and then her power would be destroyed. We in the family had worked out, over years of experience, a tactic to thwart Aunt Margaret's input, which was simply not to look at her. We avoided her gaze as if she were Medusa. If you wanted to suggest a restaurant for lunch you spoke up and searched the faces of everyone concerned, blinked as you passed over Aunt Margaret, and then waited for a response. She wouldn't, or couldn't, verbalize a negative unless as a last resort. As long as you didn't glance at any part of her body you could pass on, make progress. But if you didn't blink at the right time, or if she'd moved unexpectedly to another part of the room and you accidentally caught a view of her wilting toes, or disappointed knees, or the complete lack of your personal worth in her eyes, then you might as well move on to the next suggestion or better yet, simply ask Aunt Margaret what she'd like to do. I'll give this much to Grandma, if she didn't like somebody she threw something hard at them; Aunt Margaret pushed up her hair in back, lowered one eyelid over half the pupil, and offered you her white throat while she implored God to commiserate with her. Most people would rather take a blow to the forehead with a clock.

Now, as matriarch of the family, Margaret prodded us toward the empty chairs with gestures of resigned responsibility and careworn servitude, her hands falling like dead sparrows from the gold buttons on her bosom, from the emeralds in her ears. And although she acted as usher, Aunt Margaret was the first to sit down, taking a seat on the corner of the first row. Her husband Alf, who was hard of hearing and prayed for blindness, sat next to her. Alf's chair was short, with splayed feet, while Margaret sat in a Chippendale easy chair with boldly swept wings and broad proportions. Daddy sat next to Alf in a caned Eastlake side chair, and my mother in an ice-cream-parlor bentwood that showed red paint through a crackling coat of yellow.

I looked across the field of chairs for one of my own. Sam had taken a seat in a faux-bamboo dresser chair and motioned for me to take the place next to him, but it was a steam-bent plywood school chair and I'd sat in one of those long enough.

It's where you sit down that determines everything in life. I never choose a seat casually anymore, even when the room is empty. In college I sat down in a life-drawing class next to a boy with the prettiest blue shirt. It was the first time either one of us had seen a completely naked adult woman. I turned out to be his second. I met my first serious boyfriend at a wedding reception where there were no place cards. I sat between him and his mother and they both pulled on me from opposite directions for the next two years. I took a chair next to my former boss at a crowded conference table and he proceeded to run his claw along my inner thigh. I had to find a new job but he had to find a hand surgeon. My first husband (of one year) got up out of a chair so I could sit in it, and he still thinks I owe him. How many times have I sat down next to someone to momentarily find they smell bad, or cough, or find the weave in my socks interesting. I try not to sit next to fat people because I'm fat. I try not to sit next to skinny people because they remind me I'm fat. Let's not even mention people who look desperate, chairs that share armrests, or slatted benches. But the chairs at the funeral were filling quickly so I took a gray metal folding chair two rows behind Sam. He frowned and turned away.

Beyond the immediate family, I recognized three ladies from Grandma's bridge club, Mrs. Rodriguez and her husband from next door, and two women who worked with Aunt Edna in the school cafeteria. I wondered who was feeding the kiddies who hadn't come to the funeral. The children, and teacher who'd brought them, sat in the back row and looked for all the world as if they were waiting to begin a game of musical chairs. Mrs. Sanchez, from across the street, wore an impeccable black suit that must have been thirty years old. It looked like a copy of the outfit Jackie wore to the president's funeral. I could have invited some of my friends from high school but never felt the urge. There were several people I didn't know, a Mexican family, two ladies that might have been from Grandma's once and long-ago church, and a young boy who led an old blind man to a Boston rocker. Even the Mexicans turned as these two approached, the only blacks at the funeral. The neighborhood was all white when I was a child, but for the most part was now Hispanic, save a few old-timers who were waiting to die in their homes like Grandma.

The old man said, "That's good, Billy. You picked me a good one. I'll be all right now." The boy squatted next to him in the grass. I don't know why I felt so uneasy watching him. It wasn't as if he were going to turn suddenly and catch me staring. Maybe it was because he couldn't. I actually wondered if he was at the right funeral. He could have used a shave. That's what I was thinking when my cousin JoAnn tapped me on the shoulder and said, "That's Mr. Laurent and his grandson. He canes chairs for Aunt Edna."

"Why is he here?"

"I think he's friends with Aunt Edna."

"How do you know that?"

"I've been here a couple times when he was working on a chair. It's an amazing thing to watch. Is this seat taken?"

"No," I said. "Make yourself comfortable." Trapped, I thought. JoAnn is a whisperer to whom all conversation is a sharing of secrets, of suspicions cast and conspiracies foretold. The only thing she's sure about are the beneficial qualities of various roots, herbs, and quasi-vitamins when applied, ingested, or inhaled, and which she happens to sell.

"When were you here to meet a friend of Aunt Edna's?" I asked.

"Oh, I come through all the time." She said this as if she were admitting to pedophilia. "My main supplier is in Dallas." The people behind us leaned forward. "Aunt Edna is a ginseng nut. She uses more than I do. She can testify to its positive nail-growth effects." I turned my head and looked away, pretending she was confiding to someone else. "I can get you some for wholesale, Sarah. It will relax you, give you a tendency toward more complete fulfillment in everything you do. Have you ever had a ginseng orgasm?"

"What?" I said, too loudly.

"It's a life-changing experience."

"Speak up. I can't hear you."

"I only have so much, Sarah," she whispered, turning and smiling at everyone around us. "Over a three-day period, utilizing ginseng aroma therapy, 100-ml tablets taken orally six times a day, ginseng gel to the eyelids, combined with a thrice daily ginseng douche . . ."

"Shhh," I whispered.

She shoveled a hush right back into my ear, "Nothing completely natural should be embarrassing. That's what I tell my children when they pass gas. Farting is a natural reaction to the wrong mix of herbs and amino acids. Did you know that Vitamin B, taken in the right proportion to banana salts, can, with the application of topical oils of course, effectively reduce your risk of breast cancer, not to mention making your nipples softer."

"Here comes Aunt Edna with Grandma, for God's sake, JoAnn. Be quiet."

"I've got Kleenex if you need it," she said for my ears alone.

Brother Roberts followed Aunt Edna from the house. She carried Grandma's ashes in a wooden box that she'd painted five small chairs on, one for each side panel and the lid. Each chair was in a different landscape of flowers, field or forest. Clouds scudded through blue skies. She sat the box in Grandma's chair and then looked for a seat of her own.

"Oh, they didn't leave her a place," JoAnn whispered.

My parents and JoAnn's hadn't saved a seat. There was a moment of hesitancy, of half-risings and reconsiderations, before Aunt Edna sat in the wicker chair next to Brother Roberts and held his water glass in her hands. As we waited for Brother Roberts to begin, all our attention focused on him, a quavering voice ruffled the air between the many chairs, a voice like thin corrugated tin. It rose and fell in shallow waves. It was a voice I'd lost so long ago that it didn't sound the way I remembered it. Sister Roberts was up on the porch, her eyes closed, her hands clasped, singing Roy Acuff's "Great Speckled Bird." I'd given up church so long ago, lived away for so many years, that I'd forgotten Baptists sing with an unwary abandon, a flagrancy of love. Sister Roberts broke my heart and made me sorry for a few moments that my grandmother didn't love me, that she was already gone. I hoped Grandma was now in a place she wanted to be. My chair wavered under me, one leg sinking further into the sod. I felt grass itches working into my ankles and calves. Sister Roberts raised her arms to a revolving ceiling fan and an unseeable Jesus, and the wind blew the sparse strands of her untucked hairline flat and smoothed the loose skin of her forearms till it glistened and took her quavering voice to new levels of vibrato. It seemed that the very air was splitting, that room was being made for something to slip through. JoAnn sobbed in a feathery way, and I saw my father's body bent, as if he were a hospital straw. I marveled at Sister Roberts's gift, her ability to mollify grief by expressing it. When she finished, every chair in the vacant lot sighed under shifting weight. Old springs twanged and popped, cane and wicker cracked. The glued joints of splats and stretchers and spindles spoke a kind of brittle weariness, an appeal for humidity. A palpable dust of dissolving upholstery and dry leather, motes of human skin, and the hair of long-dead cat billowed into the air between the end of Sister's song and the beginning of Brother's prayer. This arid and infertile pollen, smelling of dry glue and fetid sweat, was somehow comforting, proof of a past, of lives lived, of moments of individual comfort spent sitting down, an old book or an old cat in your lap. But dust rising, dust falling, was a testament of some kind of change. Things had been stirred about.

Brother Roberts slammed his Bible down on the wooden stool with the report of a rifle, an act at which he seemed practiced. Yet he'd caught the tip of his pinkie between the wood and the word and almost leaped into Aunt Edna's lap to disguise the pain. We'd all been gazing at Sister Roberts, suspended as she was between two porch posts like a deflated Greek goddess, when the Bible came down and brought us to attention. Not a chair squeaked. Birds changed direction in mid-flight. Aunt Edna held the glass of water at arm's length, afraid that Brother Roberts actually would sit on her. He wrapped his good hand around the afflicted one and shook them both like a pair of dice, while hopping on one foot around the Bible on its stool altar.

"He's hurt his finger," I whispered to JoAnn.

"No, it's the power in him. His love for the Lord can't be contained. He's always like this."

He stopped suddenly. The congregation swayed in their chairs for a better view, already acquiring some of his rhythm. Brother Roberts spread his arms wide and raised his hands above his head and then proceeded to climb an unseen ladder.

"I can't get there this way, can I?" he asked.

"No, you can't," someone in the front row answered.

He took his wallet out and offered money, gray worn singles, to my father, Aunt Margaret, and to three other old ladies. No one took his bills.

"I can't buy a place in heaven, can I?"

"No, you can't," a woman yelled.

Individual hairs of Brother Roberts's toupee lifted tentatively on the wind, like the legs on one side of a spider you've incompletely crushed. His coat was too long, his tie too short. It was plain he hadn't bought a new suit since he'd retired twenty-five years earlier. He walked a figure eight, enclosing the stool and Aunt Edna, then walked a second, pivoting on the stool and Grandma's ashes. He squatted down and looked under the chairs.

"No matter how far I go, no matter how many places I seek, will I find Heaven on Earth?"

A pattern was developing here and the congregation was catching on. Four different adults and seven of the nine third-graders answered, "No, you won't," in unison. The adults who'd so answered looked at one another with satisfaction. The kids giggled.

Poor Aunt Edna sat hunched in her chair before us, as if she were being made an example of, a sinner brought up for judgment. She grimaced at each question and response.

"Who killed Elizabeth Hutton?" Brother Roberts yelled.

One of the schoolchildren shouted back, "No, you can't."

"Jesus did it," JoAnn whispered and I reached over and slapped her wrist.

"Who took Elizabeth Hutton from us? Who murdered her body? Who stomped on her fleshy heart, ran over her thinking mind with a big truck?" He looked at my father. "Did you do it?" Before Dad could answer he turned to my aunts. "Did you do it? Did you?" They both seemed frozen, the fingers of their hands spread stiffly, as if they'd just dropped a half-dozen china plates. Brother Roberts turned to all of us. "Did any of you send her away? And if not, who came and got her? She's not here, is she? We all know that. This isn't her in this box, is it?"

"No, it isn't," someone answered.

"No, it isn't. Jesus demolished this body, as he's ruining yours and mine. He's doing it on a daily basis, on a minute-by-minute basis. He'll kill us all in the name of his sweetness. Now, I'll ask again. Who murdered Elizabeth Hutton?"

"Jesus did," voices answered.

"And how do we get to Heaven?"

"Loving Jesus," voices answered.

"Is that rational?" Brother Roberts screamed. "No, it's not," he answered himself. "No, it's not," he said again, more softly.

"How do we get to be more like Jesus? We love a world we can't understand. We love a world we know we have to leave. Now, dear family, are you going to let go of your mother, of your grandmother, of your great-grandmother, as she let go of you? Are you going to bask in her memory and rejoice in her salvation? Elizabeth Hutton has gone on."

Here Brother Roberts inhabited a long pause the way a tree inhabits bark. It seemed to suit him. He seemed comfortable, ageless, almost graceful in silence. No one answered his last questions. He looked across the assembly, held his arms out as if he were being crucified, and began to quiver. His Parkinson's shaking had returned. I could almost see the leaves falling from his limbs. The old blind black man said, "Amen." Brother Roberts answered, saying, "Amen, thank you. Go in peace, Sister Elizabeth Hutton. We loved you while you were here. You've left us this fine family as a legacy: three children, five grandchildren, nine great-grandchildren. We'll be all right. We'll carry on."

He was tired now, faltering. Even the Bible looked heavy in his hands. Aunt Edna held out her glass of water, leaned forward with her entire upper body toward him. I leaned forward, too, hoping he'd take the water. It's too hard, rest, I thought. We won't leave. Instead, he dropped one arm and asked for some commiseration. "It's hot here, isn't it?" He flapped his Bible beneath his armpit.

"Yes, it is," the bridge ladies answered.

"It's a hot place to live a long life: Texas. I've never had to give a sermon on Hell to my congregation. We live in Texas. But look, here's a cool glass of water. This woman who's just lost her mother is offering it to me. She's taking care of me, isn't she?"

"Yes, she is."

"Her gesture is an affirmation, isn't it?"

"Amen."

"Life goes on, doesn't it?"

"Yes, it does," solemn voices hailed.

"I'm going to have a sip of this cool water and then I'm going to pass it on. I'm going to have a sip," and here he did so, the rim of the glass clattering on his teeth, "and I'm going to say, 'Yes.' Each of you do the same. Think of Elizabeth Hutton, have a sip of cool water saying 'Yes,' and pass it on." He handed the glass back to Aunt Edna. "We're not going to end this funeral saying 'No.' We're going to join together and finish by saying 'Yes.' We're going to affirm loss and pain, affirm healing and joy, affirm a sip of cool water. I say, 'Yes.' What do you say? Let's send Elizabeth Hutton home now. Say it with me, 'Yes.'"

Voices. My own voice. JoAnn's whisper. Aunt Edna's lips were wet and trembling. I saw my mother hand my father a Kleenex, and all around me, soft and loud, brittle and startling, the single word passed back and forth. Brother Roberts, exhausted, sat on his stool at last, smoothed his toupee, smoothed the loose skin beneath his eyes.

I looked to Sister Roberts. The small program the funeral home had printed for the service listed "Amazing Grace" as the closing hymn. She sat on the porch, her gloved hands clasped in her lap. I thought she'd forgotten where she was, that she'd missed her cue. But then, from somewhere far away, undulating in the heat off the ground like a butterfly trying to gain altitude, came the aspiring strains of bagpipe music. It might have been harsh and dissonant close by, but as the piper was unseen, and the music so distant, seeming as if it might fade away at any moment, we all felt we were on the verge of losing some beautiful thing. We wanted it to be closer. People turned their heads, looking up and down the street, and finally up to the rooftops. The music existed only on the air, and breathing it made me weep.

"Who ordered that?" JoAnn whispered.

I shook my head, running my finger under my nose. When the hymn ended, when we were sure it was gone, Brother Roberts stood again and said, "The family would like to invite everyone inside the house for refreshments."

Aunt Margaret stood up, and by the curve of her spine everyone understood she was to enter the house first, followed by not some but all present. I was on my way to escort Aunt Edna into the house but Sam beat me to it. We think alike, Sam and I do, part of our problem. We can rarely surprise each other. Wasn't it petty that I was aggravated because he took her arm? At the time I sincerely knew that he'd done this to get under my skin. She was my helpless aunt, not his. Now I had to walk into the house alone. Once again, I'd confused a funeral for a wedding. I thought I should be helping her, and he hadn't given me the chance. Sam looked over his shoulder, found me, and I shot him a calculated display of bitterness that would have made Aunt Margaret proud. He simply turned back to her, without allowing me so much as a grimace of exasperation. I thought it cold-blooded.

Aunt Margaret and Alf went inside, followed by Mom and Dad, Aunt Edna and Sam. By then Brother Roberts had stationed himself at the door so things slowed down a bit. I shuffled along next to my little brother Mike and his wife Darcy. The pair of them never seem to know anything, other than that their feet reach the ground. If you tell everyone in a room which restaurant we're all going to, they somehow miss it, and have to ask halfway there. I've explained the same Thanksgiving cherry bean salad to Darcy at least seventeen times. Mike to this day can't remember Sam's brother's name. I'll say, "Oh, John had a car wreck."

And he'll look befuddled and ask, "Who's that?"

"Sam's only brother," I'll say and shake my head. He'll grin at me and reach for the loose skin on the side of my knee. I love him but he has to be led by the hand to the bathroom.

As we stood there, listening to Brother Roberts blessing the people who'd already thanked him, Mike asked me, "Where's the cemetery?"

"I'll make a wild guess, Mikey, that it's the same one Grandpa's buried in."

"Darcy and I didn't know Grandma was going to be cremated. We thought we'd get to see her one more time."

"It was fine by me. If she still had arms she'd be throwing things at us from the casket."

"She never threw anything at me," Darcy protested.

"You weren't one of the deserters," I explained. I stepped back to let the children pass by. The rows of chairs in the vacant lot were skewed now, disorderly. Individual chairs seemed ostracized, others offended. It was as if they had nothing in common anymore, other than a general attitude toward the west. Then I noticed that Grandma's box, Grandma, was still sitting in her chair. We'd left her behind again.

I'd never been in charge of someone's ashes before. It was a simple pine box with two hinges and a clasp on the lid. No lock. Aunt Edna's decorations still looked wet. I dabbed at the corner of the lid with my finger. Dry. I picked up the box gingerly, testing the weight. Grandma weighed about eighty pounds when she died, was about five feet two. She was much more manageable now. She weighed less than my purse. I wondered what Aunt Edna was going to do with the box after Grandma was buried. It was a good size for recipes. This thought made me cackle. I was going to tell Sam about it, but then remembered he'd made me mad.

The blind man was out in the middle of the yard. His young escort seemed unsure of what to do with him. The old man held Aunt Edna's water glass in his hand. I tucked Grandma under my arm.

"Can I take that inside for you?" I asked him.

"He wasn't going to take it, ma'am," the boy said.

This startled me: that this kid thought I was accusing them of stealing a water glass.

"Of course not," I mumbled.

The old man cleared his throat. "Only black man in the entire funeral and I got the last sip of water. What are the odds?" He laughed then and held the glass out in the air, about an inch from where a sighted person would have offered it to me.

"She's got the old lady in the box," the boy said.

"This is my grandson Billy and I'm James Laurent."

"I'm Sarah Warren. I'm . . ."

"You're Edna's niece from St. Louis. You're the lady who makes Christmas ornaments. I know you, yes I do. Edna goes on and on about your ornaments." He looked at me as he spoke, looked directly at the left corner of my lips. I felt myself compressing so we'd make eye contact.

"Y'all are coming in for some lunch, aren't you?"

"Yes, we are. If I can get this child pointed in the right direction. I want to shake the hand of that preacher, too. Mrs. Hutton got a good shove toward heaven, I'd say. And that bagpiper. I want to thank him, too."

"I never saw him," I said.

"You have vision problems, too, do you?"

"Oh no," I said. "I just meant he never was in eyesight. He must be a block or two away."

"That music was from heaven."

Grandma's box was starting to bite the soft underside of my arm. "Well, I'd better get inside and see if I can help Aunt Edna in the kitchen."

"You can try, but that woman's kitchen is a one-butt kitchen. She won't let you help her. It was nice meeting you and maybe we'll talk again." He nodded and smiled at my chin. I understood then: he was making eye contact with my voice.

There was still a line at the front door so I walked around back and stepped into the kitchen. Aunt Edna turned from her sink, saw Grandma under my arm, and put both her hands over her mouth. Her eyes were still red and wet.

"I missed her so much I forgot her," she said. "Here, put her on top of the refrigerator. That's as good a place as any, since we don't have a fireplace mantel."

Edna's hands were as red and wet as her eyes. Over her dress she wore a faded cotton apron, printed with thistles.

"Can I help with something, Aunt Edna?"

"No, girl, this is a one-butt kitchen."

"So I've heard. The old blind man."

"Is James here?" She turned back to her porcelain sink, where she ran water over spoons. "He's not so old. He just dresses that way. He probably needs a shave, doesn't he?"

"If you'd just let me dry those spoons I wouldn't have to go out there and stand with Sam," I said.

She let the water run, looked over her shoulder at me for a moment. "Oh. OK, honey. Here, here's you a towel." She took one of two off her shoulder. "I'm that way myself. Your aunt Margaret keeps sending me signals and all of the sudden I can't interpret them. She's gone from crossing her legs to crossing her arms to looking up at the ceiling. Any minute she'll be whistling and we'll have to clear the house and call in the National Guard."

I grinned at my dish towel.

"It's good to see you smile, Sarah Rabbit," she said.

"I'm sorry I didn't come back and visit more often, Aunt Edna."

"We knew where you were. You had your own family to take care of."

"All the same. You and Grandma were my family, too, and I didn't make enough effort. I realize that now, now that my two are off in college. I get lonely sometimes and it makes me think that you and Grandma might have been lonesome sometimes, too, with everybody gone."

"We had a life. Don't think so much of yourself, Sarah Rabbit, that a few more visits from you would have changed things. Momma never encouraged you. I would have liked to have seen you more, but don't think of me as destitute without you. I feel good just knowing you're out there, charging around decorating the Christmas trees of the world."

"Well."

"Don't say another word."

"Well, that bagpiper made me cry."

"Honey, that spoon is dry now."

"That bagpiper made me cry." I turned and put my face against her shoulder. My tears dampened her dark dress.

"Sarah, stop that, honey." She hugged me and patted my back with a wet spoon. "Don't fret about this. Momma didn't even like you. Don't bother yourself about this."

"But why didn't she like me?" I sobbed. "All I did was go to college and move away from home. It was just a coincidence that everyone else left home shortly after I did."

"Sarah, Momma wasn't mad because you left home. That's why she was mad at your daddy and some of the others. But she didn't like you because she didn't like you."

"What?" I pushed myself away. Suddenly my eyes were very dry.

"Honey, she thought you were one of those people who pigeonhole other people. She thought that you didn't give them a chance to be other than the way you narrowly defined them. That once you made up your mind that somebody was a whisperer, or a drunk, or played a bad hand of bridge, or was a hypochondriac, you never let them improve or evolve into anything more."

"Well then, Grandma pigeonholed me."

"That's right. Don't be bothered by this." She hugged me again.

Aunt Edna smelled of processed vegetables: gallon-cans of giblet corn, sliced green beans, lima beans, pinto beans, peas and carrots, institutional vegetables that were cooked in tubs and warmed in troughs and served with slotted spoons to children pushing shallow trays. It was actually the water or thin soup left behind in the warming troughs, a pale green or yellow fluid, whose odor suffused Aunt Edna's hair and oozed from her pores. I'd always suspected that her sweat might be tinted by carrots or hominy, that on a hot day she was coated in a broth that vegetarians might survive on. She'd always smelled this way, as long as I'd known her. Was this, I wondered, pigeonholing someone? Was I smelling corn only because I'd smelled it twenty years earlier? I sniffed again. A metallic odor as if vegetables were made of tin. If this was a nasal memory it was incredibly powerful.

"What is it, dear?" Aunt Edna asked, stepping back.

"Oh," I explained, "just snot."

"Now," she said, "what's wrong between you and Sam?"

"You smell like food, Aunt Edna," I answered, driving the conversation down an exit ramp.

"I've always thought I smelled like paint." She lifted her hands and showed me her stained fingertips, which looked as if she'd just been booked for a crime. "It's my oil colors. This time it's Prussian Blue. I have a bad habit of mixing my colors with my fingertips when I'm in a hurry. There's nothing I can do about it. Once I start painting I forget everything else I know. No amount of solvent can get it out from underneath my nails. It stains my cuticles, too."

"You ought to wear gloves when you paint, Aunt Edna."

"Oh, I couldn't do that. I hate it that there's a brush between me and the canvas as it is. You don't want to tell me about you and Sam?"

"I'm still too embarrassed about it."

"OK. That's OK."

"I can't believe Grandma didn't like me because she didn't like me."

"She was a passionate person, Sarah. She hated and loved in extremes. That happens to people who are sick. You've got to imagine how it would be, stranded in a bed for the last twenty years of your life, unable to make decisions for yourself, care for yourself. I don't think she liked to be reminded she was bedridden, so whenever someone walked through her door, on two legs, she reacted violently, with a violent hate or a suffocating love."

"Who did she love?"

"She loved me and your daddy, your cousin JoAnn, her friends, Mr. Laurent here."

She looked over my shoulder. I turned to see who'd come in the kitchen. It was the young boy and his grandfather. The old man's long white cane hung in the crook of his arm. The tip of the cane, rather than a brass ferule or a rubber foot, was a porcelain furniture caster, a rolling wheel. Here was a cane for a man on the move. Later, James told me he'd designed and built his cane for his future retirement, when he planned to travel. James thought of himself as a funny man.

"Is that you, Edna?" he asked. He still had his hat on his head.

"It's me, James."

"Clear the room," he called out. "I'm gonna go hug Edna."

"Room's already clear, Grandpa," Billy said.

"What about chairs? How many of them infernal chairs are between us?"

"No chairs, Grandpa."

"All right then. Coming in for a landing, Edna. Prepare yourself to be squeezed." He crossed the room, making tiny corrections in his path, and held out his arms at the precise width of my aunt Edna's waist. He hugged her for a moment too long, I thought, the way lonely men will when confronted with breasts.

"Thank you for coming, James," Aunt Edna said.

"Who's this other with us?" he asked.

"We've already met," I said. "I'm Edna's niece, Sarah."

"We meet again," he said. "Who would have thought such a thing was possible?" And he held out his hand again. I took it, warm and supple as a dog's ear.

"Can I take your hat, Mr. Laurent?" I asked.

"You're always taking things from me, Sarah. I guess some folks think it's pretty easy to steal from a blind man." He paused, then said, "Is she smiling at me, Edna?"

"Yes, James."

"Can I feel your smile, Sarah?"

Aunt Edna nodded at me.

"Yes," I said, "if you promise not to take it from me."

"Ow, she's quick. Here, take my hand. I don't want to poke you in the eye."

I took his hand again, found little calluses at his fingertips, and guided them to my cheek. It was one of the most intimate gestures I've ever made. I held my smile while he caressed my lips with the back of his fingers. They smelled of straw. Then he touched the tip of my nose, cupped my cheek in his palm, smoothed my eyebrow, and just as I closed my eyes, he lodged his thumb in one socket, rolled over the bridge of my nose to the other eye, and finally, tiptoeing across my temple, found my hairline and the placement of my ear.

"I took your smile, Sarah," he said, letting his hand fall away, "but I'll give it back to you," and with that he smiled at my ear, a large-toothed grin that was offered with a tilt of his head. "I hope I didn't mess your makeup."

"No," I whispered. My eyes were still batting coyly. I wanted to smell his hand again, but he turned back to Aunt Edna. That seemed unfair.

"I'd say she was in a better place now, but that would be a lie and then I'd have to join her."

"Oh, James, she loved you heart and soul. Don't say such a thing."

"Sarah, me and your grandma forever argued over which of us would go to a deeper pit in hell."

"I'd bet on Grandma," I said. "She used her eyes to aim things at people. You'd have a harder time throwing a clock at me."

"Are you never going to forgive her for that, Sarah?" Aunt Edna said. "It makes you look small, not forgetting that. It was years and years ago."

"Don't get on her, Edna. I started it," James said. I would say he shook his head no, but it was more of a swaying bob, the way a parrot might shun an offered peanut. His head danced on his shoulders in an effort to influence my aunt, to calm her.

"I'm sorry," I said.

"You shouldn't always assume your opinions are shared," Aunt Edna told me. She wadded her dishrag into a ball and dropped it into the sink. It landed there with a wet thump as if it were one of my lungs.

"Now, Edna, we said we're sorry," James offered. He turned to his grandson. "Billy, you go on out in the other room and get you something to eat."

"That food is white, Grandpa," Billy answered.

"Get out there and eat some of it anyway," his grandfather ordered. "You've got to get used to it. That's what you're going to get in college someday."

"I wish I didn't have to go every place you go, do everything you do," the boy said. James rapped his cane on the floor. "I'm going."

We both turned back to my aunt.

James said, "He don't like white food."

"I didn't know black people's food was that different from ours," I said. "We're all from the South."

"Not white people's food," he said, "white food."

"Oh."

"You know, white bread, navy beans, eggs, marshmallows, mayonnaise, turkey: white food."

"Oh," I said again.

My aunt had both hands over her eyes. James couldn't notice this and I couldn't bring myself to tell him aloud. I'd tried pointing and that hadn't worked.

"That's why it's very hard for me to understand colors," he said. "You'd think all white foods would taste the same, but they don't. Strawberry and tomato, both red, taste like two different ends of a dog. There's no correspondence between color and taste. Now, Edna, I've come here to give you my condolences, and I'm sorry I've upset you."

Her hands separated from her face like things that had been glued together unsuccessfully. Both sides were wet, cheek and palm. "Strawberries and tomatoes don't taste like the ends of a dog, James," she said.

"I just mean they're that different," he answered, "even though the color's the same."

"I miss her so much already," Aunt Edna said softly. "I guess I always will."

"Things will be better with time, Edna, honey," James said. His eyes rolled back up in his head and disappeared. It almost made me swoon, all that white eyeball in the middle of his dark face. Then his pupils suddenly dropped back down, rolled to the left corner of each socket and lodged there, as if they were soccer balls kicked into the back of a net.

"Now I know why she always wanted to go first, before any of her children. It was her only fear, that Margaret or your daddy or I would somehow precede her. It's because it hurts so much. It hurts too much."

"You'll have your own life now, Edna," James said. "Your momma has finally given you your freedom."

"I could have had my freedom anytime I wanted it, James. It was always my decision, my choice to stay with her."

He shrugged his shoulders, rubbed his mouth with his open hand. All in a moment his suit became too large for him. It was as if she'd slapped him hard across his cheek and mouth. "Well," he said at last, perhaps the only word that would contain his sigh. "Well, if I can find Billy I'll be on my way. Never did like a funeral. I'm a hello man, not a good-bye man."

"James," Aunt Edna said, reaching out and taking the sleeve of his coat, "come by in a few days. I've got a little chair that needs a new seat."

"I'll come by, Edna. I wish I could do more for you."

"I'm all right, James. I just need more time. I'm afraid of being alone."

"I'm afraid of the dark," he said.

Aunt Edna slipped forward and hugged him; he brought his arms up around her shoulders, his cane flailing wildly against the cabinets.

It was then that Aunt Margaret walked into the kitchen, followed by Brother Roberts and my father. Aunt Margaret's whole body seemed to convulse as she began retracing her steps, backing out of the room, stepping on Brother Roberts, who fell bodily into my father's arms, the three of them like a train that suddenly backs up on a downhill grade. Their wheels were spinning in the opposite direction of travel. Brother Roberts, pinned between Margaret and Daddy, uttered a short, piercing, "Praise God," and then, trying to halt his fall, reached under Aunt Margaret's arm and grasped her full breast for a handhold. She looked down at his hand as if it were a sea bass suckling her breast. And then they all disappeared, dropped behind the counter next to the door.

Aunt Edna and James separated, and he asked, "What was that?"

Aunt Edna looked at me. She hadn't seen the fall either.

"There's been an accident," I said. Aunt Margaret was the first to rise. She stood up and nearly yanked her skirt off in an attempt to reassert her dignity. I think she would have tied a knot in her legs if she could have, just to impress upon everyone the fact that her virginity was, and nearly always had been, beyond reproach. Daddy helped Brother Roberts up. He was gazing into his palm as if a perfect impression of Aunt Margaret's nipple was still there.

"What the hell, Margaret?" my father said.

My aunt turned to my father, her fists still twisting her skirt. Brother Roberts was between them. She slapped his hand down, as if she'd seen evidence there as well. "There was a spider in my path," she said.

"A spider?" Daddy said.

Aunt Margaret cocked her head, and her eyes seemed to die in her skull, die and lie levelly reproachful of my father's birth.

"I'm all right," Brother Roberts said. "No harm done. For a minute there I thought I heard Him calling me to his side but I do believe I'm still in your kitchen, Edna. I'd like the family to gather, hand to hand, for one last prayer before I go."

"Well," Aunt Edna said, "we all won't fit in here. Let's gather in the living room. Come with me, James."

She took his hand and began to lead him toward the living room. Just as he was alongside Aunt Margaret, he withdrew his hand and said, "No, Edna, you go ahead. This is a family prayer. I'll wait here in the kitchen."

"No, you won't," she said.

"I think I will, Edna."

I could tell that Aunt Margaret thought James was uncomfortably close. She tucked her chin into the folds of her neck and slid her open hands along the wall behind her as if she were hiding from a prison spotlight.

Daddy said, "Anybody's welcome to pray with us, Mr. Laurent."

"Sir, I appreciate that, but this is between me and Edna and I know my place. This is a family prayer."

"Hmph," Aunt Edna snorted.

Aunt Margaret rolled her shoulder, pressed her cheek to the wall, and oozed past James and Aunt Edna, her eyes rolling wildly back, like a horse cornered in a stall. When she reached the living room the rest of my family watched her contorted body uncoil slowly to a stately repose. To those of us in the kitchen it seemed she'd just been squeezed from a tube of toothpaste with the heel of a boot.

"I don't want to make folks uncomfortable," James said.

"Let him have his way," Aunt Edna said. She turned and shunted Daddy and Brother Roberts out of the room, leaving James standing by himself.

"There's no chairs left here in the kitchen, Mr. Laurent," I said.

He turned slowly and looked out the window over my shoulder. "If you could just help me find the back porch, I'll sit on the steps."

"I can do that," I said, but I'd never led a blind person before. I took his hand. "Should I lead you, or walk beside you or . . ."

"Either of those will work, Sarah. I've never been fond of people who get behind me and shove." He paused and then asked, "Are you smiling?"

"I'm smiling."

"I wish smiling made a noise," he said.

"Here we are." I watched him situate himself on the concrete steps.

"If you could find my Billy and tell him where I am, Sarah? And tell him to bring my hat."

"Yes, sir," I said. But instead of leaving I bent down next to him on one knee. "It seems like you and Aunt Edna have a history."

"History is something you can learn from, and I haven't learned a thing," he said. "You better get on in there. Never miss a family prayer."

"Yes, sir," I said and left him there, smoothing the fabric of his pants over his knees. Billy passed me, hat in hand, as I stepped into the house. "He's . . ." I began.

"I know where he is, ma'am. He don't like to leave over the same threshold he came in."

I stood on the threshold between the kitchen and living room, looking over my shoulder at Billy, and then at my family, beginning to join hands. You walk into a room, walk out of a room, step over a threshold, through a door, into the light, into darkness. There are a million metaphors to mark a passage, to differentiate one period of life from another. Some people can break their life into chapters or episodes, but for me these demarcations would be completely arbitrary. Everything seems to flow without interruption from one state to another, without significant action or even punctuation. My life moves along in what are to me imperceptible increments. I never notice the juncture between happy or sad, only that I've arrived. I know that some people can tell you the moment they fell in love, or the precise instant they realized their life should be dedicated to Jesus. I know of no defining passage of any sort. Things come about inexorably, over great distances, through a vast accumulation of details that have no meaning in and of themselves, even if I could make them out. While I can follow and understand an entire book, I never have a favorite sentence. No aphorism seems aphoristic.

So I stepped into the circle of my family, took Sam's hand on one side and my mother's on the other, and bowed my head.

"Heavenly Father, we need help. These children here have lost their mother. They're suffering and can only think of themselves. It's hard for them to look through their tears and remember You. We know You don't care about that. You only want us to sustain each other in this crisis of memory. Death is a door that we watch everyone else go through. We don't see ourselves going through it. So we're jealous of those who go on, jealous that You're with them now instead of us. We've known them so long it doesn't seem fair that they should go away, that they should leave us, forsake us for something as inconsequential as a body's illness, for something as hopeless as the promise of Heaven. It's hard for us to understand that the dying know more than we do, that you can be sick in body and mind but not in soul. Things we don't understand make us cry. Things we understand make us cry. Why are we crying now? For both of these reasons. Because we're surrounded by love and great beauty and yearn to be surrounded by love and great beauty. These children think they've lost a love they'll never again have. But it's not so. Remind them of their own children's love. Remind them of Your gift of memory. Remind them that in exchange for suffering You've given their mother peace. Let's all make a decision to go on from this woman's house with an uncompromised spirit, an enhanced understanding, and a dedication, children, to imagine your mother as a child. Children, your mother is running into her father's arms. She's giggling, her shoelace has come untied, she's reaching up."

Holding hands, gathered in a circle as we were, no one could wipe away their tears. I looked up through a glaze of water and watched the first tears I'd ever seen on my father's cheeks fall away. My mother was crying, as were Aunt Edna and Aunt Margaret, and all my cousins were red-faced and bleary-eyed. Only Sister Roberts was dry. She held firmly to the hands on each side and beamed at her old husband.

"In Jesus' name we pray," he said.

Sister Roberts, her stockings now coiled at her ankles, began to sing. It was a song I'd last sung as an eight-year-old, a child's song. "Deep and wide," she sang, "deep and wide," and she shook the hands she held, Alf's and my father's, shook them to make them join along. "There's a fountain flowing deep and wide. Deep and wide, deep and wide, there's a fountain flowing deep and wide." Just the two lines she sang, slowly, to remind everyone, and then we joined her, "Deep and wide, deep and wide, there's a fountain flowing deep and wide." Then she stopped, just as we were all about to really get into it. Voices trailed off into sniffs, and we released each other's hands to the open air. It was then as if our hands missed the contact, because almost everyone brought their own two hands together, clasping them, interlocking fingers. Only afterwards did we wipe the water from our faces.

Our few remaining guests had stood beyond the circle of family members, holding corners of sandwiches and coffee cups. Mom and I moved to Daddy and hugged him. I hugged my little brother against the future loss of our parents, and then went to Brother Roberts. It had been a long time since I'd thanked a preacher, if I ever had. I hadn't been to a church since high school. I don't believe in God. Don't ask me how or when I came to this conclusion. It's just so. It's more a state of being than a methodical calculation. I know this may seem ironic, that a designer of Christmas ornaments has no faith in Jesus, but for me Christmas is somehow separate from organized religion. I believe in the decorated tree, adorning the natural world with objects manmade and beautiful. And I think this is a fairly accurate definition of religion if you substitute investing for adorning and ideas for objects. Which is all to say I hadn't shaken a minister's hand in a good while, because I'm quite sure they can feel atheism in your grip. Once again I fought the urge to take Brother Roberts's toupee in both of my hands to right it, and instead grasped his clasped and trembling fingers in mine and held them still.

"I'm a granddaughter," I said. "I want to thank you so much for the service and your prayers. It's made me very emotional and I haven't been emotional for a long time. I think that's good."

"I'm just an old man who makes the little girls cry," he answered. "But you only cry because you realize you were in love. I'm just the person who reminded you. It's good work if you can get it."

"But why will it evaporate?"

"What, honey?"

"These tears: they're going to dry up and I won't feel the same in just a few moments. I'm already changing."

"I don't know, dear. Maybe you have to concentrate. Memory is a lifelong process, not a summing up or a conclusion. You have to remember now and now and now and now, and if you're always remembering you were in love, you'll be in love."

His answer trailed off at last, as if he weren't even sure this was so, as if he just made it up.

"Have you had a sandwich?" I asked. "We have chicken salad, and tuna fish, and there's green pea salad and potato salad and a Waldorf salad."

Sister Roberts stood by his side now. I released his hands to hers. The skin over her cheekbones was waxen, rubbed to a dull sheen. "He never has been able to stomach foods that are glued together with mayonnaise," she said.

"I'm a mustard man," he acknowledged. "Jesus and mustard."

Sister Roberts slapped the back of his hand. "Irreverent," she chided. "Jesus and mustard in the same sentence."

"If Jesus don't know I love Him best by now . . ." he told her.

"What then?" she asked. "Then what?"

He didn't respond.

"Almost ninety and still proud," she rebuked him. Then she smiled at me. "I'll take him home and make him his favorite: an egg sandwich."

"But that's what mayonnaise is made of," I said. "Eggs."

This seemed to confuse them both for a moment, and then they simultaneously decided I was joking and began to chuckle.

"That's precious," Sister Roberts said and reached out and pinched my arm, hard. Then they began to move off toward the door.

"Did you see the car they drove up in?" It was Sam. There were crumbs of cake on both sides of his mouth. I don't know what it is about men, but at the age of forty they all lose the tactile nerves of their facial skin. They can't feel the food they've left on their face. Maybe it's shaving that does it. I reached up and brushed the crumbs away.

"It was a 1974 Impala. Immaculate. His congregation must have given it to him when he retired twenty-five years ago. Have you ever noticed how people buy their last car at age sixty-five and drive it until they die? If he lives to a hundred and twenty he'll never buy another car."

"I can't believe, after everything that man said and did this morning, that you're most interested in his car."

Sam didn't answer. He reached up and took hold of my earlobe and turned it over, as if it were a price tag on a piece of furniture.

"What?" I asked, annoyed.

"It's nothing," he said.

"What?"

"It just looked a little red."

"You just don't reach out and grab a person like that."

"You just wiped the crumbs off my cheek without asking." He held his mouth open.

I turned from him and walked. I stopped six feet away, spun on a lump of potato salad, and marched back. "You don't have the right to take liberties with me anymore," I whispered harshly, as if I were blowing into a pill bottle to get the dust out. "You don't touch me unless I ask you to. You can never again assume how I feel. Never."

He closed his eyes and inclined his head toward his shoulder, but I saw the muscles in his jaw tense, short furrows in a new garden. He actually lifted his hand to place it on my forearm.

Aloud, too loudly, I said, "No, no, no."

He lifted both palms to me, backed away, then showed his palms to several other people who'd turned toward him, as if to say he'd never touched me, would never touch me again, and then he left the house.

To show you the state I was in, I was further enraged that he'd left me standing alone in the middle of the room, that he'd made this dramatic gesture of leaving me. It only reaffirmed his clandestine departures, made them public, no longer our secret.

□ □ □

Our secret, mine and Sam's, but I'd already told my mother. So, as soon as the screen door slapped to, the first face that came into focus was, of course, my mother's, and it wore a resigned frown, as if she'd seen this type of behavior before. It made me feel like a child when I'd been unjustly accused of kicking our dog, simply because I was closest when he yelped. Everyone likes Sam. The first thing Mom said when I told her that he'd cheated on me was a listless, "The poor thing, he's lost."

"He was lost, Mom," I said. "But he turned up between another woman's legs."

"Don't say it like that," she said.

"I have to say it in the most graphic terms to make it real," I told her. "He cheated on me, he fooled around, he was unfaithful: they all sound so innocuous. When I say he put his hands on her breasts, put his mouth on her vagina, put his penis inside of her: those make it real. When I think of him lying to me, planning ahead to deceive me, the words sliding over his tongue through a thick mucous from her cunt . . ."

"Sarah, stop it. I don't want to hear . . ."

"I can't stop imagining it, Mom. But I won't talk to you about it anymore."

"You can talk to me," she said, "just don't offend me."

"But I feel so offended."

"This happens to everyone," she said.

"It didn't happen to you and Daddy."

"No, but others."

"I only care about me," I said. "I don't want to be philosophical about it; I don't want to see myself as part of a culture, or as a digit in some astronomical statistic. I don't care if everyone else has jumped off the cliff. I didn't want to. Just because everyone else dies doesn't make me feel better about dying."

"You're not dying," she said.

"I feel like I am."

"I don't know what to say to you. I'm not experienced."

"Neither am I. I just wanted you to know I'm blundering along. I just wanted you to send out a search party if I don't come back."

"Don't be so melodramatic, Sarah."

"This is my big chance, Mom. If this isn't soap opera, I don't know what it is."

"So then you're both lost now," she said, and then, "Do the girls know?"

"No, they're both still at school for another two weeks. I don't want them to know. I know how much it hurts me. It would hurt them, too."

"Is Sam going to leave home?"

"He doesn't want to. He wants to stay and work things out."

"Do you want to leave? You can come home if you want to, honey."

"I don't know what to do."

And then the phone rang. It was Aunt Edna. She wanted to speak to my father. And so my conversation with my mother ended with my father's sadness, and I went home to Sam. I slept on the sofa for the next several nights, then we joined Mom and Dad for the drive down to Fort Worth. Mom and I were mostly silent for the trip. Dad and Sam talked amiably in the front seat about whether to bomb Saddam Hussein this week or next. Mom's hands fidgeted for the entire ride and she kept trying to slip me Milky Ways and tangerines between my sighs. I arrived at Grandma's house much fatter than I'd left home.

☐ ☐ ☐

I was just now beginning to feel what a relief it was to be out of my house, so much more air to breathe, so much more food. When Sam walked out on me, after I stared down my mother's frown, I almost staggered to the food tables, to the comforting odor of mayonnaise, to vegetables that conform to serving spoons. If I'd been alone in the room I'd have plunged both hands into those Rubbermaid troughs and brought fistfuls of tuna fish laced with mayo and sweet relish to my mouth. As it was Aunt Edna beat me there, offered me a divided Styrofoam plate and a tiny plastic spoon, one quarter of a slice of bread, an olive, a cucumber wedge, a three-inch celery stick packed with yogurt and a deviled egg that she'd squeezed the devil out of. She looked at me with eyes that were all too similar to my father's and said, "Making yourself fatter won't make Sam any more wrong."

I took the ladle from the punch bowl and drug it through the potato salad, and then when the potatoes wouldn't release from the ladle, I decided it was the size of spoon I needed anyway, and dropped the whole mess on the center of my plate and made my way out the back door to the side yard and took a chair from among the dozens available. The sun made everything on my plate look pale, and almost immediately it all began to dry out or wilt, and so I ate very quickly, at last licking the chrome bowl and handle of the ladle till it glared in the bright sunshine and I could see my own broad caricatured face on its outer surface. I looked up and Aunt Edna was taking my picture.

"What are you doing?" I cried.

"I'm taking a few pictures of the assembled chairs," she said, "before we bring them all back inside. If you could stand over here, out of the way." She motioned for me to move out of the camera's field of vision. "I'm going to paint them later. I've never done a large group portrait."

I held the ladle and Styrofoam plate separately, one in each hand, at my side. The plate was so light I thought I might topple over, like two of the chairs in the back row had done.

"Do you want me to straighten up the rows?" I asked her. "Pick up the fallen chairs?"

"No, no, leave them as they are. I like the way everyone abandoned them. It will make for a good composition."

She photographed the chairs from one side, then the other, from behind Brother Roberts's stool and from the far side, stood in the street to get every last chair in. Then she took a shot from the porch and a final image of the chairs with the old house in the background. When she'd finished she stood at my side, snapping the camera back into its case. "It's funny that I never thought of painting them all together until today, until we started setting them outside, lining them up in rows. I think they look good together, don't you?"

"I guess," I mumbled.

"I'm sorry about what I said, Sarah, but you've gained some weight, haven't you, since I saw you last. You don't look healthy. I know you're upset. I used to eat when I was upset, too, then I'd get over the upset but I'd have already eaten the food. It's best to be upset when you're upset, rather than hungry."

"I'm not mad anymore," I said. "I'm full."

"You see, that's just what I mean. It's better to be mad than to be full. All the same, I'm sorry."

"I think I'm going to be very hungry for the next few months."

"Give me the ladle, Sarah."

"I'd better keep it."

"Give me the ladle, Sarah," and she smiled. "I'll lock it up till you're over this. Then we'll bring it back out and eat a whole bowl of liquid brownie mix together."

JoAnn snuck up behind us then, whispering siroccos into our ears. "All the guests have left. When are we going to read the will, Aunt Edna?"

"As soon as we get all these chairs back inside, JoAnn."

"Would you like me to light a few vanilla votives to calm everyone's nerves? Momma is on the verge of hyperventilating. There wouldn't be a charge. I've got a few in my car trunk that are half melted."

Aunt Edna turned to me. "Would you form a bucket brigade and get these chairs inside? I need to go talk to your daddy and Margaret."

"I will, but I don't know where each chair goes."

"It doesn't matter. They're interchangeable. I like to see them in new settings anyway."

I turned and looked for brigade volunteers. Sam was leaning against the fender of Daddy's car. It calms him, leaning against cars. He never slept better than when we pulled off the highway into a rest area and reclined the seats. He'd go right off and dream so deeply that he never noticed when his knees cracked the steering wheel or jangled the keys, when semis pulled alongside and their brakes hissed, or even when I got out of the car and went for a walk. Occasionally his hands reached forward and turned the wheel left and right slowly and I knew he was dream-driving. After an hour or two he'd finally wake and step out of the car as if he'd just been born, stretching and yawning, appalled at the cold or heat. I began a sentence once with, "If you paid half as much attention to me as you do to our cars . . ." and he cut me off and said, "If you paid half as much attention to me as you do to our cat . . ." Then he smirked to let me know he wasn't mad, just observant and witty. I know we save a great deal of money because Sam repairs and maintains our cars and the girls'. And it's not all fun for him. He broke his index finger once changing the brake pads on my Honda. He's a clean person, likes for his clothes to be neat, and so he's always running afoul of himself by getting a drop of oil on a pair of khakis or burning a hole in one of his shirts with battery acid. But for the most part he finds it satisfying to force a quart of oil down an engine's throat, to buy it for seventy-nine cents at Wal-Mart rather than pay two dollars at a gas station. And we use that savings to buy things we want. I use it. To be fair I use it to buy him a new shirt and another pair of khakis or a finger splint, but I use it, too. And he also loves our cat. He'd never say it out loud, but whenever she's out late Sam's up at all hours checking the doors. The cat prefers to sleep near him. It's because I roll over.

So, with a full stomach, I walked slowly out to the car and said, "Aunt Edna wants all the chairs back in the house. Will you help me?"

He didn't say anything, but nodded, and we turned in unison toward the vacant lot. My brother and Darcy joined us, then JoAnn, Uncle Alf, Mom, and the rest. While we carried the chairs into the house one by one, Aunt Margaret and Aunt Edna and Daddy cleared off the leftovers. It all seemed very sad, putting things back into their places, one more step removed from the moment when Grandma was alive. Putting the chairs back seemed to deny that anything at all had changed. By the time the vacant lot was again vacant, no one was speaking. We moved through the house quietly finding places for the last few chairs, replacing stacks of magazines, jars of brushes, and Grandma's pills. What a good shelf a chair makes. It accepts almost anything, from a book to a human behind.

By the time we were finished, the dishes were washed as well. Aunt Edna, Margaret, and Daddy all came out of the kitchen together, drying their hands. It seemed odd because I knew they must have been in that kitchen together before, perhaps fifty years earlier, washing up after dinner while Grandpa and Grandma sat in the living room. Now they came into this room and found us, their children and grandchil-dren, in place of their parents. But they didn't pause, didn't even seem to notice the change, took it all in stride. Their hands were pink and wet, the only thing that remained the same. They rubbed them dry with what seemed to me a remarkable adaptability, as if time were only water, a substance that conformed to cupped palms and that could be overcome by the power of the dishrag.

Aunt Edna snapped the red-and-white-striped towel over her shoul-der when she finished and left it there like an epaulet.

"Now," she said, "I know everyone's curious about the graveside ceremony, and why I didn't invite anyone outside the family. If every-one will take a seat I'll read Momma's will and that will explain everything."

The preamble of all gatherings, the scraping of chair legs across the floor, rose in a cacophony of maple groans and mahogany grief, and subsided in poplar burps and the resoluteness of oak against shins. The first to speak when we'd all finally sat down wasn't Aunt Edna but my cousin JoAnn. She whispered, "Did she want us to mix her ashes with Grandpa's? I know that makes some people squeamish, but I'd be happy to do it. I think it's romantic. Eternity together. I've got equipment to mix herbs in equal quantities."

"Speak up, honey," Uncle Alf told his daughter. "I can't hear you."

"Oh, Daddy," JoAnn whispered, and you could see poor Alf trying to read her lips. His own mouth made attempts to copy the shape of hers, then he'd blow air through it to hear what sound came out.

"Grandpa wasn't cremated, JoAnn," I said.

In the meantime, Aunt Margaret had crossed her legs in a fit of exas-peration. Her free foot made little jabs into the air signifying the ticking away of the last few seconds on the universe's clock. I had to admire the economy of her language.

Aunt Edna had taken a thin manila envelope from her bag. "I went by the bank yesterday afternoon and got all of Momma's things from the safety deposit box. This is her last will and testament."

"Did she have a first will and testament?" Sam asked.

"No, just this one," she answered.

"He's making a joke," I said.

"Oh. She had some silver-certificate five-dollar bills in there, and the diamond earrings Daddy gave her, and her life insurance policy. Buddy [she called my father Buddy], if you could look at that later? I can't get through it to see what it means." My father nodded. "Daddy's gold cuff links were in there, too, and his watch, which still works. It started ticking when I took it out of the padded envelope. The only other papers in there were Margaret's birth certificate and Buddy's discharge papers. I just wanted everyone to know what was in there. Of course the will was in there, too."

She pried up the little metal wings of the clasp and opened the envelope. The pages inside, rather than yellowed and brittle, were crisp and white.

"So, there wasn't a winning lotto ticket in there, Aunt Edna?"

"No, Mike."

"I'll bet the biggest secret in that safety deposit box was the date of Margaret's birth," my father said, and he winked at Aunt Margaret, speaking to her in her own language.

"I was born exactly nine months and two days after Momma and Daddy were married," she said.

"Does that mean I'm illegitimate?" JoAnn asked in a whisper that squealed with desire.

I was exasperated now. "There's no secrets, JoAnn. Besides, even if Aunt Margaret were illegitimate, you wouldn't be. It wouldn't have anything to do with you."

She rolled her eyes, leaned toward my sister-in-law and whispered, "She needs an orgasm."

Sam's head whipped around. "She's talking about a ginseng orgasm. She's selling ginseng orgasms," I protested.

"It's just a little homeopathic advice," she whispered to my mother. "All my advice is free to my family."

"What did she say?" Uncle Alf asked. "Why can't she speak up? My wife won't say anything and my daughter won't say it loudly enough."

My father stood up. "I just want to know what Momma wanted us to know, and what Edna already knows. So let's let her read the damn will." He sat back down.

"All right," Aunt Edna said. "I'm not used to reading out loud so you'll have to bear with me."

Aunt Margaret uncrossed her legs, put her clasped hands between her thighs, and bent over as if there were a bucket on the floor ready to receive her thoughts. These complex motions, involving a million firing synapses, and the abstruse machinations of the human musculature and skeletal systems, indicated to my aunt Edna that she should continue with all haste.

Grandma's will did not begin with the words, "Know all men by these . . ." or, "Being of sound mind and body . . ." or even with, "Being of vengeful mind and sickened body . . ." but with, "There's no money." Aunt Edna read: "'There's no money. Of what there is, my three kids can split it. I want Edna to have the house. I want to be cremated. I want my ashes taken to Scotland. Elizabeth Hutton. P.S.—I forgive all my children and grandchildren. Whether they can forgive themselves is a question. I apologize for all my weaknesses.'"

Aunt Edna tucked her lower lip under her upper teeth.

After a silence in which only Uncle Alf continued to hear things, my father said, "Why don't you read that again, Edna."

"'There's no money. Of what there is, my three kids can split it. I want Edna to have the house. I want to be cremated. I want my ashes taken to Scotland. Elizabeth Hutton. P.S.—I forgive all my children and grandchildren. Whether they can forgive themselves is a question. I apologize for all my weaknesses.'" Aunt Edna paused, then added, "Mrs. Rodriguez next door signed as a witness."

"It's in your handwriting," Aunt Margaret said.

"Yes. I wrote it out for Momma, just as she told me, then she signed it, then she told me to add the P.S. I asked her not to put in the last sentences but she said to put them in. Mrs. Rodriguez was real embarrassed, but she signed it, too. Momma tried to give Mrs. Rogriguez five dollars for signing but Mrs. Rodriguez wouldn't accept it."

"Scotland? Why Scotland?" Mike's wife Darcy asked.

"She didn't want to be buried with Dad?" my father asked.

"What happened to the money?" JoAnn whispered. "There was money?"

Aunt Margaret stood up and walked a question mark over the floor. She held her empty arms and hands before her as she paced, as if any moment someone had better place a big platter of explanation in them.

"I don't think it's fair for a person to apologize in a will," my mother said for my father's sake. "You don't get to accept their apology or apologize in return."

My brother stood. "I gave Grandma a book fifteen years ago, after I graduated from college and made that trip to Europe. It was a picture book, *Over Scotland,* or *Scotland from the Air.*"

"*Scotland from Above,*" Aunt Edna corrected. We turned to her. "Momma loved that book, Mike. She'd look at it for hours on end. She thought everything looked so inviting. It was easier to read than her Bible. You know how hot she always was and how she hated the brown grass and the warm wind. Scotland looked so green in the country and the stone cities so cool. She wanted to rest there. There was never any money, JoAnn, honey. I know this is all a shock, but she wouldn't let me tell anybody for fear there'd be an argument and she'd be forced to relent. I promised her I'd carry her to Scotland."

"It just bothers me," my father said, "that Dad will always be out there at the cemetery alone."

"It's not an entirely legal will," Sam said. "You can contest it, I mean, the parts of it you don't like."

I'm sure he said this last in deference to Aunt Edna keeping the house.

"Well, I'll not contest a bit of it," my father said. "It was her body. We'll do what she wanted with it. What do you have to say, Margaret? We should settle this up front, in the open, out loud."

This caught Aunt Margaret off guard, someone asking her opinion. She thought she'd already made everything clear by the tilt of her head and the attitude of her hips, the way they revolved in an elliptical orbit throwing the entire room out of kilter with the rest of the planet.

Before she said a single word, Uncle Alf asked his wife, "What'd you say?"

For someone who rarely needed to speak to get her message across, Aunt Margaret proved remarkably eloquent. "It's not what I want that matters," she began, as if speaking to a single child rather than a roomful of adults. "It's what's right and just. Daddy fully expected to spend eternity with Mother by his side, not halfway around the world. She said herself that there's no money. Who's going to pay for this trip to Scotland? And it's certainly beyond me as to why the Scottish would let a foreigner's dead body into their country. This will doesn't sound as if it was written in a sensible state of mind. I for one reject the notion that I persisted in some state that required my mother's forgiveness. The rest of you have your own conscience to deal with. Mother was bedridden for most of the last twenty years of her life. Crooked notions came into her head. It's our responsibility as her children to straighten them out. It's absurd to carry a person's body across the ocean, when it never left Texas when it was alive."

"It's not a body, Aunt Margaret," my brother said. "It's just a little box."

"It's a handwritten will, witnessed by a Mexican, and it doesn't involve money," she said. "We can do as we will. I'm for burying my mother with my father. That's what she would have wanted if she were in her right mind. Everyone knows she changed after Daddy died. Let's not let her disease change eternity for her. She loved Daddy. She lay in there in that room and her mind corrupted her past and the outside world. I say we bury her as her uncorrupted heart would have had it, next to Daddy. We can't leave him out there alone."

Aunt Edna stood up from her chair. It wobbled behind her and fell over. She was shaking, on the verge of crying.

"You're the one who's corrupting her, Margaret. Her mind wasn't diseased. It was only her body. She was just as sharp at eighty-nine as she was at sixty-five when Daddy died. She read and watched TV and had friends and thought deeply about her life, and what's more she loved you just as much the day she died as the day you were born. Now I've never been out of the state before either, but I'm taking Momma to Scotland, whether you or Daddy or the Scottish protest. You're trying to take control over Mother when she's least able to defend herself."

Then Aunt Edna turned to my father.

"Now, Buddy, you've made your thoughts known and I want you to stick by them. There's no need for you to mediate between your two sisters. I need you to stand up and hold to your opinion. You know Margaret only visited Momma three or four times in the last twenty years. And you've been busy, too. I know what Momma wanted. She longed for some place far away from here, far away from her life in that bed. And the thought of Scotland as her resting place comforted her. Her condition didn't permit her to go when she was alive. I don't know if she would have gone even if all the problems could have been worked out. For her, Scotland was a kind of heaven that she only wanted glimpses of, not any kind of real knowledge. Now, I don't know if Momma made it to heaven or not, but she's going to Scotland."

Aunt Edna turned around, picked up her chair, slammed it back down on its chrome feet, and sat down as if she'd been thrown into the seat. The effort shortened her breath. Sweat streamed off her temples, eroding channels through her base.

Daddy looked back and forth, from one sister to the other. I'd never suspected this role that Aunt Edna had suggested, that of intermediary. He'd never played that role between me and my brother, or me and Mom. He'd always stood aloof from our squabbles. It was a snapshot of his character as a child, something he'd lost or given up when he left his siblings. He'd forced Margaret into vocalizing her opinion, and now Edna demanded he stick with his.

"Margaret," he said, "you and I helped Mom monetarily, but Edna was here. She made the real sacrifice of caring for Mom on a day-to-day basis. She knew her better than you and I did. I'm going to trust her opinion. I think we should carry out the will as it's written."

"It wasn't a sacrifice," Aunt Edna said. "Momma was my best friend. I'd do it all over again. You all seem to think my life was subordinated to hers because she was sick and demanded care. It wasn't that way at all. I wanted to move back home. I wanted to care for her. I was just as happy to stay with her as you two were to move away and be with your families. I don't resent the time I spent with her. I don't resent that the two of you didn't want to help with your time. I felt lucky that she chose me. It made me special. Margaret, I won't let you or anyone else subvert her wishes after she's gone. It's the last thing I can do for her and I'm determined."

"But you'll leave Daddy alone. You'll subvert his wishes," Aunt Margaret said. Her whole frame was slack, as if speech deflated her body, made it incapable of its usual ability to communicate. I looked into her eyes and for once couldn't tell what she was thinking.

I spoke, stuttering at first, my wooden voice dragging across the floor. "Aunt Edna, did Grandma fall out of love with Grandpa after he died?"

"No, honey, no, that wasn't it at all. She still loved him."

"Then . . ." I paused, ". . . then why couldn't we send Grandpa to Scotland, too?"

Here Aunt Margaret's language rejoined her body. She slumped out of her chair to the floor like a sheet of mylar.

"She's fainted," JoAnn whispered as loudly as she could.

Everyone jumped up and surrounded the body. Aunt Margaret woke, batted her eyes like an old doll whose lids have gummed up over the years, and almost immediately thrust her hands not over her eyes but over her crotch, making sure she was still clothed. We helped her sit up, then stand up. She nodded her head to indicate she approved of these steps, then she sort of swayed in the direction of her chair so we'd know to sit her back down.

"Would you like some iced tea, Margaret?" Sam asked. "I'll get it for you."

Uncle Alf said, "Me too. I'd like some, too." He took his hand off his heart and sat down.

"I've got something to put in that tea, Sam," JoAnn said and followed him into the kitchen.

"Life's too hard," Uncle Alf said. "It's too hard."

"Well?" I asked.

"Well what?" Daddy said.

"You can't mean," Mom said, "that you want your father and his sisters to dig up their father, have what's left of him, excuse me, dear, cremated, and then take him to Scotland, too?"

"That's it exactly. Grandma and Grandpa would be together then. I thought that was Aunt Margaret's main objection."

"Leave it alone, Sarah," my brother said.

"Don't speak to your sister that way," Darcy said and slapped him on the shoulder. "It makes perfect sense to me," she said. I couldn't tell if she was aligning herself with me, or against her mother-in-law. "I'm just saying," she explained, "that I want to be buried next to you, Mike, and if you want to be buried in Antarctica I'd be buried there, too, just to be next to you." They hugged.

"I'm just glad I didn't give Grandma a picture book of Antarctica," Mike said.

Then my father, almost against his will, said, "I haven't thought about it in years, but I think Dad's great-grandfather was from Scotland, came to America as a little boy."

Aunt Edna said, "I didn't know that. Momma and Daddy told y'all all the stories and by the time I came along they were tired of telling them. That's what I lost by being the youngest."

"I can't remember anything other than him telling me his great-grandfather was from Scotland. I don't know that Dad knew anything more. I don't know when he might have come over or where he was from."

"It would be like returning your grandpa to his homeland," Darcy said.

"I'm going to be sick," Aunt Margaret said. "None of us are from Scotland. It's absurd. We're from here. Momma and Daddy both grew up in Fort Worth. We grew up in this house. We're all from here."

"But we all moved away," I said. "Only Aunt Edna stayed."

"Maybe we're from where we want to go," Darcy said.

Even Mike got lost in that one. There was a curl of hair that had fallen over Darcy's ear. She pushed it aside with complete satisfaction.

"You're living in a bright glare, aren't you, Darcy, honey," I said, but the more I thought about what she said the more my own head hurt, and the more guilty I felt. Could we possibly be from the place we want to be? Were we from the place we died rather than the place we were born? Are our aspirations our home? Maybe we are from that place to which we're bound, and that's why desire hurts so much, this longing to find a place to rest, to get home. We're not from the past, but the future.

Aunt Margaret waggled her head like a cartoon character, telling the world how I felt.

Sam and JoAnn returned with the iced tea. After he handed a glass to Aunt Margaret, I pulled him aside. "Do you think home is some place you're from or some place you have to find?" I asked him.

"What?"

"Are we defined by where we want to go or where we've been?"

"You've gone through several steps of some equation and you're asking me for the answer. I don't know where you've been or how you got here."

"I'm confused, too," I told him. "I wish you hadn't cheated on me."

"Me too, Sarah. Me too. I'm sorry."

"You don't seem like home anymore."

"I'm still here."

We looked at each other silently for a few moments, till we couldn't any longer, and turned back to my family.

"Did I miss anything?" JoAnn whispered, stepping back into the room as if it were a movie theater.

"A big chase scene," I said. "A car crash. The butler did it."

"You're a funny one, Sarah," she told me secretly. "There's herbs for sadness. There's vitamins for despair."

Aunt Margaret drank down her tea.

Aunt Edna stood up. "Well, taking Daddy to Scotland has taken me by surprise. I guess taking Momma surprised y'all. I don't know what to think about it. I like the idea of their ashes being on the same continent. It's not as if I visited Daddy's grave very often. But I did like knowing it was there, the plaque with his name on it."

"That could stay," I said, "and we could add Grandma's name to it, as a memorial here in Fort Worth."

"Daddy never suspected he'd be buried in Scotland, I know that," Aunt Margaret said softly.

"It wouldn't have bothered him," my father said. "Not being with Mom would have."

"It all seems very complicated," my mother said. "An exhumation, all the permits and permissions."

"They exhumed Lee Harvey Oswald a few years ago," Mike said. "Water had gotten into the concrete vault and he was like a mass of jelly." Darcy slapped his shoulder again. "I'm not saying Grandpa would be like that." She slapped it again.

Uncle Alf placed his hand on Aunt Margaret's shoulder, leaned down and put his lips to her ears softly. Then he yelled, "I'd want to be by you."

Aunt Margaret stumbled up from her chair, and we all backed away as if someone had lobbed a hand grenade into our midst. It was plain Alf had misjudged the loudness of his loving coo. Aunt Margaret had her palm flat against her ear to keep the ringing in. She looked to heaven and shook her head. It seemed to me that ashes from some great conflagration fell lightly upon her face.

She whispered. Even JoAnn had to lean in to hear. She whispered, "Y'all do what you will. Everyone knows Momma's done this to spite me. Alf, let's go home. JoAnn, get in the car. If I need to sign anything, send it to me. I'll sign it."

"I'll handle everything," Aunt Edna told her. "I'll let you know every step of the process."

"I don't want to know," she said. "This is the soil they were reared from. It ought to be the soil they return to. There's going to be a depression in the earth now. The country will be unbalanced. I was going to be buried next to Momma and Daddy and now that won't happen. I don't want to know any more. There's no telling where y'all will bury me. I don't know where I'll go when I die."

And with that she left the house and I didn't see her again till the end of the summer. JoAnn put a bottle of ginseng oil in my hand on her way out, telling me, "No charge."

Uncle Alf followed them, shaking his head. He stopped at the door and told my mother that he wouldn't hear a word for the next eleven hundred miles, till they reached the outskirts of Phoenix.

"Be careful, Alf," my father said.

"I can't help it that I can't hear," he said. "It makes me speak too loud. I'm probably speaking too loud now."

"No, no," Daddy yelled. "You sound just right."

"I used to could read lips, but now everybody yells at me and it distorts their mouths."

"Oh," Daddy said.

"That was 'Oh,' you see?"

My father nodded enthusiastically.

Once they'd gone we took seats again, all of us against one wall of the living room as if we were waiting in a narrow hallway. We had to lean forward to look at someone when they spoke.

Aunt Edna said, "I want to apologize for my stubbornness. The truth is I'd like nothing better than to stay here and paint all summer. I haven't the vaguest idea of how to visit a foreign country."

"Do you have a passport, Aunt Edna?" Mike asked.

She leaned forward to look at him. "No, but I have a driver's license."

"Well, you'll need to apply for a passport."

"Do you want me to go with you, Edna?" my father asked, putting his hands on his knees.

"It's your busy time, Buddy. I know that. I won't be there more than a day, time to find a place to spread the ashes, and then I'll be back on the plane."

Mike leaned forward. "You ought to stay a few days, Aunt Edna. It's just as beautiful as the pictures in the book. I was only in Edinburgh for a day and Glasgow for a day, but what I saw from the train in between them was pretty."

"He was with that other girl on that trip," Darcy said. "The one before me," and she leaned back.

"I could go," Daddy said. "I could get someone to cover for me." He leaned back against the wall.

Aunt Edna leaned forward. "I won't hear of it. You told me yesterday that you have eleven teachers to hire in six weeks."

"I'll go," I said.

"What?" Sam said.

"Aunt Edna could use some help. I'll stay here and help with Grandpa's exhumation. We'll both get passports and plan the trip and I'll go with her. If that's all right with you, Aunt Edna? If you could stand the company around here. It might take a month for us to prepare."

"It's high tourist season in Great Britain right now," Mike said. "You'll be lucky to get tickets and places to stay."

"You're not coming home?" Sam asked.

"No, I'll stay here with Aunt Edna."

"You don't have to stay with me, Sarah. You go back home."

"No, I'd like to help. I'd like to stay, if you'll let me." It was easier to do this in front of everyone.

"You're not coming home at all?" Sam asked.

"Mom could mail me the clothes I need. I have some clothes here already, and my luggage. I'd like to have this time with Aunt Edna."

"Well, I can't stay," Sam said. "I have to get back to work."

"I know that," I said. I leaned back in my chair, pressing it against the wall.

"The girls will be home from college in a couple of weeks," he said, as if this were something he couldn't handle alone.

"I'll call and tell them where I am," I said. "They'll understand."

"Honey, maybe you'd better go home for a while and then come back down once everything is settled," my mother suggested.

"Jesus Christ," I sighed. "I think I'm old enough to make this decision. Aunt Edna, do you mind if I stay for a few weeks and help with the arrangements and then go with you to Scotland?"

"Of course I don't mind."

"Then it's settled." I stood up. "Mom, I'm going to make a list of things I want sent down. You and Sam can box them up and put them in the mail."

Everyone else stood up then, as if we were all about to jump out of a plane. Sam fell out the screen door first, searching no doubt for a fender to lean against.

"Aunt Edna," Mike asked, "why does Aunt Margaret think Grandma was trying to spite her by requesting to be buried in Scotland?"

"I don't know, Mike. Margaret thinks it's always been hard for anybody to love Margaret, and so she makes it hard. Momma loved her just as much as she did me and your daddy."

My father ushered me to the back bedroom, Grandma's room. "What's going on, Sarah?"

I don't know what it is about my father showing me concern, but it always makes me cry. I feel like I've let him down. Mike doesn't have this problem. If there's something he needs, whether it's money or pity, he goes to Mom and Dad right off, fills up his war chest, and heads out again, seemingly without regret or shame. I've always felt they'd done their part by the time I turned eighteen. But now, for the second time since I was eighteen, my father could tell I needed him and had come to me. The first time was when Michelle, my oldest, had a severe case of blood poisoning and almost died. She was only six at the time. I bawled in my father's arms and let him hold me up because my own legs wouldn't support me. I told him I didn't want to live if she died. The second instance was there in my dead grandmother's bedroom when I told him that Sam and I were in trouble. I was forty-four years old and there was absolutely nothing my father could do for my problem, just as he couldn't have saved Michelle, yet I stood there in his arms and wept. I felt so guilty about weeping, making him worry. It seemed the least a person could do after crying at home for eighteen years was to not come home crying.

He said he could perfectly well understand my desire to stay away from home for a few weeks. A few weeks wouldn't cause any more damage than was already done. He asked me if I'd like him to drop Sam off in some really bad part of Dallas on the way home, which was a lot for him to offer because he liked Sam.

"No," I said. "I want him to get home to an empty house, to see what that is. Maybe he'll like it."

□ □ □

My father was a teacher for twenty-five years, a geometry teacher who became a school administrator for the last half of his career. People trusted his straightforward logical analysis of problems and the solutions he found. His hair had gone white early, giving him a bemused look rather than a distinguished one. He held his hands as if there was still chalk in them, as if chalk dust still filled the crevices in his palms that he used for erasers. He tried not to touch his clothes with his hands. So when he hugged me there was a moment of pause before he realized he could put his hands on my back without getting me dirty, that proven equations wouldn't soil my blouse.

Dad and Grandma had their falling out because he left Fort Worth for a better paying job in the Saint Louis school district. He and Mom were really just following me and Mike. We'd both found jobs there, and so Dad found one there, too. It was a question of living near his parents or living near his children and grandchildren, and he made a choice. He drew out some sort of problematical triangle and used proofs to solve his own family geometry problem. I think Grandma and Grandpa missed him badly. And then Grandpa got sick and died. Daddy had visited all through Grandpa's illness but was too late for his last visit. He walked into the hospital room. Aunt Edna and Grandma were sitting by the bed and Grandpa's body. Grandma looked up at Daddy and said, "You're too late. He had things he wanted to say to you. There were things on his conscience he didn't get to say to you.

You were his only son. You were supposed to protect him and be there for him when he was old. He had things he wanted to say to you and you were far away."

Well, what does that do to a person? At the time it made me hate my grandmother for making my father feel so bad. Because he did, for years.

Mike followed me to Saint Louis, and Mom and Dad followed us. I was the first to leave Fort Worth, the first trickle in what became a dam-bursting flood. All three of my cousins, Aunt Margaret's children, left home for jobs in Phoenix, San Francisco, and Los Angeles. Aunt Margaret and Alf followed them. Grandpa died and that left Grandma and Aunt Edna. Aunt Edna sold her house on the south side and moved back home to care for Grandma, who seemed to meander from one debilitating illness to another for the last twenty years of her life. From Grandma's point of view we abandoned her. Whose side am I on, my grandmother's or my father's? Since the day my parents joined us in Saint Louis, I've been on my father's side. But now that my two girls are in college, soon to embark on their own careers, I ask myself: Will I follow them if they both move to Seattle or Japan? Will I leave my parents here in Saint Louis to fend for themselves in their old age? I want to think that I'll be by my parents when they need me. Mike and Darcy can hardly care for a cat. I'll probably be Aunt Edna for my parents. But when my girls go, if my girls go, I know I'll take it personally. Especially if they wait till they're forty to leave and take my grandchildren with them. I'm sure that by then I will be thinking my life is somewhat settled, my family will be near me till the day I die. I'm sure that's what Grandma thought about Margaret and Daddy, and then they up and moved away simply because their children had. I was the first of Grandma's grandchildren to move away. Perhaps they all followed me. Perhaps she hated me the most, and that's why clocks flew when I visited, or perhaps it was because I'm narrow-minded and pigeonhole people.

▢ ▢ ▢

I pulled away from my father, wiped my eyes. "I'm sorry, Daddy," I said. "I feel like one of my own girls. Michelle cries over every boy who looks at her."

"I wish boys weren't so mean," he said. "I apologize for all of us."

"It's not just Sam," I said. "All of the sudden I'm really emotional about Grandma."

"Yes, me too."

"I used to hate her so much because she made you feel so bad."

"Well, I never hated her. She had her reasons to make me feel bad. But it's easy to see where your aunt Margaret got some of her personality traits. Your grandma was just as sure that everybody hated her as Margaret is."

"But I did hate her," I said. "She was right. But it wasn't fair, was it? She must have been lonely. I know I'm going to be if the girls move off. I miss them already. I miss the husbands and kids they don't even have yet."

"You can follow them," he said. "I did."

"But would you and Mom follow us again? I mean if we all moved."

"Oh, I doubt it, honey. We're pretty settled now. But you never can tell. If Michelle or Susan has a great-grandbaby we may move in with them."

"How do you choose between your kids and your parents?"

"Some people choose their kids, some their parents, some are able to make everything work out."

"I should have never left Fort Worth. I started it all. I left home. How could I have done that? Don't we all need to stay home, like Aunt Edna? I feel like we're all just a bunch of Vikings, moving around so we can pillage and burn, make a better living."

"No, honey, it's something instinctual that makes us move on. It's nothing you should fault yourself for. It's going to be an interesting ride home without you."

"I'm sorry about that. It wasn't anything I planned. But I need some time away from him, and I am worried about Aunt Edna. She hasn't lived alone in twenty years."

"Neither have you, Sarah."

"I'm trying to prepare myself for that possibility."

"Don't make all your decisions in one week. Some proofs take years to solve."

"Oh, God. I'm exhausted. If only life were as simple as geometry."

"Oh yeah! I wish you could have talked to some of my ninth-graders. They knew everything but geometry."

"Daddy, the next time you get Mom alone, I want you to tell her how much you love her, and how your life wouldn't have been the same without her. Tell her she's the most beautiful woman you've ever known."

"OK, I will."

"I'm so sorry you've lost your mom."

"It's OK, honey. I know my mother loved me, if only because she was wounded so badly by my leaving. I left out a category earlier, when I said some choose their kids, some their parents, and some both. Some people choose themselves. She could have followed us or accepted our visits with grace. She chose to be offended. But I have all that time before we left, my childhood and your childhood with her, to look back on. I loved my mother. I love her still. And I'm coming to an understanding. I feel like I'm in the middle of a novel, rather than at the end."

"I guess I need to go say good-bye to Sam before you leave."

"Well, I want to talk to your aunt and see if she needs anything. I'm glad you'll be around to help her. It's funny, Mom wanting to leave home at last, like everybody else."

"That just leaves Aunt Edna."

"I'm worried about my baby sister. She doesn't look well."

"Daddy, you and Aunt Margaret haven't looked too good the last couple of days either. It's the stress."

"All the same. I have your mother to look after me, and Margaret has Alf. Edna's all alone now."

"I'll look after her, Daddy, at least for a while."

"OK. Let's get out of this room. It's giving me the heebie jeebies, the way the bed is still tilted up like that."

"I guess I'm going to have to sleep there tonight. Aunt Edna doesn't own a couch."

"I'd line up three or four chairs and lie on them before I slept in here."

□ □ □

I found Sam with Aunt Edna in the kitchen. They stopped speaking when I entered the room. Aunt Edna took the dishrag off her shoulder and began a desperate search for something to clean. She finally lit on the accordion-like rubber seal of the refrigerator door, pulling it taut and wiping furiously at the heretofore hidden folds.

"Let's go outside and find a car to lean against," I told Sam.

"I've used every fender out there today. Besides, it's hot. We can talk in front of Edna. You'll talk to her after I'm gone."

"I better leave," Aunt Edna said. She shut the refrigerator door.

"I wish you'd come home with me. I can't make it up to you if you're five hundred miles away," Sam said.

"I'm going to go," Aunt Edna said. She dropped the dishrag into the sink between us.

"I don't want you to make it up to me," I said.

"I wish you'd stay, Edna," Sam said. "I want a witness. Just so you won't misrepresent me, Sarah, I'll say that I love you, that I'm sorry for what I've done, and I have no desire to do it anymore."

"I think Mom and Daddy are ready to leave," I told him. "You should drive some so Daddy doesn't get so tired."

"What's left for me to say?" he asked.

"I'm going to go start the washer and dryer," Aunt Edna said.

"Just stay right where you are," I snapped at her. "I don't want you to say anything else, Sam. I don't want to hear your voice. Now you know what it feels like to be left. Now maybe you'll understand how I feel."

"You two kids stop it right now," Aunt Edna said. "Neither one of you should speak to each other for a while. You go on home, Sam. I'll watch after her."

There were hot tears brimming in my eyes but I could see that Sam was furious, too. He walked out of the kitchen and the house with his arms crossed. Aunt Edna followed him to the door but I didn't. Mom and Daddy stood in the living room and watched everyone pass, Sam to the yard, Aunt Edna to the screen door, and me into the bathroom, as if they'd been waiting for just this scene, their cue to leave. Mom came to the bathroom door and said good-bye and that she'd call when they got home. I heard the front door slam, heard three car doors slam, heard Aunt Edna come inside and make her way back to the kitchen.

It was only four o'clock in the afternoon, still far too much day left to deal with, so I just sat on the toilet for another twenty minutes using up the day. I wouldn't allow anything portentous or insurmountable to inhabit that twenty minutes. The invention of the bathroom with locking door was one of the great saviors of the modern psyche. We don't follow one another into this small room so much because of the smell but because we recognize the need for some corner of the world where we can be alone. I don't think we're as embarrassed about urinating as we are anxious for a place to hide. Having to pee is just an excuse to escape from society for a few minutes. There are days when I have to go to the bathroom a dozen times, and it's not because I've had too much soda.

In the corner, above the wicker hamper, was one of Aunt Edna's chair portraits, a small canvas whose sole occupant was her own chair, the chrome and red vinyl kitchen chair repaired with duct tape. I thought it odd that she hadn't repaired the chair in the painting. It would have been so easy to do, a few strokes of red over the silver. She'd painted the chair in the vacant lot, the two big pomegranates in the background, a gray sky overhanging all. The grass was yellow, so this was a Texas winter scene, spare rather than stark. The colors didn't go at all well with the bathroom wallpaper. The room needed something brighter, perhaps in pastels rather than oil. But few of Aunt Edna's paintings were decorative in the sense that they were meant to accent a room or complement the furniture. Occasionally I'd find myself sitting in a chair with its portrait directly above me on the wall. This was unnerving somehow. I'd look up at the painting, expecting to find myself sitting in it, too. The painted chair would still be empty, of course, so then I'd feel empty, or worse, that I didn't count. It's similar to a feeling I get when I walk in front of a bank of video cameras in a department store. Everything around me is on the monitors, but often I'm not there and have to move around to find myself. Aunt Edna's paintings are like that, as if someone just moved beyond the frame or is about to walk into it. Rockers look as if they're still bobbing, their occupant just away to the kitchen for a glass of iced tea. A grouping of chairs on the front lawn seem to be waiting. Her paintings, calm and passive, still intimated a flurry of activity outside the frame. Aunt Edna's own chair seemed out of place, a kitchen chair in grass, a kitchen chair in the bathroom, the wallpaper overpowering the paint, the canvas too small for the wall it was hung on.

I flushed the toilet to cover my escape, pulled the creases out of my blouse, and stood up to find an unsatisfying reflection. Mirrors are a bathroom's only drawback. I was at that point in life when I needed to start wearing brighter clothes in order to distract onlookers from the shape of my body, the contours of my face. Crying didn't help. No one notices your clothes when you cry. I'd worn a pale yellow blouse and skirt for Grandma's service and now I looked like a Neiman-Marcus sack that had been dragged ostentatiously around the rest of the mall, stuffed with items from Women's Tall & Oversize, crumpled into an ice-cream chair at the food court, and dipped into a fountain while searching for pennies to throw. I know that's a lot for a wrinkled yellow skirt and blouse to acknowledge but it was all there. I couldn't wait to dump myself out of it. It was then I recalled that all my clothes were still in my suitcase, which was in the car presently on its way to Saint Louis.

Fits of emotion wreak havoc on my organizational skills. I miss TV shows I was going to watch, leave out ingredients from cakes, put incorrect objects in unforgiving receptacles (pouring water into the trash or storing mayo in the hamper), and often draw angels and cherubs that look like armadillos or garden tractors. The day after a fight it's best if I just lie on the couch in a jogging suit rather than make any commitments. My mind and body are overwrought with self-recriminations and lost moments where victory could have been obtained if only I'd thought as clearly as I can a day later on a couch in a jogging suit. If only life could be lived with a twenty-four-hour guarantee, where we could exchange or return the moments of indecision and apprehensiveness and carelessness for a better-fitting suit of ourselves.

As it is, as it was, I walked away from that mirror and asked my aunt Edna for a change of clothes and she brought me a jogging suit spattered and smudged with oil and acrylic, all the paint unfit for art.

"I do have my purse," I told her. "I'll go out to the mall tomorrow and get a few things, enough to tide me over till my clothes come in a few days."

"It's all right, Sarah. We're about the same size. You can wear my clothes."

But, I thought, I don't want to wear the clothes of a person eighteen years older than I am. "Thank you, Aunt Edna," I said. "I promise I'll try to be more help than burden over the next few weeks."

That evening, as we sat and talked, I examined the traces of paint on my outfit, trying to discern by the colors and gradations of shading which of Aunt Edna's works she'd painted while wearing those clothes. I see easels at garage sales, speckled with flecks of color, with the sweep of a trailing brush, and wonder what the easel can say about the canvas that's missing. I'd go to the ends of the earth to see an exhibit of artists' work clothing, Picasso's undershirt, Ingres's jacket, Homer's apron, Casatt's smock. I think that the studio floors of acknowledged masters might be pulled up and mounted on the walls after they've died, to be studied as the last vital clue to an artist's working life. I think Jackson Pollock had this idea long before I did. Aunt Edna watched me pulling at the daubs of dried paint on the sleeve.

"Everything I have is ruined with paint," she said.

"Oh no, I love it. I love everything that we drop and smear on ourselves by accident. It's a pattern we don't design but somehow represents us. I'd know one of Sam's car work shirts if I had to pick it out of a thousand oily rags."

"I'll try to keep a shirt clean as long as possible but I'll get busy and forget, and then one spot seems worse than a thousand so I'll use my clothes to wipe my fingers, to clean my brushes, even to smear the paint on the canvas sometimes. We used to talk about painting and drawing before you left so long ago, Sarah. I've missed it."

"I haven't drawn anything but my ornaments since college, Aunt Edna. Painting wouldn't have paid the bills."

"Painting isn't for bill paying. Painting is for painting."

"I know, but when you sketch Christmas ornaments all day, the last thing you want to do for fun is take your sketchbook to your kid's recital or soccer game."

"You used to send me your ornaments."

"Well, they're all pretty much the same anymore. Hallmark wants the standbys: teddy bears, Santa Clauses, reindeer, the nativity, cherubs and angels. It used to please me to see my designs on a tree. Anymore I just grit my teeth at the approach of Christmas. It used to be my favorite time of year. I can draw teddy bears in twenty-five different stances without even lifting my pencil from the paper. They tell me I'm good at it but what they don't know is it's easy for me. They congratulate me on some 600,000-unit plastic Santa and it makes me feel hollow, because I drew him in fifteen minutes."

"Some of your things are darling, Sarah. If there were other people with your talent they'd have your job."

"Oh, can it, Aunt Edna. If I died tomorrow they'd find someone else. I used to defend myself to myself in the same way. It was a challenge for those first few years after college, sending off my designs unsolicited, modeling my own ornaments, and selling them at craft shows, getting my foot in the door at Hallmark and then going out on my own as an independent designer. I think all of that was some sort of accomplishment. When that Rudolph ornament, the one where he's leading the Starship Enterprise, sold a million units, and I bought a new car with the royalties, I thought I was a real cup of hot chocolate. Then, the very next summer, not six months from my triumph, I was at a garage sale and there was one of my ornaments on a dime table. I said to the man there, "'This just came out last Christmas and you're already selling it?'"

'It was a gift from my mom,' he shrugged. 'I've always liked *Star Trek* so she got me this.' He shrugged again. 'It's my opinion that if we stopped buying each other these ridiculous gifts and donated the money instead we'd already have a cure for cancer. You can have it for a nickel if you're interested.'

"For a week I complained about that guy to Sam. 'What an idiot,' I said. 'My ornaments are collectible,' I said. 'People wait for them to come out, buy a dozen and put them away to sell in twenty years.' And that's true. Sam said it, 'That's true. Don't let it bother you.' But I know people trade in my ornaments for profit, not for the love of art. Hallmark calls them 'Limited Editions' and then stamps out every one they can sell. You know what my big seller is going to be this Christmas?"

Aunt Edna shook her head in that manner people do when they're being harangued. It didn't stop me.

"A little Titanic with an iceberg at its bow. There's a Christmas tree growing from the iceberg. There's a tiny baby Jesus riding in the stern. It's just the beginning of summer and they've already built a thousand molds to inject a million gallons of resin into; they'll make so many plastic Titanics that their sheer weight would have sunk the original Titanic. It's obscene, Aunt Edna, and I started it."

"Is there really a baby Jesus?"

"Yes, but he's removable if you don't like the idea of it. Some people are really into sacrifice at Christmas. The thought of Jesus being born just leads naturally to Jesus dying. It's inevitable. You bring the living Christmas tree into your house to watch it slowly die. Beautifully wrapped presents are ripped to shreds. Christmas lights blink. The entire year is dying before your eyes. Sam carries the tree out to the curb on his back just like it was a cross. There's a broken ornament left where the living tree was."

"Well," Aunt Edna sighed.

"You should get a cat now," I told her.

"What brought that up?" she asked.

"It was probably our cat that knocked the ornament off the tree. She likes the way they swing when she bats them. And, Aunt Edna, she loves the tinfoil icicles. She eats them. We had to take every icicle off the lower branches. You know how we found out? She was walking down the hallway early one morning. The sun was streaming in through the glass in the front door. It lit up about three inches of icicle hanging out of her butt." I collapsed in a fit of laughter. Aunt Edna smiled broadly. She put her hand over her mouth.

"What did you do?" she asked.

"Well, I had to pull it out, didn't I?"

Aunt Edna screamed and hid her face in her hands.

"Let me tell you," I cried, "Sheba didn't like that." I thought I'd shed all the tears I could that day, but more came.

"How long was it?" Aunt Edna wheezed.

"Oh, about twelve inches," I screamed. "She didn't know whether to back up or run away."

"Oh, Lord," Aunt Edna coughed. "You should feed her a whole bowlful of them before a party." I fell off my chair. I literally slipped off the edge and landed on my big butt. Aunt Edna stood up and bent over to help me up but she was laughing too hard. Finally, she just stopped, put her palms on her knees and explained, "Then, everyone could have a turn tugging on one."

"Stop it, stop it," I gasped. "I'm begging."

"You could write fortunes on them before you fed them to her."

"I'm gonna pee in your clothes," I said.

"You better not." And she stopped laughing. She made her way back to her chair. I could tell I'd said something that bothered her. I stopped laughing, too, and pushed myself up to my knees.

"What's wrong, Aunt Edna?"

"The part I used to hate most was washing Momma's sheets. She couldn't help it. We'd use diapers but they always leaked. It was so humiliating for her."

"At least it was you, Aunt Edna. It would have been worse for her in a home."

"Yes, and that's where she would have gone if I weren't here. I keep telling myself that."

"I'm so proud of you for caring for Grandma all those years. I know it will upset you to hear me say it, but she couldn't have been the easiest person in the world to support. I think the most courageous people are those who care for human beings who can't care for themselves. A hermit is a terrific coward in my book, because he won't or can't deal with other people. You didn't run away."

"It wasn't in me to run away, Sarah. You're congratulating me for my Christmas ornaments. It was easy for me. It was only hard for Momma."

"Well, she's easy now, Aunt Edna."

"I know, and it's a relief to me that there's no more humiliation, no more fear for her."

"What was she afraid of?"

"More pain, losing her mind, Alzheimer's, losing one of her children. But none of those things happened at last. She went off so easy. She went to sleep watching TV, and so did I, sitting there in the chair by her bed. I woke up when the test pattern came on, but she didn't."

"Gosh, that sounds like *The Twilight Zone*."

"Nothing eerie about it, Sarah. Her heart just stopped beating. It beat for eighty-nine years, and then it didn't. You can't expect a body to go on forever, can you?"

"No," I said. "I don't think I'll want to live that long."

"I'm so tired."

"Why don't we fix ourselves a ham sandwich? We've got all those leftovers."

"I was thinking you and I might go on a diet together, Sarah."

"That sounds fun," I muttered.

"No, I mean it. It's easier if we lose weight together. We'll make it a little contest over the next few weeks."

"Aunt Edna, I'm going through emotional trauma here. Eating is one of my only crutches."

"Well, you need to use one of your other only crutches. I'll be a crutch for you and you can be one for me. It's not healthy to be as fat as we are."

"I used to wonder at what weight would Sam take more interest in me, as if there were some number I could weigh that would make him see me differently."

"You go on a diet for yourself, Sarah, not for Sam."

"I shouldn't give you the wrong idea. Sam's never said anything about my size."

"We'll have to throw out almost everything in the kitchen," Aunt Edna said. "There can't be a spoonful of mayonnaise in this house."

"It will be harder for you," I said, "working with all that food at school."

"Honey, I got over school food twenty-five years ago. I can't smell it or taste it, much less eat it. Besides, there's only a week of school left, then I'll be free for the summer."

"Can't we start the diet tomorrow?"

"Sarah, time's a-wasting. We've both decided to make a life change. We're going to clean this house, slim down, travel to a foreign country, flutter our eyes at men, and practice art. I don't want to hang around and mope about Momma. I don't want to see you moping about Sam. There's nothing more tedious to watch than prolonged self-pity."

"My eyes don't flutter," I said. "The best I can do is bat them eight or ten times a minute." I gave her an example.

"They'll think you've been injured," she said. "OK, then, do you know how to sigh heavily?"

I sighed.

"No, no," she said. "You have to sigh like you've just seen a dead puppy on the side of the road, or like you've just given birth."

I sighed again, more poignantly.

"That's better. You might throw in a dash of longing for the past that will never be again."

"I never knew you were such a flirt, Aunt Edna."

"Oh, I'm not, but I read a lot of magazines, and they all seem to imply it's a great deal of fun. Everything I know about men first-hand I learned from the little boys in my lunch line. But from what I have seen from a distance, adult men aren't that much different than the little boys who want two milks when they only have money for one."

"What do you tell them?"

"Oh, I give them the second milk and tell them to bring the money tomorrow."

"Do they bring it?"

"Hardly ever, but when they do, it comes with a note from their mother thanking me."

"Exactly," I said.

"Exactly," she said.

We spent the remainder of the evening cleaning out the refrigerator and kitchen cabinets of anything fattening. I turned over Tupperware bowls and they barfed their contents into the trash bag. Aunt Edna got choked up when she threw out two full gallons of ice cream, Mango Peach, Grandma's favorite. By the time we were through there were four eggs, two half-empty jars of pickles, an apple, and two bottles of medicine left in the refrigerator.

"What about the medicine?" I asked.

"Leave it there for now. I need to go through the house and gather up all the bottles of Momma's pills. I don't think they should go in the regular garbage. It's amazing how many pills can accumulate. I think I could start a pharmacy with what's left."

"Maybe you could donate them to a hospital or a clinic or somewhere."

"I'll check into it."

"You know, Aunt Edna, we need to start a list. We've got a lot to coordinate. We need a calendar."

"We can do that, or we can cook this bag of microwave popcorn and eat it," she said. "It's half the fat of regular popcorn." She held it up in the air high over her head and wagged the plastic package back and forth.

"Well, I'm not going to jump for it, Aunt Edna." It was ridiculous. She was six inches shorter than I was. It was only her hair that made her look taller. My mother often said that Aunt Edna's hairdo was only limited by the length of her arms. Her hair, dyed the dark straw of a grocery sack, was always up, mounted up actually, ringlet climbing curl, reinforced with bobby pins and tortoiseshell combs. It was the same hairdo she'd had when I left town twenty-six years earlier. I think it's a style adhered to by many cafeteria and food-preparation workers because a hair net follows its contours so well. Year after year Aunt Edna had mailed out the new official school photo of herself in her white uniform. The hair and uniform remained the same. Her smile never varied. But the line of her shoulders had rounded, and her skin seemed to have lost its lushness of color, to have reverted to a sketched study that relied more on shadow and tone. Her face was not wrinkled but rumpled, as if a few minutes' spin and a good shake might smooth it out. Above all, my aunt Edna looked comfortable in her face and body, as if she'd found a place to relax. When she closed her eyes she made the room drowsy.

I closed the refrigerator door and picked up the heavy plastic garbage bag, lumpy as it was with congealed foods, liable to split and defecate pea salad. On my way to the back door I dropped the bag and made a little unexpected leap and snatched the popcorn from Aunt Edna's hand.

"Ha!" I squealed and ran to the microwave.

"You've gotten taller, Sarah," she said and followed me.

"No, you've gotten shorter," I replied. "How long?"

"Two minutes fifty seconds. I have gotten shorter."

"Everybody does."

"I never did till now, though."

I turned to her and smiled. "Was it a shock?"

"It was. I knew Momma had shrunk, but the last time I went to the doctor they measured me and I was a half-inch shorter. I made the nurse measure me again to make sure. I just didn't think I would shrink so early."

We listened to the popcorn pop, mesmerized by its randomness, by its poignant inability to fight its way out of a sack.

"Popcorn is a miracle," Aunt Edna said. "All that explosive flowering hidden away in something so hard and compact. Sometimes when I paint, Sarah, I feel like I'm popcorn. Things I didn't know were in me come out. Here, let it cool. I've got something I want to show you. It's a secret. Not even Momma knew about it."

She squatted in front of the doors beneath the kitchen sink. She opened the doors. I was still standing by the microwave. "Well, look here." I squatted next to her. Behind an assortment of sponges, rubber gloves, cans of Comet and Brasso, behind the chrome drainpipe, were stacked perhaps a dozen gallon-cans of Folgers coffee. She crawled under the sink and struggled to bring one of the cans out into the light. "They're so heavy," she huffed.

"What is it?" I asked.

"Money," she said earnestly.

"Whose money?" I asked. "There *was* money," I accused.

"This is my money, not Momma's." She burped the plastic lid and pulled it away to reveal a full gallon of dimes.

"Dimes," I said. Sam had a big jar of pocket change at home, too.

"This is my lunch-line money," she explained. "The kids brought it to me."

"Aunt Edna, you didn't embezzle all this change from the school?"

"Of course not. I replaced every penny I took out of the till. It's all silver, Sarah. I started at the cafeteria in 1958. They stopped making silver coins in 1965. As the kids brought the silver coins through the lines to pay for their lunches, I'd tease out the silver and some of the other old coins."

"All of these cans are full of silver? They're full?"

"Full to the top. I've got two gallons of silver dollars, three gallons of half-dollars, five gallons of quarters, three gallons of dimes, a gallon of buffalo nickels, and two gallons of wheat pennies. The kids are going to pay for our trip to Scotland."

"Oh, Aunt Edna, I can pay for my trip. You should save this for your retirement."

"I am. This was my last year. I retire in a week."

"But why didn't you say anything earlier? You're only sixty-two."

"I'll miss the kids, but I'm ready to retire. I've got a lot of painting to do."

"How much is all this worth?"

"Oh, it's not gold, but I'm hoping some of them have a rare date and will be worth more than just the silver. I'll have to get a coin book."

I plunged my hand into the open can. Beneath a thick layer of Roosevelt dimes were Mercury dimes and even a few Barber coins. "You collected these one at a time?"

"In the early days, I'd put my whole paycheck into the till. Later on they petered out. I had to be very diligent. But you'd be surprised by how much is still out there. And I think the kids sometimes pilfered mom and dad's collection to buy their lunches."

"All the time I thought you smelled like green beans you were smelling like money."

"Oh, it's not that much, Sarah, but I hope there's enough to get the four of us to Scotland and two of us back. I'd hate to use any of the estate money for those expenses since Momma left me the house. I'd like your daddy and Margaret to get a little something."

She put the can back under the sink.

"That money's been under the sink all these years?"

"Yes, it's the only place in the house Momma never went. She didn't like kitchen work."

"Why did you have to hide it from her?" I asked.

"I didn't have to, but it would have preyed on her mind. She was always worried someone was going to take something from her, especially later on. If she knew we had a silver horde she'd have never slept."

"I probably owe Grandma an apology," I said. "I do pigeonhole people, and I pigeonholed her, especially after Grandpa died and she made Daddy feel so guilty. I put her down as a mean, selfish hypochondriac."

"Well, you weren't too far off, but you'd have to include depressed and betrayed, and above all in love. You have to be madly in love to feel betrayed. People you don't care about can't betray you. She was debilitated by love, felt unworthy, and so she made herself unworthy.

Somebody at work would do me a slight and it would make her so mad. She'd try to get up out of bed, collapse back down into it, and then complain, 'I wish they'd come down here. I'd give them a piece of my foot.' Your daddy would come for a visit and she'd cry and cry after he left, tell me how beautiful he was, then spend the next week saying, 'He's gone from me, but I know he's still alive. He's still walking this earth. What would I do if I lost him?' She only said mean things to a person when they were with her. Afterwards she'd say nothing but good, never seeing her mistake, never remembering how she chastised them in person, unable to comprehend why they weren't eager to return to see her. Then in the very next moment she'd turn on herself, because, well, she was always there in person, wasn't she, and talk about how unworthy she was of attention, how impossible it was to love anyone so crippled with arthritis and inconstancy, how even my own daddy died just to get away from her. She never said a bad word about you after you left, Sarah. I mean, not long after. Sometimes it took a few moments for her anger to wear off."

"She treated you badly, didn't she, Aunt Edna?"

"I tried not to take it personally. If I hadn't been here, it would have been someone else she treated badly. This isn't very good popcorn conversation, and it's good popcorn, isn't it?"

"Yes. I think I'm going to sleep on the recliner tonight."

"We'll get that hospital bed out of there soon and get you a good bed."

"It's just that she died in that bed," I said.

"I know, honey. It's all right."

It's funny how, after someone in your family dies, you notice their features and mannerisms in those left behind. Were these always there, or were they transferred or taken on at the moment of death? I could see my grandmother in Aunt Edna's hands, in her pronounced cheekbones, in the way she never looked at you at the beginning of a sentence, and ended by locking down on your eyes in an almost accusatory way. I supposed, after my father died someday, I'd see him in Aunt Edna, too. She was the youngest of her immediate family and would have to contain all the memories of her siblings and parents in facial tics and bone structure, until it passed onto the next generation. Sam does this with his cars, transferring gearshift knobs, seat cushions, and cup holders from one car to the next so that some feature of the earlier car is always retained in the present one. Sometimes, if you focus on that gearshift knob, or the radio he's scavenged and re-installed, you can forget where you are, in the new car or the old, perhaps in one he sold ten years earlier. I looked at Aunt Edna's face and watched it slowly change from her mother's into her own and then occupy a plastic evolutionary state where she could have been either person. A day or two later, when James Laurent showed up to work on Aunt Edna's chair, the first words out of his mouth to me were, "You sure do look like your aunt Edna." In my state this alone would have been unnerving, but heightening the effect, I'll remind you, was that James was blind.

□ □ □

When I woke the next morning, Aunt Edna had already gone to work. The kids' breakfast had to be ready by seven-thirty, which meant she rose at five and was at her station by six. The thought of forty years of this appalled me. But her recompense was that her workday was over at two in the afternoon.

Mom called at noon to tell me they'd arrived home at 3:00 A.M. and that she'd go over to the house and get some things off to me first thing in the morning. I asked her how the ride home was and she said, "Fine."

"Fine?" I said.

"Well, we didn't talk about you and Sam, Sarah. He wasn't in any mood for that."

"What kind of mood was he in?"

"He sulked for a while, then we talked about that new laser teeth-cleaning method and what new cars would be out this fall. Then we stopped at McDonald's in Oklahoma somewhere, and then I went to sleep. It was dark."

"Did Daddy say anything to Sam?"

"This is between you and Sam, Sarah. You can't ask your father to intervene."

"I'm not. I'm just asking if he said anything to him."

"They talked about the cars."

"But was Daddy nice to him?"

"He was civil."

Finally, a word I could relish. Daddy had only been civil with Sam. That would show him what an asshole he was. Guys can tell when other guys are only being civil with them. They'll get them a beer but they won't open it before they give it to them. It makes them feel like hell.

I spent the rest of the day and much of the week making phone calls, trying to make plans. There wasn't much I could finalize. I couldn't schedule our flight to Scotland till we found out how long it would take to get Grandpa exhumed and cremated, and Aunt Edna wanted to make these inquiries at the funeral home in person. I did find out it would take four to six weeks to get our passports, and when I told Aunt Edna this she had to sit down.

"I'm sorry," I said. "I didn't know I'd be staying that long either."

"No, it's not that, Sarah. I just didn't have any idea it would take so long to leave the country. I wish Momma had chosen Vermont or Colorado."

"There's something else," I said. "We can't just fly over there, get off the airplane, dump the ashes, and get back on the plane. The fares are almost a thousand dollars cheaper if we stay for a week. I mean, if we're going to spend all this money, I think we should stay a few days anyway and look around."

I'd glanced at Grandma's book, *Scotland from Above*, as I sat in her recliner that first night, and it was a gorgeous country from on high. I'd been to Mexico and Canada but never to another continent.

"Yes," Aunt Edna said. "I could take a paint box, I guess."

For a moment I pictured her there with her easel in a green field, painting Scottish sheep, until I realized it would be chairs in the field rather than sheep, Scottish chairs among the thistles.

Aunt Edna walked to and from work. Manuel Jara Elementary was just at the end of the block. When I visited my grandparents as a child, I used to sit on the front porch and watch the schoolchildren stream by morning and afternoon. It was unsettling to think about all the other kids in the world I didn't know, how effortlessly they moved along without my friendship. When I first saw them coming down the sidewalk I was sure they were from my school, that they were on their way to see me. As each student passed, each as unrecognizable as the last, I shrank further and further back into my chair. The fact that a few of the girls waved at me made no difference. The world was suddenly vast and unpredictable. Just how many children were there? How many schools? Was there enough milk?

I sat and watched them pass the week after Grandma's funeral with the same sense of a world existing beyond me that managed without my help or even my knowledge of its existence. Why should a seven-year-old walking down the sidewalk with a book in his hand, a very thin book, remind me of my own ignorance? I can't know everything. I can't oversee everything. It's my own arrogance that unsettles me, the assumption that my life should matter.

When Aunt Edna came home from school we'd take her little car and run errands. We went down to Barnes & Noble on University and bought a couple of travel guides to Scotland, even though Aunt Edna insisted *Scotland from Above* would be sufficient. I told her I wanted something that relied more on a street-level view.

We drove out to Michaels near Ridgmar Mall where she bought a few tubes of acrylic paint, some sable brushes, and a variety of water-color and sketching pads. Much of this, I found later, was for me. She dumped these supplies, along with a box of pencils, erasers, and charcoal, in my lap, with orders that I draw nothing that wasn't from life while I stayed with her. In other words, no angels, cherubs, Santas, or elves were to darken the pages of my sketch journal. If I wanted to paint a subject I was to look directly at it in strong light and look at it often, at least once every three brush strokes. I should probably do a pencil study, a watercolor for mood, and an oil sketch before I even thought of working on a canvas I intended to frame.

"Can I paint something besides chairs?" I asked.

"Don't be smart," she said.

On Wednesday afternoon we had an appointment at Northside Funeral Home. Aunt Edna dressed as if she were attending a funeral. "Well, I'd feel strange, walking into a funeral home in a loud red dress," she said. "It's always quiet in there." I wore one of Aunt Edna's better warm-up suits, pink with a maroon racing stripe down the leg. Northside had carried out Grandma's cremation just a week earlier, so when we walked in they assumed we'd come to handle the interment of her remains next to Grandpa. When the receptionist found that wasn't the case she had us sit down in the foyer while she called the director. Aunt Edna held her purse in her lap, but leaned over it to examine the legs of her chair, trying to discern if the chair was a subject worthy of pencil, pastel, or oil. She made these inquiries repeatedly over the summer, inspecting chairs as if they were horses, running her hands along their fetlocks, pulling back a lip of upholstery to judge tacks. In Scottish pubs she picked up chairs and turned them over to see their undersides. One waitress thought she was looking for gum and told her the chairs were cleaned regularly. In the funeral home she leaned toward me and said, "These chairs aren't even real mahogany. They're stained. It's enough to make you suspect their caskets."

A tall man in a dark blue suit with even darker blue hair approached us down the length of a long hallway. I knew he was coming for us but he wouldn't say so. He waited till he was within whispering distance and said, "I'd be so glad to be of service to you."

"I talked with Mr. Evans before," Aunt Edna told him.

"Mr. Evans is off today. I'm Mr. Heffernan," he calmed her. He tilted his head knowingly, reassuringly, soothingly. His expression was a denial of all personal joy, his recompense for our loss. "Won't you step back to my office?" he pleaded softly. We walked down the long hallway on carpet that suppressed the notion that we were earthly beings, that gave us the sensation we were floating toward nothing so firm as a commitment. He held the door open and closed it behind us, and I'd swear the latch was muffled with cotton balls. He sat at his desk without making a sound, without disturbing a single pencil, paper, or dust mote, because there was nothing on the broad expanse of his desktop, not a single thing to sell.

"My father," Aunt Edna began, "is in your plot number 1162. My mother passed away last week and asked that her remains be scattered in Scotland. We've decided to take Daddy to Scotland, too. So we'd like to have him exhumed and cremated, so that he's more portable. And we're sort of on a tight schedule."

"I see," Mr. Heffernan said, but he didn't really see. He peered into his clasped hands instead of looking at us. "Would you like us to sell your plots then? This service we provide without fees of any sort."

"Do you take a commission?" I asked.

"We don't take a commission. We refund to you the total cost of the burial plots. How many plots do you own?" he asked.

"Wait a minute," I said and put my fingertips on Aunt Edna's arm. "Would we receive the amount that you sell the plots for?"

"You receive 100 percent of your original cost," he said. His words sounded like individual bean bags thrown into a pillow.

"Let's see," I said. "How can I ask this question differently. If you sell our plots for a thousand dollars, do we get a thousand dollars?"

"Sarah," Aunt Edna shushed.

"I think we'll sell them ourselves," I said.

"I don't want to sell them," Aunt Edna blurted out.

I blew air through my nose in disdain. "They sell the plots for ten times what they sold them to Grandpa for twenty-five years ago and keep the profits," I explained.

"I'm not here to sell land, Sarah. If you'd just let me handle this. I'm sorry, Mr. Heffernan. I'm interested in getting my father exhumed and cremated. Can you tell us how we can go about that?"

"We need to remember this is a business, Aunt Edna, and not a church."

"All right, Sarah."

"We may not be a church," Mr. Heffernan said, "but we do provide a private chapel for your needs. And we are a service company. If you're not happy, we're not happy." He absolutely refused to become disgruntled. He'd seen all classes of bereavement and had made unflappability his highest goal. "Certainly we can help you, Edna," he cooed. I wanted to see how far his fingers had to be bent back before he started begging for momma.

I can look back now and see why I was in such a state, but at the time all I knew was the world was an evil place where my Grandpa's dead body was hovered over by profit-takers. I know now that I was simply hungry. I'd been on Aunt Edna's diet for three days. It consisted of a small bowl of oatmeal for breakfast and a tuna fish sandwich (made from low-fat bread and nonfat mayonnaise), for lunch. I was still trying to drag a shred of tuna from that tight place between my last two molars. When you're hungry the tiniest bit of food can occupy your attention for hours. Dogs know this. I didn't want to brush my teeth for fear I'd dislodge and spit out something I might get to eat later.

"How long will the whole process take?" Aunt Edna asked.

"I'd say approximately one month. We'll have to get a permit from the Texas Department of Health, and then all concerned parties will have to sign it."

"Concerned parties?" I asked.

"Are you the only surviving child?" he asked Aunt Edna.

"No, I have a brother and sister."

"Well then, they'll have to sign as well. Then we'll need a certified copy of the death certificate. We'll disinter the body, remove it from the casket, and send it to the Forth Worth Medical Examiner. We'll get a permit from the local registrar along with a set of cremation papers. We'll return the ashes to you in a plastic box, or you can consider purchasing an urn. We have an urn showroom if you'd like to take a tour."

"No, that's all right," Aunt Edna told him. "Can we scatter their ashes anywhere we want to?"

"We're taking them to Scotland," I said. "Can we take them on the airplane?"

"To Scotland? That's a long way from Texas. Common carriers are required to accept human remains for transportation. Here in Texas you can scatter remains in the ocean, or above five thousand feet from an airplane. If you want to scatter on private property you must get permission from the owner. I have no idea what the rules are in Scotland. We had one client who had his remains spread under a deer feeder. He loved to hunt. A fisherman had his ashes poured into his favorite bass lake. Have you decided on a specific site in Scotland?"

We looked at one another and shrugged. I said, "My grandparents didn't kill anything that we want to feed them to."

□ □ □

Later that evening, after a supper of vegetables and cantaloupe, I brought out *Scotland from Above* again and asked Aunt Edna if Grandma had favorite pages or a certain section she lingered over. Edna couldn't recall anything. I had the idea there might be a place name underlined or a silk bookmark at a historic site she admired.

The book was heavily worn, the cloth backing buckled at the spine. But there wasn't a bookmark, or notation, or the slightest pencil mark throughout. She had turned down the corners of three pages. At first I thought these were simply places where she'd stopped reading, but there was hardly any text to read. I walked through the entire book in thirty minutes. I had to decide which page she'd intended to mark by bending a corner. Was it the page the ear was bent toward or the page on the other side? I bent a few pages to see what I'd do, what I intended. I always bent them toward the page I wanted to mark. That left us with the city of Edinburgh, and a photograph of Glencoe Pass in the Scottish Highlands, and the small village of Plockton on the west coast.

"What do you think about these three places?" I asked Aunt Edna.

She looked at the photos rather disinterestedly and said, "They'll do."

"Which one?" I asked.

"You wanted to see the country. It's a small country, isn't it?"

"Spread their ashes in three different places?"

"That way we'll know we at least got part of her where she wanted to go. I wish I'd just asked her."

"I better look at a map. We're going to need a map. The maps in the guidebooks are too small."

"You make me nervous when you talk so fast," Aunt Edna said.

"Am I talking fast?"

"I can hardly keep up with you. It's at least a month before we get on the airplane and you just used the word 'map' in three different sentences."

"I like to plan ahead. I like to be organized. It keeps my mind off food."

"Go put some pebbles in your mouth."

"Aunt Edna, I think our diet is too harsh."

"The stones will keep your mouth occupied and they're low fat. They'll trick your mind and you won't be hungry."

"You're starting to sound like JoAnn. Do you really buy all those herbs and vitamins from her?"

"Just enough to make us both happy."

"What?"

"It makes JoAnn happy when I buy some little something. That's all it takes, a couple of dollars. You, on the other hand, require hours of counseling. You have to be talked into being happy. You have to be persuaded."

"I do not."

She opened her purse. "Here's two dollars. Be happy."

"That's ridiculous."

"It works for JoAnn."

"JoAnn's simple."

"That's bad apples, Sarah. You shouldn't judge another person's journey to happiness after they've arrived."

"Now you're starting to sound like Darcy."

"Darcy's a smarter person than you think she is. Just because she's sweet doesn't mean she's dumb."

"She married my little brother, didn't she?"

"There you go again. You have this attitude that anyone who hasn't followed your path, thinks the way you do, is dumb. Last time I looked at a map there were a dozen different roads leading into Fort Worth."

"What?"

"I know you think I'm dumb."

"I do not, Aunt Edna."

"You do. You were afraid that undertaker was going to hornswoggle me today and you jumped in and caused a scene."

"I didn't think you were dumb, Aunt Edna. I just didn't think you knew what I knew."

"There would have been plenty of opportunities to take me aside and whisper in my ear before I handed that man my life savings. You jumped in before you even gave me a chance to show I can take care of myself."

"I was just trying to help," I said.

"These are my parents, Sarah. I've been taking care of them for years. I wouldn't let anybody hurt them, even after they're dead. Now, here's a question. You're all worried about maps. That will be easy compared to speaking Scottish. How are we going to learn Scottish in a month?"

"Scottish?" I whispered.

"Yes. I don't know the first word of it. We'll have to get a tape recorder and at least learn how to ask where the bathroom is."

"Aunt Edna," I said, "they speak English in Scotland."

"They speak English in England, Sarah. They speak Scottish in Scotland."

"Are you making fun of me, Aunt Edna?"

"No. Don't they?"

"I think they've been speaking English there for a few hundred years."

"Oh," she said. She looked at me somewhat vacantly. "I've been worried about that ever since Momma made up her will."

I scratched at the arm of my chair.

"I guess you can interrupt me anytime you want," she said and smiled. "I'm not dumb. I'm just ignorant."

I smiled back, the corners of my mouth working ripples into the pond of my cheeks.

□ □ □

The next afternoon we went for our passport photos at Kinko's on Camp Bowie. "Mother and daughter?" the clerk there asked.

Before I could say a word, Aunt Edna replied, "Lord, no. I'm only eighteen years older than Sarah. I'd have been a child having a child."

"Y'all just look alike," the boy said.

"I'm her niece," I explained. "My mom was seventeen when I was born. Of course, that's a big difference from eighteen."

Aunt Edna pulled off her hair net and wadded it up into a little ball. She stood on the strip of tape the boy indicated. "Am I supposed to smile?" she asked him.

"If you feel like it," he answered.

"I just want my government to get the right impression. I'm not going to Europe for drugs or espionage."

"Aunt Edna, most people don't go there for drugs or espionage."

"Where are y'all going?"

"To Scotland," I said.

"You can buy marijuana in Amsterdam," the boy said. "They have cafes there where you can buy it legally."

"Really?" Aunt Edna asked. She blinked when he took the picture. She looked at me. Her eyes were the size of quarters. "How far is it from Scotland to Amsterdam?"

"Why?"

"For the . . . you know."

"Aunt Edna."

"It's just an herb, Sarah. It's good for certain kinds of illness."

"Well, you might be able to buy it there, but you can't bring it back to the United States."

"No?"

"No."

"Well, never mind."

I stepped on the tape. He took the picture while I was still glaring at Aunt Edna. To this day my passport photo makes me look like I'm blind, my pupils locked into the corners of my eye sockets. Aunt Edna smiles in her photo, even though her hairdo was viciously cropped.

□ □ □

That evening, as we sat eating a plate of vegetables fresh from the freezer, a black woman about my age knocked on the door.

"Well, where's your daddy?" Aunt Edna asked her.

"Oh, he's in the car, Edna. He wants to know if you still want your chair fixed."

"Of course I do. I told him I did, Thelia."

"He's acting like his feelings are hurt. You know how he gets."

"Thank you, Thelia. I'll come out to the car with you and bring him in. Come back for him in a couple of hours. That chair needs a whole new seat."

I sat with my plate on my knees all through this. Aunt Edna came back in a few minutes with James on her arm. He had a sheaf of cane under one arm and a toolbox in his free hand.

"What about making Thelia come to the door," she said to him, in that tone that implies you shouldn't dare to answer or explain.

I stood up when they came in and said, "Hello, Mr. Laurent. It's me, Sarah."

He put his hand out, I shook it, and he said. "Hello, Sarah. It's me, James. You sure look like your Aunt Edna."

"Thank you," I said, as if it were some other word I meant, as if he'd just given me his wet dentures.

"Now, you sit right here and I'll go get my chair," Aunt Edna said.

"Can I help you with your things?" I asked.

"No, if I set them down I'll know where they are. If you set them down there'd just be a lot of searching and floor patting and people telling me 'to your left' or 'to your right' or 'you're standing on it.'" He moved his toolbox to the floor and began to arrange his materials. "I like to be close to the earth when I work. All men should work on their haunches, sweeping the earth with their palms when something goes missing. How's your aunt been doing?"

"Good," I said.

"I've been worried. It's hard to lose your momma."

"I'm sorry," I said. "'Good' was the easy, polite thing to say. She's coping. When I'm around she seems OK, but I'll come into the room sometimes and she's staring off into space."

"You know, Sarah, people say that all the time and I've got no idea what it means."

"It means she's so deep in thought that her senses don't transmit information."

"Like a leper," James said.

"Well, I see what you mean, but usually there's no physical harm done. And she's cried a couple of times. I've heard her crying in her bedroom at night. I've been sleeping here in the living room on the recliner. Aunt Edna gets up at night and checks on me two or three times. I think she's doing it out of habit, the way she used to check on Grandma."

"Here she comes," he whispered.

Aunt Edna walked in, carrying an old Empire side chair. The caned seat was rotten and had collapsed.

"Just because you're blind doesn't mean I can't hear whispering, James," she said. "This is my house. If secrets are being told, I want to be in on them."

"No secrets, Edna," he said.

I picked up Aunt Edna's plate, stacked it on mine, and started toward the kitchen.

"Y'all having dinner?" James asked. "I can't smell a thing."

"That's because it's hard to smell an ice cube," I said. "Aunt Edna and I are on a frozen-vegetable diet."

"Well, come here, Edna, and let me feel if you've lost any weight."

"You just set about your business, James Laurent. I've got a scale."

"Well, don't lose too much. I wouldn't be able to find you."

"Just hush and fix my chair. Do you want a cup of coffee?"

"I do."

"I'll get it."

There in the kitchen I told her, "He was just asking how you were."

"I know."

"Did you know he was coming tonight?"

"He comes when he comes. It doesn't matter. In this house there's always a chair to be fixed."

We both stood over the coffeemaker while it made little consoling sucking noises. After about two minutes of watching it, I said, "I'll finish watching it."

"OK." She took off her apron, and then she looked into the chrome of the Vent-A-Hood and touched her hair in two places.

"He can't see your hair," I said. "He likes you for who you are."

She dropped back down on her heels. "I pay him good money to fix my chairs."

"Hmph," I said.

"And he likes me."

"I'll watch the coffee."

"I'll go in and see how he's getting along."

"I'm watching the coffee."

"Do I smell all right?"

"I'm not going to smell you. I'm too busy watching this pot fill with coffee. You probably smell like coffee."

"Oh, good," she said, and left.

□ □ □

I thought about my aunt having a little flirt in the living room until the indifferent phone on the kitchen wall turned its shoulder to me. Sam had been at home for almost four days now and hadn't called. Of course, I hadn't called him either. The few times it had rung I'd let Aunt Edna answer in case it was him, just so I'd have a few seconds to compose myself. There were things he needed to know. I had three potted plants, behind my kitchen sink, that needed watering once every three days. The toilet in our bathroom sometimes runs after you flush it. I'll go in there an hour after he's gone to work and it will still be running. I wore my cashmere sweater out the night before we left and if he were to wash it he'd surely throw it in the dryer, too, and ruin it. I'm not there to remind him to feed the cat or call his goddamned wife.

I'm sorry I've spent so much time talking about myself. But I don't think my perceptions of Aunt Edna would be valid if you didn't know how I was feeling at the time. I know everyone is interested in Aunt Edna. I know it's not humble to think your own thoughts are valuable enough to put them down on something that lasts as long as paper. But I really think that biographers, even if they're writing about George Washington or Jesus, ought to tell how they were feeling at the time, what happened to them over the months or years they worked on their book so you'll know how their life affected the work, whether they were talking about themselves or their subject. If you don't know where I was at the time you'll never understand why I didn't turn Aunt Edna in. I feel like I've waited my whole life to write about Aunt Edna, and of course, I have.

When the coffee finally finished dripping, and the phone on the wall presented a final rebuff, I took three cups on a tray into the living room. Aunt Edna was on her knees next to James. He was running his hands over the chair, counting the holes around the perimeter of the seat. He'd already cut out the old cane, which lay in shattered bits in his lap and on the floor around him.

"Now," he asked, "do you want the same pattern in the weave or something else?"

"I want just what was there."

"I could put a dog's head in there."

"Just the regular weave."

"Some people don't like to sit on a dog's head, especially if his tongue's lolling. I wouldn't charge you nothing extra for a dog's head."

"James, that chair is a hundred and fifty years old. That hexagon pattern is fine with me. If you can do it."

"What's that 'if I can do it'? There's no pattern I can't weave in straw, cane, hickory, or hemp. 'If I can do it.'"

"I know your fingers are old and those holes are small," she said. She looked at me and winked.

"What?" he said. His hands stopped moving.

"It's no problem for me to go out and cut a piece of plywood to cover that seat," Aunt Edna told him. "I could just tack it down with four or five nails."

James smirked. "My momma taught me not to tease blind people. What about yours, Sarah?"

"And short people," I answered. "You shouldn't tease short, blind, or fat people."

"You want the plastic cane or the natural, Edna?"

"Natural."

"Well, Sarah, if you'll take this cane into the kitchen and put it in a steamer for me, just like you'd steam broccoli. You have to steam it or it'll snap and splinter on the bends. Give it about fifteen minutes after the water goes to boiling."

"The steamer is in the drawer next to the stove," Aunt Edna said. "There's a big one. Use it. Use the tongs to handle the cane. If it won't go in the pot, just drape it over and move it from time to time."

I had the distinct impression I was being sent from the room. I felt as if one of my daughters had asked me to go bake cookies for some boy who was visiting, just so I'd be out of the way. I wasn't in the way. I just wanted to watch.

While the water boiled I sat at the kitchen table and sketched the pot and stove on a little blue napkin. At first I drew upwardly undulating lines to indicate the steam, but then I realized I was simply drawing angels again. My lines didn't look like steam at all. They were just a generally accepted notation for steam. They were cartoon lines, shorthand. I tried again, erasing the lines, using the flat of the pencil to shadow the entire area of steam, then using my fingertip and the eraser to remove patches of darkness and lighten the values where the steam was brightest. It wasn't steam but it was closer, angrier, more anxious, hotter. It was more like me. I knew I'd somehow lost this pleasure: the way a pencil enabled me to forget that I was alone. But

I didn't think it would be so easy to find again, not as easy as fifteen minutes and the backside of a blue napkin. It's possible to live happily for hours between a pencil point and the surface of paper, your life drawn out to a thin, highly tensile line.

I carried the limp cane back into the living room on a platter, set it down next to the chair. Aunt Edna and James were in two adjoining chairs, the backs of their hands touching. James turned to her, brought his hand up to his mouth, and said, "Shhh, I think she's coming back."

"Hmpf," I said. He giggled.

"Aunt Edna, I need a sketch pad."

"There's a new one on my bedside chair. Use any of the pencils or brushes you want. There's charcoal and watercolors in that cabinet by my easel."

"I have a pencil," I said. "I'm going to conquer the world with this pencil." I showed her my napkin.

"What's that?"

"It's steam and a pot and your stove."

"Oh," she said.

"That's encouraging."

"Oh, it's good, honey."

James was down on the floor again, holding the chair in his lap like a puppy. "Here, Edna, give me an end of that cane."

"It's hot," she said.

"We've got to hurry now," he told her.

She used the hem of her skirt to pick out the end of the cane and put it in James's hand.

James threw the chair in his lap about three feet up into the air. "Lord God, Ernie Hoover, Maybe Spilee, and Jimmy Jackson," he yelled.

"Well, I told you it was hot, James," Aunt Edna said. "Are you burnt?"

"I just didn't see it coming."

"Was that cussing, James?" I asked.

"I don't say no bad words, Sarah. I don't."

Aunt Edna looked up at me. She was holding James's wounded fingers. "Jimmy Jackson sold him a bum house. Maybe Spilee broke his heart. Ernie Hoover was a boy in school who snuck up and hit James in the back of the head with a pipe."

"And the 'Lord God,' Edna?" he prodded.

"The Lord God made him blind."

"I don't say no bad words," James said.

"James never curses," Edna affirmed.

James tied a knot in one end of the cane and pulled the other end through one of the holes in the corner of the seat. "See that, Sarah. That hole is drilled with a wedge-shaped augur so the knot will lodge up in there and won't pull through." He worked quickly, his fingers continually counting holes, his free hand pulling the cane through and threading the far side. He was drawing. He used little wooden pegs in the holes to hold the cane in place. It seemed like an incredibly complex game of Battleship. The pattern started to build on the second pass. By the fourth pass the hexagon stars were beginning to take shape. He must have used a hundred feet of cane to build a 12" x 12" seat. "Now don't sit on this chair till that cane draws up or you'll never get up. When it dries you'll be able to bounce a bowling ball off of it."

"How long have you been doing this?" I asked him.

"Oh, about forty-three years now. I used to have a little shop and people brought the work to me. Now I travel to the customer. Nowadays you have to think of service to keep your business afloat."

"Is Aunt Edna your biggest customer?"

"Well, I used to have a string of drugstores and ice-cream shops, a few restaurants. There's still a few companies that make cane-bottom stools and rockers, but they're so cheap people throw them away or nail down a fiber seat rather than pay me to repair them. I guess my biggest clients now are the antique shops. They all know me and know I do good work. My worst problem is getting a ride. Now that Thelia works the day shift, it's catch as catch can. The buses don't go all the places they used to go. But I don't need many jobs to keep me in ready cash. If I've got barber money I'm doing all right. I like to give my boy, Billy, a little something now and then. You met him at the funeral. He'll walk me to some of my jobs."

"James lives with Billy and Thelia," Aunt Edna said.

"In the bum house that Jimmy Jackson sold me. Every summer the back bedroom breaks off and you have to stuff towels and coats in the crack to keep the moths out. Then the ground will soak up in the fall, the house will close up, and you can't get your coat back out of the crack. It's a bum house and I've been saying so for twenty years. I didn't wear my best coat all winter because the house wouldn't let go of it."

"Do you have a Seeing Eye dog, James?" I asked.

"I never did trust a dog. They've tried to give me a dog. You have to feed a dog. A dog will grow."

"I'm thinking about going down to the pound and getting Aunt Edna a cat," I said.

"A cat?" James said.

"Don't get me a cat, Sarah," she said.

"But you like cats."

"I do, but I don't want one."

"Why not? It would keep you company."

"Cat's the only thing I can't hear," James said.

"I just don't want a cat," Aunt Edna insisted.

"That's not true," James said. "I didn't hear Ernie Hoover when he snuck up on me and hit me with that pipe in the back of the head. Do you want to feel my head where Ernie Hoover slapped me with that pipe?"

Aunt Edna bobbed her head at me.

"Sure," I said.

James bowed and said, "Give me your hand and I'll lead you to it." He placed my fingertips in a hollow on the back of his skull. It gave me the willies. "My barber knows how to hide it so I have to guide people there. That hole's been there for almost fifty years now and I've suffered no ill effects."

"Why did Ernie Hoover hit you in the back of the head with a pipe, James?"

"I took away lead cornet in our school music club. I think he was wearing only socks. That's how he snuck up on me. But I heard that pipe when he swung it. The end of it whistled before it made the swale in my head. He got worse out of it than I did."

"What happened? Did he go to jail?"

"No. After he hit me, he turned and ran away. He ran as fast as he could right into the edge of the door to my room. To this day he's got a scar down his forehead, across his nose, and over his lower lip. Couldn't play the cornet for the rest of the year. I got to play his solo as well as mine in the school program."

"What school did you go to, James?"

"Fort Worth Colored School for the Blind."

"Ernie Hoover was blind then, too?"

"Run into that door, didn't he?"

"How'd he know where to swing the pipe to hit you?"

"Well, I was sitting at my desk. He'd been in my room lots of times before. He knew I was a studier. Blind people have a pretty good sense of where something is if they've been there before. But the door to my room used to swing in the wind. It must have closed a bit when he passed by. That's what foiled his perfect crime. But that pipe proved my daddy wrong. He'd always said I just needed a good sharp rap to the head and I'd get my vision back. I was just as blind after as before and he had to admit he was wrong about that. It doesn't do any good to hit a blind person in the head in an attempt to restore their vision. You got some daffodils in here, Edna?"

"I've got a whole bouquet in the kitchen," she answered.

"Who's giving you flowers?" he asked.

"The school board sent them to her for her retirement," I said.

"Retirement?"

"Tomorrow's my last day," she told him.

"But when did this happen? You lose your job?"

"I just decided it was time. You never know what's going to happen to you. Momma started getting sick at my age, and Daddy was almost dead. I want to spend some time painting, doing what I want to do."

"Those kids are going to miss you, Edna. I know they will. Everybody at that school's going to miss you."

"It's just a block away, James. I can visit if I get homesick."

"I'm not worried about that," he said. "I'm worried about all those leftovers you got for me. I've had several good leftover meals here. What's going to happen to those?"

"You'll just have to eat fresh," Aunt Edna said, smiling.

"Leftovers are better," James said. "A bean gains character in the icebox. I'll take a cold fried chicken over a hot one any day."

"Please," I pleaded, "no more talk about food. I'm going to take a handful of crackers out on the back porch with me and eat them while I draw that mimosa tree, Aunt Edna. There's still some good light left. Y'all don't worry about me."

I left them there and spent an hour climbing through that sprawling tree, using the slanting evening light and the nub of my pencil to define an entangling mass of shadow that no bird could ever fly through. Too dark, too dark, I kept thinking and used my eraser to make sniping attacks on the tree limbs, to show that light reflected there. There's light everywhere, even in the darkest recesses, and only light can make a shadow. Even if the source isn't on the page you still must feel its presence. So I made little marks, retraced, swept graphite dust up into a cloud with my thumb, then shot light through it all with my eraser. Here's the sun. It's millions of miles away, but also in my right hand.

A car pulled into the driveway. I couldn't see it but heard the crack of gravel beyond the backyard fence. Aunt Edna and James stepped out on the back porch a moment later. As she walked him toward the gate he said my name three times and then said, "You call a person's name three times when they're up to magic. It gives them good luck if you're for them, bad luck if you're against. What's it like to draw a picture, Sarah? I can't get your aunt to tell me."

"It makes you powerful, James. I might draw you tonight, and then you'd be in my power."

"From what I understand it's hard to see me in the dark. I might be hard to capture." Then he turned to my aunt at the gate. "I'll be here in my best suit. I'll wear my best suit for you. I usually only wear it for dead people, but for you I'll make an exception."

"Go home," she said.

"Going home," he said. Then he yelled out, "Thelia, honk the horn, honey, so I can find the car. Going home."

Aunt Edna came back through the gate after they'd gone, her arms folded contentedly on her stomach. She sat down next to me with a sigh.

"What?" I asked.

"It's so hard to believe that he can't see. I've known him for two years now and I still ache over it."

"It doesn't seem to bother him."

"Let me see what you've done." I handed her the sketch pad. "Oh, that's nice, Sarah."

"I'm losing the light. The light wouldn't stand still."

"It never does. I get so aggravated with it sometimes. It's like a cat."

"Why?"

"I tried to draw a cat once, this little stray that used to come by once in a while. He'd hang around on the front porch and out in the yard. Every time I thought I had a fix on him he'd get up and move somewhere else, or roll over and lick his leg. I started eight different sketches and finally gave up. The light will do that to you."

"What's all this about James, I mean, leaving by a different door?"

"He's a strange person, Sarah. I haven't yet figured him out. He has superstitions that I've never heard of before. At first I thought they were black superstitions, that I hadn't grown up in that culture and that's why I hadn't heard of them. But they're his own. He's made them all up himself. He was working on a chair for me once and cut his thumb on a staple. He put his thumb in his mouth, sucked on it, and then put it under his armpit. 'Got to hide a wound,' he said. I asked him if he wanted a Band-Aid and he said no, hiding it would do just as good. And not another word of explanation. If he comes in the front, he leaves by the back. If he comes in the back, he leaves by the front. It's so the bad thoughts he leaves outside a house when he arrives won't be able to jump back on him when he goes home. He tricks them. There's that thing about saying names three times. He folds his money president-in before he puts it in his wallet."

"How does he know which side the president's on?"

"He doesn't. You have to tell him. If you ask him why, he tells you that if you fold them president-out, they'll escape. Fold them president-in and they multiply. You know what my favorite thing about him is?"

"What?"

"I'll leave a room and come back in. While I was away, if he's not working, he'll have found the sunspot in the room, just like a cat. The light is forever on his face. He looks like a painting."

"Wow," I whispered.

We sat in the darkening, the concrete porch becoming cooler, the bugs starting to work up toward the moon. We didn't speak for minutes,

simply kicked our feet out into the air, then let our calves bounce off
the concrete on the backfall.

"He was in a good mood when he left, wasn't he?" Aunt Edna
asked.

"Why was that, Aunt Edna?"

"I told him I'd think about it."

"Think about what?"

"He asked me to marry him."

I couldn't help it. I gasped. I wanted to stuff my fist down my throat
to retrieve it but it was too late. I turned to look at her, my eyes wide,
trying to take in all the available light. All I could get out was her name,
her full name, "Edna August Hutton," as if I were presenting her to the
Queen.

"Well, it's not as if I haven't been asked before," she said.

"He's asked you before?"

"No, other men have asked me, Sarah."

"What are you going to answer? I mean, should you answer now?
Shouldn't you wait? I mean, Grandma just died, and tomorrow is your
last day of work. It's an emotional time."

"I told him I would think about it. That's what I'm doing."

"But, Aunt Edna, you just spent twenty years taking care of Grandma. Do you really want to take on another handicapped person?"

She pushed herself up. "Sarah, did you ever consider that I might
marry him so he can take care of me?"

I stood up too, the graininess of the concrete leaving its impression
on my palms. "I'm sorry," I said. "It just took the wind out of me. I had
no idea you two were this far along. I thought it was flirting. I hadn't
even considered it."

"Why hadn't you considered it?"

"Because he's black and you're not."

"That's right," she said.

"I know."

"He's black as midnight."

"He is."

"And you know what? To him, I am, too. It's only you and I that
see the difference."

"I really like him. I'm over the shock of it now."

"He is sweetness itself."

"He is."

"He only wants to be around me. There's not a lot of people in this world who have that desire."

"There's me," I said.

"You don't count."

"I do too count."

"You're family."

"Which makes it all the harder for me to like you. You have to count me."

"OK," she said. "I'll count you, but I'm counting James, too."

"Of course. You could count a cat, too, if you'd let me get you one."

"Not now."

"James ought to have a dog."

"You shouldn't try to play matchmaker between the animal and human kingdoms," Aunt Edna said, which was such an odd thing to say that I had no reply. We stood on the porch listening to crickets flirt with their own kind. On the next street an older child called out and a younger answered. As the day's heat faded, the grass itself seemed unburdened. The backyard, coddled by moon and mimosa, swathed in bug song, seemed to sway and moan, to mew in longing. Up until I was sixteen or seventeen, before my social life made my grandparents' backyard disappear, I played here with my brother and cousins. I climbed the mimosa and drew the squirrels that screamed at me for doing so. The yard seemed smaller now, of course, but just as whole, containing all possibilities. Strange that it should to a woman of forty-four. I knew I'd never climb that tree again. It made me shiver to think that thirty years had passed since I'd physically chased someone my size. How could I have let that much time get away without running as fast as I could occasionally? I turned to my aunt, who was young when I last hid behind the mimosa. I realized that she'd been just as cognizant of time passing this whole week as I was at that moment.

"Wow," I said softly, "a proposal. Tonight. Right in there?"

"He got down on one knee. I was sitting in the little pine Windsor. He said, 'Please, Edna darling, would you consider marrying me?' He said it this way, 'Ednadarling' as if it were one word."

"It's so exciting," I said. "We should eat a cookie."

"You've already had extra crackers."

"Jesus, Aunt Edna."

"All right. I'll split one with you."

□ □ □

I lay in my recliner that night, surrounded by chairs huddling around me as if for protection. I felt as if I were their source of light because all their shadows fell away from me. Cars passed quickly along Refugio Street, and empty chairs swirled around my room like sparks off a fire. Light, light, light, I dreamed, naming good luck and bad. I drew a flower whose reflection fell in water to the left, its shadow falling to the earth on the right. The stalk bowed away from me in the wind. But all these dark lines representing light flowed back toward me, became bundled and common in the shaft of my pencil, and splintered again in the bones of my fingers and the veins of my arm. The point of a pencil in contact with any surface contained the known and unknown universe. I woke in the middle of the night and imagined drawing James in the dark, crosshatching all the things I didn't know about him, the way he thought about Aunt Edna, till the paper was blank with blackness, save for two tiny reflections of light, my eyes in his. Then I thought, when I can see him, he'll be able to see me. That's what happens when you draw someone: the sitter knows you better than you know them. You've given yourself up in brush strokes. I know that Helga understood Andrew Wyeth far better than he knew her. But it's his desire, his yearning to understand her that draws us to him. He's desperate for understanding. And if you can keep from shying away from someone who's desperate, you're attracted to them. That's why some artists can paint self-portraits and some can't. I knew I'd been in the latter group since I left college, since I began drawing fairies for money.

□ □ □

In the morning I counted money and baked a cake. Aunt Edna had set me to the job of sorting her silver. She'd bought a book of coin values recently but hadn't even torn the plastic off yet. It was a bigger job than I'd imagined. Beyond the variation in dates and condition, the coins came from different mints: D for Denver, S for San Francisco, and if there was no mint mark it came from Philadelphia. This made me wonder if everything in the world without attribution was from Philadelphia. All unsigned art and all orphans were from Philadelphia. (Well, such was my condition while smelling a baking cake. I meant to surprise Aunt Edna at school with a chocolate sheet cake, a little retirement party.) I began with the dimes, using the entire surface of the kitchen table as a dime-sorting tray, continually reordering stacks of coins as a new date or mint mark would surface from the coffee-can bank.

I had to make a little pile for misfits, coins that had a hole drilled through them, coins too worn to read the date, dimes that had plainly lain on a road for years before someone picked them back up, one side scratched featureless. There were coins that had been bent, punched, dyed, and hammered thinner than a dime, coins melted, epoxied, and bitten. These misfits were by far the most interesting, so important that they were worn as personal adornment, or were once lost and then found, or were shattered remains of accident, art, or experiment. I knew we'd get nothing more out of them than their silver content, the value of weight. I decided to ask Aunt Edna for these dimes. I'd drill a hole in each of them and make a charm bracelet, by alchemy transform silver to art, create a personal talisman that would ward off random acts of damage. I'd shake my wrist at adulterers and make them turn away, the sound of silver against art deafening them with its change-making ring. I'd shake my wrist at lunatics and make them rational, shake at the blind and make them see.

I'd follow in James's path and make up my own rules. He lived so much more inside than most of us, and his lack of vision gave him so little understanding of cause and effect that he'd created his own set of commandments to follow. Perhaps his rules weren't so much superstitions as they were simply arbitrary, simply his.

Sometimes, when you step off the curb, a big truck slams by, sometimes it doesn't. Without your eyes, where's the cause and effect? I pulled up to an intersection stoplight, my fingers drumming the steering wheel to Sonny and Cher's "I Got You Babe," and my husband's car crossed before me. I honked. A woman in his passenger seat turned toward me for a moment and threw a cigarette butt to the pavement. He looked, too, but kept on driving. He didn't wave. I was stuck there at the light. It took forever to change and when it did the car behind me had to honk at me to get me to move on. I turned in the opposite direction Sam had gone, and I've moved farther away from him since. I'd been blind, but I knew what that woman's cigarettes smelled like. It was in his clothes, the upholstery of his car. He'd told me it was from hanging out in the break room at lunch. The woman didn't recognize me when I honked. She thought I was honking at someone else. I wanted to send her pictures: this is what I look like, these are our daughters, this is what we look like together in front of our house. I wanted to scream at him: How can you kiss someone who smokes? You've told me a hundred times how stupid people who smoke look, how awful they smell. Why doesn't she know what I look like? I wondered, if James were to wake up one day, his sight restored, would he start screaming at all of us, asking us why we betrayed him?

There were too many dimes. They slipped from my fingers, fell on the floor and rolled. Stacks tilted and coins rode each other to the table in a rush to stability, abandoning the order I'd imposed. I believed this was because the smell of the cake was overwhelming. It made my stomach ache, my hands tremble. I pulled it from the oven and set it on the stovetop to cool, then had to leave the house or I'd have scooped it into my mouth with burning fingers. I walked two blocks to a convenience store on the corner of Twenty-fifth Street and bought a Diet Coke and sat on the curb and drank it. To tell the truth, I'd thought almost as much about food that week as I had about Sam. I wanted to be a good diet buddy. I know it's easier when you diet with someone, all that moral support, exchanging of recipes, all that water-drinking, scale-avoiding, bowel-minding shared effort. It just seemed so much easier for Aunt Edna. I wanted to use the excuse of my personal trauma, that I needed more sustenance rather than less, but hell, her mother had just died, and she was able to push her plate away without complaint. That morning I realized she had James as an impetus. She was thinning down for a wedding dress. So I baked the cake and would serve it to her, and she couldn't deny me a part of it, a simple piece of cake to celebrate her retirement. By the time I got back home the odor had dissipated somewhat. I'd left both front and back doors wide open. I whipped up a vat of chocolate icing, spread it over the cake in its aluminum pan, and then used the only color of food dye I could find in the kitchen, orange, to write "CONGRATULATIONS, EDNA" with more icing. I snapped a sheet of Saran Wrap over the pan and walked to her school.

The school was just as I remembered it. I hadn't attended there but had played in its yard and slid down its fire escapes on weekends and after school as a child. Grandma used to tell Mike and me to watch out for the little Mexican kids, that they liked to pick fights. But we never ran into other kids at the playground. They seemed to avoid the place after hours just as I did my school at home. It was like going into work on the weekend. I stepped into the front door and was overcome. The entire school smelled like Aunt Edna. I checked in at the office, with its low windows and counters and chairs, and on my way to the cafeteria passed a classroom that reeked of the sawdust compound used to soak up vomit. All the children were in class. Cork bulletin boards, mounted at the level of my knees, lined the hallways. I looked for notices of Aunt Edna's retirement on them, posterboard flowers signed with glitter. What a world to live in, I thought, every explanation, every decision, had to be made clear to the lowest common denominator, in height and rationality. There was a poster asking that you wipe your cheeks after getting a drink from the fountain. Another explained the importance of clean nostrils. I looked down at my cake. Between CONGRATULATIONS and EDNA, in an artistic reversion to my Hallmark ways, I'd sculpted a little orange bunny. It was plain to see I was at home in these hallways. I suddenly wished my own girls were still in elementary school rather than college. Even though the cake was close and warm, the air at my nose was thick with canned corn and Salisbury steak. By the time I reached the cafeteria, I was running my palm along the painted cinder blocks so I'd know where the wall was when I swooned. I walked through a field of chairs that made me feel a giant among women, so large that no diet would see me back to the size of normal humans. There was a window, a foot square, in the swinging stainless-steel door that led from the cafeteria to the kitchen. I peered in. There were five women inside, all about Edna's size and all with the same hairdo. Their hair nets gave their heads a brainlike quality. They moved like drones from one task to another, their white uniforms tight and wet at the level of a sink's rim. They all seemed so intent that I felt I should knock. When I did, they all looked up in the air as if they'd never heard this sound before. It was then I knew that they were more accustomed to sudden screams and yelling, that swinging doors and pounding feet were the norm, and that a timid knock on their door must suggest imminent disaster. Aunt Edna looked up from stacking huge aluminum trays on a rolling carrier. I pushed open the door and waved, recognizing two other ladies from the funeral. Aunt Edna looked worried. Someone turned off water that had been blasting down into a steel sink. The air in the room was incredibly warm and humid, as if everything in it was being not only sterilized but scalded. Aunt Edna came toward me along the tray counter, wiping the stainless bars with a rag as she came.

"What is it, Sarah? I looked up and saw you and all I could think was there was something wrong with Momma. Then I remembered she was gone and I was relieved. Isn't that queer?"

"I didn't mean to scare you. Look, I baked you a retirement cake." She looked at the cake, reached over the counter for a plastic spatula and, with one clean jerk of the Saran Wrap and two quick swipes with the spatula, removed all the writing. I was holding the cake pan with both hands so I couldn't slap her. She stuck the spatula into her uniform pocket and turned to the other women. "Everyone, this is my niece, Sarah. She's baked us a cake." As they moved toward us, she turned back to me and whispered, "They don't know I'm retiring. Keep it mum."

This was the first time in my life anyone had ever used the phrase, "Keep it mum." I was so stunned I forgot my main intention, which was to eat as many pieces of cake as I could in as short a time as possible.

"What's the occasion?" one of the ladies asked.

"Chocolate doesn't need an occasion," I said. "It works in all circumstances." Then I thought to say, "Just celebrating the end of another school year."

"I'll say," one of the women said.

On the way home, as I wiped at my face with my fingers and then licked them, the way a cat does after a meal, I tried to comprehend why Aunt Edna wouldn't want her fellow employees to know she was retiring. I'd seen the flowers and card from the school board. I knew she had actually given notice. But she hadn't told James and now she hadn't told her friends. As soon as I'd had a single slice of cake, she'd ushered me out of the kitchen and on my way. I'd counted on carrying the leftover cake home, but she said she'd take some to the principal and office staff, that way she could wash the pan before she brought it home.

"What a good idea," I'd sneered.

She simply responded, "Sarah, Sarah, Sarah."

She got home several hours late that day, pale and tired. "So many things to wash and put away at the end of the year," she explained.

"I'll make dinner tonight," I said.

"Well, not much for me. I'm not hungry." At first I was concerned for her health, but then she added, "I had too much cake."

This just made me mad. Even if I did cook it for her.

"Why haven't you told your friends you're retiring?" I asked peevishly.

"Oh, Sarah, they'd have gone on and on about it, given me presents and parties. I didn't make the decision until just before Momma died, so I haven't been keeping it from them for long. They'll all find out, one by one, over the summer and there'll be no big fuss."

"But you deserve a big fuss," I said peevishly.

She took off her hair net. It left a long pink crease high on her forehead, as if her scalp had been surgically removed and replaced. She sculpted her hair with her hands, pushing it up and pulling it out. It seemed to expand like a balloon.

"Did James call?"

"No."

"He's supposed to call to let us know if he can get a ride Sunday or if I need to go pick him up. He's having Sunday dinner with us."

"Do you want me to go out that night so you two can be alone?"

"No, Sarah, James and I have eaten dinner alone before. I had to sneak out of the house to do it, but I did."

"Why did you have to sneak out of the house?"

"Well, Momma didn't mind James working here and she even suspected he was fond of me, but if she'd known I was fond of him, well, she would have been hurt. He used to pay as much attention to her when he came by, as he did me. He'd go into her room and say, 'You sure are pretty today, Mrs. Hutton.' Momma couldn't help herself. She'd smile and then call him a 'lying black bastard.' Oh, it made me cringe. But James didn't mind. He got her back good. He said, 'Us black folk oughtn't swear at one 'nother, Mrs. Hutton." Momma was flabbergasted. 'I'm not black,' she howled. James turned to me. 'She's not black?' I had to put my hand over my mouth. 'He's teasing you, Momma,' I finally blurted out. James said, 'She sure sounds black. I'd have sworn you were as black as coal, Mrs. Hutton. That means I'm in an old white lady's house. Well, it's an accident, but as long as I'm here, could y'all guide me to your silverware drawer?' Momma's eyes got big as cereal bowls and from that day on she made him work on the chairs in her room, so she could watch. She told him it was so she could keep her eye on him but it was really because she liked him. From time to time he'd say, 'I wish you'd get your eye out of my back, Mrs. Hutton. It's starting to hurt.' Momma would giggle till she couldn't breathe."

"She would have been upset that you were going out with a black man?"

"Oh, some of that, I'm sure, but mostly she would have been afraid that I was going to leave her, that somebody else had my attention."

"Well, you're free now," I said. I'd gotten over the cake.

□ □ □

That night was my last on the recliner. In the morning the Goodwill truck arrived. Two men carried out the hospital bed, Grandma's wheelchair, her bathtub seat, and a half-dozen bags of clothing. I'd gone through the plastic bags of clothing, looking for things I might give my girls. I found a little sweater for Michelle, and a scarf for Susan. Much of the clothing was Aunt Edna's: sweaters, wool pants, a couple of coats. She'd taken the opportunity to do her own closet cleaning.

"Some of these things are nice, Aunt Edna," I told her.

"You're welcome to any of it, honey. I'm tired of it all."

I dug through and found a nice cotton sweater and a wool-blend vest. I'd finally received a box of my own clothes from home and had jogged right out of Aunt Edna's suits. She couldn't watch the hospital bed leaving the house, but stayed in her bedroom while I held the doors open for the men. At last they pulled down the sliding door on their truck, handed me a receipt, and left. Aunt Edna came out then, her eyes red and still full of tears.

"Somebody will get good use from that bed," I told her.

"I know."

As soon as we'd finished carrying Grandma and Grandpa's original bed frame and mattress in from the garage, Aunt Edna dusted her hands and said, "Now, I'm going to let you make your own bed. I've got an appointment with a chair and a paint box and a canvas I've already primed." Her entire mood had swung. She'd gone from being weepy to a state of rapturous anticipation. It was a transformation that I'd see dozens of times that summer. Her troubles were soothed by painting, by the thought of painting. But I don't want to give the impression that painting didn't trouble her, too. She took her art seriously and went through a range of emotions with a brush in her fist. You can still see this in her canvasses. She'd get so upset sometimes that she would turn her brush around, grab it by the bristle end, and jab at the canvas, make little indentations and sometimes even tears before she'd go back at it with the paint.

That morning she carried a chrome and steel kitchen stool, the kind that has a backrest but also steps that fold out from beneath the seat, to the backyard. By the time I was through making up my bed, she had the stool hung from a limb of the mimosa. The bottom step didn't quite reach the ground. It was unsettling to see a chair in that attitude, suspended from a cord, a step stool that couldn't be climbed. As she set up her easel and paint box, she kept her eyes on the chair that was swinging slowly in the wind.

"Do you mind if I watch, Aunt Edna?" I asked.

"It will cost you a cup of tea," she said without turning to me.

"I'll start it brewing right now." By the time I returned she was already laying on a thin ochre ground. The legs of the chair were chrome, but dull with age; the seat, backrest, and footsteps were yellow, but the paint was bubbling at the edges of all this sheet metal as if rust were heat. Her painting was representational. She didn't show the stool in midair in a surrealistic manner, poised statically among clouds. The chair hung on a cord from a tree, just as she saw it. By the time the water was boiling she'd already set in proportions and had begun to sketch in the tree, the cord, the outlines of the stool. She spent the entire day there, worked through lunch and the heat of the afternoon. I kept her supplied with snacks, switched from hot tea to iced as the day warmed, and never commented on what she was doing, or asked questions. I'd get up from time to time and go sort dimes. I took a half-hour nap. She continued to paint, wiping her hands on her T-shirt, mixing and building layers of color. She'd slap a brush over her forearm to clear the paint thinner from it, spraying her pants and shoes. Every once in a while she'd sigh and say, "I need to let it dry," or "Leave it alone, Edna, leave it alone," and then she'd go back at some detail and this would lead to a total resurfacing of one area, which would lead to another. She squeezed paint out of a tube as if she were throwing a glass into the fireplace. As the day proceeded the wind died away, the stool stopped swinging and seemed to inhabit a stillness that no earthbound chair could. Aunt Edna worked on a rubber footpad of the stool intently, her face inches from the canvas, saying, "There, there," then she'd back away and say, "Shit," and return to it. A tiny bug landed in the paint, drowned there, but she didn't pick it out, simply painted over the body. She was satisfied with the perspective and the composition, but the patches of color embittered her, made her palette a swirling spectrum that she repeatedly scraped clean and built again. Her foot went to sleep beneath her and she stomped it awake, pacing back and forth, refusing to step beyond her easel toward the suspended stool. The thumb protruding through the palette was encrusted with paint, a writhing worm trying to break out of an earth of which it was a part. When the light started to go, she had to quit. Aunt Edna's paintings are rarely dark, are often so suffused with light that the color is blanched. She dropped her arms to her side, her last wet brush describing an arc on her thigh. She turned to me and said apologetically. "It'll take another week or two. I have to let this dry a bit so the brush strokes will hold. I'm worn out. I haven't gotten to work this long, uninterrupted, on a picture in years."

"Thank you for letting me watch," I said.

"Sarah, honey, I didn't even know you were there. When I paint it's just me and the chair. I don't hear a thing. If you ran a fire engine between the easel and the chair I wouldn't see it pass. I wouldn't smell the fire. When Momma was alive, I used to set a kitchen timer to clear my head of the paint fumes so I'd go check on her every once in a while."

"Why is the chair hanging by a rope, Aunt Edna?"

"I don't know. I've just painted so many sitting on their four legs. It seemed the thing to do."

"That painting over the TV, the bow-back Windsor, why does one leg turn into an electric cord?"

"I don't know. I knew I was going to hang it over the TV. Maybe that's why. It seems like everything in the house is plugged into that socket behind the TV. I know it doesn't make any sense that the picture would be, too."

□ □ □

I know that the catalog notes and museum placards like to speak of the "inherent symbolism" in her pictures, that the "allegorical content" is akin to that in Dürer's woodcuts and engravings. It's probably heresy to say she never meant anything so specific. Just because something in her mind happened to predict a planetary conjunction doesn't mean she intended it. Just because a chair leans against a lamppost doesn't mean it's found the light. Later that week I found a very rare dime among the thousands she'd collected. I showed her in the book: for every million or more 1916 Mercury dimes minted only a few Denver coins were struck. "It's incredibly rare," I said. "It could be worth over a thousand dollars if the condition is good enough."

She shrugged her shoulders and said, "Well, good, that will pay for one of our tickets." I kept going on about its rarity, what impossible luck brought it from a child's hand into hers. She said, "Rare doesn't mean impossible."

It's possible that even though her paintings suggest the world to us, they were only chairs to her. A stool suspended by a single cord doesn't mean her life hung in the balance. Perhaps all the things we see don't emanate from her but from us. She wasn't a source of light but a sponge. We're all writing our own biographies and calling them the life of Edna Hutton. If we only knew more we wouldn't have to interpret clues and invest meaning. But I feel that no matter how much information I give you, even if I tell you everything I know, you'll need more, and simultaneously wish you knew less. All you really want is to interpret and invest and gossip anyway, to use knowledge as a basis for invention. The best explanation I've heard so far is that somehow the very sparseness or emptiness of her pictures enables them to act as Rorschachs, that they invite speculation but can only reflect it. Her life may or may not be represented in her pictures. I can't tell you what every painting means. She enjoyed the process of painting them and I know she never envisioned the vast audience they've reached and somehow speak to. The only thing that's right about her paintings being in a museum is that they're together. She worked knowing they'd hang in her house, not on the anemic canvas walls of a gallery. They mean different things there. They were painted for a specific environment, and like an altarpiece removed from a Renaissance church, they're out of place and seem gaudy and unusual, separated as they are from their context. I think all the attention would have frightened her. I think she'd just want everybody to sit down.

□ □ □

James never called, but showed up with Billy on the front porch the next evening. They'd walked the two miles from their home.

"Why didn't you call? I'd have come picked you up," Aunt Edna said, holding open the screen door.

"Good day for a walk," James said. "A little more practice and I'd be able to get here by myself, if Billy wouldn't take a different route every time."

"He's too proud to ask for a ride," Billy said.

"Son, I told you," James said.

"Billy, I'll bring him home. Do you want to stay and eat with us?"

"No, ma'am. I've heard all Grandpa's stories and there's a ball game this evening."

"There's always a ball game," James said.

"How about a pop to take with you?" Aunt Edna asked.

"All right."

"Don't you go home by that magazine shop," James ordered.

"I was just looking at the sports magazines, Grandpa."

"I know what you were looking at. I'm going to have a talk with that man in there."

Aunt Edna handed Billy the can of soda. "Thank you for bringing him, Billy."

"You're welcome, Mrs. Hutton. He carried his coat all the way here and didn't put it on till I told him we were close."

"You can go on home now, son," James said.

"I'm going home," Billy said.

Aunt Edna turned to James after the boy left and said, "Give me that coat. It's almost ninety degrees and you're wearing a coat."

"I told you I'd wear my best suit."

"You don't care what I look like. Why should I care what you look like?"

"Don't say that, Edna. I'm a vain man. I've been told I'm a good-looking man."

"I'm not saying you don't have points. I'm just saying you don't have to dress up for me."

James turned to me. "Sarah, you're looking nice today."

"Thank you, James. It's an Armani suit and the pearls are from Tiffany's," I said.

Aunt Edna turned James around, taking off his jacket. When he was facing her, she reached up and pecked him on the cheek. "Thank you for walking so far to see me. Sit down right here. It's right here behind you. I'll get you a glass of iced tea."

"That would be nice," James said. "Sarah, are you having supper with us?"

"I am. Aunt Edna is having spiral-sliced ham, mashed potatoes, spinach, and rolls. It'll be the best meal I've had in a week."

"I'll trade you my spinach for your rolls."

"You don't have to eat the spinach if you don't like it, James," I told him.

"It's awkward, people finding out what you like and don't like. A man ought to be grateful for any kind of food, but I think I'd just as soon starve as eat a spinach leaf."

"I can't eat lima beans," I confided.

"We're going to be good friends, Sarah. I can tell. You know blind people can see things sighted people can't. I can tell right off when a person's to be trusted. You're a trustworthy person."

"I wish I had that ability. I wouldn't have married my husband."

Aunt Edna came back with the iced tea. "I think I met your husband at the funeral, Sarah. Very few people will approach a blind person. They don't know how much mind you have without eyes. But he walked right up and put his hand in mine and we had a nice little talk."

"There's no one Sam's afraid to talk to. He's good at it. Too good at it. He's funny and he's handsome and he has to share it. Do I sound bitter? I'm trying to sound bitter."

"This house smells like paint and potatoes at the same time," James said.

Aunt Edna gave me the evil eye, so I stopped talking about failed marriages. "Aunt Edna's been painting up a storm," I said. "She's got half a dozen canvases going at once."

"When I was in school they took us to a house and let us touch the paintings and the sculptures, the old vases. I'd be running my hands over that art till I bumped into the hands of one of the other students and that would startle me, to think about other hands making things, like I'd bumped into the artist's hands while he was making it. To me it's people's hands that are works of art. Every hand is different, and everybody makes their own hands with the kind of work they do, the kind of life they've lived."

"I have a friend who lost part of one middle finger working on an oil rig," I said. "When he shakes hands with you the nub of that finger tickles."

James shook his head as if he were being forced to bite down on spinach. "Lord God, Ernie Hoover, Maybe Spilee, and Jimmy Jackson, I'd hate to lose a piece of my hand. I read with my fingers."

"Tell me about Maybe Spilee, James. What did she do to you?" I asked.

"Maybe Spilee broke my heart," James said. "Maybe Spilee was the first girl I loved, and I've loved girls ever since. Maybe was in my school. We dated, but she said it was foolish for two blind folks to get married. You always love things that disappoint you, Sarah. Never forget that. I've been in love with women ever since."

After dinner I left James and Aunt Edna alone. They sat on the front porch for a while, then they came back inside and watched an episode of *Murder, She Wrote*, which James liked because Jessica, Angela Lansbury, always thought out loud. I walked through the room once or twice. They sat in chairs side by side holding hands. James's head was tilted as if he might be sleeping, and Aunt Edna didn't watch the TV, but watched James and listened as he did. She took him home after the news, and by the time she got back I'd had two glasses of water with lemons, and big tears were running down my cheeks.

"What's wrong, Sarah?" she asked.

"I'm sorry," I said. "There's nothing wrong. I'm just sick of being pitiful. It's Sunday night and I've been sitting here waiting. And I'm miserable with envy because you're in there sparking with James and holding hands. It's been a full week now and still Sam hasn't called or anything and I won't call him but I can't stop crying."

"My God, Sarah. I thought there had been some terrible accident." She sighed.

"I just don't understand why he can't do things right. He hasn't called."

She sat down across from me, the dimes rolled and stacked between us. "Stop this bawling, Sarah. I'm ashamed of you. It isn't as if one of your daughters has died."

"What a horrible thing to say," I said, but I did stop crying.

"Well, you've got to place this sadness in perspective. There are worse things in the world that could happen to you. Well, Sam cheated on you. So what? You're not hungry, your children are healthy, and guess what, he still loves you. I haven't got time to put up with someone who likes feeling sorry for themselves. People who feel sorry for themselves are boring. The amount we can love is infinite. Only our ability to receive love has its limits. I know you love Sam a lot. That's why you're hurt. But don't grieve because he hasn't given you everything. You wouldn't want it. You couldn't live under it. Everyone has this vision that a true lover would think of them constantly. Why would you want that? It's stifling. So his love wasn't perfect. Maybe his love for you isn't all-consuming. He isn't blinded by love for you, but he still wants you. Isn't that better? He wants you in the light of day, flaws and all. Who wants somebody that's blind?"

"You do."

"I'm talking love blind, Sarah."

"But he lied and cheated. He put his penis in another woman. You can't take his side."

"That's all he put there, Sarah. He took it back out."

"And put it back in, and took it out, and put it back in, till he exploded inside of her. It's the same way we made our girls."

"He's sorry, Sarah. I heard him say he was sorry."

"He's sorry," I said.

"If you hate him so much, why are you sitting here crying because he hasn't called?"

"I'm crying because I won't call him. I'm crying because I can't forgive him yet."

"I'm going to ask you to do a favor for me. When you do decide to call, don't tell him you forgive him. It's not a word that should pass between people who love each other. Momma used to tell me she forgave me when I was late, or decided to go out for a bit. Whether I deserved it or not, I resented it. Swallow your forgiveness and just say hello."

"I'm sorry, Aunt Edna, I didn't mean to spoil your evening with James."

"Nothing is spoiling anything with me anymore, Sarah. I've decided to do as I please. I'm going to paint and I'm going to get married."

I put my hands flat on the table as if something had shaken the house. "Aunt Edna," I whispered, leaning forward.

"I'm tired of mighta oughta shoulda."

"I can't believe it. This is so great. We're going to have a wedding." I got up and hugged her.

"James was so nervous he made me nervous," she said. "All evening we sat in there and he didn't say a word about it and then I thought, well maybe he didn't ask me, or he's forgotten he asked me. So we were sitting there watching TV, hadn't spoken about anything for ten minutes, and I just said, 'Yes,' and he said, 'Good,' without even pausing and that was it. We didn't even set a date or make any plans. I took him home and we kissed at his door and now I'm wondering if any of this happened."

"Sure it happened. I saw y'all sitting in there. I saw you leave to take him home, and I saw you come back. This is all corroborating evidence. We'll hold him to it."

"No, I have to talk to him. I've realized since he said, 'Good,' that there's things I want."

"He'll give you anything you want, Aunt Edna. It's James."

"I want to get Momma and Daddy settled first. And I don't want a courtroom wedding. I want your daddy and Margaret to be there. We can have the wedding right here at the house. We can plan to have it a week or so after you and I get back from Scotland. That will give me about a month to paint unmolested."

"Aunt Edna, you'll be able to paint after you're married, too."

"It's just so hard to believe in having two happy things at once."

"I wonder how Aunt Margaret is going to take this."

"What do you mean?"

"Well, when she saw you and James hugging after the funeral service she lost control of her legs. She was afraid to get near him."

"James?"

I nodded.

"Well, she'll have to get over it. I know she was upset about Momma and Daddy going to Scotland, but she can't have anything against James. I want her to be here. I want all of you to be here."

"How will James's family take this?"

"I don't know. Thelia seems to like me. She'll have a home to herself when James moves here."

"James will move here?"

"Well, yes. This is my house."

"He's said he would?"

"I just assumed he would. He's always talking about his bedroom cracking off the house. I've got a good bedroom."

I smiled, then asked, "You're not waiting to get married because I'm here with you?"

"No, Sarah. I want to get you and Momma both out of the house before James moves in." She threw her thumb over her shoulder at Grandma, who was still atop the refrigerator.

"Aunt Edna, would you never have married James if Grandma hadn't died?"

"James would never have asked me. He knew where my priorities were."

"Then we can look at him as Grandma's last gift to you."

She put her hand over her mouth so that she had to breathe through her nose. Tears welled up in her eyes.

"Oh, Aunt Edna," I said, "I'm no good at all."

She took her hand away long enough to say, "I miss her so much," before she walked off toward her bedroom. I followed her and by the time we reached the hallway she was able to breathe normally, to pause before her day's work, which sat drying on a chair there, and say softly, "I'm going to switch to acrylics. They dry so much faster than oils."

□ □ □

Aunt Edna woke the next morning in a panic of planning. At first I just thought she was agitated because this was the first true day of her retirement but she said no, she'd always had summers off. None of the other cooks were at work that day either. She said I might look for that kind of response in late August when school started again, but that otherwise I was to believe her when she told me what she was panicked about. She made me call the airline at seven-thirty in the morning and order our tickets to Scotland for two weeks earlier than we'd planned. I told her we might not have our passports by then, but she said we'd just push back the reservations if that was the case. I told her there might be additional costs but that didn't sway her either.

She said, "I'm so mad at the government. I pay taxes my whole life and it still takes them a month to print my passport."

"Well, they have to do a background check, I guess," I said.

"A background check?"

"To see if you're a terrorist or a convict or something."

"They don't just check to see if all your taxes are paid?"

"Maybe that too. It might not take as long as they tell you. The fellow at the post office said he's seen them come back in as little as three weeks."

"There's no chance that they wouldn't let us back in the country once we've left it? Because if there is, we need to take James with us."

"They'll let us back in, Aunt Edna. What's got into you?"

"It just seems like there's a lot to do in the next couple of months." She put her hands on the back of a chair and bent over it. "My back is sure aching this morning. That's what two days straight in front of an easel got me. Let's go for a walk and maybe that will work it out."

"Let me scoop up the rest of this paint thinner," I said sourly. We'd switched to skim milk from 1 percent. I'd accused Aunt Edna of washing out her smallest white brush in a gallon of water and pouring it over my cereal.

When Grandpa was alive, half the men on his street worked at General Dynamics. They carpooled to work. But now this had become a very low-income neighborhood, predominately Hispanic. Almost every driveway had a car in it that seemed to be built of parts. If there were two doors on a car, they were different colors. If there were four doors, one of them was missing. In many yards the grass had given up to the feet of children and chained dogs. We walked along a cracked and heaved sidewalk. There were places where silt had washed over the walk and dried into a thin, brittle cake.

"I started painting chairs when the first poor family moved here," Aunt Edna said. She stopped in front of a house, put both hands on her lower back, and pressed.

"Why then?" I asked.

"The family that sold them their house took the window air conditioners with them. I guess the new family couldn't afford to replace them. Anyway, they brought their chairs out in the yard every evening and sat in them till it was cool enough to go back inside. I'd walk to work early in the mornings and their chairs would still be there, grouped in a little arc facing the street, dew glistening on the arms and seats. I was just overcome. I used to look forward to walking past those chairs every morning. They were none of them the same. All different. Sometimes they'd be full of leaf fall from a windy night. Sometimes there would be one less chair or one more, a stranger or a guest. Beer bottles and pop bottles sat empty at their feet. Maybe one chair would be tumped over. Sometimes there would be a broken-down car, a car with its hood up or a wheel off, and all the chairs would be grouped around it. Those chairs just seemed to make everything a spectacle. They seemed to be interested in me, too, a little crowd gathered to watch me go by every morning, just to see what I'd do or what I was wearing. Little things like that can make you feel like you're enough. And you are, if you notice them."

We walked. She pointed out chairs, a single on a porch, two under a tree. In a vacant lot, next to a large house, two weather-beaten couches faced one another. There was a dog asleep in each.

"It's hard to fit a couch on a canvas," she said. "They hump up and blow out and won't be contained. A chair fits."

"When I was in school, Aunt Edna, we had to read John Ruskin's drawing book. One of his first lessons was that you shouldn't draw the things you love."

She looked at me with her mouth open, her brow channeling all her derision down the bridge of her nose. "Well, I don't know who John Ruskin was except a masochist and a fool. Why shouldn't you draw the things you love?"

"Because of the associations they have. You're influenced inordinately by their associations and your work would be skewed in some way."

"Exactly," she said in triumph. "Nobody should make up rules about art, not even for beginners. I mean you could explain about mixing colors or how to trim a brush or any technical thing, but telling somebody not to draw what they love: he should have been shot."

"Now see," I said, "you knew immediately how you felt about that. I've been trying to decide for twenty-five years whether I thought he was right or wrong or somewhere in between."

"It comes with age, Sarah. You get tired of standing in the middle. You see the same disasters occurring again and again and you get tired of indecision and moderation and committees and you just decide to be a dictator."

"A dictator?"

"Yes, Momma is a pretty good example. Even after she's gone, she's having her way."

"How's your back, Aunt Edna?"

"Better."

We turned a corner and started back toward Refugio Street. Squirrels skittered before us, found safety in the trees, then barked at us. We seemed to be the first humans they'd ever seen. The day was rising in billowing waves of odor and warmth and dust. A pair of blue-robed concrete Madonnas stared at one another from opposite sides of the street as if they were one-upping each other over their son's accomplishments. Weathered strings of Christmas lights still hung in sagging garlands from gables. We were surrounded by mysteries of nature and theology. I'd never thought of myself as a religious artist before, but I was. I was the last in a 2,000-year-old line of artists reworking the icons, performing the tiniest of sacrileges generation after generation, until Christ became Santa Claus, the apostles, elves. If I'd made this leap all in one step, all by myself, it might have been laudable, but I gave myself the task of reinterpreting Santa's belt, Rudolph's eyelashes. I needed to take a bigger leap. I needed to have a vision.

"I wish I could find something to paint that satisfied me as much as chairs satisfy you," I said.

"Paint chairs," Aunt Edna suggested.

"I think you've cornered that market," I said.

"Any subject is inexhaustible."

"But I want something of my own."

"Paint end tables. There's a field that's totally unexplored." She smiled. "It doesn't matter what you paint, Sarah, but your manner of treating it should be respectful."

"You need to write a manifesto, Aunt Edna."

"No, I don't. Just because I take a stance doesn't mean it's right. I have second thoughts all the time. I just get tired of them. I don't have the energy anymore to consider them. One of the things I'm not going to reconsider is marrying James. As soon as we get back to the house I'm calling your daddy and Aunt Margaret with the news."

"It's still early in Phoenix," I warned her.

"We'll call Phoenix first then. Catch her before she's put on her face."

□ □ □

It didn't go well. My father was startled but recovered, and promised to be there when she picked a date. He would give her away. But Aunt Margaret, it's safe to say, acted as if she'd been assaulted with a wire brush. I only heard one side of the conversation, of course, but there were long pauses where I knew she was trying to force her contorted facial expressions and bodily shock through the narrow phone lines. At last the line went dead and we took it that Aunt Margaret had fainted, managing to place the phone on its cradle as she fell.

"She said he was a black man," Aunt Edna told me. "I told her he knew that. Then she asked me if I knew what color I was. That's when I didn't say anything for a while. She said I was lonely and grasping for companionship and I should come out and stay with her and Alf for a while. That's when I told her I couldn't do that, that Momma and Daddy had to be handled."

"Is she coming for the wedding?"

"She doesn't know. She said Alf wasn't feeling well. She'll let me know. I knew she was a prejudiced old nag but it just hacks me no end that she thinks James is marrying up, like I'm some kind of catch because she's my sister."

"I think you're a catch," I said.

"Then she told me I felt sorry for James because he was blind. That's when I told her I felt sorry for Alf because he was deaf, but that didn't keep me from loving him."

"But Aunt Edna, what was it that made you tell her to go to hell? I couldn't help overhearing."

"She told me to make sure I made up a prenuptial agreement. She said James might be after my money and the house. Can you believe it? She said then I'd be living out there with her full-time, whether I wanted to or not. Did I say 'go to hell' loud, Sarah?"

"You remember when Brother Roberts was yelling? It was like that but snappier."

"Well, no wonder she dropped the phone. I'll call her back in a week and ask how Alf is and apologize. But I can't do it now. She gets me so worked up. I'm going to get dressed and go for a drive."

"I'll go with you. I want to pick up a few things."

"Sarah," she said, "Momma didn't always require constant attention. I had occasion to go off by myself sometimes and I still need to do that, be off by myself."

It took me a second or two to understand. "Oh," I said, "sure. I understand. I can go anytime."

"I'll be back before lunch."

"Take as long as you like. I'll start working on the quarters or the nickels. I've got some phone calls to make."

"I'm sorry I'm so anxious."

"Go," I said, "go."

□ □ □

Aunt Edna and I had agreed not to weigh ourselves until we were ten days into our diet so we wouldn't be discouraged. She'd been a rock of

consistency, rarely cheating, and on top of the diet had given up coffee and tea because JoAnn told her the caffeine was overwhelming her
systems with "anesthetic vapors." At ten days I'd lost four pounds and
she'd lost six. She tried to console me by saying her last week at work
had been especially active and suggested I try some form of exercise.

"We can walk," she said, "get our stamina up for sightseeing in
Scotland."

I nodded, sourly envious of the two pounds.

□ □ □

Daddy and Aunt Margaret got the disinterment authorizations back
to us by midweek. Aunt Margaret attached a terse little note to hers,
telling Aunt Edna to be sure and attend the body at each transfer or we
wouldn't know who we'd be scattering in Scotland.

"You and your aunt," Aunt Edna asked, "where do you get this
mistrust of morticians?"

"It's death and money, Aunt Edna, our species' two most mysteri-
ous subjects. I think if we got back to that time when we all buried
our own dead on the family farm we'd have a more balanced understanding of life. That's why I like this idea of spreading Grandma and
Grandpa's ashes. I think we should dig the hole, build the casket,
carve the tombstone for our loved ones. The idea of someone else
doing it seems intrusive and disrespectful. Paying someone to dispose
of remains doesn't seem humble. If we can do it for our dogs and cats
and goldfish, why not our loved ones?"

"Sarah, how are you and I going to cremate Daddy?"

"I know that requires special equipment. But a shovel isn't too
special."

"There are laws, Sarah, about embalming and concrete grave liners."

"I know, I know. We've made the laws so we have an excuse not to
feel bad about not doing the work ourselves. I just wanted to say that
spreading the ashes is a step in the right direction. That's another gift
that Grandma's given us."

"If you don't stop talking about the things Momma has given us
after she's died, I'm going to slap you. As far as I'm concerned, when
I die, I don't want my family to be out somewhere digging holes and
sawing up plywood. I'd rather you spend time helping one another
than burying me."

"Aunt Edna, I know you fought to take Grandma to Scotland, but do you resent going, even though you think it's the thing to do?"

"Not at all."

"I mean, you're putting off getting married to do this."

"Sarah, I cared for Momma for twenty years or more. A few more weeks doesn't bother me. I'm not one of those who forget the twenty years their parents spent raising them." I didn't know if this was a jab at her siblings or the world at large. "Besides, I want to see one foreign country before I die. I mean, I looked at that book for years, too, just as Momma did, but it never ever seemed like a possibility, another place in the world to visit, at least not while Momma was alive. She never would have allowed someone else to take care of her. And now that I know they speak English there, I'm much less anxious about it. I'm ready to be on my way."

□   □   □

On the following Sunday the phone rang and, for the first time in two weeks, it was for me. Both my girls had come home from college in automobiles packed with dirty clothes, and I wasn't there to help sort. Sam had simply told them I was helping Aunt Edna and that I was going to Scotland with her. Their phone call was one long complaint. Michelle was on the kitchen phone and Susan on the extension in her bedroom. "Why aren't you here? When are you coming home? I could have gotten a job on campus if I knew you weren't going to be here. There's no fabric softener. Dad wants to work on my car so I can't go see my friends. I need a copy of my birth certificate. Why can't Aunt Edna go by herself? There's stacks of mail you haven't opened. Couldn't you come home for a while and go back later? Dad used a metal fork in the Teflon pan. That economics professor I hate gave me a C. You should be here when we come home. They want me to work on Saturday nights. Before we ever even kissed he put his tongue in my ear. I need a new pair of brown pumps."

When I told them their aunt Edna was getting married and that I wanted them to come for the wedding, they asked why. It was my fault. My children had hardly heard of her, much less met her. Bringing them to Fort Worth to meet a grandmother I didn't like never seemed urgent.

"She's part of your family," I said. Then to make it more intriguing, I added, "She's marrying a black man and he's blind."

"Why? That sounds weird."

"Because she loves him."

"Did your grandma leave you anything?"

"No. Look, I really like my aunt Edna. You'd like her, too. She's still painting, Susan. I want you both to come. I want you to take care of your father for me in the meantime."

"I don't know if I'll be able to get off," Susan said.

"How did your last project in art class go?" I asked her.

"I got a B minus. She said I worked too deliberately. She said I didn't flow into my work. It's the exact same criticism she wrote on my first drawing, that I was too literal."

"Well, I want to see it."

"I didn't bring it home with me. My car was packed."

"Susan!"

"Mom!" she mimicked.

Michelle, my oldest, who'd graduate the next year with a degree in political science, asked if everything was OK.

"Sure," I said. "I'm really looking forward to Scotland."

"You've never been interested in Scotland before."

"No, I've never wanted to travel anywhere before, but now I do."

"Don't you want your mail?"

"It will keep."

"Dad said to tell you the people from American Greetings called."

"OK."

"Don't you want their number?"

"Not really."

"Mom!"

"I'm just taking a few weeks off, Michelle."

"But you don't do that," Susan said.

"It's a family emergency," I explained. Susan hadn't declared her major yet, but I knew it wouldn't be art, even though she was talented. She'd choose marketing, as I had.

When they asked if I wanted to speak to their father, I told them no, I'd just spoken to him and I'd catch him next time. I told them to call me every couple of days, telling them it was so I wouldn't run up

Aunt Edna's phone bill, but it was really so I wouldn't have to speak to Sam if he answered. Nothing makes you feel more rotten than lying to your kids.

□ □ □

James came over for dinner almost every day. Thelia would usually bring him by and Aunt Edna would take him home. It seemed to me that when he had work, he talked about it and when he didn't, he talked about the news. You get used to having a blind person around, you really do. I know that sounds patronizing, but I was uncomfortable at first. I walked heavily so James would know I was leaving or had arrived. I made attempts to describe things by the way they smelled rather than the way they looked. I spoke loudly, as if he couldn't hear well. I wore too much deodorant, because I thought James's remaining senses must be very strong in compensation for his blindness. I took up whistling so he'd know I was happy. I went around the house with a piece of chalk and outlined furniture on the floor, so that if a piece were moved it could be returned to the same spot. I knew that joke about Helen Keller and moving the furniture. Aunt Edna wanted to know who'd murdered all her chairs, who'd murdered the TV and the kitchen table.

I'd never really looked at a black person before, growing up as I had in an unofficially segregated neighborhood and school. Although I felt self-conscious and rude at first, I quickly settled down to a comfortable state of staring at James, and he never seemed to mind. Aunt Edna frowned at me from time to time but she was just as fond of staring at him as I was. He was a very handsome man. The room would go intensely quiet and James would turn to one of us, say, "What?" and we'd both sham a, "Nothing," as if we weren't counting the hairs on his forearms. Occasionally his eyes would wildly flutter like moths around a bare lightbulb. It would make my joints go weak, such abandon in an otherwise placid face. His skin wasn't black but burled, reflected light from every angle like hair, returning it drenched with texture, dyed with darkness. The rims of his eyelids were abruptly pale, like the hinged edge of a door that was overlooked and never painted. There were deep maroon dots under each eye. His hair was short, compressed over the ears where his hat sat, and not yet white although it soon would be. He always wore slacks and black shoes, a long-sleeved white shirt and on Sundays a coat and tie, a thin silk navy blue tie whose knot seemed especially severe and compact. His tie made me think of Sam, who can't tie a tie unless he stands in front of a mirror. James couldn't even comprehend what a mirror was, and yet he could tie his tie. He ate his food as if the table were a drafting board and he was designing a jet engine. All of his movements were precise, intricately planned. He never seemed to be afraid. I began by watching him as if he were my two-year-old, but within days didn't think anything of asking him to fix the kitchen timer when it refused to sound off. He took it apart down to its constituents, bent something, oiled something else, put it back together. I yelled a question at Aunt Edna, where's the garlic salt, and James answered, "First cabinet to the right of the sink, second shelf, behind the salt and the toothpicks." Toothpicks, I thought, those must have hurt when he first found them.

"He sits down to pee," Aunt Edna told me. "There's never any overspray."

"Maybe he wipes the rim afterwards," I said.

"No. I've never heard water against water. He must sit down. He's the most thoughtful man the world's ever made."

"Aunt Edna, do you and James have knowledge of each other?"

"That's none of your business," she huffed, then huffed, "No."

"I'm in the way, aren't I?"

"No. We'll wait till we're married. It's not as if some inadequacy in that department would deter me. We'll never speak of this subject again as long as I live."

"OK. I'll bet he's pretty good though. I mean, really good hands."

She put her hand over her mouth to hide the fact that it was wide open. "If you don't shush, I'll slap the snot out of you."

"Do you want me to get you some birth control pills?" I giggled. "I buy them for my girls."

She frowned. "I'm going to pull a tinfoil icicle out of your butt if you don't hush. Do you really buy them birth control?"

"Since they were fifteen."

"Were they having sex that early?"

"No, but I didn't want them to have to come to me the day they started, and I don't trust teenagers with condoms."

"Why not?"

"They get too excited. It's hard to insert a mechanical step between heavy petting and intercourse. Michelle can barely work a Band-Aid. I can just imagine her fumbling with a condom."

Aunt Edna pinched her bottom lip with her thumb and forefinger and nodded slowly. "Did you have an unwanted pregnancy, Sarah?"

"No, but I figured the odds of two generations in a row being lucky weren't good."

"It just seems so reasonable," she said. "I'm proud of you, Sarah."

I can't tell you how good this made me feel. Aunt Edna was the first person outside of my husband and mother I'd shared this confidence with. Sam had said that it might be a bad idea, that even though the girls might be protected from pregnancy they'd still be susceptible to the diseases of an unhindered sex life. Even my mother, who always listens for doom but never cups her hand to her ear because she doesn't want to let on, suggested the girls might grow up too quickly.

▢ ▢ ▢

Thelia and Billy had dinner with us the following Sunday. Billy ate in a kind of stunned silence, even though there wasn't any white food on his plate. Thelia barely had time to compliment the food when Aunt Edna asked her if she'd considered providing Billy with birth control.

"Aunt Edna!" I screeched. "I'm sorry, Thelia," I said. "We've been talking about my daughters. I had no idea she'd bring it up now."

James was smiling into his plate.

Thelia's fork was in her mouth and she seemed unable to pull it out.

"Did I say something wrong?" Aunt Edna asked.

"Edna, honey, it's not polite . . ." and here James broke down and laughed, "It's not polite to invite a black family into your white house for the first time and ask them if they're trying to hold down their numbers." He slapped his open palms on his thighs and then held his stomach.

"Well, I didn't mean it like that at all."

"I know you didn't. That's what makes it so funny."

"You said he's starting to look at magazines and he's about that age," Aunt Edna said.

"What magazines?" Thelia asked.

Billy became as compact as the knot in his grandfather's tie.

"Now, Thelia," James said, unable to stop smiling, "I thought he stayed in that magazine shop too long last time we were there but I don't know what he was looking at. Let's not embarrass him anymore."

"Were you looking at those dirty magazines, William Lee?"

"No, ma'am. That man in there won't let kids back in that corner."

"Unless you sneak," James said.

"We're going to have a talk when we get home, young man."

Aunt Edna said, "Sarah gave her daughters birth control pills when they were fifteen."

"Aunt Edna!" I screeched again.

James said, "Best if this boy don't know there's girls out there with birth control pills, if you know what I mean." He bobbed and whistled.

"Grandpa," Billy whined.

"I'm not saying nothing else," James said.

"Mrs. Hutton, I haven't told you yet how sorry I am that your mother passed," Thelia offered, and for once I was grateful that someone switched the subject to the death of one of my relatives.

"Thank you, Thelia. I guess I'm nervous. I just know we haven't talked about your daddy and me getting married and I'm worried about how you feel about this. I'm sorry, Billy. I want you both to call me Edna."

"Edna," Thelia said, and then sighed. "I've been preparing myself for a few years now for Billy to bring a white girl or a Mexican girl home some day. He goes to a school where 75 percent of the girls are white or brown. I'll admit, it did take me back when it turned out to be my daddy rather than my son. If Daddy don't care that you're white, then I don't. My mother's been dead for almost fifteen years now. I don't have any fears that you're going to try to be my momma or that Daddy is trying to replace her. And I guess you know you're marrying a blind man, that I'd be worrying about him even if he wasn't blind. But I trust his judgment. Y'all were friends a long time before you decided to do this. Daddy's always happy after he's been over here. There are things

I want to teach you how to cook, things he likes. We're going to miss him, miss having a man about the house."

"I'll be the man, Momma," Billy said.

"He's right," James said. "He's a capable young man. I won't worry about Thelia if Billy's there. Edna, I told Thelia she could shut off that back bedroom, just let it crack and fall off the house after I'm gone."

"Well, you're welcome here anytime, Thelia," Aunt Edna said. "And you too, Billy. There'll always be a pop in this refrigerator for you."

"What do you say?" Thelia asked him.

"Thank you, ma'am. Mom," Billy said, "But I don't have to marry a white girl, do I?"

"Of course not," she answered.

"Because white girls are white," Billy said.

"That's enough out of you," Thelia said, lifting her finger.

"It'd be better if everybody was like me," James said. "Better if everybody was blind."

As Thelia and James and Billy were leaving that evening, Thelia paused in the living room and said, "Edna, you've sure got a bunch of chairs. Daddy told me you did, but when he trips over one or two of something he's pretty sure the world is infested with it. But you've got a bunch of chairs."

As soon as they were out the door, I confronted Aunt Edna about revealing the confidence I'd shared with her and she said, "How was I to know it was a confidence?"

"It was about fifteen-year-old girls and birth control," I said.

"I thought you were bragging," she said. "From now on, before or shortly after you tell me a confidence, you must say, 'This is a confidence, Aunt Edna,' and I'll hold it till the day I die."

"So you have no ability to discriminate on your own?"

"Not if you're the kind of person who's embarrassed about doing the right thing. Now if you'd told me you'd stolen a pop from the store, or offered your daughters to a pimp, I'd know not to spread the news."

□ □ □

At the end of our second ten days, I'd lost another four pounds and Aunt Edna had lost another six. There was a definite smirk on her face as the needle rattled to a stop. Well, I thought, she has more incentive than I do. People often dieted before their weddings, rarely before a divorce.

□ □ □

We drove out to the cemetery to stand witness at the disinterment. Two men used a small backhoe to dislodge the flat bronze marker and the concrete block it was embedded in, then the backhoe began lifting soil from the grave and depositing it on a green tarp. The lid of the concrete vault was only a couple of feet under the surface. The teeth of the backhoe's bucket scraped across it repeatedly, and I had the strangest urge to climb the nearest tree. We were both worried that water had infiltrated the vault and that Grandpa, like Lee Harvey Oswald, had been preserved as a quivering mass of jelly. So we were prepared for the worst when the lid of the vault was pried free. The men wrapped a chain around the lid and lifted it out whole. Aunt Edna and I stepped gingerly to the edge of the grave. Grandpa's copper casket gleamed in the light, dry as the day it was put there twenty-four years earlier.

I'd come home from college to watch Grandpa die, to attend his funeral. One thing about cancer is that it gives the family plenty of time to gather. He'd died of liver cancer and so went to his grave as yellow as the blade of a tape measure, his body as desiccated and light as a dead cricket's. My father kept comparing him to a piece of painted lumber that's been hollowed out by termites. You pick it up, expecting it to have some form of substantiality, and almost throw it across the room because it's so light. Your feet, which you'd planted firmly to sustain and shift the weight, prickle with the effort to keep your balance. If Grandpa's body was light, the guilt my father carried staggered him. He'd commuted from Saint Louis to Fort Worth for weeks, leaving work and driving all night to spend the day with his father. He'd nap in the afternoon and then drive back to Saint Louis the next night in order to be back at work in the morning. Mike and I were both in school. Dad and Mom had bought a new home. He'd just moved from teaching to administration and felt some responsibility to his school district. On one of the nights that Daddy was driving back to Saint Louis, Grandpa woke up and was especially vibrant. He asked for my father, was disappointed that he wasn't there, and slipped into a coma hours later. He never regained consciousness for the last three days of his life. So Grandma sat in front of Grandpa's casket at the graveside service and wept bitterly at her loss, after lashing out at my father because Grandpa had left things unsaid. I asked my father what could have been so important and Dad said there was nothing, that he and his father knew and loved each other well, and that his mother was only angry at death. He tried to explain to her how sorry he was, how he had tried to balance the needs of both his families, and finally he got mad at death, too, and told her that his anguish was just as valuable as hers, that he wouldn't allow his grief to be diluted by guilt. They didn't speak for two years.

The men slipped straps beneath the casket, winched it up to a gurney, and rolled it into the hearse for the journey to the funeral home. We followed them there, watched the unloading process, and were asked if we wanted a viewing, but Aunt Edna told them no. She signed more papers. The body would go to the medical examiner now, and from there to the crematorium. I asked Aunt Edna what would happen to the casket.

"I don't know."

"It must have cost a fortune."

"I think it did. Do you want it?"

"No."

"I'll tell them to put it in storage for us. Then if we need a casket we'll have one."

"We could use it as a planter or an ice chest," I said, "and save the storage fees."

"That's not funny, Sarah. I know what we'll do. We'll have them put it back in the grave. We own the plot. Then when we need it we'll have it disinterred. They can't charge us extra because they'd have to dig the grave anyway."

She struggled with this, unsure if it was an insight or another morbid joke.

□ □ □

Between all our errands, between cremation papers and registrars and estate lawyers, before and after James's visits, Aunt Edna continued to paint her portraits of chairs. I know now that this subject wasn't unique to her. Van Gogh painted his chair with a pipe in its lap, Matisse painted a large canvas of an armchair that Picasso didn't like because he thought the chair was going to swallow him. Monet did a lithograph of a chair, and Wyeth a watercolor called *The General's Chair*, a chair draped with a uniform coat. Dutch still lifes frequently are dominated by an old chair, and there is that famous fifteenth-century Netherlandish drawing of men shoveling chairs, which is what I occasionally felt like doing to Aunt Edna's collection. The difference is that Aunt Edna painted chairs exclusively. If there were something else in her portraits it was only happenstance, or perhaps some tool of composition. She painted chairs in the form of actual portraits, the background a single tone. She painted them as part of a landscape and in family groupings. There's one canvas depicting three chairs stacked one upon another, one of chairs draped with white sheets, a series of chairs balanced on other objects: balls, candlesticks, cat's tails. I think of a chair now as a perfect sitter for a portrait, never fidgeting, slumping, or complaining, never tiring. A chair has patience, a chair can wait. Its arms are always open, always inviting. Since chairs are designed to accept a human body, they can be a metaphor for one. We went to a couple of yard sales that summer. Aunt Edna enjoyed collecting her chairs almost as much as painting them. She told me she'd bought chairs because they reminded her of a friend, and that she'd bought chairs and then went searching for a friend who'd sit in them. She would invite people into the house, into a room with twenty-five chairs, and say, "Find a chair," to be funny, or she'd simply ask them to take a seat, just to watch them choose, to see which chair appealed to them.

In Pittsburgh residential neighborhoods in which parking spaces are at a premium, there's a custom of placing an old chair in your parking space while you run an errand, holding the space for your return. It's a respected reservation, especially if you've removed snow from it. They don't use garbage cans, or orange crates, or cones, but chairs, because they're personal. You just don't move someone's chair. It's a taboo that countless slapstick comedians traded on. This is all just to say that I know some have speculated that she painted chairs because she had to stand up all day at her job. Well, she stood up all day in front of her easel, too. She didn't paint chairs because she was tired and longed to sit down.

For the two weeks prior to our departure for Scotland, Aunt Edna devoted herself to a single canvas, working from the photographs she'd taken of her massed chairs the day of Grandma's funeral. There were no people in the pictures, of course. The chairs attend each other, row upon row, shimmering in the heat. It's plain that something's happened, that something's been left behind. It's a large work for Aunt Edna, thirty-six inches wide by forty-eight tall. The chairs face the viewer, except for Grandma's and Aunt Edna's, whose backs fill the foreground. You almost don't know they're chairs at first, they're tones so close to that of the earth. The chairs beyond are carefully delineated and although the rows roll over one another like breaking waves, each chair is a crest all its own. I can easily pick out the folding metal chair I sat in that day, the bentwood Sam sat in, my father's place. The tones are for the most part faded and neutral, as old chairs are wont to be, but occasionally she laid on a richness of color that's breathtaking and it brings your nose to the canvas to see how such a thing was technically possible. I know that these effects are accomplished by a blending of tones or an unusual juxtaposition of clear, limpid colors. I know this and yet I'm still drawn to these moments in the picture, easily a dozen of them in this single work. They are so vibrant that when I squint at the painting it reminds me of a constellation, points of light in an otherwise darkened firmament.

Aunt Edna worked in an almost brusque manner in the mornings, but by lunch she began to choose smaller brushes and bring her face closer to the canvas. Usually at two-thirty or three in the afternoon she'd take a nap. I realized that all the distractions of the past few weeks and my presence had interrupted this habit, that she'd probably always had a nap after school. She'd work another hour or two after awakening, gradually backing away from the easel till her extended arm and brush couldn't contact the canvas anymore. Then she'd say, "Oh, well," grimace or smile, and wash her brushes.

Even though I'd been working every day as well, I still didn't have Aunt Edna's stamina, the ability to paint for hours on end. I had to break it up with the counting of silver, an occasional movie, or trips to Asel Art Supply or Michaels for paper. The purchasing of art supplies is at times far more enjoyable than art making itself. It offers and promises endless accomplishment, while a finished work is unflinching in its indifference to the artist. I drew, from time to time, Aunt Edna's windows, from the inside looking out and vice versa. I couldn't decide whether I wanted to paint what I saw through the window, the window itself, my reflection in it, or all three. My ideas were much more complicated than Aunt Edna could approve of, but then she sighed and said, "But everything has to seem complicated before it can seem simple."

"But can a shadow be reflected?" I asked her. "Does a reflection cast a shadow?"

"You just have to look harder," she answered. "Maybe you should try a stained-glass window. You can't see through them. You just have to remember that light and shadow can't exist without each other. It's the line or the area where they blend that's going to make your picture."

"You're talking about technique, Aunt Edna, and I'm talking about ideas. I have to figure things out for myself."

"Hmph," she snorted, "a self-taught artist is one taught by a pretty ignorant person."

"Who said that?"

"I did."

"No, you didn't. I've heard it before."

"Well, then, I repeated it. It's a shadow, or a reflection, of the last person who said it. It still applies."

"Ha, ha. Well, who taught you then?"

"I went to art classes at Suzy's Cozy Creations on River Oaks."

"Suzy's Cozy Creations?"

"It's not there anymore, but they would sell you the paint and brushes and canvas and then explain how to paint. I painted a barn, and an old truck in a field, and a vase full of flowers. Then they went out of business. I sold those paintings for real money, too, at the school fair to raise money for the new jungle gym. That jungle gym's long gone now. Anyway, Suzy was a good teacher. I think she relied too much on nostalgia subjects but she knew the difference between shadow and light."

"I give up. I'm going to go count half-dollars, Aunt Edna."

□ □ □

While Aunt Edna painted or cooked dinner, James would help me with the coins. I'd check dates and mint marks and he'd count, stack, and roll. He once put a handful of dimes and quarters in his pant pocket and then did a hokey pokey dance around the kitchen. "Hear that?" he asked. "I haven't heard that sound in thirty years or more. These new clad coins don't ring in your pocket like silver did." I filled both pockets with silver and joined James, jitterbugging between him and the refrigerator. The coins vibrated against each other and rang like crystal.

"Now that's music," I said.

James sang while he danced.

> Momma need a nickel for the store
> Sorry little baby we're too poor
> Momma gimme dime and I'll tell a rhyme
> Sorry little baby there's no time
> Momma need a quarter for my school
> Sorry little baby I'm no fool
> Momma need a dollar to give to God
> Sorry little baby here's the rod
> Momma need a penny for the show
> Sorry little baby there's no more
> Sorry little baby there's no more

James bounced, I bounced, the room seemed filled with silver tambourines. Aunt Edna turned from the stove and gave us a glorious smile and I told James, "She's smiling, she's smiling, James."

"I knew she was."

"Sing the song again," I huffed, getting my exercise, making feints at the cabinet doors and all the food behind them. And he did.

□ □ □

I asked Aunt Edna later if James ever talked about his wife.

"Oh, yes," she said. "He was in a great deal of pain after she died. He missed her so. Thelia and Billy moved in with him and he felt like he was a burden to them, that they'd adjusted their lives to suit his."

"But what about her, his wife? What was she like?"

"He carries a picture of her in his wallet. He'll show it to you. That's what we do with the pictures in our wallets: show them to people. It doesn't matter that he can't see it. He can hear you when you tell him she was pretty."

"Was she?"

"Oh yes. It's an old black-and-white photo, just limp with wear, but she had a beautiful smile and a way of tilting her head. He still loves her. I wish I could have met her because he makes me love her, too. I mean, that there was this other person like me, this person who loved James the way I do."

"You're not jealous?"

"I'm going to give him my picture to put in his wallet, too. I can't tell you how much pleasure it gives me to know he'll be showing my picture to people. They'll say I'm pretty because they'll want to please James."

"You are pretty."

"Oh, bosh. But I'm not bothered by my looks anymore, not since I turned sixty. Once we reach this age everything concerning looks seems to even out. Old age has allowed me to be as beautiful as most women."

"Then why are you trying to lose weight?"

"For my health, Sarah. You're lucky, for you it's for your health and your looks."

"Well, thanks a lot. You know, sometimes I feel like I've come to discipline camp. Instead of allowing me the luxury of a little self-pity I have to diet, exercise, study, and bear up to brutal honesty, and all because Sam couldn't keep his thing in his pants. Why should I have to improve because of his mistake?"

"It doesn't have anything to do with Sam's mistake. You're free to do as you please, Sarah. I don't care if you and Sam get back together or not. You're distant relations to me. Maybe I give my opinion too freely, but it's my opinion; you're not bound to it."

"But I want you to like me. I want you to like my drawings."

"Why? I don't care if you like my work. I only care if I like my work."

"Aunt Edna, you're impossible."

"I think we're all impossible, and we're working to prove otherwise."

"What does that mean? We're trying to prove we're possible?"

"Yes, trying to prove we're not dead."

"Jesus, Aunt Edna, I'm not trying to prove that. I'm trying to prove I'm right."

"That's a lost cause, even if you are right, but to each his own," she said lightly, as if we'd been arguing over ice-cream flavors. Criminy, she's my white whale. She heaves me to this day. What Starbuck cried to Ahab on the third day of the chase: "Moby Dick seeks thee not. It is thou, thou, that madly seekest him!"

□ □ □

There were days when James had no caning jobs, and then Thelia would drop him off at Aunt Edna's on her way to work. By and by he was learning the house. It wasn't only a memorization of the number of steps and the turns involved to reach the bathroom, but a familiarization with details that I'd never concerned myself with as a sighted person, and so I couldn't understand why James was interested in them. He made us set out a step ladder so he could climb it and put his hand on the ceiling. He traced the moldings along the baseboard, using his hand as a caliper to measure width and depth. He knocked on the plaster, sounding the walls, and blew into the electrical outlets. I felt like everything he touched told him something I'd never be able to understand. Though he'd lay his cheek against a windowpane and I'd know it felt cool. While Aunt Edna painted, he had me give him instruction in the use of her stove, including putting his hand near the burning pilot lights so he'd know where to check if he ever smelled gas. We followed the same course with the water heater and the furnace, but he had to guide me through these.

"I'll need to caulk these windows," he told me. "There's a draft that comes through some of them, some of that outside trying to get inside. That isn't right in a house. It isn't right for things to slip in without knocking."

Once, while he helped me count quarters, he asked in a whisper, "Where'd all this money come from, Sarah?"

"I thought you knew," I said.

"I knew that white folks had all the money but I didn't know they kept it in gallon coffee cans. All this silver smells like coffee, smells like cocaine money."

"It's Aunt Edna's savings, James. She picked it out of the change drawer at school over the last forty years. She'd exchange new coins for the old silver."

"You're joking me."

"No, I'm not."

"She never said a word. That's the saddest story I ever heard, saving her retirement a dime at a time. All this and she's got the social security coming, too."

"You're marrying into real money, James. She'll have a pension, too. She's participated in the teachers credit union retirement fund."

"And I thought I was just marrying her for her looks."

James was fond of baking cookies from scratch. He was skilled in the home arts, from cooking to ironing to mending, and had unusual knowledge of stain-removal remedies and glue formulas made from ingredients at hand. He and Aunt Edna once argued over the individual merits of their favorite cooking and sewing-machine oils.

I was never more startled than the day he found a pack of playing cards in a drawer, brought them to the kitchen table, counted and shuffled them, then spread them out in a fan before me and said, "Now, pick a card."

I started to laugh so hard I couldn't breathe.

"Pick a card," he ordered. I pulled out a card. "Now, look at it," he said with a frown. It was the Queen of Hearts.

"OK," I said. "Now what?"

"Tell me what it is."

"It's the Queen of Hearts."

"Jimmy Jackson, you're the easiest person to trick I've ever met. You're not supposed to tell."

"You asked me."

"It's sleight of mind that fools people, not sleight of hand. You can't feel sorry for me because I'm blind. I'll hit you with a pipe if you do that."

I stopped laughing. "OK, James."

"You've got to stop reminding me where things are and stop asking if I need something. I do have a voice. I'll ask."

"OK."

For news he listened to the radio. For entertainment he read books printed in Braille. One of my most cherished memories is of Aunt Edna and James sitting side by side, a book spread open across their laps, James guiding Aunt Edna's fingers over the raised print and whispering the meaning in her ear. He read her paintings in the same way, brushing his fingertips over the topography of dry paint, the furrowed impasto, his hands alternately flowing with or stumbling across her brush strokes. "This one seems angry," he'd say, or, "This painting shouldn't have stopped at the frame."

At some point he gave all his friends Aunt Edna's phone number. He was more popular than I'd thought. If the phone rang after he arrived in the morning we just let him answer it, because more than likely it was for him. A few calls were business, but for the most part they were from friends, men and women his age. I accused him of being a bookie one afternoon after the phone rang three times in succession.

"It's just the network," he explained. "We all check up on each other."

"Could I be in the network?" I asked. "I never get phone calls."

"The network is just a group of us old blind folks," he said. "We keep each other company, talk about the news, gossip."

"Well, I guess you're a hot property about now," I said, "getting married and all."

"There's going to be a lot of people bumping into each other at the wedding," he laughed. "They're all wanting us to set a date, but I keep telling them we're not sure when y'all will be back from Scotland. I wish you didn't have to go, especially since Edna thinks her momma put that in the will for her sake."

"Put what in the will for her sake?"

"Taking her ashes to Scotland. Edna thinks her momma thought she was in love with Scotland, since they always looked through that book together. She thinks maybe your grandma misinterpreted her interest. But she can't be sure, so she's going no matter what."

"I wish we could all understand each other better, James. I wish we could know for sure what the people we love want."

"Hard to know when they don't know. My grandson has a different idea every day. I get caught up to him, think I know him by evening, and then the next morning he's a different person."

"People get more stable the older they get," I said.

"I wish that were true, Sarah, but it's not. I'm a long way from figuring out your aunt. Everything she does seems sort of magical and remote to me. I feel like there's firecrackers going off all around. She's quick-tempered, sure-footed, full of resolve one minute and the next she's lolling on my shoulder like a child. One moment she's taking care of me, the next I'm taking care of her. We haven't reached an equilibrium yet, where we're taking care of each other without thinking about it."

"It will come," I said. "I know you can't see her eyes, James, but when you're around they crinkle like tissue paper. She acts like one of my teenage girls who has a new boyfriend. I feel like I'm caught in the middle, between a gushing aunt and a gushing daughter, and I've forgotten how gushing feels."

"How are you and your husband getting along?" he asked.

"I don't know," I said. "We haven't spoken in almost a month now. The girls say he's upset. They know there's something wrong now. Did you ever cheat, James?"

"Not that I know of."

"What's that mean?"

"There were a few times when she didn't say much while we were underway. Could have been anybody in bed with me, I suppose." He smiled. Then he added, "People make mistakes, sure enough."

"That's what he said. But there are repercussions for mistakes. His mistake made him feel good and me feel bad."

"He probably feels bad, too," James offered.

"I'm sorry I asked you about cheating. That was rude. If Aunt Edna had been here she would have told me so."

"She's got definite opinions," he said. "I tried to tell her what to do to that chicken in the oven and she said that would never happen in her house."

"What'd you say?"

"Told her to slip some kalamata olives under the chicken skin, let them bake there. It gives a real good flavor to the bird. She said it looked like the chicken had tumors and took them out. She's got opinions. I hope to never cross her, knock on wood." He rapped the arm of his chair three times.

"Why are you so superstitious, James?"

"I'm just hedging my ignorance, Sarah. People with eyes tell me about all these things out there, things I can't know about: airplanes, the moon, a cliff. Most humans have five senses. Who's to say there's not something out there a sixth or seventh sense wouldn't understand? Maybe we're all disabled, and someday a child will be born who has six senses and he'll be able to tell us what we're missing, where the dangers are. Maybe he's already been born, maybe he was Jesus or Mohammed or somebody else we stomped on or put in a crazy house. Superstition doesn't cost me anything. I use it for free."

□ □ □

Grandpa was ready to go to Scotland before we were. He didn't require a passport. Aunt Edna and I picked him up at the funeral home. He was delivered in a plastic tub. From there we went straight to the Craft Mall on Hulen where Aunt Edna bought another little pine box. The tub fit inside perfectly. She spent a couple of days painting chairs on its sides and lid. I must say Grandpa weighed much less than Grandma. We both noticed this but didn't comment upon it, simply tested the weight by lifting the box on our open palms, the same way you'd feed a horse. When Aunt Edna finally finished the little casket's decoration she placed it on newspaper on the back porch to dry. James arrived later that day and she asked him to put Grandpa up on top of the refrigerator with Grandma. James was six inches taller than both of us and wouldn't need a chair.

"Your mother's on top of the refrigerator?" he asked.

"Yes."

"She's been up there all this time?"

"Yes."

"Why didn't you tell me?"

"What?"

"Don't seem right her being in the same room we cook and eat in. I've been baking bread and cakes. What if I'd mistaken your momma for flour?"

"Oh, James," Aunt Edna said.

"We'd all be cannibals," he said. "If anybody found out, they'd take us to jail. If there were any cookies left, I mean after they used them as evidence against us, you'd have to throw cookies all over the fields of Scotland to spread your momma's ashes."

"Stop it right now," Aunt Edna said.

"Can't we put them on top of the TV or in a closet? I won't like thinking of them looking down on me whenever I open the icebox. I'll feel like I'm stealing their food."

"You're the strangest man I've ever met in my life," Aunt Edna stammered.

"Somebody's got to consider these things for you people that don't."

"All right, I'll put them under my bed," she said.

James crossed the room to the stove, began to arrange ingredients for a loaf of bread. "Could have been eating an old white lady in a cookie," he muttered and shook his head.

□ □ □

A couple of days later I woke up early, put on my housecoat, and as I often do at home, put on the coffee even before I peed. As I headed back to the bathroom I noticed that both Grandpa and Grandma's boxes were on the floor just outside Aunt Edna's bedroom door. That seemed strange. It seemed less strange after I peed, when upon returning to the kitchen I found James there in his pajamas. I was so grateful he was blind because he couldn't see my jaw tumble.

"Good morning, James," I finally squeaked out.

"Good morning, Sarah. This coffee does smell nice."

"Sleep well?"

"Very well, Sarah."

"I would have sworn to the police that Aunt Edna took you home last night."

"She did. But we sat in my driveway for a while and then she decided to bring me back."

"So that's why Grandma and Grandpa are out in the hall."

"Can't seem to find a good place for those folks." He smiled and left the room with two cups of coffee.

Later that morning, after Aunt Edna dropped James off at an antique shop on Vickery to do a three-chair job, we talked at the kitchen table. I was stacking buffalo nickels, most of which were undatable due to heavy wear.

She said, "It's not right to talk about it."

"No," I said. "It's a betrayal."

"James would be so upset if he knew we talked about it."

"If he knew," I agreed.

She leaned forward and whispered over the worn nickels, "Last night, in my bedroom, I told him I wanted to turn the lights off and he said, 'The lights are on?' and I said, 'Yes,' and he said, 'Is the door closed?' and I said, 'Yes, but I'm bashful,' and he said, 'Edna, I can't see you,' and I said, 'But I can,' and he said, 'You've never seen yourself naked?' and I said, 'Of course, but I've never seen us naked together,' and he said, 'Well, Edna, are we ugly?' and I said, 'Of course not,' and he said, 'We don't feel ugly,' and I said, 'I don't care, I'm turning out the light,' and he said, 'All right, all right, you go ahead. Then neither one of us will be able to see. I was hoping you would tell me what I was missing, and I said, 'And we're not talking anymore after I turn out the light,' and he said, 'We're not?' and I said, 'No,' and he said, 'But that's a good part,' and I said again, 'No,' and he said, 'What about hearing and smelling?' and I said, 'No listening or smelling either,' and he said, 'Should we even be in the same room, Edna?' and I said, 'I'm turning out the light. I'll be right back,' and he said, 'I just hope we can find each other again once you do,' and I said, 'Shhh,' and he said, 'Shhh,' and then I turned off the light."

"I thought you were saving yourselves till the wedding?"

She straightened up in her chair. "I changed my mind. It's possible those passports will never come. Sarah, there are immoral things I'd never do except out of necessity. And James sure seemed like a necessity last night. You won't tell your daddy, will you?"

"Of course not. This is a confidence."

"I'd hate for him to think less of me."

"Aunt Edna, Daddy would never think less of you. You could murder half of Fort Worth and he'd come to your defense. He's just like that."

"I know. That's why I don't want him to think bad of me. Momma never wanted to cause him any trouble and I inherited that from her."

"She gave him the guilt trip of his life," I said.

"Yes, but she didn't mean to. She couldn't help it. I'd suggest we ask him to do something for us and she'd just go frantic and beg me not to bother him, thought he had more important work to do. It was because he was a man. If he was a garbage collector, she'd have thought his work was more important than mine."

"She didn't feel that way about Aunt Margaret?"

"No, she just didn't want her around."

"I can understand that."

"I'm thinking about getting on the phone and telling Margaret that James and I shacked up last night. I'll tell her I didn't turn off the light."

"But you did turn off the light."

"She doesn't have to know that."

"All of these little conspiracies between us," I said. "It's like we trust each other."

"I guess we do," she said. She said this as if surprised, as if she'd found something in her purse she'd put somewhere else.

□ □ □

"Well, I apologize to the United States of America," Aunt Edna said when our passports arrived four days before our scheduled flight. She'd returned from the mailbox for almost two weeks with a look of complete disgust, slandering her government, regretting every dollar of tax she'd ever paid. Now that the passports had arrived almost a week before promised she was at peace with her country once again. We both examined these documents closely, feeling an overwhelming sense of prideful citizenship, and an inherent responsibility to be good representatives of our nation.

Aunt Edna said, "The president trusts us to go abroad."

"They don't just let anybody have these," I told her.

"No?"

"Well, maybe they do. I guess they're willing to let anybody out of the country. They just don't allow criminals and anarchists to come in."

"Anarchists and criminals?"

"You know," I said, "known civil disrupters, drug dealers, murderers, museum slashers."

"But we're not any of those."

"No, we just have to make sure we don't become one of them once we're outside the country."

"It seems very risky, this leaving the country. I don't even like going to Dallas."

"Oh, Aunt Edna, don't worry. Scotland isn't nearly as far from Fort Worth as Dallas is. Dallas is full of city people. When I went off to college I met people from Dallas and every one of them had Caesar salads three times a day: breakfast, lunch, and dinner. They have traffic jams in Dallas, Aunt Edna. They put their city council on the radio and it depresses their entire population. I'm sure Scotland is much more like Fort Worth than Dallas is."

"Well, that makes me feel better," she said.

But she didn't feel better. She was anxious. Twice during the last week before our flight she left the house on errands, making some excuse to go alone. At last I accused her of my suspicions. "You're visiting a tanning salon," I said. She seemed stunned. "You don't have to be embarrassed about it, Aunt Edna. You have much more color than when I arrived a month ago."

"You can tell?" she asked and held her palms to her cheeks.

"They've done a very good job," I said. "It's been very gradual. But I don't think those machines are good for you."

She looked down into her lap. "It's embarrassing to be vain," she said.

"It's your wedding. Don't be ridiculous. My girls lie out for weeks, buy new clothes, and spend a fortune on makeup for a simple date."

"I just feel so pale up against James," she said. "I don't want us to seem so different when we're standing up there."

"Aunt Edna, the beauty of it is that you and James are different."

"But you say that you and Sam are different."

"That's different," I said. "Do you know he's never once been to a museum with me? Whenever there's some exhibition I want to see he'll tell me to go ahead, it would cost too much for him to go along. If I tell him it's free, he'll tell me he wouldn't get anything out of it. When I tell him you can't get anything out of a bucket without putting your hand in, he asks me if I've ever been to one of his car shows."

"Have you?"

"No."

"Then he's got a point."

"Cars aren't art."

"Art can contain cars, Sarah. You shouldn't reduce art to paint and brushes."

"Why do you continue to back him?" I asked.

"Once again, just because I'm against you doesn't mean I'm for him. You keep making that leap by yourself. I'm too tired to argue with you. I need you to come to some of these conclusions on your own."

She left me standing in the living room, my mouth open, my hands clenched, my feet spread far enough apart so my body could accept a bull's charge. Instead, I slowly tilted over and fell into a chair.

□ □ □

Rather than sell to an individual dealer, we took Aunt Edna's silver to a weekly coin auction in Arlington. We carried the shoe boxes of rolled coins into the auctioneer's office, and when we both turned around to go back to the car for more, he said, "There's more?"

I explained, "All the coins were in fourteen one-gallon coffee cans, but when I rolled them up they filled twenty-six shoe boxes."

He called his secretary then, put a brick painted like a dollar bill in front of the door, and we all carried in the boxes.

"I misunderstood," he said.

"I've already made an inventory sheet," I said. "Here's a list of about 200 individual coins, the ones that I feel are worth more than the value of their weight. And here's a list of the rolled coins." Aunt Edna just sat in front of his desk listlessly, so I told him how the silver had been collected. She nodded.

"Do you have some idea of the value you have here?" he asked.

I didn't want to guess for fear of making a fool of myself or getting Aunt Edna's hopes up.

"Well," he said. He left the room for a moment and returned with a bathroom scale. "I have to apologize for the crudeness of this technique. We have a bullion scale but it's for delicate measurements. It only goes up to twenty-four ounces." He placed one of the shoe boxes on the scale. We all bent over to read the meter as if we were determining our own weight. The pointer vibrated to a stop at thirty-two pounds. He went back to his desk and poked at a printing calculator. "Silver is at $6.24 an ounce this morning. That one box represents 512 ounces or $3,194.88. How many of these boxes are silver?"

"All but four of them. Two are full of old pennies and two of old nickels."

He prodded the calculator again. "Then I'd say you have a minimum of $65,000 in simple bullion value. Now, we'll get more than that. The coins usually have some numismatic value. As far as these coins you've separated out, they'll bring whatever they bring. I'll have to grade and mount them separately. But I'll go by your inventory so that we account for everything. Here's a contract stating our responsibilities and our commission. You'll get your check approximately one week after the sale."

He continued to speak while we read the contract, but I think we were both too stunned to hear or read. Aunt Edna held her hand over her chin. It's always hard to appreciate the way small things can accumulate, how minutes become years, and dimes dollars. It all seemed to cave in on Aunt Edna at once, this realization. A tear spread along her eyelid and slipped down her cheek at varying speeds, as her expression changed. I put my hand on her back.

"I just didn't know it would be so much," she said. "It was a few coins a day. Some days there were no coins. I should have sold them earlier, Sarah. Momma could have gotten some good out of them. It was just a hobby for me."

"I'm glad you're pleased," the auctioneer said. "Most people are disappointed. They think their pocket change will change the world. But I have to tell you, Mrs. Hutton: I've never seen this level of dedication, over such a span of years."

"It was just one day at a time for me," Aunt Edna told him.

"One of the dimes is a 1916D," I pointed out.

"The same year my father was born," he said. This wasn't the response I'd anticipated. He looked up at me from the coin. "Oh, it's a good coin. I think we'll do very well with it. I've got several collectors who've been searching for this. People collect coins for all kinds of reasons. For some the design is important, for others it's the date. We have one lady coming in who's trying to get a complete set of U.S. coins for the date that her father was born, and a complete set of German coins for the date her mother was born. You see, her mother was born in Germany. She also buys proof sets for each of her grandchildren's birth years. It's her way to deal with time and money."

I was a little annoyed at this speech that didn't have anything to do with us, but Aunt Edna answered, "The last thing all this money bought was food for children." She didn't elaborate. He nodded at her and smiled.

"I'll tell them that at the auction," he said. "I like that."

This is how she could make you feel: I was interested in the value of a coin and she was thinking about hungry children.

□ □ □

Her anxiety about the trip told in her upset stomach. What began as small soughing burps that she could cover with her fingertips grew to great air-ripping, gravel-throwing, ship-sinking expostulations that carried on for seconds. She'd apologize and smile after each one. Finally we got her some Gas-X and this helped.

"You need to eat more," I told her. "Your bowels are hollow. Diet or no diet, wedding or no wedding."

"It's only a couple of weeks till the wedding," she said. "I'll eat after that."

She'd lost another six pounds over the last ten-day period, while I'd only lost three.

"Well, you're going to have to eat on this trip. We'll do a lot of walking and you'll have to keep your strength up."

"I'll be all right."

It wasn't as if either of us were wasting away. We'd both been big women when we started the diet. We would have had to lose five pounds every ten days for several months before anorexia worries would set in.

With tickets and passports in hand, we were able to make plans for the wedding. Aunt Edna wanted to be married at home, but James wanted Brother Roberts to officiate. We all, Aunt Edna, James, Thelia, Billy, and I, sat on the front porch one evening after dinner, making up an invitation list.

"Why do you want Brother Roberts?" Aunt Edna scoffed.

"He's a good preacher. He believes what he says and he's so old I think he's closer to heaven than most of us."

"He goes on and on and on," Aunt Edna said. "He'll talk his way into the bed between us. If he can get everybody fearful, guilty, and sad he feels like he's done a good day's work. Short and sweet is what I want."

"You could write your own vows and hold him to them," Thelia suggested. She turned to me, "Oh, look at that frown on her face, Sarah. Here's a woman who's gonna get what she wants."

"It might just be gas," I said. "My girls used to frown like that when they had gas."

Thelia and I left Billy and the wedding couple on the porch to their plans. The mosquitoes had come out and I felt I had little more blood to offer. I started the coffeepot, grimaced at a rice cake. Thelia sat at the kitchen table with both of her palms flat on the table.

"Are you going to stay for the wedding, Sarah?" she asked.

"Of course."

"Is your family coming down?"

"I don't know yet."

"There'll just be us on our side. I'm an only child. Billy's an only child. Daddy has a brother but he lives in Louisiana and isn't feeling too good. There'll be a few of Daddy's friends there."

"Well, I don't think we'll overwhelm you, Thelia. I'm sure my parents will come, but I don't know about Aunt Margaret and Uncle Alf. I want my girls to come."

"I could invite Billy's father but I'd have to raise him from the dead."

"I didn't know he'd died. Aunt Edna told me y'all were divorced."

"Oh, he's not dead, but if I ever saw him again he would be. I heard a saying about boats once that applies to marriage real well. They say the happiest day of your life is the day you buy a boat, and the second happiest is the day you sell it. I was really happy the day I got married, and I was almost as happy the day I got divorced. He wasn't a good husband or a good father or even a good employee. He was handsome. I'll give him that, but the only reason he had looks was because they were given to him."

"How long were y'all married?"

"Two years."

"So Billy doesn't know him?"

"He came by once after we got the divorce. Billy was four. He brought the boy a *Star Wars* toy for kids ages nine to twelve. I asked him, 'How long did you think you'd been gone?' He said, 'Not long enough' and we haven't seen him since."

"I sure like your father, Thelia," I told her.

"Everybody loves Daddy. I think part of my problem is I can't find a fella as good as him. What's wrong with your fella?"

"I don't know," I said.

"Has he got a job?"

"Yes."

"Does he ignore your kids?"

"No, not at all."

"I know it's none of my business, but does he hit you?"

"No," I said. "He had another woman for a while."

"I'm sorry. I didn't mean to make you feel bad. Some people like to talk about it. Makes them feel better."

"It makes me sick at my stomach to talk about it."

"Did he go to live with her?"

"No, he's at home with my girls."

"He won't give her up, though?"

"Yes, I mean he says he has."

"Did he apologize?"

"Yes," I said.

"You don't like him anymore?"

"I don't trust him anymore, Thelia."

"I guess it's hard," she said, "trusting somebody for such a long time and then not trusting them. I only trusted my husband for about a month before I switched over to the not trusting. It wasn't a very big ditch to jump."

"It must have hurt all the same."

"Not so much. He didn't cheat on me. He was just worthless. Like a bad check. Somebody gives you a bad check, you get mad about it and then throw it away."

"Is James upset that I'm here?" I asked.

"Not that I know of. He thinks you're helping your aunt."

"Well, now you know. I'm just hiding."

"Everybody needs a place to hide sometime. I'm sort of glad Daddy is moving. Now Billy will have somewhere to go when we fight. He can come over here and sulk for a couple of hours till he's ready to come back home. Are you going to invite your husband to the wedding?"

□   □   □

So I called home that night, a day or so before Aunt Edna and I left for Scotland. Sam answered.

"It's me," I said. He didn't respond, but he didn't hang up either. I could hear his measured breathing. "We're leaving soon," I said. "We'll be there for five days."

"So you're coming back," he said.

"I don't know," I answered.

"I meant from Scotland," he said. I couldn't respond then. "I already know you're thinking about not coming back to me, Sarah. I thought maybe you'd decided to stay in Europe for a while. The girls told me you've started painting and drawing again, and that Edna's getting married. You'll need some place to go, some place to stay."

"How are the girls?"

"They're a little bit pissed, I think. I told them what I did."

"What did they say?"

"Susan said and did the same thing you said and did and Michelle hasn't said anything yet. I think she's stewing on it."

"Michelle's always been better prepared for disaster," I said. "She's wiser."

"I love them both. Both reactions seem to work on me."

"You shouldn't have told them," I said. "You didn't have to tell them for my sake."

"Sarah, they know we haven't spoken in a month. They knew something was wrong. Besides, I told them for my sake, not for yours."

"They haven't spoken to me about it."

"They've known for a week. They probably don't know how to. They want to be reassured and they're afraid you might not be able to do that for them. I'm afraid of that, too."

I didn't answer and the phone line hung limply between the poles from Saint Louis to Fort Worth for minutes. When he spoke again the line snapped taut.

"I don't need an answer, Sarah," he said.

"OK," I whispered.

"What?"

"OK."

○ ○ ○

Aunt Edna had been packed for a week. While I caught up, she spent our last day at home in front of her easel with James at her side. The piece she worked on, and didn't finish till after we returned from Scotland, is perhaps the most colorful of her career. We'd shoved, kicked, and rolled Grandma's overstuffed recliner, unwieldy as a dead moose, out into the backyard. Aunt Edna had then draped an old patchwork quilt over its bulbous proportions. To this day this painting makes me uneasy. The chair seems to suffocate beneath the quilt. It seems there might be a body beneath the covers. The patchwork of color is so random that the idea of a chair, its regularity of form and solid consistency, seems unreasonable, on the verge of collapse.

I asked Aunt Edna that day where the quilt came from and she told me that Grandma had had it for as long as she could remember. All the color you see in the painting is in the quilt. I can't imagine ever using it on an actual bed. It would overwhelm a room. You'd wake up beneath it and think the world had shattered. Draped over Grandma's chair, it seemed to cast it into a storm made up of shards of stained glass, to throw it through a cathedral's window. I didn't feel, like Picasso, that this chair might swallow me, but that it might rent me were I to come too close, that if it were to swallow me it would spit me back out torn and broken, a bright and scattered object. I walk around this painting like a dog, wary of the hand holding out food toward me.

This was the first time that I saw Aunt Edna bring out a second chair to her easel. She sat in this one. She lowered the legs on her easel and sat behind it, peering around the canvas at the quilt-draped recliner as if she were looking under the bed for a rapist. James sat next to her, alternately reading, napping, asking Aunt Edna what she was doing.

She'd answer, "Putting in some red," or, "Working in a green."

I heard him ask once, "What's blue?"

Aunt Edna's brush caught on a piece of sky as if it were barbed wire. She turned to him. "How am I going to explain 'blue' to you?"

"By explaining what it is to you."

"But it's not a texture or a smell or anything you can relate to."

"Textures and smells and sounds all make me feel some way. How does seeing blue make you feel? I can understand how you feel."

I'd been out in the backyard taking clothes off the line. I sat on the concrete porch with a blue laundry basket on my lap.

"Well," Aunt Edna began, "blue makes me feel cold sometimes and warm other times. When it's next to yellow I'm happy. I've always wished my eyes were blue but they're not."

"Why do you wish that?"

"Because the sky is blue and on clear days your eyes would reflect that light and be even bluer, more intense. I'd be more like the sky, more like light. Blue makes me feel included."

"That's good," James said. His face tilted up, seemed to ascend in a slow spiral, as if a gown were being lowered over his head and shoulders. "Maybe when you come back from Scotland we can talk about red."

She said, "But maybe it will be green first. I am anticipating green."

"I will anxiously await green," James said. "I feel there must be a great many secrets in green."

His face seemed to be caught on rising air and then it fell again like something the wind wished to coddle. Aunt Edna turned back to her work, applied her next brush stroke hesitantly, then brought the brush, thick with color, back to her face and peered into the pigment as if it had just alighted there. For a moment I thought she might put it in her mouth.

Landscape □□□

GRANDMA AND GRANDPA were in the overhead storage, and in our laps lay Grandma's big book. I gave Aunt Edna the window seat. We'd landed in London on an overcast day and were now on the short jump to Edinburgh. We'd flown all night from DFW and to my surprise Aunt Edna slept soundly for almost six hours, while I mentally counted the bones in my own back over and over. In an airplane seat my vertebrae seem to grow more numerous (like Ingres's *Grande Odalisque*) as well as larger, the way a handful of marbles seems to when you put them in your mouth. While most of our fellow passengers from Fort Worth to London were Americans on vacation, the shuttle flight to Edinburgh was full of British business-men in black suits. It was early in the morning, but they seemed an unusually dour lot, sitting quietly or reading the *Financial Times*. Aunt Edna and I felt we'd been given a solemn escort to our funeral, that as soon as we'd come across the border a troop of honorary mourners had joined our column.

We'd come across the big water on American Airlines, but the shuttle was a British Airways flight. Our sugar was delivered in indi-vidually wrapped cubes. The stewardess had an accent. When I was asked if I'd like a pastry I stared at the woman for a full ten seconds before I decided that 'yes' would be an acceptable response; even if I didn't understand the question I should take a few chances. I should answer yes to every question I received while in Scotland and see what came of it. Aunt Edna asked me, "What did she say?" and before I could answer I had no idea, I was handed a pastry with a dollop of something yellow in its center, a tiny bread palette of sunshine.

I looked at Aunt Edna. "I'm not on a diet this week," I said. When Aunt Edna was asked the question she shook her head and did not receive the pastry, which is how we found out we'd been asked if we wanted a pastry. Before we came to understand English as it was spo-ken here, we took advantage of our numbers, enlightened by this first happy trial, and always answered once in the affirmative and once in the negative. In this way we were usually able to decipher our interrogator. I would answer, "Yes," and Aunt Edna would respond, "Well, no." If Aunt Edna didn't get cream in her coffee occasionally, she also didn't have to have her shrimp cocktail coated with mayonnaise.

We descended into Scotland from above, with an aerial photograph of Edinburgh in our laps, but it didn't look the same. It had changed from a city of water and light to one that looked like fog. The first thing we saw of Scotland was the concrete porch, the airport runway from a height of about twenty feet. Aunt Edna and I wanted to clap for our pilot's heroism and skill but our solemn escort, whose demeanor was one of uncompromising pity, gathered their dark raincoats and gray umbrellas and led us to the burial ground in a procession silent and well-ordered, our first queue. A tall man helped Grandpa and Grandma down from the overhead, each in their own handled Dillard's shopping bag. I'd never contacted Scottish authorities about bringing ashes into their country, for fear there'd be red tape of some sort. The boxes had passed through the scanners at DFW without any problems. I'd been afraid that ashes might look like plastic explosives to an X-ray machine, or that they might hold some memory of bone and the attendant would recognize something from his previous line of work in a hospital lab.

Ours seemed to be the only luggage on the çarousel. As soon as they'd seen us safely into the country, our lugubrious pallbearers had disappeared. I had a single suitcase on wheels, while Aunt Edna carried an old vinyl American Tourister that had belonged to Grandpa, and an artist's backpack that not only held her paints and brushes but also a collapsible easel and folding chair. Along with the pair of Dillard's bags and our jackets we had quite a load. We walked into Scotland as if we'd stepped aboard a sailboat for the first time, wary of each step and under the firm impression we could fall off. I noticed the tile on the floor, the shoes of other women, the unusual wrappers of candy bars, advertisements whose graphics seemed somehow off. We'd pick up a rental car here in two days, but for now we only needed a taxi to take us to our hotel in Edinburgh, and a way to pay.

I stopped in the middle of a concourse and Aunt Edna bumped

into me. I turned to her and grinned. "Here we are," I said. "You see, they're all speaking English."

"You're not supposed to stop and gawk," Aunt Edna said. "The pickpockets will know we're tourists."

"Aunt Edna, they're going to have to undress us to our underwear to pick our pockets." We were both carrying our traveler's checks in money belts beneath our blouses.

"They can do it," she said. "You'd be surprised at what people can do."

We worked our way to a bureau de change, and while Aunt Edna provided screen cover with both of the Dillard's bags I exchanged a hundred dollars. I knew the rate would be exorbitant at the airport but I didn't know how much the taxi into Edinburgh would cost. The British coins were lumpy and muted in my hands after I'd dealt with so much worn American silver.

Outside, the fog had risen somewhat. There was a bit of grass in a median beyond the taxi stand, and Aunt Edna considered it attentively for a few moments, as if it might possibly do for her parents' final resting place. Throughout our first day in Scotland she looked for a place to deposit the ashes the way a dog frantically searches for a place to go when it gets off an airplane; almost anywhere will do, a rug, a mat, even on the run.

We were both very happy to hand over everything but Grandma and Grandpa to the taxi driver. Aunt Edna winced every time she picked up her heavy bag. If airports are the same the world over, are one nation scattered, it really only took us thirty seconds to reach another country by taxi. We were already on the far side of the road. Our driver, despite the fog, blitzed through a pair of roundabouts, totally disorienting me, so that direction seemed to have no meaning. I looked at my watch and thought it should be going the other way round, too.

"Green, green," Aunt Edna said and pointed to the roadside. "If it's this green in the fog . . ."

I didn't care about the grass. I tried to focus on the rules of the road, how to make my way back to this spot on the planet by paths diabolically circuitous, mind-bendingly mirror-imaged. I decided James was right: only superstition could make sense of it. I watched the driver's hands on the wheel (which was on the wrong side of the car—I knew I'd be driving on the left, but didn't realize I'd be sitting on the right), noted the placement of turn signals and lights. I'd studied a guide to road signs, but here they seemed much more remote, the colors less stark, and there seemed to be more direction printed on the road surface itself than I'd been led to believe.

"You'll quickly get the way of it," our driver reassured me. "Everyone lets you know when you misstep. Just be mindful of the pedestrians. They all have minds of their own. It's the tourists you have to watch. And don't be afraid to use the blaster. That's what it's there for."

"The blaster?" Weapons?

He beeped the horn.

We rushed through city streets, slithered between buses.

"It doesn't look the same as in the book," Aunt Edna whispered.

"We're way down in the picture," I said. "We're looking at these buildings from below rather than above."

"I don't think Momma would have liked this. There's fumes and noise. There's people."

"Things look different from above and below."

The streets were busy with people, cars, dogs, and all the rules that separated them. The fog made everything wet. Even the trash in the gutters was gauzy and seemed to follow rules, staying to the gutters. I pointed out the tiny brilliant gardens in front of homes, a pastry shop, a McDonald's, the ubiquitous stone. Aunt Edna held Grandma tightly in her lap.

"No wonder the British love watercolor," she said. "Their subject and medium are one in the same. Everything's wet. That stone building looks like it's about to puddle."

"It's been there for ages," I told her, "always on the verge of puddling."

Just as things were about to get really interesting, as we were arriving in the heart of the city, our driver turned off to the left and took us through a warren, then a grid, of back streets till we arrived at a block of stone houses, one of which was our inn, Dukes of Windsor Street, just below Calton Hill: "Just a short walk to all the main sights of the old and new towns." I'd booked two nights. There was an unprepossessing brass plaque beside the glass door.

"Look, the sidewalk is made of stone slabs," Aunt Edna said. "This whole city is made of rock. We can't spread Momma and Daddy on rock."

"We know there's gardens, Aunt Edna. You can see them in the photos. There's big gardens."

We stepped into a small foyer with a grand spiral staircase. There were brochures on a small table, next to an unusual telephone with a slot for coins. Soon a door at the back of the hall opened and our hostess welcomed us. She led us up two flights of the steep staircase, asking when we'd like breakfast.

"Oh, whenever it's convenient for you," Aunt Edna said, huffing.

"No, you're on holiday. It's to be at your convenience," she answered.

"How about eight?" I asked.

"Eight it is. Brilliant. We serve a continental breakfast: cereal, juice, and croissant. Would you prefer coffee or tea?"

"Yes," I said.

"No," Aunt Edna said.

"Here's your key to the room and another for the main entrance. You'll find it locked after 10:00 P.M." She swung open the thickly painted door to our room; twin beds, a blond wardrobe in one corner, a chair in the other. "Your bath is en suite as you requested. Are you familiar with Her Majesty's plumbing?" We both must have looked as if she'd asked us to slap her on the bottom. "Well," she said, "before you step into the shower, pull this chain. That will turn on the hot water. Then once you're in the shower, press this button on the box only once, and turn the dial to the temperature you prefer. Where are you from?"

"Fort Worth, Texas," I answered.

"I dare say then that you'll find the toilet works in much the same manner as yours at home."

We nodded. It looked familiar. She motioned us out of the cramped quarters of the bathroom. We came to a small queue between the two beds. Here she opened the curtain to our lone window. The yard and garden beneath us was almost as narrow as our room. We looked out on several gardens in fact, bordered by high stone walls. Each garden had a small shed and a dog. We could see through the windows of other houses, whole banks of windows in banks of houses under one slate roof. Once our hostess was away we brought in our luggage. There was no room to pass each other. The wardrobe seemed to hover over us like a great tree, and the chair was of the sprawling type. Aunt Edna immediately fell in love with it.

"It's our first Scottish chair," she said. "I'm going to capture it." Even before unpacking, she took out a pad and began to sketch. It was hard for her to get enough distance in the little room, but she managed by perching on the bedside table in the far corner, drawing the chair from above. I washed my face, changed clothes, peed, and she was still drawing, having moved from sitting on the nightstand to standing on it, scotching herself in the corner so she wouldn't fall as she scribbled furiously.

"Aunt Edna," I ventured, "we'll have this room for two days. This isn't your last chance to draw the chair. Let's go out."

"Maybe when we come back we can push that bed over next to this one so I can get a better view of the chair." She climbed down. "Shouldn't we take Momma and Daddy with us?"

"Why don't we just look around today? If we had them with us we'd feel pressured. If we find a good place we can go back. I want to see the castle and I'm hungry."

"Well, I have to get ready. I can't just go out like this."

I sat on the end of the bed and waited. I wasn't used to waiting for my traveling companion. Sam was the one who sat on the bed waiting for me. It seemed she took an inordinate amount of time in the bathroom. I heard half a dozen bottles opening and closing. The toilet flushed twice. The sink ran continually. This foreign city was all before me and minutes seemed to fall off the opportunity of exploring it like tiny silverlings plunging over a waterfall. Edinburgh had been there for thousands of years yet I was on the verge of missing it while Aunt Edna brushed her teeth. I was looking down at my hands when they were suddenly brought into relief by light.

"Aunt Edna," I yelled, "the sun's coming out. The whole world is changing."

"Almost done," she hollered back. "I can't get that Conté crayon from underneath my nails."

At last we hit the pavement. It was good to get the kinks out of my back. I felt as good as I had in years, physically. I'd lost sixteen pounds over the last month and felt up to the walking since I'd taken up the habit of roaming through Aunt Edna's neighborhood. My legs felt strong, my body light.

The sun and a fresh breeze from the west were beating away the fog and low clouds. My jacket seemed just right in the morning air.

We were overwhelmed by the abundance of stone; pavement, sidewalk, curb, cornice, lintel, roof. What wasn't of stone was cast in iron: mailboxes, benches, lampposts. It seemed a very solid, heavy city that no mere raindrop would ever dislodge. We had a small map, but the lady at our inn said to just keep climbing and we'd find our way to the castle. I showed the map to Aunt Edna, pointed out all the green areas. Above us on Calton Hill were towers and domes. Down Leith Walk were shops and eventually the ocean. We successfully completed our first street crossing, stepping out onto the pavement as if it were mined, as if we might be struck from below or above rather than from the left or right. Every corner we turned offered some massive architectural edifice. Whether it was bank, hotel, or post office, every building was imposing, strikingly overscale, a true monument. Government buildings were usually classically stark, hotels embellished with Victorian frill. Only the shop fronts were modern, sheets of glass held in place by stainless-steel framing. Beyond the Royal British Hotel we got our first clear sweeping view of the Royal Mile and Edinburgh Castle. It was as if all the clothes were suddenly blown from our bodies. We stood still in the middle of the sidewalk, looking up at tier upon tier of stacked stone, crenellated towers, marching chimney pots, a city clinging to and climbing rock toward a castle. It seemed the architectural encrustation on the back of a long sleeping dragon. This view gave every mannequin in the shop windows of Princes Street erect nipples. Edna was aghast. "They'd never allow those nipples in Dillard's," she said. The remains of fog groped along the castle walls. Crowds of commuters and shoppers coursed around us. The photos we'd seen hadn't prepared us. We finally began to stumble along, our eyes up, our feet tripping over cigarette butts and spent gum. I came to a complete lack of understanding of a species that could simultaneously build such a city and then spit gum on it. We walked past Waverly Station and the Scott Monument and turned up The Mound. Both the Royal

Scottish Academy and the National Gallery were to our left; to our right, sweeping away beneath the castle walls, were the Princes Street Gardens.

"Oh, Momma was right," Aunt Edna said.

We leaned against a stone wall and looked down into the vast lawns and the pockets of flowers. Scattered trees vibrated in the breeze.

"It's beautiful," I said. "We didn't have to look very far."

"Let's go back for the ashes now, Sarah."

"Aunt Edna, there's a medieval castle above us. There's two huge museums right here. And my stomach is empty."

"All right, all right, but we're not here to just sightsee. We have a job to do."

"That's not what James told me," I said. "He told me you think Grandma wanted to be scattered in Scotland because she thought you wanted to come here."

"It's possible," she said. "We may be on a fool's errand. But I can't take that chance. And even if that's the case, that she did this for my sake, I couldn't turn her down. It was the only thing she could give me. She thought I was poor. So this trip is either a duty or a gift and I'll accept it on either count."

"Why didn't you just ask her, Aunt Edna?"

"It didn't occur to me till after she was gone, and even if it had, I don't think I would have said anything. It wouldn't have been very humble to ask her if her last thoughts were of me. And if I was wrong it would have made her feel bad, that she was thinking of herself and not me."

"We're here," I said. "We've already found a beautiful spot. Maybe there's another. I think we should get the feel of the place before we leave her ashes here. That museum may be full of ugly paintings. That castle may have been the home of tyrants. We need to find out. There was something back there on Princes Street called a Boots and they had snacks."

"I want a peppermint," Aunt Edna said. "I've got heartburn and I think a peppermint would soothe it. Do you think there are any paintings of chairs in these museums?"

"You see, we need to know these things."

Off my diet, I bought a Milky Way bar and a Pepsi. Aunt Edna found a bag of peppermints. I wasn't ten feet from the store when I discovered there was a 3 Musketeers inside my Milky Way wrapper. What an odd mistake, I thought. I didn't even know both candy bars were made by the same company. I don't care for 3 Musketeers bars. I went back into the pharmacy, or chemist's, and too embarrassed to return the first item I bought in Scotland, I simply bought a second Milky Way bar. It, too, had a 3 Musketeers inside. The whole batch must have been miswrapped. I now had two opened candy bars I didn't want. I took them back to the clerk.

"Look," I said, "there's a 3 Musketeers in this Milky Way wrapper and I really wanted a Milky Way."

She was young. Very short black hair. Skin as smooth and white as a lightbulb. She looked into the end of the candy bar I'd bitten into. "I'm sorry," she said.

That's right, I thought.

"But," she continued, "that's what a Milky Way bar looks like."

"But there's no caramel in it," I asserted.

"There never has been."

"Yes, there has. It's my favorite candy bar. I've been eating them since long before you were born." All of this subterfuge, I thought, simply to save the price of a candy bar. I'd be damned if we'd leave my grandparents' ashes here. I'd heard of Scottish tightness but this was too much. A young man stepped behind the counter with the clerk. He had on a dark blue vest.

"Is there a problem?"

"My Milky Way has a 3 Musketeers inside of it. I wanted a Milky Way."

"Are you from America?" he asked.

"What has that got to do with it?"

"Many American candies are packaged under different labels than they are here. You understand, we call a French fry a chip, you call a crisp a potato chip. Yes, I believe what you want is a Mars bar."

I followed him back to the candy rack. He tore open the wrapper, broke the bar in half, and held it up for my inspection.

"That's it!" I whooped. "I'm so sorry. I didn't know."

"It's my pleasure," he answered.

"What do you call 'arsenic' here?" I asked.

"Arsenic," he said, his brow curdling.

"That's a relief," I said. "I'd hate to order a cup of coffee and poison myself."

I'd left Aunt Edna on the sidewalk outside. "What took so long?" she asked.

"Things aren't what they seem," I told her.

"They never are," she mumbled around a peppermint and we set off.

At Edinburgh Castle we peered over another stone wall to a lower terrace, an area of manicured grass containing the tiny headstones of castle pets. Some graves were over a century old. It was unsettling to be looking at battlements and weapons and regiments and then to be confronted with the immaculate grass over the beloved body of a dog. Later again, in Greyfriars Kirkyard, we saw another pet's grave, Greyfriars Bobby, a Skye terrier who stayed by his master's grave for fourteen years after his master died. There were no flowers on his master's grave, nor on David Hume's, the famous Scottish philosopher, but Greyfriars Bobby's stone was mounded over with fresh and withering cut flowers. Loyalty itself is remembered far longer than the idea of loyalty. These little graves, in and of themselves, were enough to win Aunt Edna and me over to the Scottish people.

With little time to sketch, Aunt Edna took photographs of chairs whenever she came across them: in cafes, castles, antique shops. These chairs were often under people, and she had no qualms about asking clerks and docents to get up and give their chairs better light. These people in turn seemed to pay closer attention to the form and construction of the chair they'd always taken for granted. Almost all were obliging and afterwards wouldn't immediately sit again, as if their new regard for chairs made them more circumspect, less able to simply collapse. At Holyrood Palace a tour guide cautioned Aunt Edna about photography inside the Queen's home, but when he found out she was an amateur artist, he said he shared her "affliction," looked over his shoulder left and right comically and said, "Right on, squeeze one off quick, dearie."

We found another green area next to the palace, a ruined cathedral. Its roof, the vault of the blue sky, allowed green grass to squirt around the edges of tombs set into the floor. But as the property was owned by the Queen herself, rather than a municipal or state government, we thought it bad manners to spread human remains on her lawn without her permission.

It was a full day, from the castle to Greyfriars and then down the Royal Mile to Holyrood. We'd stepped from one stone to another across Edinburgh, as if crossing a creek. Among the Scottish accents were many American voices, and we wondered if everyone from back home had come to dispose of their parents' and grandparents' remains that summer, wondered if the natural erosion of Scotland's soil wasn't being replenished by all the seed she'd sown in other lands, even if that seed were only pictures in a book, or the misapprehension of desire, or the fallibility of love. By the end of the day Aunt Edna and I both found ourselves at home in this city. The people seemed so concerned about preserving their past that we wanted to become a part of it. We were bringing our people back to a place they'd never been before. It seemed odd to appropriate Scotland as a homeplace simply because we desired a memory as solid as stone. We were beginning to feel that if we left Grandma and Grandpa here, they'd be well cared for. And that when we returned we'd have a real claim to this place, that desire for a home was birthright enough, and loyalty proof of citizenship.

By the time we made our way through the palace grounds Aunt Edna was thoroughly pooped. We took our place on a stone bench with a view of Holyrood Park. Beyond the trailing edge of the Salisbury Crags, across a bog and mounting meadows, rose Arthur's Seat, a rocky promontory.

"We could take the ashes up there," I told Aunt Edna. "Then they'd have a view of Edinburgh from above. I'll bet you can see all the way to the ocean from up there."

There were tiny flecks of color descending the slopes, people whose homeward trek was all downhill.

"I haven't got the strength to get up there," Aunt Edna said. "I've never been this tired in my life."

"Why don't we take a taxi back to the hotel? We'll rest a bit and then find a nice pub for dinner."

"I'm sorry, I'd like to walk but I'm just give out. Before we go I want you to use my camera and take a picture of me on this bench. I've never seen a chair made out of rock."

"I imagine the first chair was a rock," I said as I snapped the shutter.

"That, or another human," she answered. "I feel like somebody's sitting on me right now."

"Here, give me your bag and jacket and lean on my free arm and we'll stagger off together."

"It won't look good," she giggled, "us walking into the pub in this condition."

"Do you think there'll be men at the pub?" I asked.

"If there's not we'll go to another."

"Aunt Edna," I hushed, "you're a promised woman."

"I am, but I never said what condition I'd arrive in. But I'm mostly interested for you."

"I didn't come to Scotland to find a man." I hailed a taxi whipping up Horse Wynd.

As Aunt Edna crawled into the backseat, she said, quite audibly, "You could get a gigolo." The driver glanced up into his rearview mirror.

"Windsor Street," I said, "Dukes of Windsor Street Hotel. It's on the other side of Calton Hill." I shut the door.

"I know the street. It's very respectable, I'm afraid. I could take you down to Leith now, and there . . ."

"Dukes of Windsor Street," I repeated.

"Very good."

I glared at Aunt Edna. She shrugged and looked out the window. Still, I could see the corner of her mouth rise and the full reflection of her smile in the door glass, a smile she gave herself but which she aimed at the city of Edinburgh rushing by. She seemed older in the reflection, the black windows and soot-darkened stone of Calton Road passing behind her eyes.

I dropped Aunt Edna and our bags off at our room and then struck out again. I wanted to climb Calton Hill. It was just a short march across London Road, through the Royal Terrace Gardens, and then up into the grass. I had to pause a couple of times before reaching the monuments, waiting for my wind to catch up to my feet. I stopped at the National Monument, or Scotland's Disgrace, the half-completed replica of the Parthenon, intended to memorialize the dead of the

Napoleonic Wars if subscriptions hadn't fallen short. It's probably much more famous in its incomplete state than it ever would have been as a full copy of a Greek temple. To the southwest was Nelson's Monument, a stone telescope turned on end as if to peer deeply into the heart of the planet, to all things dark and tomblike, magnifying the unknowable. Below the City Observatory is a monument to the dead philosopher Dugald Stewart and across Regent Road another to Robert Burns. They've all been given a view of Scotland from above. From Calton Hill I could see all the way out to the Firth of Forth, a broad sheen of bay, and all around me lay the city, beguiled by the approach of evening. The skyline was pierced by many church spires and clock towers and weather vanes and lightning rods. Edinburgh seemed like a dangerous place to fall on. The morning fog returned disguised as evening fog, and as I stood there lights began to flood the castle from below, to highlight the city's churches, so that Edinburgh and God might not be lost in the dark. So many people had come and gone here. Aunt Edna and I were the very latest. There were so many remembered that I realized there must be a reciprocally large number of forgotten. Some people work their entire lives in hopes they'll be remembered in rock. I want to say that Aunt Edna, however famous she is now or will become, wasn't one of these.

□ □ □

We had our dinner on Rose Street. We followed a man in a tweed cap, who smoked a heavenly mix of cherry tobacco in a pipe, into a pub whose sidewalk chalkboard announced, "You'll not be finding haggis here!" A hostess in a short black skirt and net stockings told us there was a table coming available if we wouldn't mind waiting at the bar. The bar was immediately before us, crowded with old men. Before we took two steps forward, two stools were vacated as if we'd reserved them. Their former occupants stood up, beer in hand, and continued to talk to the other men around them. It was so nonchalant, so effortless, this action, that Aunt Edna and I both paused for a moment, looked at each other to remind ourselves we were two fat girls, before taking our proffered seats. I ordered a half-pint of Guinness. Aunt Edna ordered a Scotch.

"What whisky would you prefer?" the bartender asked her.

"This is my first Scotch," she answered. "I want a good one."

"I'll get you a Macallan." He returned a moment later with Aunt Edna's dram. "Now, try that."

"What a pretty color it has," she said and laid the rim of the glass to her lower lip, let the whisky slide to her open mouth slowly, the same way you pull on a ribbon that will unfurl a bow.

"It's the peat that makes the color," the barman told her once she nodded her approval. "Or the sheep urine in the peat."

"What a dumbass you are, Michael," said one of the men who'd stood up for us. "It's the barley."

"It's the casks they store it in," said another man sitting next to Aunt Edna.

"The color of Scotch is a direct gift of God to the Scottish people," the other standing man said. "Nothing else can explain it."

They were all smoking and I was about to choke to death.

"Bourbon has a fine color," Aunt Edna said.

I noticed it hadn't taken her long to shake off her nap.

"Bourbon?" the man next to Aunt Edna scoffed. "You cannot even get drunk on that color of whiskey. It's little more than beer. What did he give you, dear, our stupid friend, Michael?"

"A Macallan."

"A fine choice. But have you had a Laphroaig or a Bruichladdich?". She shook her head. "I've just had this one."

"You mean to say this is your first Scotch ever?"

She nodded. "It's very good."

"Michael." He slapped the bar. Michael approached. "I want a ring of six glasses placed before us, just tasters, mind, a different Scotch in each. I don't want to know what they are. This young woman and I will try to discern the difference. We are going to hold a little class here, the most important learning opportunity of her life."

"Oh no," Aunt Edna said.

"It's all right. It'll go on my tab. What part of America are you running away from?"

"Texas," she answered.

The hostess put her hand on my shoulder. "Your table is ready, dear."

"Oh, don't leave now," the man pleaded with Aunt Edna. "You'll not go back to Texas with this much ignorance of whisky. We need you to start converting the other heathens in Texas, the Bourbon drinking, never to be inebriated."

"You go ahead, Sarah," Aunt Edna told me. "I'll be along in a bit."

"Do you want me to order anything for you?"

"No, I'm not hungry. You go ahead. I'll be right along."

I was shown to a table that was about fourteen inches in diameter. If I leaned over it and put my cheek on its oak surface I could see Aunt Edna's back in the next room. The man had his hand on the back of her stool. I went through my Guinness and had three leaves of iceberg lettuce and a little hard tomato that squirted unpierced from beneath my fork. This, along with two slices of cucumber, went under the alias of a salad. I had another half-pint. I had an order of fish and chips. Still Aunt Edna did not come. Once I heard her laugh above the laughs of a dozen laughing men. Then I had something called Sticky Toffee Pudding, which made me not only forgive the salad and the oily fish but Aunt Edna and the woman Sam puddled in. I ordered a second piece. The waitress smiled and suggested I have a dram of Scotch with it, as one flavor enhanced the other. I'd already had one orgasm so I ordered the Scotch so I might have a double. The pudding was something like a thick ginger cake with warm butter and brown sugar poured over, and then the whole sublime creation was drowned in cream. I took a bite of pudding, sipped the single-malt Scotch, took a bite of pudding. I didn't care where Aunt Edna was, nor did I care where my husband, daughters, or even my money was. I would eat Sticky Toffee Pudding in this pub, in this chair, every day for the rest of my life. Let my husband have all the women he wanted. Let my daughters choose the wrong majors and men. I no longer cared if I could draw, but let me drool.

As I scooped up the last bit of cream from the bottom of the bowl, Aunt Edna sat down at my little happy round world of a table.

"He's asked me to go off with him," she said.

"What?"

"What would you think of me if I went off with him?"

"Aunt Edna, your face is flushed."

"I know it is. I mean, I can feel it. But I don't think it's only the Scotch. I think it's the man paying attention to me."

"You don't even know him."

"It doesn't matter."

"But what about James?"

"I love him more than I love me. But there's this other here now who can see me and James will never know. I'm alive tonight, and who knows, tomorrow I could be dead."

"It won't be worth it in a week, Aunt Edna."

"What if I said I can't help myself? What if I did it? Could you still love me?"

"Of course. Don't be ridiculous."

"Would you leave me here alone in Scotland?"

"Of course not."

"He didn't ask me to go with him. He was a nice man."

"What?"

"I just told you he did to see what you'd say."

"Why? Are you drunk?"

"I'm just wondering why you can forgive me for cheating on the sweetest man in the world and you can't forgive Sam for cheating on you."

"You are drunk."

"I am not."

"You need some food. I'm going to order you a Sticky Toffee Pudding."

"A what?"

"A Sticky Toffee Pudding. You're supposed to eat it with a dram of Scotch but you've already had the Scotch so it will have to mix below."

My stomach full of pudding and Scotch, I told her, "It's not the same. You didn't cheat on me. You cheated on James. Sam cheated on me. For it to be the same you'd have to ask James if he could forgive you."

"Has Sam asked you to forgive him?"

"Not in so many words."

"He should ask you in so many words."

"I don't want him to do that. I don't want to humiliate him anymore."

"Look, we're both away from all that and we're having a really good time, right?"

"Right."

"When the pudding comes we'll clink bowls to toast Grandma and Grandpa and their new home."

"I don't feel very good," Aunt Edna said.

□ □ □

At eight the next morning Aunt Edna, while still abed, said, "I can't remember any of the chairs in that pub. I know there were chairs. I sat in one, didn't I?"

"I'm exhausted. I was so tired when we got home last night and then I laid awake for hours."

"It's the lagging jet. It's three o'clock in the morning back in Fort Worth."

"Let's sleep some more."

"Today's the day we spread some of the ashes, Sarah. Get up. If I can do it, you can. I need you to help me figure out that box on the wall of the shower."

When she swung out of bed and stood up, she immediately fell back down, her body collapsing like the bellows of an accordion. The sound she made, too, was a musical note interrupted and then simply air expelled through open valves. I don't remember my own actions, but I was suddenly on the floor at her side, one hand on her back, the other cupping her forehead. She breathed heavily for a few moments and then said, "I'm OK now."

"What was that?" I whispered.

"The first sign of old age, I guess," she said hoarsely. She pushed up off her knees and sat on the bed. "It must have been the Scotch. I haven't felt that way in a long time, like somebody punched me in the stomach."

"Do you want a glass of water? What should I do?"

"Didn't Sam ever come home drunk?"

"No, not really."

"Well, I have. I'll be all right. I have something in my purse for this. I'll be better after a shower."

"Maybe you should leave the door open a bit. I promise not to look unless I hear a big crash."

"Bosh. Don't worry." She paused, her hands on her knees. "Sarah, what are you going to do after my wedding? I mean, where will you go?"

"I don't know," I said.

"Why don't you stay with us? Stay with James and me."

"Oh, Aunt Edna, I appreciate it, but James will want you all for his own and he deserves that. I'll find some place. I have to come to a decision sometime, don't I?"

"Well, you'd be welcome is all. You're right to take your time with your decision. There are so many things to consider when you're thinking about losing someone you've been with for most of your life. I just wish you could forgive poor Sam. It would make me feel better about my life."

"Why is that, Aunt Edna?"

"By the time you get to be sixty-two there'll be plenty of things you can look back on and hope you were forgiven for, that's all. Judith McElvay, my head hurts."

"Who's Judith McElvay?"

"She was my supervisor at school when I first started at the cafeteria."

"Forty years ago?"

"Yes. She made me clean out all the grease traps my first week. I threw up three times in two days. Then come to find out there was a service that came every Friday with a big vacuum truck to do what I'd been doing with a cup tied to a stick. She never did explain why she did that to me. It's all right. I had her job in five years."

"Did you ever forgive her?"

"I'm still working on it. I can still smell that grease in my nose."

"You know, Aunt Edna, you don't smell like a gallon of green beans anymore."

"I don't?"

"No, you smell like a smoky lady who needs a shower. Each whorl of your hairdo has caught up a puff of cigarette smoke."

I steadied her walk to the bathroom and stood there while she shut and locked the door. Again there was a great deal of bottle opening and vial snapping. I knew my own father often chewed a Vitamin C tablet but Aunt Edna seemed to have taken JoAnn's remedies too far. Perhaps it took a great many herbs in pill form to combat a hangover.

When Aunt Edna finished her shower she seemed much rejuvenated, though she still looked like hell. Our breakfast came while I showered, and after eating we were off with Grandma and Grandpa under our arms.

By the time we reached the Princes Street Gardens a light mist was falling. The castle above us was decapitated by fog. Dark stone walls climbed into thin gray water. The gardens themselves seemed muted, less green. Every flower cupped a tiny pool of gathered mist, or held jeweled droplets at the tip of each stamen. I was somewhat depressed by the heaviness of the sky, the dampness of the earth, until Aunt Edna turned to me with a smile I can only describe as one of gracious acceptance.

"The world is feeding," she whispered. She said this as if we were the first people ever to see some rare butterfly mating. She said this as if we'd come to these gardens through great trials, that we'd parted thick fronds of jungle growth to find the ancient elephant dying grounds, a horde of priceless ivory ours for the taking. She took Grandma's painted box from a plastic bag and then smoothed the bag on the short grass next to a bed of pale blue delphiniums. She knelt on this bag. I did the same with Grandpa's box and sack. I'd wondered about the mechanics of this operation, how we'd deposit the ashes. We couldn't just dump them out in a single pile. It would look like a fire-ant mound. And how were we going to mix Grandma and Grandpa's ashes? By hand? Aunt Edna opened Grandma's box and removed the plastic container. The lid of this tub was sealed with tape. She carefully removed the tape, folding its sticky side back in upon itself and placing it in her purse. I did the same.

"What now?" I asked.

"I've brought this little spoon," Aunt Edna said, taking a small silver spoon from her pocket. "It was Momma's baby spoon. It was the only one I could feed her with toward the last, all she could take of medicine or food at one time."

Across the handle of the spoon, in a heavily worn script, was the word "Lizzy." Aunt Edna popped open the tub and dipped the little bowl of the spoon into Grandma's ashes. The ashes were powdery gray, almost as fine as talcum. Then she sprinkled them lightly over the bare soil between the flowers. The ashes immediately darkened and seemed drawn into the earth. She dipped once and twice, then motioned for me to open Grandpa's tub. She dipped there once and twice, spreading his ashes over Grandma's. She moved from tub to tub, placing spoonfuls of ashes at the bases of individual flowers, as if she were tossing bread to a group of ducks in a pond, making sure every duck got something.

"Grandma and Grandpa are finally together again," I said.

"They're more together now than they ever were," Aunt Edna said. Then she said, "She was the love of my life. I miss Daddy but she was the love of my life." I rubbed her back. She continued to spoon out the ashes until about two-thirds remained. "That ought to do it for here."

"It's so nice to think of them together in this beautiful place," I said. We closed the tubs and put them back in their little painted caskets, pushed our own bodies up from a knee-indented planet, the remains of prayer.

"If Momma's in heaven," Aunt Edna said, "she's looking down on us just as if we were in *Scotland from Above*." She looked up and scanned the embroiled currents of mist and fog. She looked back at me and shrugged.

"We're in between," I said.

"I'm glad you're here, Sarah. It's good that we both know where they are. I'd hate to pass on and think no one but me knew exactly where they were."

"I'll write it down in my journal," I said. "And someday I'll bring my girls back here and show them the spot so they'll know, too." I said this to make her feel better but the saying of it made me feel lost, made me feel powerless in the face of time and distance, as short-lived as a transplanted flower in a public garden.

We took a taxi back to our room and had the driver wait while we stowed Grandma and Grandpa away again. Then the day was ours. We began at the Scottish National Portrait Gallery, which is overrun with portraits, in the same way that Aunt Edna's house was overrun with chairs. My favorite was painted on a corrugated panel so that perspective worked a diabolical misdirection; from one angle the portrait of a placid lady, from another her earthly end: a hollow gray skull. In the gift shop I found a mouse pad imprinted with a photo of the butt of one of Canova's marble Graces. I thought this rather ingenious and for a moment actually considered it as a gift for Sam. I wouldn't be bothered if he ran his hand over this other woman's ass.

Later in the day, at the National Gallery of Scotland, I stood for minutes transfixed by Sir Henry Raeburn's *The Reverend Robert Walker Skating on Duddingston Loch,* painted in 1784. The minister, in black pulpit attire, including stockings, peaked hat, and long coat, is striding across the surface of the frozen lake, arms crossed over his chest, one leg extended, and completing a lovely crescent of human movement through a Turneresque background of hills and pink light. His movement was so effortless and fluent and so incongruous with his demeanor and clothing and occupation that he seemed to have broken free from one life and entered another. I backed away from the painting and watched young children try to assume his pose because it looked so inviting. I could assert that there is something more here than a skater, this man of God walking on water, skating before a luminous background of diffused light that could emanate from dawn or dusk. But it could simply be a preacher skating. They could simply be chairs. Backing away from the portrait, I realized it was hung at the far end of a series of arched portals, that it was framed and framed and framed and framed in a gesture of reverence for the work of art.

We had our dinner at Chez Jules, a French restaurant in Craig's Close off Cockburn Street. A clerk at the National Gallery recommended the restaurant's sole and proximity. The narrow close was as steep as a fence post. When we finally reached Chez Jules we were too tired to climb any farther. There were only a few tables, pressed closely together. The patrons were young and dressed in black, body-hugging materials. Our bright plastic jackets seemed obtrusive so we shucked them, but there was very little we could do about our faces. The bar and the door to the kitchen were inches from the back of my chair. I felt in the way every time the waitress moved between them. After two days in Edinburgh we felt more comfortable with the accents, ours and theirs, but our waitress, a beautiful black girl from Jamaica, had us on our toes again. It was as if someone had melted English around a peppermint stick. Everything she said came out cool and curled and lovely, every word a ribbon twirling in the wind. I had the Special because I recognized that word, special, and Aunt Edna ordered the sole. We were still unaccustomed to the languid quality of the restaurants and cafes, the length of time it took a waitress and then your food, to arrive, the nonchalance of the staff when it came to receiving payment for their services. Rarely did patrons seem to be in a hurry. The waitresses always seemed very busy, but never attentive. Yet when we were served it was with the utmost concern, as if they were quite sure they'd made some mistake and might be incapable of correcting it, but give it a try they would.

We were each given a bit of toasted bread with a triangle of salmon at its center crowned with a single caper. We heard French beyond the kitchen door. More patrons crowded in. There was no room for their packages, jackets, and umbrellas, and so they leaned them all against their legs and ours. A beautiful college-aged boy sat next to me, introduced himself, and then asked if I'd watch his bag while he went to the loo. I will forever love this loo word now. His smile was as bright as the inside of a refrigerator at midnight. When he returned he immediately picked up the conversation, holding out his hand and asking our names, repeating his own, Jonathan. Aunt Edna had her sketchbook out, working on a drawing of a bar stool. This never failed to draw attention.

"That's very nice," Jonathan said. "Are you attending University here?"

"Oh no," Aunt Edna said.

"Well, you have a facile hand. You sketch better than most of my students."

"Your students?" I asked.

"I'm a lecturer at Edinburgh University."

"How old are you?"

"Thirty-two now, I'm afraid."

I actually calculated the difference in our ages. "You look much younger," I said.

"Thank you. It is difficult sometimes to attain the degree of respect you'd like when your cheeks are as rosy as mine." He smiled that re-frigerator smile again. Everything inside looked delicious.

"You lecture on drawing?" I asked.

"I tutor life drawing and screen printing, and occasionally I'll lec-ture on Italian Renaissance painting."

"I took a life-drawing class when I was in college," I said.

"Did you like it? Do you still draw as well?"

"I was uneasy there. I think I'd do better now. I've taken up my pencils again lately. My aunt's been helping me."

He looked at Aunt Edna's sketch again, said, "Do you mind?" and took the pad from her. He flipped back through the pages. Aunt Edna looked at me while his head was down and she frowned. He looked up at her, as if he'd heard the frown, and told her, "I'm sorry, but these are brilliant."

"Oh, bosh," Aunt Edna scoffed.

"I'm quite certain," he said. "These decisions you've made, here, and here, the way this line leaves off and takes up again without fault, this shading where there shouldn't logically be any: it's very unusual and quite breathtaking."

"Bosh," Aunt Edna said again.

"What is this 'bosh'?"

"She thinks you're toying with her," I said, and smiled, pushed my hair around behind my ear.

He turned back a few more pages, scrutinizing each page for a moment, looking up at Aunt Edna, and then going on. Finally he said, "Chairs are marvelous, aren't they? Almost human. What other series have you done?"

"I don't understand," she said.

"To what other subjects have you devoted such concentrated studies?"

"I only draw chairs," she said.

"Chairs only?"

"Yes."

I wish now that Jonathan had asked why, but he didn't. He simply tilted his head and smiled at her, as if he now perfectly well understood. He'd simply been doltish for asking.

"It's breasts with me, I'm afraid. I never tire of drawing a breast." He looked down at the table, pushed a menu over an inch, then looked up brightly. "Well, yes, where have you been, where are you going? Are you starting with Edinburgh or are we your last place to visit?"

"We've been here for two days," I said. "We're renting a car tomorrow morning and driving to Glencoe and then on to Plockton on the west coast."

"I'm from Udny Green. Toward Aberdeen. It's too bad you can't get up our way. It's beautiful country. Castles on every hill. We've a mort house in our cemetery that's very famous."

"What's a mort house?"

"Have you not heard of the Resurrectionists?"

We both shook our heads, readying ourselves for a religious harangue.

"The body snatchers?"

"No," I whispered, in a dead imitation of JoAnn.

"Well, at the beginning of the nineteenth century, Edinburgh's medical school was becoming renowned, attracting many anatomy students who required bodies for dissection. William Burke and William Hare, living in the Grassmarket, supplied these bodies to an eminent physician by the name of Robert Knox. It seems the demand outstripped supply so Burke and Hare began to murder vagrants, perhaps tourists, people who wouldn't be missed, and sold the bodies to the good doctor, who didn't ask questions. You see, the usual way of business was to remove freshly deceased bodies from their graves. That's why there are watch houses or towers built in early cemeteries. The mort house in my village is a rather plain, circular stone building without windows, but with a heavy pair of doors that require four keys to unlock. Bodies were placed on a turntable and allowed to become, let us say, unsalable, before they were removed in succession to their plots."

"What happened to Burke and Hare?" Aunt Edna asked.

"Hare informed on Burke, who was executed. Dr. Knox, it is said, got away with murder. It all happened just over the high street there. But those were the good old days. Little worry now. You just want to be sure you'd be missed if you were to go missing, eh?

"Then there's our local Jekyll and Hyde, in fact, the very same that inspired Mr. Robert Louis Stevenson's tale. Edinburgh's not all museums and festivals and gardens. It's the hoary past that brings most tourists here: the throat of Mary, Queen of Scots' secretary slashed at Holyrood, our Jekyll and Hyde executed with a device of his own design."

"Who was he?" I asked.

"Well, the point is he's all of us, isn't he? This particular version, Deacon Brodie, was an upstanding member of the community, a 'pillar of the Church' as the guidebooks say. By night, he was a thief. He took impressions of the local shopkeepers' keys while they were at the pub and plundered their wares in the evening without sign of entry or exit. An amateur inventor of sorts, he was hanged on a gallows he'd designed. Then he tried to cheat the rope by wearing an iron collar beneath his shirt. A wily fellow, who lived in two worlds."

"He lived in one world," Aunt Edna said. "Everyone just thinks there's two."

"Are you represented by a gallery, Edna?" Jonathan asked suddenly.

"Oh, heavens no." She squirmed.

"You should think about it. I'm a fairly good judge and you seem ready. It wouldn't hurt you to share your work. It's not as painful as you might believe. It can actually be quite pleasurable. I agree with you that art should be, primarily, for the benefit, the catharsis, of the individual artist. You know, doing it because you love it, not so somebody else will. But there's nothing wrong with letting others appreciate your efforts, even if you do consider that a by-product."

"Well," Aunt Edna said, and glanced away.

I looked at him and smiled. "I'll work on her, Jonathan."

He left before we did that night, wishing us good luck on our journey. He wasn't yet beyond the door when Aunt Edna leaned over our tiny table and whispered harshly, "He would probably draw your breasts if you just asked him to."

"What?"

"He's twenty years younger than you are, Sarah."

"Twelve," I said and then added, "What of it? It's not like I just left with him. I'm sitting right here with you."

"He was interested in me," she said.

"I know that. So why bring my breasts into it?"

"Well, if you'd leaned over and touched your shoulder to his one more time . . ."

"What?"

"I'm just glad your daughters weren't here."

"My daughters weren't here. That's just it, Aunt Edna. It's just you and me. And if you want to know, no, I want you to know, whether you want to know or not, the idea of that fellow drawing my breasts really does sort of give me a thrill."

"That's just what I thought. The same kind of thrill Sam might have wanted."

"You're vicious. There's a difference between desiring and having."

"There is not."

"There is too. Desiring hurts. Having feels good."

"Desiring lingers. Having ends it. And in Sam's case, then it hurts again. There's not two worlds. There's one world."

"Are you finished with your meals?" our waitress asked, her voice like syrup with words of fruit.

"Oh yes, it was delicious," Aunt Edna answered, her demeanor abruptly blurring, changing from bright oils to muted pastels.

"Coffee then?"

But we declined, although her voice made this seem impossible. Outside, as we carefully stepped down the dank close, that is, after we both scanned the alley for any sign of Mr. Hyde or of Burke and Hare, I asked Aunt Edna, "What's all this one-world, two-world stuff? Are you trying to tutor me in some ancient oriental philosophy?"

"Don't walk so fast, Sarah. It's just that everyone thinks there's two kinds of people, good and bad, and I think there's one kind."

"Which is it? Are we all bad, or is it just Sam?"

"You know what I'm trying to say. Everybody is susceptible, under the right circumstances, to an unfortunate decision. What if that Jonathan had really courted you, really. I think you would have left me with that waitress in a flash. I'm not even sure I could find my way back to the hotel."

"I would never abandon you, Aunt Edna. How could you think I'd let you walk these streets alone? I would have met him later at a pub. Didn't you want to just cup his cheek in your palm? And that smile."

"I've got a boyfriend, Sarah, and you have a husband. If you'd let it, this could be an opportunity for you and Sam to start over, start fresh. I can't bear it any longer: I am on Sam's side."

"I knew it!" I yelped. My voice echoed up steep stone walls. "I knew it, I knew it, I knew it," I whispered.

"I believe in second chances and sticking by the people you love even when they hurt you."

"What if you don't love them anymore? What about that?"

"If you don't love him, then you should have broken it off long ago and none of this ever would have happened."

"So it's my fault either way?"

"If you don't love him."

"I don't know. Perhaps I don't love him now as a result of what he did."

"I don't believe you can love and not love a person because they hurt you. There'd still be the love with the hurt. The hurt wouldn't dissolve the love. It would make the love and the hurt more intense."

I couldn't decide whether to cry or throw a fit. I finally said, "Aunt Edna, no one is going to talk me through this to a conclusion. One day there will be a conclusion and I probably won't know which day that was until years later."

We walked on silently, past the museums to Princes Street. All the shops were closed but the sidewalks were full of strolling couples, young and old. It took blocks for me to realize I was a member of a couple as well.

I said, "I almost told that waitress that you were engaged to a black man."

"Well, Sarah, why in the world?"

"Because I'm trying to be a part of this place, have a connection to it."

"She would have thought you were out of your mind."

"I know. That's why I didn't do it. It was just this absurd urge I had to be related to this city in some way, to that beautiful girl, her voice."

"Oh, Sarah, honey, I didn't realize how far away you are. You already belong, Sarah. You're human. You don't have to find a reason to smile at someone. Just smiling works."

"I just feel like I'm from away," I said. "And it's so beautiful here. I want to be from here. I want to be from almost anyplace except my own past."

"Fort Worth isn't so bad, honey."

"Oh, no, I love Fort Worth. I'm happy to be from there. It's nice to watch these people when you tell them you're from Texas and all the cowboy movies they've ever seen light up their eyes."

"You're right. I can't talk you out of your past."

"No, me either."

"Do you think it's too late to call James?"

I looked at my watch and counted back. "No, it's only five o'clock at his house."

"I didn't think I'd miss him this much. Do you want to talk to him when I call? His voice is very soothing."

"It is, isn't it? What a nice man you're marrying," I said. "What a lucky girl."

◻ ◻ ◻

It took us some time to decipher the telephone system in the hallway of our hotel, but with the help of two operators, several thick coins, and my credit card, Aunt Edna finally reached James. I left them alone.

I lay on my narrow bed and allowed myself the luxury of thinking about the young tutor. He may have been interested in Aunt Edna's sketchbook, but he'd smiled at me several times and once touched the back of my hand. The second time I leaned toward him he pushed back. His hair was clean but unkempt, perhaps it had needed trimming for weeks. It kept falling over his eyes. The way he had of moving it away, raking through it with one hand, revealing the crease between his eyebrows and the paleness of his brow, the way his hair immediately began to fall again, taking away the paleness in a slow, measured way: it had been everything I could do not to touch him with my hands in some way. His clothes were dark; neither shirt nor jacket had collars. It didn't seem to me that it would be hard to find him again, this man who went to French restaurants alone, who freely talked about art, who paid more attention to me than he did to the beautiful Jamaican waitress. Of course, I was far too big to be drawn in the nude. Unless it were to involve drapery, perhaps a great swathe of linen covering the floor and the lower two-thirds of my body, only the upper torso revealed. Well, I've gone too far here, I know, but it's a survival instinct, allowing yourself to think that some part of you is desirable. I wanted to think that Jonathan could find that in me, appreciate it. I knew that Aunt Edna and I were leaving in the morning, and I'd never see him again. I knew that the women he studied were the same ones I'd drawn in college: students, girls so relaxed with their bodies that beauty seemed to lounge across them, and clothing seemed peripheral, merely decorative. They were mildly bored with nudity, and even if their proportions weren't classical their bodies fit their skin, and no line I drew seemed as natural. I never allowed myself to meet them, to become their friends, because I was an artist and they were simply models. They weren't as ashamed of their nudity as I was of drawing it. I couldn't draw them because I couldn't draw resolve, or carelessness, or confidence, or anything else I lacked at the time. I knew I'd never become that kind of body now, but I yearned to be that carefree, to be consciousless of my body in any state. As it was my body hung around and constantly followed me. But I did think that perhaps I was ready to reveal my shoulders, to pull the linen tautly around my back and gather it beneath my breasts, and let Jonathan look at me intently while I simply stared into the blankness of a wall, or examined a green vine climbing up the mullions of a loft window.

I went down and called my girls after Aunt Edna was through with the phone. They'd made me promise I would. I hadn't spoken to them since they'd learned of their father's transgressions and I wasn't looking forward to it. I didn't know how I'd respond if they started to ask questions. It seemed to me that this was between Sam and me. Michelle answered and immediately called her sister to the extension.

"Where are you?"

"We're still in Edinburgh. Tomorrow we'll rent the car and go to the Highlands. I'm pretty nervous about driving on the wrong side of the road."

"Just stay on the side that the oncoming cars aren't on, Mom," Susan said.

"I will, but there're these roundabouts."

"I talked to one of my friends who spent a year in Oxford. He says if you get disoriented on a roundabout you just stay on it, keep going around and around till you know where you are, which exit you want to take, and then you get off."

"Wow, that's a great idea," I said. Then I told them about everything I'd seen, about spreading the ashes in the gardens, about the stone, the museums, the gum, and the monuments, everything but Jonathan.

They said "unhunh" and "really" half a dozen times. Neither one of them was interested in traveling. They wanted to get out of school and make some real money. They talked about their summer jobs, the clothes they'd bought with their paychecks, how boring home was compared to college. Michelle started to tell me the plot of a movie she'd gone to see the night before and I realized that both my girls were intensely interested in their own lives. They weren't boring or mindless, but devoted to the specifics of their lives. I hadn't been interested in my own life for a long time. While I was having this little personal mind twist, Michelle had come to tears.

"What's wrong, honey?"

"I just want you to come home to Daddy. I don't want you to be apart. It's not right. I just can't stop crying about it. It hurts so much. I can't stand it that you're both hurting." Then she broke off and all I could hear was my daughter sobbing a few feet away from the phone.

"Are you still there, Susan?"

"Yes, Mom. She's pretty upset."

"I know, honey. I guess you are, too."

"I'm pretty mad at Dad. I cook his supper every night but I don't talk to him much."

"Please don't be that way with him, Susan. You'll break his heart. I don't want y'all to take sides. This is between your dad and me. He shouldn't have told you. Don't treat him badly."

"It makes me sick to think about him being with someone else. If he'd do that to you why wouldn't he do it to me, you know, find some other daughter to love."

"He'd be physically incapable of that, Susan. He loves you two more than he loves himself."

"I guess you thought that about him before he betrayed you, Mom."

"I want you to stop thinking about him like that. He's your father and deserves your respect. Go tell your sister to stop crying and get back on the phone."

I listened to her walk away from the receiver while I blew hot air in snorts from my nose. Why both of their reactions made me mad I can't now explain. It seems like one or the other should have pleased me. Both girls got back on the phone but neither would do more than breathe into it.

"Now, look," I said, "this is between me and your dad. He's still your dad and I'm still your mom. It doesn't affect how we care about you two. Now we're going to work this problem out in one way or the other. Whatever happens we're all still in love with one another."

"I thought you'd be together forever, Mom," Michelle blurted out, crying again.

"Michelle, honey, we might yet. I just don't know. It's going to take some time. He and I are both hurt. We feel bad about hurting each other and hurting y'all and it's going to take time to work out what we want from each other."

"He wants you to come home, Mom," Susan said.

"Well, he says that, but I'm not sure either of us knows what we want. I don't. And I don't want to talk about this with my daughters. I want to work it out with me first and then we'll see if your dad and I can work it out."

"I'm sorry Dad hurt you," Susan said.

"I'm sorry too, Mom," Michelle sniffed.

"I love both my girls so much," and then I started to tear up. I caught each breath the way you'd snatch litter blowing down the street. "OK, so I want to see both of you at the wedding in a couple weeks. I want you there and we'll talk some more. I don't care what your bosses say: you come. If you lose your job I'll hire you for the rest of the summer."

"We'll be there, Mom," Michelle said.

"Can I bring a friend?" Susan asked.

"Susan, just shut up," Michelle snapped.

"Who?" I asked.

"Scott Grayson. I met him this summer at work, Mom."

"God, Susan," Michelle whispered.

"Sure," I said, "if he wants to come. I'd like to meet him."

"I haven't asked him yet. I waited to ask you first."

"Sure, bring him. I'll call you when we get back to Fort Worth. I'm having a good time. I wish y'all were here with me. It's so beautiful and the people we've met are so friendly. I never knew I'd like traveling this much."

"Be careful, Mom."

□   □   □

When I opened the door to our room I surprised Aunt Edna. She was sorting through a mound of medicine, a dozen or more pill bottles heaped on her bedspread. She quickly scooped them all up and dumped them in her bag.

"How many medications are you on, Aunt Edna?"

"I'm just looking for something to help my back."

"Do you take that many pills a day?"

"No, some of them are JoAnn's herbs and I have a few of Momma's leftovers. I thought I had a bottle of James's pain prescription he got the last time his hands flared up."

"His hands flared up?"

"Once in a while the muscles in his hands hurt."

"You're not supposed to take other people's prescriptions," I said, apparently still on the phone with my daughters.

She stopped searching and stood up, both hands pressed into her lower back. "Sarah, I'm not mixing medicine. After taking care of Momma for twenty years I can quote long lists of long words that don't mix in the human body. I know exactly what works and what doesn't. I just want a pain pill for my back." By the end of this speech there was water in her eyes.

"I've got some ibuprofen," I offered.

"I don't think that's going to do it. I don't know how much more climbing and walking I can do."

"Do you want to go see a doctor tomorrow morning?"

"No."

"We'll be in the car most of the day. There won't be much walking."

"That's good. I'm going to go sit on the toilet." She took her pharmacy with her.

□ □ □

I made my first mistake getting into the rental car. I sat down, keys in hand, and felt immediately that something was amiss. There was no steering wheel in my lap. It was over on the other side of the car. This made me guffaw. Aunt Edna, loading the turtleback, just gave me a blank stare as I got out of the car, rounded it, and got back in.

"That's not making me very comfortable," she said.

"Just get in," I yelled. I was still giggling nervously.

She slammed the hatch and joined me up front. "We don't know where we are," she said.

"What?".

"When you don't know which side of a car to get into you are completely lost. We can only get more lost from here."

"How can we get more lost than lost? Lost is a limit. Lost has nowhere to go but found. Thank God it's an automatic. Thank God, Sam wasn't here to see that first step. We're just going to take things slowly, familiarize ourselves with everything. Fasten your seat belt. What's that?"

"My sketchbook."

"You're going to draw while I drive?"

"I was just going to touch up some of these chairs I've seen over the past couple of days. We've been in such a hurry that some of them don't have shadows."

"Aunt Edna, don't you want to see Scotland?"

"I'll look up occasionally."

"I need you to help me navigate and make sure I'm on the right side of the road."

"Oh, all right." She humphed and spewed. "I thought I was going to get a chance to work while we were here, but it's been rush, rush. Well, time's a-wasting, let's go."

"I'm not sure this car is going to turn left when I turn the wheel left. Maybe that's backwards, too. Give me a minute. Everything is on the wrong side."

"Put your brush in the other hand," Aunt Edna said. I clicked on the windshield wipers and watched them oddly weave and I quickly became disoriented. How did they avoid becoming entangled? I snapped them off.

"What did you say?"

"Put your brush in the other hand. Turn the canvas over and paint on the back."

Her eyes were as dull as crevices in bark. "Once again," I said, "I seem to have missed something."

"You just have to imagine your life as it is lived in a mirror."

I shook my head.

"When you see the other cars coming at you, do you think you'll aim for them?"

"Of course not."

"Then start the car. Let's go."

"I'm just telling you I'm at a nervous pitch. I'm really uncomfortable."

"I think you're excited. I've always known traveling would be like this. We're lost. We'll not find our way out of this parking lot till we start rolling."

"Aunt Edna, we've got all the time in the world. Would you give me a break? I just want to find the turn signals and adjust my mirrors."

"I wish I had a magazine," she said.

I pulled away from our parking space at the airport rental lot as if I were leaving the earth itself. It was incredibly hard to overcome almost thirty years of habit. It was as hard as believing that my husband cheated on me, that he didn't love me. My left hand pulled away from my right, which isn't good practice when they're both gripping a steering wheel. I ran an internal mantra: stay left, stay left, stay left. We followed another car out of the parking lot and around the two roundabouts at the entrance to the airport. A man in a dark suit drove the car in front of us, one of the mourning businessmen we'd flown with into Edinburgh two days before. I hit upon the plan of following him for the rest of the day, making all his sales calls with him. If I stayed bolted to his bumper I'd never be on the wrong side of the road. Merging onto the A8 and then the M9 took a great feat of will: I could not believe that other cars wouldn't be using the ramp to exit. Once on the carriageway I saw that there was a barrier between us and the oncoming traffic and I realized they'd planned for our arrival. I remained in the slow lane, checking my gauges and mirrors as a fighter pilot would. Aunt Edna arranged her hair in the visor mirror.

"You're certainly a cool one," I told her.

She shrugged. "No pedals or steering wheel over here. Not much different than being in an airplane. I've got little control over my life."

"I've got our entire route highlighted on the map. Every road change we make is circled. It's about a hundred and fifteen miles to Glencoe."

"With a road like this we'll be there by lunchtime. Why are we staying there? We could drop off some of Momma and Daddy and keep going."

"I thought you were tired of rushing?"

"I'm never going to be satisfied, am I? It's disappointing, this late in life, not to be satisfied. I don't think it's my life's fault. It's my personality." She flipped up the visor and sighed. "I'm sorry about my short temper. I've never been dissatisfied or disappointed in you. I'm grateful for your companionship. You've moved away from home and traveled halfway around the world to help me and I've been short with you. You've lost interest in your job, your girls have left home, and your husband has been unfaithful, and I've only thought about myself. I'm sorry."

"Well, I appreciate the apology," I said, "but somehow it doesn't make me feel much better. Thanks for laying it all out in an orderly fashion for me. You can take out your sketchbook now."

"Can I?"

"I've got six miles under my seat belt now. We'll be on the M9 for some time. Do you want me to tell you when we pass a castle or a palace or when we're about to hit a truck?"

"Oh, Sarah, this is your adventure. I'm just on a delivery, along for the ride."

I tested the horn. It burped a very nasal European "fronk." Aunt Edna settled down with her pencil. The road was smooth but from time to time she'd give a little yelp of excitement as a line wandered from her intention, as if her pencil were a dog on a leash. She'd hold her breath for moments longer than I thought healthy, and then expel it with her pencil point lifted from the paper. Once she looked up at me, smiled, and said, "I've never done this before. You'd think it would be irritating but it adds something. The shadows vibrate. They seem to have a life of their own."

"Like Peter Pan's shadow," I said.

"Everything behind us looms up, doesn't it?" Aunt Edna said. "Everything behind us seems bigger than it did at the time. I like the idea of the past being separate and still alive."

The road beyond was remarkably litter free, the grass in the margins as green as boiled broccoli. Our little Vauxhall was relatively new and smelled of fresh plastic and Scotchgarded fabric. When a truck thundered past, I felt the familiar shove and suck of its shouldered air and immediately was more comfortable. The only difference between this and an American highway was a freewheeling sense of desperation. People might pass from any side. I myself might discover a new country.

"What do you think of that green?" I asked Aunt Edna.

"It's too green," she said. "It's florescent and painful. It's the same green they find when they clean an old painting, and you realize that life fades and tarnishes. Their lives, the old painters' lives, were just as colorful and vibrant as your own is today and they were lost. It's too green."

The buildings along the highway gave evidence that Scotland wasn't only past: corporate headquarters, industrial works, modern multi-unit housing. There were colorful plastic toys lying in yards. Occasionally the stench of rubber or propane filled the car. Ravens stood sentry along the roadside, barely flinching when cars flashed by, their feathers momentarily going blue when they turned their backs to the onslaught of wind. I read every road sign for clues to my future, scanned the advertising on trucks as if it were hung in a museum. I can look back at a map now and tell you we passed Linlithgow, went through Grangemouth and Stirling, but I only saw a landscape of motorway margins and what access the highway allowed. Frequently old stone caught my eye, a hedgerow, fields, but I wouldn't dare hold to them for fear of something that moved. I had few doubts that the road could end far more abruptly than I could brake. So I watched it and the things that lived on it. Highway construction signs showed little men shoveling a little pile of dirt. There were frequent posted warnings: "Traffic Queuing Ahead," and curiously, "Police Speed Check Ahead," as if the highway department were undermining law enforcement. At one point I could choose between Glasgow and Stirling and my body actually shivered with unexpected opportunity. Church spires ghosted through my peripheral vision as if they were on horseback. I pressed a button that I thought would spray soap on the windshield. It did so, but the manner in which this was accomplished made me shriek. The cleaning fluid for the rear window shot all the way over the roof of the car and splattered on the hood and windshield. The rear wiper brushed dryly over the glass. I pressed this button many times over the next couple of days just to give myself a start.

Aunt Edna looked up as we passed the great upheaval of Stirling

Castle and said, "Oh," as if she'd forgotten her purse. I gave it about two seconds of my attention and turned back to the motorway because my first exit was coming up somewhere in the next five miles: the things we miss in the hegemonic anxiety and tunnel vision of the present.

Aunt Edna popped another pill as we exited onto the A9.

"What was that for?" I asked. She'd taken it without water, without a noticeable swallow.

"My medicine, Sarah, and I wish you'd leave me alone about it. I'm not a child, eating everything under the sink. I promise not to take anything I don't need. I've got a little headache."

"It was ginseng, wasn't it, a little ginseng orgasm."

"Bosh, drive the car."

We finally left the relative comfort of the dual carriageway at the A820. Here the road had only two lanes, and I was allowed only half of these. It suddenly seemed as though roads that placed high-speed vehicles within feet of one another, that allowed them to go in opposing directions, were a flagrant disregard for life. All roads should be like those in cities: one way. We motored slowly through farmlands the three miles to Doune. Only two cars passed us in all this way. The fields on either side of us were lush, littered with the remains of sheep-nibbled turnips. Rock walls, rumpled by big oaks, stumbled over rolling hills, separating sheep. The rumps of the sheep were brightly painted: vermilion, blue, orange.

"That doesn't seem a proper canvas," Aunt Edna said.

"You should paint a sheep," I suggested. "You could sit on a sheep."

We came into Doune at fifteen miles per hour and this was all too fast. We were headed upstream and had turned off onto a narrow branch, a rock-strewn tributary. The houses were gray stone with white windows. Occasionally a building was whitewashed. The signs over storefronts were simple almost to the point of modesty, as if they were embarrassed by the act of trade. There were cars parked on each side of the road, cars coming at me, and the space to pass completely inadequate. The more I slowed the more the oncoming cars seemed to accelerate. The actual passing was more like slashing, a bright steel and glass throat cutting. Trucks parked in the middle of the street, forcing passing cars into games of chicken in the single lane left. To sheer amazement we came through unscathed, cleared Doune, and emerged on a somewhat wider thoroughfare, the way a cork emerges from a set of rapids. The sun bore down making everything brittle and distinct.

"Do you think all of their towns are so narrow?" Aunt Edna asked. Her pencils and sketchbook were scattered on the floorboard.

"I suppose they were built for carriages, not for four lanes of parked and charging cars."

"You're going to have to be careful."

"That's what I've been trying to tell you. Scotland's going to be a gantlet."

"Well, I'm too young to die, Sarah."

"You're too young? What about me?"

"You've lived a happy, productive life: a prosperous career, two daughters in college, a husband who loves you."

"A half hour ago you used those same examples to explain why you pitied me, Aunt Edna."

"I guess it all goes to show you how different things can look from the other side, in a different light. You don't believe that Sam loves you in the same way that Momma didn't believe I loved her. You think his love should be pure as light."

"Well, shouldn't it?"

"Light is made up of many colors. Even light isn't pure, but you can still read by it."

"You and Darcy are the queens of long-distance metaphors."

"You know what I mean."

"Grandma didn't believe you loved her either?"

"She knew I loved her. She was just ashamed of being sick, ashamed of taking so long to die. How far are we from Glencoe?"

"Still about eighty miles, and it'll be smaller roads from here on."

"I'm going to get the big book out so we'll recognize it when we get there."

"It's a valley in the mountains. There'll be eight or ten miles of it. There's a river running down through the middle, so it's going to be hard to miss."

We began to climb outside of Doune, passing through the haunts of Rob Roy. The countryside was green and rich and meticulous.

"Do you feel like you're from here, Aunt Edna?"

"No, Sarah."

"I mean, what Daddy said about our ancestors maybe coming from here."

"I recognize the air I breathe, but that's all."

"We should have done our genealogy before we came."

"We had little enough time for that."

"I know, but I feel like I'm missing something, that there's more here than we've found. What if we have relatives here and we're driving past their houses as we speak?"

"More than likely they're happy we're passing by. Hard enough to keep close family happy to see each other, much less distant cousins."

"You're just a bundle of contradictions," I said. "Last night you told me all I had to do to be accepted was smile at strangers."

"You shouldn't listen to me, Sarah. I don't know where I get off. I get mixed up lately. I don't think I'm senile yet, just too emotional. I'm bitter one minute and overjoyed the next and I don't know how I get from one to the other, what lives in that interval. Sometimes when I'm painting the whole texture of a work will change from one brush stroke to the next, change in the time it took me to dampen my brush."

"What makes you happy?"

"Working, taking Momma where she wanted to go, taking you with us, but mostly James, James and painting."

"How is James?"

"He said he was lonely, said he could feel I was a long way from Texas. He said we've only got twenty-five years left with each other and I need to get back home. Then he told me a joke."

"Well?"

"Well, it's a sex joke."

"OK."

"The *New England Journal of Medicine* has reported that they've discovered a food product that completely inhibits the sex drive in women. He said he was going to make sure I didn't eat any of it."

"What is it?"

"Wedding cake."

"Ha, ha, ha. Very funny."

"He laughs a lot at his own jokes. I like that in a man."

"Sam does that, too."

"Once, I pulled two dollars out of my wallet to pay James back for something. There was a piece of lint that came out of my billfold with the money. James felt it and said, 'What's this?' and I said, 'Lint,' and he just broke apart laughing, saying, 'Been a long time since you paid anybody back, hasn't it?' He laughed about that for three days. He's almost always ready to laugh and he'd just as soon laugh at himself as anybody else. It's like he hasn't found anything funnier than being an old blind black man."

"I've never heard him say a pitiful thing about himself, other than that thing about God making him blind."

"He told me he doesn't miss his sight at all, that he couldn't miss something he never had and couldn't hope to have. And then he'll get all disappointed over a losing lotto ticket, a one-in-a-million chance."

We were on the road into the Highlands. There were grand, bald mountains in the distance. The road ran like kinked ribbon from a spool through planted pine forests and hay fields. Big round bales of hay wrapped in black plastic huddled along the verges of fields like apocalyptic presents, only to be opened at drought or blizzard.

"I could live here," I whispered. Aunt Edna didn't respond.

Ben Ledi rose on our left, Ben Vorlich beyond to the right. We climbed alongside a falling river, and by now Aunt Edna, too, gaped at the luxuriousness of the terrain, its persistent invitation to be hiked over. Sheep were everywhere, walking more proudly than I'd ever given them credit, bunked in twos behind rocks, one using the other's orange flank for a pillow. Tufts of wool decorated every knot and barb of wire fences. Beyond Lochearnhead the hills rose more steeply and freshets leaped out of gullies into a boiling river. It seemed the only thing more powerful than gravity here was green, the color itself climbing rock and tree trunk and fence post. Only running water itself moved too quickly to be grown over by moss and lichen and grass.

"Where is everybody?" Aunt Edna asked. "It's so pretty here. Why aren't there more people living here, more houses?"

"The Clearances," I told her. "The Highland Clearances. There used to be many more people here, more farms."

"I've never been to a place where there were less people than there used to be."

"In the late 1700s and early 1800s the landowners evicted most of their peasant tenants in order to bring in more profitable herds of sheep or to create vast sporting estates."

"Where did all the people go?"

"Some to the cities, some to the coast, and I guess many of them were forced to immigrate. When Samuel Johnson and James Boswell came through on their tour, Johnson was appalled by the displacement. He called it, 'this epidemick desire of wandering.' I love that phrase."

"It sounds like he didn't understand. Maybe it should have been 'this epidemick regret of wandering.' They had to leave this beautiful place."

"But many of them came to America, Aunt Edna. They went to a place where they couldn't be arbitrarily evicted."

"Still, it was their home."

"They thought it was. It never was in a real sense. They were squatters, just like me in my marriage."

"Oh, Sarah," she sighed.

We drove down a long valley toward Crianlarich. The mountains were scored, rivulet-ridden. Streams of scree pooled at the bases of gullies and the water worked its way through the rocks the way a cat moves through the legs and stretchers of chairs beneath a table.

Before Tyndrum, the fields lay rumpled like a great blanket had been thrown across the land covering a still-sleeping body. The grass seemed to grow in strata, terrace upon terrace scored in the hummocks, the work of the pacing sheep.

We stopped at the Little Chef in Tyndrum. I pulled into a parking space, turned off my lights, and reached down to put the car in park but Aunt Edna beat me to it. Her action had been involuntary. The gearshift, for her, was where it should have been. I looked at her. She looked at me, then the gearshift, then me again, and said, "Oh, sorry."

I grinned. "That's OK. If it takes both of us, that's OK."

She seemed tired. I was beyond my jet lag by this time but she was still working under its burden. I asked about her headache and she said it had gone, but she ate little all the same. I had peas, mashed potatoes that were so inundated with butter they were bright yellow and delicious, and a Somerset pie: pork and spiced apple in a scrumpy sauce, cooked in pastry. Aunt Edna had a bowl of chips and drank a

Coke, which she proceeded to burp for the rest of the afternoon. After each burp she'd say, "Oh, that was a good one," or "Oh, that's better." They were colon cleaners, great ruddy base knuckle-scraping chest vibrators that changed the air pressure in our small car.

"Something's going to let go if you keep doing that," I told her.

"I wish it would," she said. "I wish I could burp out everything bad in me. I'd burp out forgetfulness and nausea and that affected way I paint kids' chairs when I come upon them because I think they're all cute. I wish I could burp out the way I keep mulling over mistakes, as if there were something to be done about them."

"You could patent that burp. I'd like to burp off pounds and feeling inadequate and indecision and the memory of Sam at that intersection."

"It's such a shame that burping only works on Coke and bananas."

Beyond Tyndrum, Beinn Dorain disappeared into a bank of mist. Its flanks were creased by gully after gully, seemingly only yards apart, as if gravity were ceaselessly trying new ways to find the fastest way down.

Aunt Edna turned the pages in *Scotland from Above* and looked up at the mountain.

"That's not it," I said.

We passed the Bridge of Orchy Hotel and began a steeper ascent. The mountains were reflected in a sweep of loch whose surface caught tufts of wind and made the planting of evergreens on the lower slopes shimmy. The road wound through a hummocked pasture that was more lake than field. Tiny islands rooted a single stark shrub. This was Rannoch Moor, from which we'd descend into Glencoe. The landscape glistened with patches of reflected sky, water that awaited the last thirsty man. Half the moor lay in shadow beneath the higher mountains.

The vegetation became sparse, the evergreens and scrub spindly. Monuments of natural stone rose from boggy ground. As we began to descend into the valley of Glencoe the surface of the earth was plainly skinned to the bone. Scree resembled lava flows. Everything was cut from rock, made from rock, broken off rock. A line of telephone poles stepped down on our right and seemed as out of place as jewelry on a skeleton. The rock was scabbed over with lichens brown, gray, yellow, and white, the scabs overlapping each other with a licking greed. The road used the River Coe's path at one point, squeaking through stone bulwarks. This seemed to make the water mad. It boiled and caromed beneath the bridge. To our left were the Sisters, a triumvirate of mountains time-scoured and water-scored, mounting up in progressively steeper cliffs.

"Here, here, here," Aunt Edna screeched. "We're in it. It's that mountain and the river below it. We're in the picture."

I pulled over at the next available spot of gravel. It was dark here. The valley was a narrow sluice that blocked out light. Mists skulked around the mountains' middles and their very tops were obscured in clouds. In this gorge there was very little place to look but up. All I could think of these summits was, "There is a place I'll never go." Aunt Edna got out of the car with the book. She laid it on the hood and looked between it and the mountain. The photo was taken from a balloon. It showed the valley in winter, the grass brown, the bracken rust. Snow capped and drizzled down the mountain. But we were plainly in the photo. Even the gravel pullout where we were parked was in view, where Allt Lairig Eilde, a rough waterfall of a stream, joined the River Coe. We seemed small there. The landscape was raw and overpowering and I wanted to look for someplace to hide. If God did not make Glencoe, then He was born there. What had been a bright and mild summer day outside the valley was shadowed and damp within.

"Anywhere here, then," Aunt Edna said.

"Let's go down to the hotel first," I suggested. "I want to put on my tennis shoes and a sweater. After we check in and rest a bit, we'll drive back up here. It's only a few miles to Ballachulish."

"OK, I'm tired, too. I don't see how so much green can live with so much bare rock."

"Did you see the moss and lichen on the rocks?" I asked as we drove down the fissure. "It's like daubs of thick paint on a palette."

Although everything around us mounted up on high, it also seemed to be leering down, imminently flowing down. And although there were innumerable places to hide, there was nowhere to hide. Our car rolled downhill with its own weight as sole impetus. As the valley descended, the mountains became taller. Sheep, tiny white specks against the gray rock, were trying to escape without the aid of wings. At Loch Achtriochtan the valley floor opened up a bit and eventually, following the river, we saw Loch Leven laid out at the base of the mountains, darkly gray, a bit of the ocean that had chiseled its way into the stone. We made our way to the Isles of Glencoe Hotel, where the receptionist told us the valley of Glencoe was very "dreigh."

"Dreigh?"

"Dreary and doleful," she explained. "Will you want dinner?"

"Do we have to reserve now?"

"We like to give Chef some idea, but he can always squeeze in two more. Join us if you can." She passed us our key card and we bumped up a flight of carpeted stairs with our luggage to the room, which overlooked the loch.

"They actually have a name for the way that place makes you feel," I said. "You want the near bed or the far?"

"I want the one next to the bathroom. I think I'll have a little nap before we take Momma and Daddy back up into the valley."

I got into bed with my Scotland guidebook. "Do you want to hear about Glencoe?"

"Read it to me. If my eyes are closed, I'm still listening."

I looked at her and raised my eyebrow. "I'll just give you the highlights as I come to them. The mythical Scottish giant Fingal lived in the valley. There's a witch, Bean Nighe, who washes clothes in the River Coe. If you spot her you'll die soon after."

"In Gaelic, Glencoe means 'Valley of the Dogs' but many people still know it as the 'Valley of Tears' after the massacre of 1692."

"The massacre?"

"In the early morning dark of February 12, in a driving blizzard, 120 members of the clan Campbell rose up and slew their hosts, the Macdonalds. Thirty-eight men, women, and children were slaughtered and thrown on the dung heaps. Many more perished in their flight into the frozen mountains. It's said that even two centuries later some Macdonald innkeepers wouldn't board a Campbell."

"It certainly was an abuse of hospitality," Aunt Edna whispered. "I'm going to sleep now, Sarah. I want to be rested when we take Momma up."

"I'll be quiet." I punched my pillow and fell back to the guidebook. My grandparents' ashes would be compost to a soil already thick with human fertilizer. Here, unlike the gardens we'd chosen in Edinburgh, their remains would work up through root and blade, burn green and inviting, become sheep fodder and woolstuff, and be dropped again, perhaps on higher ground.

Aunt Edna slept, and whined softly from time to time, like a window in the wind. Her head lay unmoving upon her pillow, coddled, a lifetime's practice in protecting a hairdo. The revelations to come were just that to me, complete revelations. I watched for no clues, as you may be doing as you read this, and had no suspicions. Things that now seem obvious to the reader who is aware of my aunt's story, those of you who've seen the television segments or read the many magazine and newspaper articles, are only recognizable to me in hindsight. I've presented events as they occurred, to the best of my ability and memory. Perhaps the details I've reported so far are skewed by the events that would follow. Perhaps I recall the witch, Bean Nighe, rather than the tiny flowers that bloomed from fissures in the rock of Glencoe, because my hindsight is a dark and acute vision.

When Aunt Edna woke up, she washed her face and came out of the bathroom drying her hands. "Did you see that Roman cippus in the National Gallery, Sarah? It was a little white marble box for remains."

"I must have missed it," I said.

"It reminded me of my little boxes. We've been carrying people around in boxes for just forever, haven't we? But I don't think mine will ever be in a museum."

"If it was a Roman box, it was probably two thousand years old," I said. "You've got to give art some time to get to a museum." This was the only reference that my aunt ever made to the idea of her work being seen by someone other than a member of our family. I'm glad I said what I did. It gives me some comfort now, to think she might have had hope.

We drove back into Glencoe early in the evening, the whole valley in shadow and threatened by fog. Green reached up into the cliffs, up into the northern escarpment, till there was no handhold left. I felt like a dog, cowering below its master, afraid to look up in more than quick glances. Parking in the same gravel pullout, we carried the ashes into the thick grass, descending slowly down a footpath toward the river. I let Aunt Edna lead. There were other hikers in the valley, carrying staffs, wearing leather boots and bright windbreakers. When Aunt Edna saw them approaching down the trail, she broke off into the untrodden heather. She walked slowly, and so to give her time to get a few steps ahead I bent down to touch the grass. Grandpa rested on my knee. The groundcover was as thick as cotton in an old mattress, the ground itself whipped, porous. All five of my taut fingers disappeared into the loam up to the webbing. Soon I noticed water pooling around my sneakers. I looked up and saw that Aunt Edna was stepping from tuft to tuft, holding Grandma in both hands. She turned back to me.

"It's wet. It looks dry but underneath it's wet. I want to go to the middle of the picture. We need to get close to that river."

"It's just going to get wetter," I said. "The ground is like a sponge."

"We'll have wet feet then," she answered. "Wet feet isn't a catastrophe. You get them wet in the shower everyday."

She walked toward a small knoll, a rise upon which stood a single sheep. His black face turned to her abruptly, and Aunt Edna kept marching, the box held out before her firmly, as if it were an offering. The sheep stepped forward, but then thought better of it and bolted. Aunt Edna crested the knoll and kept marching, down through a boggy area where the water reached our ankles, up another rise and along a line of lichen-encrusted boulders that led to a low dense copse alongside the River Coe. Here she stopped and sat on a low sloping stone. We'd walked for perhaps twenty minutes. I caught up with her and saw that the rock she sat on was surrounded by rabbit dung and deer scat, brown pellets of varying sizes.

"Your butt's getting wet," I huffed.

"I don't care," she huffed back.

The water below us was dark and clear at the same time.

"I hope we don't see Bean Nighe down here," I said, sitting next to her.

"Who?"

"The washerwoman. Are we here yet?"

She looked around, and down at the box on her knees. "We're here."

"The river sounds nice, doesn't it?"

"I feel like it's flowing right through me, cold and fast."

Her voice shifted and burbled, seemed unstable, like dishes stacked haphazardly in a box you were carrying. The rims of her eyes were red.

"Oh, Aunt Edna," I whispered.

"I don't want to open the box," she cried softly. "I don't want to give up any more of her. Sarah, when Momma died it was as if my only child had died. When I first began to care for her, I was as resentful as anyone would be when their adult life was taken from them. But after a couple of years I came to see she couldn't help who she was. She was like a child and I grew to think of her as my child. I was forty years old then. I knew that I wasn't going to have a family, my own baby. So I was grateful for her, the way she needed me and asked my advice. She was my child."

She sobbed for a few seconds and I put my arm around her.

"It seems so unfair that she had to die. I've never had to give anything up before its time, except Daddy. How would you feel if you lost one of your daughters?"

"She lived a good, long life," I said, unable to respond to so direct and hurtful a question.

"I know, I know. She had more than lots of people get. I just miss her. If you weren't here, I don't know what I'd do. These poor Scottish people would have an old pitiful woman on their hands."

"Don't be silly. Where's the little spoon? I'll start with Grandpa."

"I didn't bring it, Sarah. I want to use my hands. If you'll just hold the boxes open for me, I'll do it."

"Are you sure?"

"Yes, it's what I want. I don't want anything between us."

"OK."

The water had leached through my pants and I felt like there was nothing between my skin and the lichen-layered stone. I held both boxes on my lap as Aunt Edna opened them, scooped ash into her moist palm, turned and spread them like feed before a flock of birds, pitching the ash in long falling arcs, a sweep of dust that actually lingered in the air before falling, and in falling mottled the blades of grass with specks of gray. She took from both boxes and mixed in her gathered palms and flung the ashes up and away. Tears fell from her eyes to her nose, and she wiped them away with the sleeve of her jacket. She took small pinches in her fingertips from each box, mixed them in a single cupped palm and said, "I wish I could mix my own ashes in with hers. I'd like to be with her, too," and she turned and flung her hands away from her body, the ashes smoking the air for a dense moment, her ache made visible.

I closed the lids of the boxes. "That's enough for here," I said. "We need to save some for Plockton. Let's go down to the river."

I took her caked hand in mine and led her around the copse to the bank of the swift river and plunged her hands into the water and washed them, as if she were my child. I moved my hands through hers, wiping the ash from her skin, turning her darkened nails into the current, using my own to clean under them. She used her wet hand to brush away the last of her tears, and squatting there on the riverside, she said to me, "Sarah, I've seen that Bean Nighe, that washerwoman."

"What?" I actually looked up and scanned the far bank of the river.

"She's you, honey. I don't need to keep this from you any longer. I don't know why I've kept it from you. Habit, I suppose. I kept it from Momma for so long. It's silly to be ashamed of dying. I always told her so. It's nothing we can help. It's nothing I can help."

I let her hands go. "I don't understand," I said and stared at her.

"Sarah, I've got that damned old cancer. I've had it for months. That's why I've got all that medicine. That's why I get so tired and can't eat very well. It's in my pancreas and it's spreading to my liver. The medicine they give me helps some but it's starting to be pretty hard to hide. I mean the medicine is becoming ineffectual."

"We need to get you home," I said. "Why are we here? You should be in a hospital having treatment."

"Sarah, slow down. They gave me the option of chemotherapy and radiation and a life span of four or five months, or none of that and a life span of three months. The second option gives me the time and health to do this. It's the same cancer that Michael Landon had and if he couldn't beat it with all his money, I won't either. I didn't want to spend my last four months in hospitals. I didn't want to lose my hair." She actually smiled at me. "When I get really bad toward the end, you can put me in the hospital so I won't be such a handful for you and James."

"James," I said, but couldn't say anything else, my throat tight and hard.

"He doesn't know either," she answered.

"But you were going to get married."

"I still hope to. If he'll have me after I've told him about this. If I can bear to tell him. He'll just say my name three times and that won't work."

"I'm such an idiot," I said.

"No, you're not. I was good at hiding it, but I know I couldn't get away with it forever. I'm tired of hiding it. I might need your help to walk back to the car."

"I thought you were just getting curmudgeonly like Grandma did when she got old. You weren't going to a tanning parlor back home then?"

"No, honey, I was going to see my doctor."

"Are you in pain all the time?"

"Yes."

Well, I lost it then, rocked back on my haunches into the smooth wet stones of the riverbank, covered my eyes and just wept. Aunt Edna put her hand on my upraised knee and gently swayed my leg back and forth, as if she were rocking a cradle.

□ □ □

We made our staggering way out of Glencoe under the indifferent gaze of the Three Sisters, Buchaille Etive Mor, Buchaille Etive Beag, and Bidean nam Bian: mountains ravaged by wind and water and hoof and the sheer weight of time, whose vertical rocky faces belied their irreversible slouch toward level. The River Coe ceaselessly carried the Three Sisters to the sea. The death of this landscape was inevitable. Yet the scale of time made me look over my shoulder at the rocks above me and feel belittled, and somehow I thought the mountains less than indifferent, only haughty. "We were here when your great-great-grandparents were born and died, we'll be here when the woman on your arm dies, and we'll be here long after you die." I suppose I should have been comforted by the resilience of the landscape, especially now that my grandparents were part of it, but I was only sullen.

We paused and rested twice on the way back uphill to the car, stood in the wet grass breathing heavily while the water worked up between our toes, already trying to carry us away to the sea.

Aunt Edna said, "It's strange. My body was always a comfortable place to live. Lately, it's not. I feel like I've moved away from home. It's bad light in this valley, isn't it, Sarah? Things are darker than they should be. You wouldn't want to paint in this light. The main thing I regret is you'll treat me differently now. You won't argue with me."

My answer for a time was silence. We drove back to the hotel. I was simply stunned and unable to formulate any sentence that wouldn't make me cry. Aunt Edna immediately seemed frail, withered. Her weight loss wasn't a preparation for a wedding dress but only a complete lack of hunger. In dieting with her I'd been competing with cancer. The whites of her eyes now seemed faintly amber. Her uneasy stomach was a gaseous trumpeting of death's imminent arrival.

She answered questions I couldn't articulate. From time to time, as I drove, she'd look to me and speak as if in response, although I'd never spoken a word. "I didn't tell James because I didn't want him to love me out of pity.

"I didn't tell you or my friends at work because I didn't want the last few months of my life to be an unremitting wake.

"I didn't tell Momma because I knew it would hurt her too much."

This last I had a response to. I pulled into the little gravel lot at the Isles of Glencoe. Aunt Edna put the car in park. Still I couldn't help my eyes from brimming with tears. "In a way, she was lucky that she died before you had to tell her."

"I know," she answered. "I've thought about that, too. She died a couple of months after I found out. I was so relieved that she wouldn't have to watch me die, too. She'd been watching herself die for so long. It would have killed her to know I was dying."

Repeatedly that evening I asked if she was sure she didn't want to turn back and go home, forego the final distribution of the ashes. We could leave the rest here in Glencoe, I suggested. Or I could bring the remainder back later, on my own, take them to Plockton as we'd planned. But she was adamant.

"It's only another day, Sarah," she said. "The one thing that makes me feel good is carrying out Momma's wishes."

"But we don't know if they are her wishes. Not really. It was just three crimped corners in a book."

"But we made a plan and I want to stick to it. Maybe our plan is just as important as her wishes. Maybe our plan is her wish."

That night, after showering and donning dry clothes, after dinner in the hotel restaurant, I made Aunt Edna lay out her medicine on the bed and explain the purpose and dosage of each. I made her define pancreatic cancer, the progression of the illness. I made her tell me why radical treatment wasn't a viable option. I tried to be as organized as I could, taking notes in my sketch pad.

"That's an awful waste of a good sheet of drawing paper," she told me.

"How am I ever going to draw again," I said listlessly.

"Well, I hope you won't stop, just because I'll have to."

"My hand is trembling now. And there's nothing but field mice and evergreens and elves in my hand anyway. I draw a window and it looks like an elf's window."

"I wish I could make you happy before I go," she said. "You have to learn to believe what you see."

I slept in her bed that night, my hand covering hers.

◻ ◻ ◻

When we'd driven west into Glencoe the planet seemed to have dropped out from underneath the landscape. Between the ever-protruding rock, the forage, tough and fibrous, seemed as if it could only serve primordial beasts. The light took too long to come, and the dark arrived earlier than it should. I look back at that passage now as a trial. We had to suffer Glencoe to be worthy of the rest of the Highlands. For beyond Glencoe the mountains spread out, had room to squander on slope and field and planted forest. There was distance.

We got an early start and were driving along the eastern shore of Loch Linnhe in shadow as the sun struck the far shore. A steel trawler and a tug with barge worked against the tide bound for Fort William. Aunt Edna kept making me stop the car so she could snap a picture out the open window.

"I wish I could show these to James," she said. "It's the kind of light that allowed the world to be born. It's the kind of light that almost makes a chair invisible, because every rung and stile reflects with such intensity. If it weren't for the faint shadow beyond, you wouldn't know there was a chair."

I stopped for gas at Fort William. It was the biggest town we'd come to in 150 miles. I didn't know if these weren't the last gas stations we'd see in the Highlands. The map empties out beyond. Ben Nevis towered behind the town, bald and windswept and wearing a halo of sun-broached mist. Aunt Edna got out of the car and stood by me, leaned against me, as I pumped the gas.

"Close your eyes," she said.

"Why?"

"You've got to learn to see out of someone else's eyes."

"Why?"

"So we can tell James about this."

I closed my eyes and leaned against her. I could hear cars gearing down as they approached a nearby traffic circle. There were fumes from the gas nozzle and beyond this, fumes of coal smoke. Two men were talking at another pump. Their voices cut in and out as cars shushed by so that their conversation seemed to take intuitive leaps. The nozzle was cool and solid in my hand, Aunt Edna's shoulder warm and soft.

"What does the air taste like to you?" she asked.

"I think this is the wrong place to be tasting the air."

"It tastes man-made, doesn't it?"

"Yes."

"We'll try again later."

"Can I open my eyes now?"

"What if I said no? What if you weren't allowed to open them again, forever?"

I opened them anyway and looked at her. She was already looking at me. I said, "James is so happy right now. He doesn't know you're going to leave him."

"I'm going to go inside and buy something I've never bought before."

"What?"

"I don't know. I haven't seen it yet."

I topped off the tank. Wow, it was expensive. It's lucky things are so close together in Scotland. Aunt Edna bought a bag of Maltesers and was upset when she opened it to find they were only malted milk balls, something she had back home.

"Here, you eat them," she said.

"Aunt Edna, was our mutual supportive diet only a ruse to cover your weight loss?"

"For the most part, but you really do need to lose some weight. But here, have these, you're on vacation."

I threw them over my shoulder into the backseat.

"That's my girl," she said.

"You're infuriating," I said.

Beyond Spean Bridge we passed a stone pen crowded with Highland cattle. Their eyes were concealed behind long russet locks. Short, broad, mud-frocked, they seemed as unperturbed by passing cars as the thousands of sheep we'd passed, to whom we were nothing more than wind in the trees. We saw a sign that read "Concealed Church Access Ahead" and Aunt Edna remarked, "Oooo, I like the idea of that. It's like they're going to jump out and get ya."

We crossed the Caledonian Canal, and although Loch Ness, only seven miles away, was a strong draw, Aunt Edna said, "We don't have time," rather matter-of-factly, and we turned west at Invergarry toward the coast and Plockton.

The drive up from the great glacial rift that contains Loch Ness and Loch Lochy, nearly splitting off all of northwest Scotland, to Loch Duich and Plockton, all fifty miles of it, is perhaps the most beautiful I've ever taken. Loch Garry and Loch Loyne were like lakes of fog seen from above. The road from there is stream-chased. By the time we reached Glen Shiel the jeweled density of the landscape wouldn't allow me to drive more than a few miles per hour. Even Aunt Edna commented, saying if we'd been able, we should have walked. Perhaps it was the sun behind us that made us feel we'd escaped from Glencoe. Everything before us was lit, each blade of grass and hummock of heather distinct. Color never seemed less remote. There seemed countless shades of green and russet and purple.

"You could place a chair out there and not even notice it," Aunt Edna said.

We rounded a curve near the bottom of Glen Shiel and found a ram leading us down the road. His wool trailed along the blacktop. Entangled in his coat were three tree branches fully six feet long. Bracken rode his back and leaves were woven into his cheeks and flanks. He was a walking thicket, animal made vegetable. He swept the road on all sides and behind and seemed bent on staying in its middle, the only trail he'd found that allowed him unfettered passage.

"We should help him," Aunt Edna said.

"It looks like he's going home to me," I said. "We'd need shears and a saw to free him anyway."

"His past made visible," Aunt Edna sighed. "All those things you regret dragging along behind you, catching on other things as you pass by. But very little has happened to me that I didn't choose. Everything I wear I bought."

"Well, you're a lucky woman, then," I said. And immediately felt guilty for it.

But she said, "I feel that way, too. Up till now I've always been very healthy. I wouldn't have wanted to linger through old age the way Momma did, trapped in her bed, her body always tired and ill-fitting."

We crept around the ram slowly and flashed our lights at other cars coming up the valley. Loch Duich ate up what was left of Glen Shiel and lay in the grass sated and still. We skirted the lake's flanks in the same way that I avoided conversation. Everything I thought to say or remark upon seemed to hold larger meaning, seemed obtrusive, sure to wake the swollen silences.

I hadn't slept much the night before. I'd lain awake listening to Aunt Edna's sleeping, which she seemed to come to with some relief now that she'd made her confession. She wasn't carrying the burden of dying alone anymore.

We both broke our silence when we came upon Eilean Donan with gasps of pleasure. The castle, ancestral home of the MacRaes, perched upon an outcropping of rock off the shore of Loch Duich and was connected to the mainland by a stone bridge. We pulled into the visitor parking lot, sat in the car, and gaped.

"I'm glad I have seen that," Aunt Edna said.

I looked at her and smiled. The castle, the color of seaweed and seagull nest, rose from the lonely rock itself. The arched bridge leading to the island became rock wall and graveled path, which, in turn, became turret and keep and slate roof and chimneys of stone. I imagined that even the carpets and furniture inside were sculpted from island stuff, mussel shell, and seal bone. I opened the guidebook.

"It's been here since the thirteenth century," I told Aunt Edna. "Do you want to go in?"

"No, it's enough to see it from here. It looks like there'd be a lot of stairs in there to me."

"I'll bet there's some old chairs in there."

"I'll never paint all the chairs I've got in my head already. Let's go on to Plockton. I want to get things settled."

I reached over the seat and brought back *Scotland from Above* and placed it in her lap. "It's not far now."

As the road looped and tucked into the Highlands, BBC 3 would go out and swing back in with music, then dissolve to static again around the next curve.

"The sheep trails in the grass," Aunt Edna said, pointing at their criss-crossed intricacy.

"Yes?"

"They're like crosshatching in early Italian drawings. They're mesmerizing. Do you think they've been there for hundreds of years or do they change every season?"

"I don't know," I answered.

"It would be something to stay here long enough to know that. Maybe you'll come back some day."

We turned off the A87 at Balmacara, taking the smallest road we'd been on yet. I didn't have to chant my mantra because the road was only wide enough for one car. Occasionally small gravel or pavement turnouts, signposted "Passing Place," gave one the opportunity to duck out of the way of a speeding truck. The road was bordered by rock walls on both sides, emphasizing direction. I felt as if we were in a log chute to Plockton. Cresting the high point of this five-mile-wide peninsula, we could see the ocean beyond to Raasay and the Isle of Skye. Tiny boats gusseted the sea in the distance: oil tankers. The road itself was bent through a landscape rent by bulldozers or some lasting primeval frost heave. Down through Duirinish, we fell into Plockton from a high ridge as if dropped there by a bird. I drove slowly into town, my foot on the brake. We passed a school yard ringing with children's voices, dozens of voices raised in thrill.

"Oh, oh, oh," Aunt Edna yelped. "I've missed that. Wait here for a moment." I stopped the car, she rolled down her window, and we listened. "It sounds the same doesn't it, even though we're in another country, thousands of miles away. Do you remember the sound, Sarah?"

"Yes," I said. We couldn't see the children. They were beyond a wall, behind the school, in some sort of wild game of running and shouting.

"Our windows in the cafeteria are high, but they're always open. During recess we would turn down the radio and listen to just this. It's so invigorating. A few minutes later they'd all come in for lunch, winded and rosy-cheeked, their knees green, so hungry. I hope our hotel is close to here."

"It should be," I said. "It's a tiny place."

I let the car roll on. We passed a couple of craft shops. At the bottom of the hill was the ocean. A single row of stone houses rimmed the harbor, only the lane and a stone wall between them and the sea. A steep hill rose behind. Across the water were forests and an escarpment of the Highlands. There were a couple of small islands before us, one fairly close by. As we walked along the stone houses and shops, some whitewashed, the Plockton Hotel painted black, I watched Aunt Edna eye the islands. They occupied the center of the photo in *Scotland from Above*. Between the lane and the water there were occasional gardens, built up with their own sea walls. In several grew a variety of hardy palm tree, incongruous against the stark hills across the harbor. Waves met the stone below us like the rustling of feet in another room, as if someone were on their way to find us. The doors and window trim on the stone houses were brightly painted, usually red but sometimes blue or green, small strokes of color against a stark white and roughly textured exterior. There were small sailboats in the harbor, riding to moorings, their masts seeking camouflage in the trees on the far shore. We looked for our bed and breakfast and found it in a small white house beyond Plockton Shops, An Caladh. While Aunt Edna waited, I walked back and moved the car. We were shown to our upstairs room, which coveted a tiny window facing the bay. The window was in a dormer, so only one of us could look out at a time. On the little table between our beds was a card announcing our host could speak Gaelic if the need arose. This seemed exotic, not to mention handy.

"What a strange and wonderful place this is," I said. It seemed so trim against the unmanageable sea.

Aunt Edna was at the window, blocking the light. "Do you think we could get someone to row us out to that little island?"

"Is that where you want to put the ashes?"

"Yes."

"There's lots of boats here. Maybe we could hire someone. If not, we'll swim."

"Oh, Sarah. I'll bet that water's ice cold."

"Let's go test it."

"I'm not swimming to that island."

"It's only a joke. We'll find a boat. We'll go down to that little shop on the corner. The one where we were parked. They'll know some-body with a boat."

So we did that, walked down to Mackenzie's and bought a *Scots-man*, two postcards, and asked a white-haired gentleman about hiring a boat to the island.

"This one here?" he asked. "Just off the harbor wall?"

"Yes," I answered.

"Well, there's no need to hire a boat. If you've time to wait a couple of hours, the tide will be out and you can walk there."

"All that water will be gone?" I asked, incredulous.

"You're from very far away, deep in the heart of America, aren't you?" he said

"Yes. Missouri," I said.

"Texas," Aunt Edna said, not wanting to be lumped in with Mis-souri.

"We have a terrific tide here. If you'll wait to the low you won't wet the bottoms of your shoes. It's only an island for half a day at a time. I've always wanted to see the Alamo, myself."

His hair was remarkably unruly for being so short and white. His pink face seemed perpetually caught between expressions. But with the word "Alamo" it hung onto a grave smile. "Our Culloden is your Alamo," he told Aunt Edna, "except that in your case, the cause was finally won." And then he did a remarkable thing. He put his hands flat on the counter and sang, "The stars at night are big and bright," and here he raised his hands and clapped four beats, then resumed, "Deep in the heart of Texas." Aunt Edna and I were stunned. "I worked in a uniform factory during the war, mostly women there, and we'd sing to pass the monotonous time. That was one of our favorites. Yet we were made to stop singing that particular tune because the clapping slowed production so."

Aunt Edna and I stood there in the tiny shop, smiling and wavering slightly.

"Well, I see you've had a surprise. Go on about your business. Don't spend more than an hour or so on the island or you'll be trapped till the next tide." There were two other white-haired pink men in the shop. They nodded. I wondered if all three of them worked in that tiny room.

Before we left, Aunt Edna bought an ice cream. We stood at the sea wall and looked at the water between us and the little treeless island a hundred feet or so away. Aunt Edna licked the melted ice cream from her fingertips and said, "That's the best thing I've had in days."

"Better than Sticky Toffee Pudding?"

"I think so. Let's go get the boxes."

"Aunt Edna, we'd be standing here for hours with the ashes. That's a lot of water to move. It's going to be awhile before we can walk out there. I can still hardly believe it will happen."

"Then I want to go back to the room and work. I feel good today. I have a chair in my mind that I've never seen before."

"Let's stop for a ploughman's lunch at the Plockton Hotel."

"I just had an ice cream."

"Well, I didn't. I'm hungry."

"Well, I don't have time for two lunches. You stop and I'll go on back to the room."

"An ice cream isn't a good lunch."

"You're confusing me with your daughters."

"What?"

"You're not the boss of me."

"I'm just saying you should eat to sustain yourself."

"I'd rather eat to enjoy myself. I might take up smoking, too. It doesn't matter now, Sarah. Don't worry about me."

"How can I not worry about you?"

"I'm going to die soon. There's nothing you can do about it. There's no sense in worrying."

"You're impossible," I huffed.

"I'm glad you're arguing with me, though. Have your lunch. I'll be in the room."

"I'll be there as soon as I'm done."

"Don't hurry. I never feel lonely as long as I've got a pencil and a piece of paper."

□ □ □

I sat at a table just inside the door, near a window with a view of the harbor. I watched the tide between bites as if I were on stakeout and the ocean was my main suspect. There was a phone near the bar. I could call anyone in the world, release myself from the burden of sole knowledge, as Aunt Edna had released herself by telling me. But I knew this was her story to tell. There was James to be informed, my father and Aunt Margaret, Sam, my kids. We'd all gather again in the vacant lot next to the house, the same group of mourners in the same mourning chairs. If James still wanted to marry her, would accept being made a husband and widower again, then perhaps they'd have a month together, a sorry bedridden month of medicine and body aches and hospitals. As I turned my gaze from the ocean to the phone and back again, I realized I'd become involved in a tragedy that couldn't be avoided. I felt I had to get hold of myself, to be as calm as possible for Aunt Edna, since that seemed to be what she wanted. It was amazing to me, at this late date in her illness, this close to the end of her life, that a pencil could overcome her loneliness.

The waitress approached with another small pot of tea and placed it on my table without a word, even though she could plainly see me sniffling. I thought that if I ever left Sam I'd have Aunt Edna to visit occasionally, a home to return to in Texas. I'd lost that option. The tide was receding. It would be a much closer swim to America now, wouldn't it? Or no, the tide would be high there when it was low here I supposed, the distance between the continents just the same.

"Was your lunch all right then?"

The waitress was there again, a box of tissues in her hand. She held it close by and moved closer in offering it, so the other patrons in the pub wouldn't see.

"Oh, thank you," I said, and wiped my eyes. She was my age, her hair was short and combed back over large ears from which suspended pearls. Her sleeves were pushed back on her forearms, and there was a line of water across her blouse where she'd leaned against a wet counter. "It was a delicious lunch," I said.

"It's hard to foul bread and cheese," she shrugged. "It's a lovely day, isn't it?"

I looked out the window again. "Yes, it is."

Then she bent lower. "Crying's a lovely thing, isn't it? I had a good boo-hoo this morning myself. My daughter wasn't accepted to the school we were all hoping for. A silly thing to cry over but I felt better after. I think it's an evolutionary ingredient, crying. It helps you survive. I think the fittest are those who cry. Have you had enough or will there be something else?" This last question, I surmised, was about food. "You didn't like it at all, did you, dear. Not a crumb left on the plate." She smiled.

"I like to eat," I said.

"Another evolutionary ingredient," she affirmed, this sympathetic Darwinist, and she was off.

□ □ □

Aunt Edna had her sketchbook in her lap, its upper edge propped against the windowsill. She sat on her upturned suitcase.

"The water's leaving," she said.

"I know. What are you working on?" She leaned back so I could see. An immense ladder-back, only its upper slat and finials visible, was cresting the escarpment on the far side of the bay. I raised one eyebrow, lowered the other. To tell you that I was only interested in technique, the weave of her pencil strokes that made shimmering water, is my only excuse. I did not ask why the big chair was peeking over the mountain, or about to surmount it, or whatever. Perhaps it is simply a mountain and harbor superimposed over a chair. Aunt Edna was rarely responsive to questions about the ideas behind her paintings but would talk openly about color and texture and light and any of a thousand other things to do with the moment of work. What brought her to that moment wasn't something she felt comfortable communicating. I'm not comfortable with it either. My best advice is to visit the museum, look through the catalog. Almost all of us have found her paintings and drawings increasingly elusive. The more we try to define them the more they slip away. Perhaps someday someone will bring an understanding, some peace to the discord. For now they're only beautiful. As Mr. Coates has said, after viewing the first exhibition every day for a month, he still found them enormously tantalizing. I confess I did not see all of this at the time. I do now. She was my curious aunt. Many of us have a relative who fashions canes from sticks, or collects driftwood for collages, or writes poetry. It's easy and common to dismiss them as intelligent, lovable eccentrics. I respected her knowledge of technique and wanted to learn from her, but to me her canvases weren't originals or masterpieces, they were Aunt Edna's. I can't be trusted to spot genius. Listen, people weren't snapping up van Goghs while he was alive, either.

The day was too beautiful to stay indoors. I picked up my own sketch pad and left Aunt Edna to her work. I hadn't been beyond our bed and breakfast and so took a hard left outside the door. Plockton sat upon a small peninsula jutting into Loch Carron. I wanted to stand at the peninsula's very tip, go as far as I could go and be completely surrounded by water. I'd rarely been anyplace where my only choice was to turn around and go back. The row of houses along the harbor made a lazy reversed S curve inland. I followed the road across the neck of a low point of land occupied by many houses and came upon a finger of water that had cut into the rock. There were four sailboats there, hard aground, perched on their keels, lines leading off their bows to shore, and off their sterns to anchors in the mud and seaweed. It was almost a surreal vision, these boats seemingly tied off quite unnecessarily. The tide had receded enough that I could make my way along the uninhabited northern shore. I crossed a narrow patch of grass, ducked under a black sailboat and its web of tethers. It seemed more like a barrage balloon than a boat. There was brush above me and trees on the hill beyond. I stayed near the high-tide mark, the whiter stone, because the rocks below were slippery with a black gloss of growth and dark tendrils of weed. I was doing not bad work for a fat lady, picking my way, climbing over big rocks that had fallen from low cliffs, my gaze intent upon each footfall. It was something new for me, scrambling over a seashore. The intertidal zone was as pungent as orange peel but muckier, of course, as if things were born and died there every hour, a slosh of corpse and afterbirth and ongoing sex. I hiked for perhaps fifteen or twenty minutes and found myself where I wanted to be. You are from that place to which you're bound, I reminded myself. There was a rock that seemed sculpted for my butt and so I put it there and placed my sketch pad upon the easel of my knees. I could see a great way up Loch Carron to the west. Kishorn Island and the mountains of Applecross were to the north. There was water before me and all around. Current poured around the tip of the peninsula, bound for the open sea. I breathed deeply, short of breath, full of pleasure. Aunt Edna was right. I needed to lose weight to travel lighter. I needed to do it for me. Still, I knew the next time I was near Sticky Toffee Pudding that I'd feel the eating of it was for me, too. I liked this new view of landscape. I'd become enamored of movement. Even if it was only a few feet left or right. Traveling, being bound, made the pauses more poignant. I realized I'd only have this view for a short time and then I'd be gone. Just as Aunt Edna realized she had only bare moments to draw Plockton Harbor and the chair of her mind. I capped the eraser on the tip of my pencil with a tiny worn seashell and with this un- accustomed balance used a lighter, finer line to draw the far shore. There was a narrow white band at the foot of the hills where they entered the water and this white band was all that separated moun- tains and the reflection of mountains. The only difference in the two scenes, beyond their orientation, was that wind worked on one and not the other and so I worked chiefly on a semblance of wind, trying to make my pencil not represent but imitate wind. I worked here for at least an hour, I believe, because at some moment I looked up and there were thirty more feet of foreshore. When I got back around to the boats a man was there looking at his hull.

"Is the tide all the way out now?" I asked him.

He turned around, looked at the water, and said, "It'll be another hour before the turn."

So back on the lane I turned up a trail behind the row of houses lining the harbor. The backyards climbed steeply to the path I walked and were the complete opposite of the trim face of the lane. The grass was uncut, brush abounded, garbage cans and compost heaps over-flowed. The backsides of many of the houses needed repointing and paint. Curtains didn't match. It was vaguely unsettling.

The path led back down to the school, but recess must have been over. The street was quiet. At Mackenzie's I could see that our way to the island was almost clear. Only a narrow sluice of water worked the gravel on the near shore. I started back up the lane toward An Caladh but met Aunt Edna halfway there. She carried the two painted American cippi, which are now exhibited in the Coates Museum.

"Where have you been?" she asked, clearly upset.

"Just walking. We've got plenty of time."

"I didn't know where you were. I looked up and realized you hadn't been with me for hours. And then the island almost wasn't an island. You shouldn't leave me alone for so long. We're in a foreign country. I almost had to do this by myself."

"OK, Aunt Edna," I said. "OK, I'm here now. What happened to never being alone when you had your pencil and paper?"

"I was done with it and then I thought about everything and it wasn't the pleasant thought I sometimes have and, I don't know, I was just afraid for a while and you weren't there."

"I'm sorry," I said, and I took one of the boxes from her. "I'm sorry. I should have thought."

"We want to get on the island as soon as we can so we aren't stranded."

This was absurd. The island was only a few hundred feet from where we were presently standing. She was worked up. I walked her down to the small concrete boat landing directly across from the island. There was still a narrow slick of water blocking access.

"Just sit down here. I want to take my sketch pad back to the room and get my other shoes. I won't be five minutes."

"Hurry," was her only response.

"The tide works gradually," I told her. "It's not like someone slam-ming a door. We could have a picnic out there and still be off with time to spare."

"If you're not back in four and a half minutes, I'll do it without you."

"Aunt Edna?"

"I have to get this done before I die."

"All right," I said. "I'll be right back."

I returned in my wet sneakers, still inundated with the River Coe. I also had a hand towel stuffed in the back pocket of my jeans. If she was going to use her hands again I wanted to be prepared. I took Grandpa's box under my arm and held Aunt Edna's free hand. The beach was alternately stony, weed-covered, and muddy, but generally firm. There were a few shallow tidal pools that we avoided as if Nessie might be living in them. The island was merely a low outcropping of rock covered with a few inches of soil, enough to support grass that looked as if it should be growing on a golfing green, and a thick mix of short shrubbery. There were rabbitlike trails, feather litter and mussel wreck, an occasional pale cigarette butt, and the dense odor of all this soil stuff and its fertilizer, the dreck of seagulls.

We found a patch of grass that seemed grazed and here Aunt Edna spread the last of the ashes. She used her hands. I held the boxes open and she took from them alternately. Her eyes rimmed red and she looked at me and said, "I hate to let her go," and, "This is the last of her." She bent down on her knees and cast the final cloud of dust beneath a shrub yellow in flower. Her face fell to her knees and she cried softly and so I bent down, too, laid my palm flat on her back and looked out across the low foliage at the harbor and the hills beyond. I looked into the windows of the houses lining the harbor to see if we were being watched.

"We've brought them to the center of a beautiful place," I whispered. "They're the stuff that islands are made of and we'll always remember them."

"I hate to let her go," was all she could say.

We crouched there for a long while, as if we were trying to hide.

"Do you want to stand up now?" I asked after she seemed to settle some. "We can walk to the far side of the island and wash your hands. There's still some ocean there. I brought a towel to dry your hands."

She didn't respond and so I bent lower, both of our faces near the grass, and I saw then that she could not speak because her fingers were in her mouth. Tears coursed over them.

"Oh, Aunt Edna," I shushed. My first response was to treat her as one of my children, to yank her hand from her mouth and brush away the dirt from her lips with my thumb, but instead I let my own face float gently down into the short grass where I lay and watched the tears run off her face onto her gray hands and leave pale trails of flesh there. Finally, I murmured, "That's OK, that's OK," and I reached over and grasped her hand firmly and took it from her mouth and she let me do this. "Let's go to the water now," I said.

We washed her hands in a tidal pool that was somewhat warmed by the sun. I dried her hands with the towel and used that salty dampness to wipe her face, the dark creases in her lips. She walked with her head down, my arm over her shoulders, back to the room. I put her to bed late in the afternoon. For some time I watched her sleep.

□ □ □

We never spoke of the events on that little island in Plockton Harbor. To this day I don't know the island's name or even if it has a name. All I can say is that Aunt Edna woke refreshed, rejuvenated, relieved.

"I feel much better now," she said, sitting up on the edge of the bed. "My responsibilities are almost over. The rest of my life is for me, Sarah. I'm so happy we've done all we could do for Momma. I'll only miss her for a month or two more, and hopefully I'll have James to help me through that time. You and James. But if I died tomorrow I'd feel like I've done my life's work. I think it's a rare thing for a person to feel content, don't you? And I do. I'm a lucky person."

"You're a lucky person," I agreed. "Because I'm not content right now."

"What are you?"

"I'm hungry."

"Then let's go eat. But you should fix your hair first," she said. "You look a mess."

For our final evening in the Highlands we ate roast Angus beef, boiled potatoes, creamed turnips, and a tomato stuffed with skirlie: something oatey, salty, strong, and delicious. I preferred not to know more, so never asked the waiter.

"If we were to ever eat here again," Aunt Edna said, "I would try the chicken stuffed with haggis or maybe the salmon."

"There's no Sticky Toffee Pudding on the menu," I said sadly.

"We'll have one last night in Edinburgh. You can have it again there.

And you can come back one day. I want you to come back to see how things are, how they've changed. You seem to like this traveling."

"I didn't know that I would, but I do." I wanted to talk to her about traveling, but it seemed odd, contemplating things I'd do when she was gone. I suppose I didn't believe her when she said she wasn't resigned, but content. To this day I am still an unbeliever.

In the pocket of her jacket, Aunt Edna found a small sable brush, and throughout dinner she repeatedly dipped it in her water glass and drew invisible chairs upon her absorbent napkin. She'd tilt her head as if there were actually something to be seen there in the tight wet weave of the cloth. Finally, unable to stand it any longer, I asked, "What is it?"

"It's the only important thing, the work itself. I want you to stop worrying about what your pictures look like for now. You should just enjoy holding the brush or pencil in your hand, the time spent."

"I do. I think I do."

"That's the most valuable thing. If you wait for outside approval, for anybody's approval, especially mine, it will be a long time coming, won't it? Especially with me. I'm going to die before I like your paintings. Many other people will, too."

"Thanks," I said, uncertainly.

"So you have to like the moment of working or your work will be valueless. I know I would have liked your work, someday, if I'd had the chance."

"Thank you," I said, quite honestly. "But you could have just lied and told me you like it now."

"I've never lied to you. I've kept things from you, it's true, and I regret it. If I told you I liked it now, your work, you'd have nothing to look forward to. Someday, you'll be in the middle of a painting and you'll know, Aunt Edna would have liked this."

"Ever since I found out about Sam I feel the whole world isn't worth trusting. I look at everything suspiciously, and since you've told me about the cancer I'm even worse. I feel like nothing is stable. I hear those schoolchildren screech with pleasure and I know they're going to die. The last thing I want to do is love someone else because I know they're untrustworthy, too. I've turned into a cynic and I hate cynics worse than I hate liars."

"It seems so odd to hear you say those things, when I know I'll miss everything, even liars and cynics. I already miss them. Cynics seem so adorable right now."

"I thought you were content?"

"I'm content to miss them."

It was almost ten-thirty by the time we left the Plockton Hotel. The island of the harbor lay dark and surrounded by water. A two-car train rushed along the far shore, incongruous in shape and sound and light with the black hills beyond. The engine began to strain as it took on the grade.

"We could have come here by train," I said.

"Maybe next time."

□ □ □

That night, lying in bed, I worked up my courage and asked, "Aunt Edna, are you awake?"

"Yes, honey."

"What would you have done with your life?"

"Oh, I would have taken care of Momma just as I did."

"No, I mean what would you have done if you could have lived another twenty years?"

"Yes, I would have taken care of Momma until she passed away."

"You don't understand."

"Yes I do. I know if I'd lived longer she would have, too, and I would have cared for her until she died."

"You think she guessed you were dying?"

"No. I have this one last confidence, Sarah. If I'd lived, she would have, too." I heard her turn onto her side. "When I found out my case was terminal I put Momma to sleep. It would have killed her if I'd died first anyway, an unfamiliar person taking care of her. She never wanted to outlive any of her children, even Margaret, much less me or your daddy. That's all she ever wanted from God: to die before her children. So I made that happen. I mixed some pills in with her other medication over a few days. She was never in pain. And she left in her sleep. I can die now without any remorse. You see, knowing how Momma felt, the only thing I wanted was to go after Momma did. We both got our wishes."

My voice was dry and caught on the stiff edges of words, but still I asked, "She didn't know what you were doing, Aunt Edna?"

"Oh no, I would have had to explain I was terminal, that I only had the few months to live. If I'd explained why I was putting her to sleep it would have done away with all the good of putting her to sleep. She died without any physical or emotional pain, knowing her children were all still reaching on into the future. We don't have to talk about it now. I know you'll have questions and I'll answer all of them. But I hope you'll keep my secret at least for a while. There's only a few weeks or so left. I'll tell the police later on, before I lose the ability to tell them. I promise. Later on comes so quickly. You'll find that out when you get old, when you're about to die. I know we're as far from home as we'll travel. That's why I've waited to tell you."

□ □ □

I have as hard a time writing now as I did speaking the next morning. I'd spent little more than twenty-four hours coming to terms with Aunt Edna's death. Yet her death was natural, beyond human control. She wasn't struck down in an untimely way by a drunk driver, wasn't dying of accidental poisoning or from a gunshot. I'd had a friend who'd died of cancer, another under treatment for breast cancer, and my own grandfather had died of liver cancer. However horrible and unfair it seemed, I could wrap my mind around Aunt Edna's illness and death. She herself was able to cope with it. But my grandmother's death had, apparently, none of these characteristics. It was unnatural in any explanation not involving Aunt Edna's psychology. Grandma was bedridden, arthritic, and had heart disease, as well as a multitude of minor ailments, many of which may have been psychosomatic. But she did not die on the day the four winds suggested. She died on the day Aunt Edna suggested. Whatever the circumstances, however we feel about the viability of my aunt's concern and reasoning and her mental health at the time, foregoing all the current apologists, it stands that she did not euthanize her mother, but murdered her.

The next morning, after I'd lain awake most of the night rearranging my view of the world and left it in a jumble, we sat down to a very organized full breakfast: eggs, bacon, sausage, tomato, cereal, juice, tea, toast, and a bit of smoked fish, not to mention the attendant butter, jam, sugar, and cream. Aunt Edna ate as heartily as I'd seen her in weeks. We sat at a large round table with the only other guests, an elderly couple from Australia. In the way that all outside events tend to relate to one's own problems, the aged gentleman proved to be a retired police officer. He'd served in England during World War II as a training officer for military policemen and had brought his wife back to Britain for a two-month holiday to see all his old haunts. He still had the air of a swashbuckling officer, a ready wit, white handlebar mustache, and was quite unperturbed and too well-mannered to allow two silent women to destroy a conversation. He was able to speak continually without ever losing contact with his breakfast, in a consummately choreographed engagement of knife, fork, and tongue. He related several incidents where baton prowess and physical strength determined the outcome of struggles with gigantic sergeants and drunken privates. Aunt Edna and I hadn't said a word to each other, much less to this man. At the high point of another completely surmountable conflict between military police and ration rioters, I held my hand up and asked Aunt Edna openly, "How did you kill Grandma?"

She looked first at the stunned and suddenly silent couple and then turned to me quite calmly and said, "Muscle relaxers. Twenty-two pills over three days."

I turned back to the policeman. "Go on."

"I know when I'm being made a joke," he said. His wife put her hand on his shoulder and not another word was said among the four of us.

As we packed, I looked out the tiny window. The tide was all the way in again, the island once again an island, what was left of my grandparents inaccessible.

The night before, after we'd returned from dinner, I'd spent a half hour with the map of Britain and quite by accident found Udny Green, the little town Jonathan was from. The town with the mort house. Then, scanning the map further, I came upon a castle called "Hutton-in-the-

Forest." I showed the map to Aunt Edna. I was so excited. "It's our castle," I said. "We should go there and at least buy some tea towels and bookmarks. But that's strange; it's in England, not Scotland."

"We don't have time," Aunt Edna said. "It's too far away."

I was so disappointed. We seemed unprepared, unable to adapt, so short on time. "We'll never know where we came from," I said sadly.

"It doesn't matter," Aunt Edna teased, "we're here now. We know where we came to."

In a sense I still feel that the past is unavailable to us, that we continually arrive without knowing how we got here.

But I knew how we got to Plockton and followed the same route out, the single-lane road over the hill to Balmacara. There I rejoined the A87 and began the long drive back through Glencoe to Edinburgh. Our flight to London left early the next morning. We drove along silently for some time. I was waiting for Aunt Edna to fill things in, just as she had after telling me about the cancer. And sure enough, a few minutes after we'd left Balmacara she spoke.

"Sarah?"

"Yes."

"Honey, I think we're on the wrong side of the road."

There was some indecision at first. Everything was suddenly unfamiliar. Then I swerved back to the left in a tire-squealing snap. I realized I'd been driving on the right, on the wrong side of the road, for at least three miles, around curves and over hills. I'd almost killed us both. Half a minute later we passed an oncoming car. That's how close we'd come to a head-on collision: thirty seconds. I'd come off the single-lane road at Balmacara and joined the main road just as I would have back home in Texas.

"I'm sorry," I said.

"I've got you flustered," Aunt Edna replied. "Do you want me to drive?"

"Not on your life," I said.

"But my mind isn't struggling and yours is. I've had weeks to come to terms with the things I told you about the last couple of days."

"I'm a wreck now, but I'd be a complete wreck if you were driving."

"Well, I don't want to but if you're unable, I will."

"I'm able. I just have to concentrate. Just don't say anything unexpected."

"I don't have anything left."

"Good."

"That breakfast has made me sleepy. If I fall asleep you'll wake me up when we pass through Glencoe. I want to see it one last time."

"Go to sleep. I'll be all right now."

"I trust you, Sarah." And with that she closed her eyes and settled in. She'd sleep a great deal from then on. Although she'd have occasional good days, for the most part the life left to her was a simple and thorough progression to dehydration and death. She grew more weary every day, and often fell asleep in the middle of a spoken sentence, or with her brush suspended in midair. Twice I found her asleep in front of a canvas, the wet brush flowing into her lap or thigh, staining not only her clothing but her very skin.

As I drove along that morning, I never thought, My God, I'm in a car with an insane woman. But I considered everything else. She'd done away with my grandmother for the silver coins. It wasn't Aunt Edna's money but Grandma's. She'd done this thing so she could spend her last weeks with James. Grandma would never have approved of their union. She hated her mother, had hated her for years, and finally had had enough. Yet all of these conclusions, this simpleminded conjecture, seemed empty and groundless and finally untrue.

What would the police do to a confessed murderer who was going to die in a matter of weeks anyway? Convicted killers were put to death in Texas every month, but the process took ten years. Talk about empty threats. But I hated to think they'd lock her up, that she'd spend her last hours in a prison hospital rather than at home. Even at this stage I was mentally preparing for her home care. I looked at her as she slept, wondering if I was strong enough to carry her from a chair to a bed.

I thought, what am I missing now? For weeks I'd mistaken terminal cancer for colds and a dyspeptic stomach and the infirmities of age and grief. For years I'd lost contact with my own husband. And for an entire career I'd accepted congratulations and favor for work I wasn't proud of. I lived in a world in which love was uncompromising.

Following this creed we, my family, sometimes lied to one another and more appallingly, we lied to ourselves.

Aunt Edna didn't stir till we arrived at Glencoe. I parked in the same gravel wayby and touched her shoulder. "We're here," I whispered.

She roused herself, leaned forward, and peered through the windshield. "It's not the same place," she said.

She was right. The valley glistened in the sun like wet paint. The blue sky was reflected in the emerald grass and seemingly in the stone itself. The cataracts of rock seemed altogether scalable, as if they were made to be climbed, were asking to be climbed. There were brightly clad hikers everywhere, sprinkled across the canvas of mountains in flecks of color as if an artist had slapped the stem of her brush against her wrist. The many small burns and ravine-riding freshets didn't seem so much to score the landscape but to gambol in it, as if this were water's favorite place.

"It's just an Eden, isn't it?" I said.

"Rest in peace, lovely Momma," Aunt Edna said, and smiled at me.

I was overcome by a nauseating sense of the macabre. It seemed to me then that time enjoyed birth and death. Time couldn't get enough of it. I said the thing, then, to Aunt Edna that I still regret, even though I think it's true. She told me once never to say anything to Sam that was irreparable. "Like what?" I'd asked her. "Like anything you wouldn't be able to forgive if he said it to you." The thing I said to her in Glencoe: "Grandma had a right to her pain."

She let it go. She shrugged and said, "It's done now, Sarah." She didn't, as she could have, say, "Who would have come to care for her? You? She didn't even like you. Your father or Margaret? She wouldn't have allowed it. She would have lived in grief, grief for her only loving daughter left, and then she would have died a slow, neglected death in a nursing home. I knew her. I loved her. You didn't."

"It's done now, Sarah."

My aunt Edna and her mother were a couple. Sam and I were a couple. When Sam and I had problems I wanted the whole world to know about it. I wanted public bereavement, and Aunt Edna's almost daily input. She carried the responsibility of her relationship alone.

We continued on to Edinburgh and arrived in the early afternoon, taking the same room below Calton Hill. After lunch, Aunt Edna wanted to rest. I packed my backpack with enough water and supplies to last an afternoon in the city. Aunt Edna closed the curtains and lay down. She watched me get ready and asked if she could use my pillow while I was gone.

"How are you feeling?" I asked.

"Will you come back, Sarah?" she answered.

"Of course, I will."

"I'm afraid now."

"Of what?"

"Of everything."

"I just need to take a walk. I'll be back in a few hours."

"OK," she said.

"I thought I'd find an art supply, see what kinds of things they have here."

"Buy lots of cobalt," she said. "You can never have enough cobalt. Maybe they have a different blue. Buy all the blues."

It felt good to be out walking after driving all morning. It was Saturday. Princes Street was crowded with shoppers. I moved through the people as if I'd been doing it for years and crossed the street at the Scott Monument. It was all uphill to Chez Jules. I paused at the door, pretending to read the menu on the wall of the narrow close, while my breathing eased. When I finally calmed down, I stepped inside but found the restaurant empty. A waitress said, "I'm sorry, but we won't open again till five-thirty." She wasn't the Jamaican girl who'd served us before.

"Do you happen to know Jonathan?" I asked. "He eats here often, I think. He's an art professor at the university."

"I'm sorry, I don't, and I'm the only one here at present. Perhaps you could call again when some of the others are here this evening?"

"Thank you," I said and left.

The university itself was plainly marked on my map, only a couple blocks south of High Street on South Bridge. Once there, I stepped into the first door that had a university logo posted. I was in some sort of academic office for foreign students. There was a very young girl, an Indian, at a desk. She was, I realized, probably Susan's age.

"Hi," I said. "I'm looking for an instructor and I only know his first name."

"Yes," she said, "is he in this office?"

"No, he's in the art department. His name is Jonathan."

"I have a directory of everyone connected with the university, but it might be best if you just walked over to the Department of Art." She gave me a photocopied map of the campus and circled the art center. "You'll have much better luck there," she said, her voice a creamy liquid poured from porcelain.

I was at the art center in five minutes. Another student at a front desk. "I'm looking for an art professor. I'm afraid I don't know his last name. It's Jonathan something. He teaches life drawing."

"Yes," he said. "That's Mr. Merritt. I'm afraid he's not scheduled for classes today. I can give you his office number and you can reach him there . . ." He looked at a chart. ". . . between ten and two on Tuesdays and Thursdays."

"I need to talk to him today. My flight home leaves tomorrow morning."

"Home phones aren't published in the university directory, but he may be listed in the city directory." He opened a phone book, wrote out a number. "You can use ours if you'd like." He pointed to a phone on the next desk. This opportunity approached more suddenly than I'd expected. I walked slowly to the desk and took off my backpack. I rang the number with, as you'd expect, some trepidation. Jonathan answered on the third ring.

"Yes?"

"Hi. This is Sarah Warren. I met you at Chez Jules a few nights ago. I was with my aunt. You looked at her sketchbook."

"Oh, yes, yes, I remember."

"I just wanted to thank you for being so kind. My aunt was very appreciative of the things you said."

"Well, she's quite good. There was nothing to it, really. We all have to approach art with some goodwill, don't we?"

"I was wondering, Jonathan, if I could come by and speak to you."

"How did you find me, Sarah?"

"Well, I'm standing in the arts office at the university just now." And here I did the thing that I'm ashamed of now and that I was ashamed of before I did it. I traded on my aunt Edna's cancer. I said,

"Jonathan, my aunt is dying. This will be her last vacation. If I could just have a few minutes of your time. You seemed so kind."

"Yes, but I don't know what I could do for . . ."

"Oh, I'm not calling for help of any financial sort, and I don't want you to see her or anything. I'd just like to drop by for a few minutes to talk about her work, what I'm to do with it once she's gone."

"Of course," he said. "I'd be glad to help."

He gave me the address: the Pollock Halls of Residence, off Dalkeith Road. I took a taxi there.

His flat wasn't much larger than a dorm room. He supplemented his pay by overseeing a group of students. The residences were post-war construction, low and remarkably plain beneath Arthur's Seat. The aluminum-framed windows were without mullions and made his flat seem vulnerable to the sky and weather. He took my light sweater and asked if I'd like a cup of tea.

"Yes, thank you." While he filled the teapot and set it to heat, I walked around the small living area. There was a bath and bedroom through a heavy gray door. The kitchen faced the living room, which was hung with a half dozen of his own drawings and paintings, all nudes, male and female.

"These are wonderful," I said.

"Oh, thank you," he said. "Wonderful and unsalable. My flat is always decorated with the rejects of the latest exhibition."

"I can't believe that these are rejects. They're lovely. I do want to thank you for being so kind to us the other evening. It was nice to get to know a real citizen, I mean other than our bed and breakfast hosts or a waitress."

"Believe me, Sarah, I'm the one who's grateful. Americans are so open to conversation of that sort. They don't seem to need to live in your village for twenty years before they say hello. And besides, it was nice to speak with adults. I'm with children most of the day."

"Children?"

"Students. And they're all living in that world of 'tell me who I am and tell me quick.' Please sit down."

I took a dull green armchair near the glass end of the concrete-block room. There was a blanket draped over the back of the chair, not one of Ingres's oriental throws or even a white linen sheet, but an expanse of blue microfleece. It was incredibly soft and sensual for plastic.

"I'm sorry to hear this thing about your aunt."

"She has pancreatic cancer, and perhaps only a month or two left."

"It's such a shame. Her hand is so facile. Lovely lines and that ability to create texture with a minimum of strokes. It's almost impossible to teach. I really was amazed to find it in her sketchbook. Is there a large body of work? How long has she been drawing?"

"Yes. Her house is full of paintings and drawings. The attic is stacked with canvases. I haven't even begun to go through them. She's been at it for at least thirty years."

"Not an artist when she was young?"

"Not that I know of."

The water began to whistle and Jonathan went after it. I pulled the blanket around my shoulders. The room was cool. Almost immediately I was warmed by my own body heat. I reached up and out of the blueness around me for the cup of tea.

"I'm very fond of her," I told him. "But in a while, all there will be left is her work. She has no children. She just lost her mother. That's why we're here in Scotland, to scatter her remains. In a month or two, I'll be doing the same for Aunt Edna. I want to feel responsible. I'm hoping that making myself responsible for her body from now until she dies, and for her work afterwards, will help me heal."

I started to tell him about my own troubles with Sam, the girls leaving home, my work, but for some reason I held off. I wanted to remain anonymous to some extent.

"Are you an artist as well, Sarah? Have I already asked you that?" He sat down across from me on a small white stool. He wasn't as handsome as he'd been in the dark corner of the restaurant. Still, his mouth was luxurious and the lashes of his hazel eyes were long and curled. His black hair looked as if it hadn't been combed for a week. There was charcoal on his fingertips. I'd interrupted something.

"I used to be an artist, but I lost faith."

"Ah, that's too bad. But Art, like Jesus, will always take you back."

"I hope so," I said. "Were you working when I came in?" I gestured at his hands.

"Oh, yes, I'm always piddling, hoping my hand will come up with a subject my mind can't seem to find."

"Would you like to draw me? I mean," and here I gathered the blanket in my fists, "I mean, I know what your subject matter is. Would you draw me?"

I stared at him because I knew if I looked away he'd say no.

"What are you going to do about your aunt's work, about the way you feel about her?" he asked. And while he was asking, he reached across to a table and withdrew from a stack of art papers a sheet of heavy stock that was riddled with dark thread and bits of rag detritus. The paper was pale yet seemed ancient. He didn't acknowledge my request other than to set about it as if I'd asked him to mend my shirt.

"I'm going to cry for a long while, I think. There are extenuating factors." I shifted under the blanket. He clipped the paper to a piece of thin masonite and then began to rummage through a drawer for something.

"If you'd like, you can disrobe in the other room. Keep the throw. Then come back and take any pose that's comfortable to you. Have you done this before?"

"No."

"It's very simple. When you come back just sit as you were in the chair there. I have a new box of charcoal here somewhere." His voice faded off to a murmur.

I stepped into his bedroom, dropped the blanket on the floor. I was absolutely beyond trembling to a state of vibration. I unbuttoned my blouse and laid it out carefully on the bed. There was a mirror above his dresser and I took pains to avoid it. I kicked off my shoes. Then removed my slacks: as always the gaping hole of the waist seemed voluminous from above. I slid off my socks and unclasped my bra. I wondered momentarily if the removal of my panties was really necessary, as you always do on a visit to the doctor when you're there for a cold, but finally slid them off as well. I quickly covered as much of my body with the blanket as possible so I couldn't see it. I'd been encouraged by Jonathan's drawings. The models weren't perfect human specimens; they were sometimes old, obtuse, symmetrical in parts but not as a whole. Whether this was the way they were, or a result of

Jonathan's vision I didn't know. Perhaps only the drawings of beautiful people sold. I realize that my actions here seem out of character. They did to me, too. All I can say is that writing about these events is far more tense, more revealing, than disrobing ever was. I held the blanket closed with one hand and pulled that fireproof, leaden door between the rooms open. Jonathan had moved his stool farther away from my chair.

"Yes," he said, "just as you will. Make yourself comfortable."

I sat down. "What should I do with . . ."

"Why not pull your legs up into the chair with you. I know it's chilly in here. Your toes are pink with cold. I'll try to be as quick as possible. There. That's fine. Do with the throw as you will."

I still had it wadded closed at my neck. I let my fingers open, and looked down, watched the blanket reside. My skin, in the strong light, reflected blue. It seemed corpse-like. Jonathan sat on his stool and propped the masonite drawing board on his thighs. I shrugged the blanket off one shoulder and it gathered in folds in my lap.

"That's very nice," he said, rising slowly. "May I adjust you somewhat, Sarah?"

I nodded. He put his board down and walked toward me quickly.

"Just here . . ." He moved my jaw down a bit so that I might face him directly. "I want you to look straight at me when I'm drawing. And here, may I . . ."

He took my hand, which had gathered more material and re-formed into a fist, opened it, cupped the fingers and palm, and placed my hand under my right breast. He never touched me anywhere but on my hands.

"There," he approved.

I said, "Yes," and he went back to his stool.

He worked quietly for several minutes, his arm and hand never jerking but never still. I turned once and looked out the window. Perhaps only someone high up on Arthur's Seat with a telescope could see me. My mind was oddly detached from my body, which sat naked in front of a man I didn't know.

He asked, "So what are you going to do?"

"Is it possible to live in a continual state of I don't know?"

He smiled and continued to work. I don't know how long I sat there, curled in that chair, nude to the waist, but I wasn't cold anymore and I never broke out in a sweat. Perhaps forty-five minutes, perhaps an hour. At last he said, "That's good. You can get dressed now if you'd like, Sarah. I'm going to work a bit on the shading while you change. Off you go."

When I returned, Jonathan was spraying a fixative over the drawing. I went to his side. The tones were lighter than I'd imagined they'd be. Having watched the sweep of his extended arm, I thought I'd come out dark and somewhat contorted, heavy. I was timid before my unabashed gaze.

"Thank you," I said.

"You're lovely, aren't you." He didn't pose this as a question, but as a gift.

"Thank you."

"I'll tell you what you can do with one of your aunt's drawings: send one to me someday in return for my offering you this."

"I can have it? I don't mind paying for it."

"No. Send me a small drawing someday. I'll be getting the better of the trade."

"You really think she's something, don't you?"

"I've been teaching for ten years. I haven't had a student yet who can match her draughtsmanship, much less her way of choosing which lines to draw."

I walked away slowly that day with my prize. I thought of sending it to Sam, this drawing, my direct gaze. But even that piece of childish revenge couldn't overcome my desire to own it, to keep it a secret. I look at this sketch now, a year later, and my gesture is neither one of offering nor ownership, but simply of support, weight coddled, my hand as home. From that day forward my own desire and ability to draw were enhanced, as if allowing myself to become a model enabled me to choose a subject as well. I know that at this late stage my own work is still a compendium of the droll and hackneyed but to me it is the best I can do and so it's comforting and compelling, the way any day's work is. I continue to work to improve.

I may have posed that day, gone to the extreme limits of my character, simply as a way to avoid my aunt and the thoughts of the thing she'd done. I walked slowly all the way back to the hotel along the continuous row of shops that is Clerk and Nicholson streets. On South Bridge I did happen upon an artist's supply and there purchased pencils, a small and exquisite set of watercolors in a dovetailed mahogany box, and a tube of cobalt as a sort of rabbit's foot. I lingered in James Thin's Booksellers, and in a tartan shop on the Royal Mile, where I bought each of my girls a Stewart scarf of merino wool. I stayed away as long as I decently could, thinking this would be the last day of my own for the next couple of months.

Portrait
□ □ □

AUNT EDNA WAS STILL ASLEEP when I got back. She didn't want to go out to dinner and slept through most of the next day: on the flight to Gatwick, during our three-hour layover, and all the way home to Texas. We left Scotland as we'd arrived, in a thick fog. I never confronted Aunt Edna again with what she'd done. She knew her act was illegal; that's why she'd held it secret for so long. But I knew she also felt she'd done the right thing. She had no remorse. She felt she'd taken the last responsible act of not only a daughter but of a mother. On one of the many occasions during her last weeks when I asked if she was in pain she responded, "My body hurts, but I'm not in pain because Momma's not in pain. There's no present or future pain for her and that makes me feel good."

We arrived early in the evening, passed through customs where the agent asked if we'd brought anything home that we hadn't taken with us. No, I thought, I'm bringing back the same murderess I took with me, and she's returning with the same cancer. We'd left the car in the long-term parking lot and so drove ourselves home, though the placement of the steering wheel seemed strange, the right side of the road somehow unsettling.

"It's good to be back home," Aunt Edna said. "I've missed this much sky."

"It sure is hot. How can it still be this hot?"

The work on the overpass at 820 and 183 didn't seem to have progressed at all during the week we were away. License plates hadn't changed. No new stores had opened. When we turned onto Refugio Street, the same toys lay in the same yards, the blue-robed Madonnas continued to beseech or forgive.

The only thing that seemed different from any other return home from the grocery was that there was an old black man sitting in a chair on our porch, and he rose when he heard our car.

"There he is," I said.

She only responded by a deep and almost silent moan of longing that I recognized from my memories as a teenager. James stood at the edge of the porch and waited for her, his cane hooked over his forearm, his feet mincing up and down in anticipation like a puppy at a fence.

"I knew the sound of that engine blocks away," he hollered. "I've been waiting two hours. Y'all are late. Thought maybe you'd decided to stay in old Scotland."

I helped Aunt Edna from the car, and then I leaned against the fender much as Sam would, while they had their moment. It came to me then that my journey to Scotland was done, and I was overcome with a desolate sense of loss and arrival. Aunt Edna hugged James from the lower stoop so that her face was buried in his abdomen. Her shoulders shook slightly.

"Well, there now," James said. "You're home now. No need to go on like that."

They went inside the house. I took our bags out of the backseat and sat them in the grass. The old house shimmered in the heat. We were coming on toward night and bugs were beginning to rouse. I laid my suitcase back in the St. Augustine and opened it wide, to let all that cool Scottish air out into the Texas evening. The sweater and jacket I'd worn all week were folded there on top. Beneath were my guidebooks and maps, scarves of Scottish wool, a couple of shells from the beach at Plockton, every receipt and candy wrapper, tufts of heather pressed in a book, Jonathan's drawing, and my own sketches. Of a sudden my suitcase seemed so valuable, filled as it was with these treasures. I snaked my hand down through the clothes and paper and into a plastic bag. My sneakers were there, still damp from the waters of Glencoe and the Hebridean seas. It was strange to think of all those people who were still trudging through the Highlands or the streets of Edinburgh, knowing I wasn't missed. But I missed me there. And missed the simple movement through new space, missed the anxiety of lostness. If I found anything that summer it was this love of travel, outbound and in, which also made me appreciate the interval between journeys, my time at home, wherever that is.

I finally carried our bags inside and went almost straight to bed. Although it was only 8:00 P.M. in Fort Worth, my body seemed to have remained in Scotland where it was 2:00 in the morning. James and Aunt Edna were talking in the living room as I fell asleep. I could have cried about James, so full of anticipation and joy, so unaware.

◻ ◻ ◻

Of course I was wide awake by three and had the immediate thought that I was lying in the same room my grandmother was murdered in, vulnerable and alone, with the sole knowledge of the crime. I was, in fact, an accomplice at this stage. As ridiculous as this sounds I actually considered writing down the facts and sending them to a lawyer with instructions to open the envelope in the event of my sudden death. The only way to combat such early-morning paranoia is to get up from the horizontal and take action, even if it's only to brush your teeth. I put on a robe and went to the kitchen to start a pot to boil. I'd bought a little box of English tea at Gatwick with the last of my change. It was so hot that we'd left the air-conditioning on all night, but I found the back door open, the kitchen warm. I thought James had forgotten to shut the door when he went home the night before. As I started to swing the door to, I saw a darker hump in the night, a faint outline of black on blue, the subtle work of starlight.

"James?" I said.

"It's me, Sarah. You're up early." He spoke without turning.

I groped my way outside and sat next to him on the concrete. My feet couldn't quite reach the ground.

"I'm wide awake," I said. "It's 9:00 A.M. in Scotland and I'm still there. Why are you up?"

"This is my favorite time of summer, between two and four, cool enough to think, quiet enough to listen. I take a little nap in the afternoons so I can be up now."

"I was going to make some tea. Do you want a cup?"

"I want to know what's wrong with your aunt Edna. Did she meet somebody over there?"

"Meet somebody? No."

"Something's wrong. She even sounds different. Feels different. Smells different. Things weren't right in there. She's too quiet."

"Did she tell you she was sick, James?"

"Yes, she said she wasn't feeling good. I hope she gets better soon. We've got a wedding in five days. I don't know that this trip was a good idea."

"She had to go, James. It made her feel good inside. But she's sick. She's not going to get better. She's been hiding it from all of us and she only told me because it's getting too hard to hide. She has cancer, James. It's untreatable."

He lifted his hands slowly to his eyes and softly rubbed at them. "I knew it was so," he said at last. "I knew I was coming to the end of something rather than the beginning. If she'd told me before, I wouldn't have let her go. Oh, Lord. What kind of cancer?"

"It's in her pancreas and it's probably already in her liver, too. She's known about this since before Grandma passed away and at that time the doctor said she might have three months, so that means she might only have a few weeks left. I'm going to stay and take care of her."

"Why wouldn't she tell me?"

"She doesn't want you to be disappointed. She's afraid of everything now, I think."

"God, help us," he whispered, "God, help us. It's my fault. I badgered her into loving me, marrying me. I said sweet things and ignored silences and was more happy than I should have been around her. Sarah, I'm not as wise or congenial as I pretend to be. I'm just that way around Edna so she'll be fooled into loving me. How can you say serious things to a jackass? She had to hide it from me. What am I going to do? I knew something was wrong. I knew it blocks away. I should have been able to tell she was getting the cancer. I should have been able to tell her body was getting too hot."

His fists were wet.

"Old eyes aren't good for nothing but tear ducts. Doesn't seem fair," he said. "Nothing seems fair. She cried too easily this summer. I thought it was the loss of her mother but she was losing all of us: her momma, you, me, her friends at work, all those children. She's been crying about all of them. We're only losing her but she's losing all of us."

"I'm sorry, James."

"Don't seem fair I should have to go through this twice. First time almost killed me. I don't think practice helps, do you?"

"No."

"What are we gonna do? What are we gonna do?"

"I don't know," I said. "I'm so sorry."

"Can't no doctor fix it?"

"She says no. It's the same cancer Michael Landon had," I said. "With all his money and fame he couldn't beat it."

"Who's Michael Landon?"

"Little House on the Prairie," I said. "The actor."

"I don't know him."

"Little Joe Cartwright."

"He's dead?"

"Yes."

"I didn't know that."

"It's dark out here," I said.

"Is it?" James asked.

"Yeah."

"Dark in here, too. Dark everywhere. I'm gonna go back inside now and lie down next to her, Sarah."

"OK," I said, and helped him find the knob to the screen door. Then I sat back down. A single small jet coasted over, bound for Meacham Field. Beyond it, mingling with the stars and mimosa leaves, were the lights of half a dozen other airliners, either just leaving or landing at DFW. The night sky was full of human beings, and almost all of them were on a separate itinerary, oblivious to the problems and passions of not only those on the ground but of the person across the aisle. It's a blessing, this ignorance, the only thing that allows us to survive. How does God weather the accumulation of sorrow?

□ □ □

The warmth of the night air finally made me drowsy, that and the desire for sleep itself, the only way I knew to avoid thoughts of James's pain. Aunt Edna woke me by sitting on my bed softly, in the hollow between my knees and elbows.

"Wake up, sleepyhead."

"What time?"

"It's almost ten o'clock. Sarah, I went to bed and James did not know and I woke up and he knew. He came to understand while I slept. It was the easiest way for me."

I sat up, pushed myself away from her, and leaned against the headboard. "I'm sorry, Aunt Edna. I've got a big fat mouth. It was just unbearable for him not to know."

"It's all right. It was too hard for me. I was thinking about jumping in front of a truck rather than telling him. But I couldn't because I have that other responsibility."

"I didn't say anything about Grandma."

"I know."

"I won't."

"I know."

"Aunt Edna, we don't have to tell anybody else. The body is gone. There's no evidence." She shrugged slightly. "It was Grandma's idea, wasn't it? To be cremated?"

"Of course."

"If you tell anyone else, they're going to ask you that."

"Let's worry about that later. I've been to the post office to pick up the mail. Guess what's in this envelope."

"It's from the auction house. I forgot all about it what with . . ."

"Yes. Me too."

"Well?"

"Shall I open it?"

"Right now," I said. I shoved the sheets off my legs. "But where is James? What about James?"

"He's gone home. He's pretty upset. He'll be back soon."

"What about the wedding, Aunt Edna?"

"He wanted to get married today. I told him Saturday would be soon enough."

"How are you this morning?"

"I feel better. I felt better after you knew and I feel better now. But I'd just as soon not tell everybody else yet. I want a happy wedding. You can all cry at my funeral but I want a happy wedding."

She put her thumb under the loose flap and tore the envelope across the top. There was a pink computer-printed check and a long itemized payment stub inside.

"How much?" I asked.

"The check, after all commissions, is for seventy-nine thousand, three hundred twelve dollars and forty-two cents."

"Wow," I whispered.

"If I'd known it was that much I'd have bought a better grade of canvas and more brushes a long time ago."

"That's a lot of lunch money," I said.

"It multiplied in those cans. It doesn't seem like it should be that much."

"What are you going to do with it?"

She pushed herself off the bed. "Time to get up. We've got a wedding in four days."

"You're not going to tell me what you're going to do with it?"

"Sarah, honey," she said, "I'm going to return it." And she walked from my room.

□ □ □

James did return later that day, dressed in dark slacks, a long-sleeved white shirt, and a narrow blue tie. He sat in one of the recliners and alternately wept and read a massive Braille Bible. He'd hold Aunt Edna's hand for long stretches, while she repeated softly, "Stop that, stop that. I won't let you stay if you don't stop." Occasionally she'd take a break and go off to the kitchen to make some coffee or biscuits for him, and I'd take her place.

He whispered to me, his eyelids squeezing off tears as if they came from a dropper, "I wish cancer was catching. I wish I could get it from her." And this made me get all weepy, too, so that when Aunt Edna came back she openly frowned and silently motioned for me to leave the room. There was another day or two of this with James, but he more or less became his old self as the wedding approached. On Thursday he wore work clothes, matched khaki shirt and slacks with a white undershirt, and mowed the lawn, constantly sweeping the grass with his bare foot to see if he'd missed anything. The two garden beds off the front porch took his attention for most of the day. He and I went to Calloway's and bought a dozen blooming potted flowers, which he planted on each side of the walk.

"How's that look?" he asked me.

"Looks good."

"Smells better. We'll have to watch my friends at the wedding."

"Why?"

"Blind people are always stepping on flowers," he said and smiled at my left breast.

Aunt Edna cleaned house, rested, cleaned house, rested. I couldn't get her to give it up. Finally, after my continuous badgering, she shouted, "Sarah, this may be the last time I'm able to clean my house and I'm not going to leave a dirty house for someone else. I've always liked cleaning my house. Let me clean it."

□ □ □

Sam and the girls arrived the day before the wedding. I was expecting them, and when they first pulled up in front of the house I let the corner of the curtain fall and walked slowly back to the kitchen. I didn't want to meet them outside in all that sunshine. The doorbell rang and I waited for Aunt Edna or James to answer it. I wanted to be engaged, doing something when they arrived so they wouldn't think my life away from them was all holiday, so I quickly took a cantaloupe from the refrigerator, sliced it open, and began to eviscerate the poor thing. When Susan and Michelle came into the kitchen I made a big show of drying my hands. They hugged me one at a time, all smiles. Then I braced myself for their father but instead, behind the girls, was this tall awkward boy.

"This is Scott," Susan said. "He works with me." She beamed at him as if height and awkwardness were feats of intelligence. Michelle turned away and rolled her eyes. But it was odd for me because I saw myself in Susan's gaze, saw the thing I'd lost, and I was hurt, and envious, and wary for my daughter, and then I was smiling and shaking his loose grip.

"Mom, you've lost weight," Susan said.

"Well, thanks for telling Scott I used to be fatter," I said, still smiling. "Y'all sit down here at the table and I'll show you our pictures of Scotland. How'd Susan talk you into coming to a family wedding, Scott?"

"I'm just a stupid person, Mrs. Warren. I've got no more brains than a cow."

"Scott!" Susan drooled.

Michelle, standing behind them, opened her mouth wide and stuck her finger in it. I thought that was pretty funny. They sat down and I put Cokes in front of them. "Where's your dad?"

"We left him on the front lawn with Aunt Edna and Mr. Laurent."

"I guess I better go say hello." Michelle followed me into the living room.

"You can't ever leave me alone with them again," she insisted. They were practically doing it in the backseat on the way down with me and Dad, right there in the car. If they'd just grope and smack it wouldn't be so bad, but they have to talk, too. Mom, a word of warning: Dad has changed his hairstyle."

"What?"

"He's parting it in the middle again, like he did when he was my age."

"Oh no," I said.

"It looks pretty weird on an old guy."

"He's not so old. You're just really young."

"Well, I warned you. Christ, I left my Coke in there with them. I'll have to go back and get it. Do you have any sunglasses on you?"

"Get out of here."

"I haven't been so disgusted with Susan since I found her sucking on that little dog turd when she was a baby."

I laughed out loud, remembering her face at five, when she brought me her three-year-old sister, the poop still clutched tightly in her fist. I hugged her again. My girl was taller than me. "I've missed you so much," I said.

"Me too, Mom. We've all missed you."

James had his hand on Sam's shoulder and was explaining to him the best way to go about driving a car. Sam had the four fingers of each of his own hands shoved only two knuckles deep into his pants' pockets as if he might need them suddenly. His hair was parted in the middle, but it was also cut very short. It gave him that barbershop sheen, a turn-of-the-century snappiness. He had on a brilliant white long-sleeved shirt and looked altogether dapper. It was the most ridiculous thing I'd ever seen. I had an almost overwhelming urge to get a comb and move that part over where it was supposed to be.

I stepped up and asked James, "When have you ever driven a car?"

"When I was a young man I worked hauling hay in east Texas. I couldn't wander around in those fields searching for bales so they put me in the truck and I drove up and down, back and forth through the hay fields while the other boys threw the hay on the truck. Almost all of those hay fields were cotton fields lying fallow, so I could feel the old furrows in that steering wheel and drive a straight line. I ran into a creek once because they didn't tell me to stop, but that's how I learned to drive, in a Ford double-A truck. That was a hot summer, but I think it's hotter now, don't you, Sam?"

"It's always hotter now than it was yesterday," Sam answered.

"You're right about that," James said. "And that just means it's going to be hotter tomorrow. I'm glad this wedding is inside."

"Well, come inside right now, old man," Aunt Edna said and took his hand.

"All right, all right, there goes my hanging-out-with-the-boys days, Sam."

"We'll be right in," I said.

We watched them till they were in the house. I put my hands in my pockets, too, and walked back toward our car. It was in the shade of the big oak at the street.

"You look nice, Sarah," he said.

"I've been walking a lot, trying to eat better. What in the world have you done to your hair?"

"Oh, I've just been parting it differently. Trying to see somebody else in the mirror. You know. Doesn't look right, hunh?"

"It doesn't look like you."

"I know. Just different."

"It looks OK."

"It's nothing I can't change."

"What about this Scott? Michelle said he was all over Susan in the backseat."

"It was her on him if it was anything. I saw one peck in the rear-view mirror. Michelle's just jealous of her little sister. He seems like a nice kid. He has a job and a car. Calls me 'Sir,' which sounds strange. Maybe it will just be a summer thing."

"We'll have to watch him. Susan looks at him the way I looked at you when we first met."

"Then I'm glad for him. He's a lucky kid."

"You understand that I'm staying here tonight? I'm not coming out to the hotel. There's still too much to do here before the wedding in the morning. And I'm not coming home after the wedding either. Aunt Edna asked me not to tell anyone till later but I need to tell you now why I'm not coming home. She's got cancer, and she's not going to live through it. I've really come to love her so much, Sam. So I'm going to see her through it, her and James."

"How long?"

"She might have a couple of months. But I don't know. She gets weaker every day. And she's lost a lot of weight already."

"I could tell. Who else knows?"

"Just you and me and James. Aunt Edna wants a happy wedding."

"Jesus Christ," Sam said. "Poor James." And then, "I'm sorry, Sarah. I mean, for you too."

"I know. People keep abandoning me this summer."

He bowed his head then, shoved his hands further into his pockets. "You're worried that Scott's going to treat Susan like I've treated you."

I looked down the street at children playing with a wheelbarrow. "Yeah, I guess, someday. But I worry every time she gets in a car, too."

"I'd beat him within an inch of his life if he hurt her," Sam said, and smiled. "I should have let your dad do that to me. Maybe you'd have forgiven me by now."

"No, that might have helped you but it wouldn't have helped me. Sam, I'm never going to forgive you for what you did. I'll think about it the day I die."

"Are you going to be able to live with it, though?"

I took this to mean 'Are you going to live with me?' So I told him the truth, which was, "I don't know. I don't know. Something brought us to that. I'm going to think about it for a while, Sam. You can't push me."

"I'm just in limbo, too," he said.

"Neither one of us has been alone yet," I said. "We don't know how we are. By the end of the summer the girls will be back in school and Aunt Edna will be gone. Maybe when we're each alone, we'll know where we are."

"I know where I am, Sarah. I made a mistake. I'm sorry for it. I just need you to come home. That's as plain as I can make it."

"It's not that easy for me. I wish you hadn't told the girls what you'd done. I didn't want them to be mad at you."

"What, and let them think that problems come out of the blue? I'm willing to take responsibility for this, Sarah."

"Sam, all I know to say is I'm not the same person anymore. You don't even know if you love me, you couldn't, because I'm not the same person I was at the beginning of the summer. And I don't think I'm through changing. You shouldn't commit to someone when you don't know who they are."

"We are already connected by those two young women in there. We made them together."

"I know, honey. I know. But they're made. They're finished to whatever extent we can finish them."

"I guess I've got to stop talking. I'm not getting through to you and I'm just causing more damage."

He jerked his hands out of his pockets and walked around me and between James's rows of flowers and into the house. That's how I am, too, when I don't get the answers I want. Somehow I never even got to the part of the conversation where I told him that I wanted to be an artist again, how I loved to travel.

□ □ □

Just after Sam and the girls left for their hotel, Momma and Daddy arrived. We put them up in my room and I moved out to one of the lounge chairs in the living room. JoAnn and Mike and Darcy would all arrive an hour or two before the wedding the next day. Aunt Margaret called to say that Uncle Alf wasn't feeling well so they wouldn't be coming. I held my hand over the mouthpiece and whispered to Aunt Edna, "Please, let me tell her."

"No," she whispered back, "I wouldn't want her to come because of that. She's more comfortable away and I want her to be comfortable. Can you imagine the body she'd wear for pity's sake? She'd be like Millet's gleaners, all hunched over with worry's burden. It would be as if she had cancer. Let her come later."

That evening, as we all sat in the living room after dinner, Daddy asked Aunt Edna how she was feeling. "You look worn out," he said.

James immediately put his hands under his thighs. It's funny, this way men have of concealing their hands when they're hiding their feelings.

Aunt Edna countered, "I may not look good, but I'm happy. I'm so glad Sarah and I took Momma and Daddy to such a beautiful place to rest. I don't think I'll ever be more relaxed than I am now. The house is clean. Momma's at peace. I'm getting married tomorrow morning. I used to only feel this way for a half hour at a time, just after I finished a picture. Then I'd have to start worrying after the next picture. But I don't feel that way now. I feel like I'm going to be happy for a long time."

"That's wonderful," my mother said. "You've done it, James."

"Yes," he said, "women just have that response to me." He laughed for a brittle three seconds.

"Buddy, I want you to give me away in the morning. We're going to set the chairs up here in rows, and James and I will stand in front of the TV. I'm not going to walk down an aisle. I'll just come out of the bedroom and you can stand up and then sit right back down."

"You're bringing Brother Roberts back?" Daddy asked.

"Yes, James likes him."

"I like him, too," Daddy said.

"Edna," James asked, "have you seen my prescription? I know I left it here. My hands are all bound up again." He explained, "Lifetime of caning chairs. I have these muscle relaxers that help. When you're young you never think of your work as a hazardous occupation. It's just work."

I told him, "James, medieval and Renaissance artists often poisoned themselves with their art by pointing their brushes in their mouths."

"Well, that's just nasty."

"I think it's all gone, James," Aunt Edna said.

"Now, now," he crowed, "there was more than half a bottle. I left it here months ago. You didn't throw it out, did you?"

"I'll look but I think it's all gone."

"I try to keep a bottle everywhere I go so I'll always have it," he told my mother and father.

I followed Aunt Edna into the bathroom and shut the door behind us. "You used James's pills," I accused her.

"Yes," she said, putting her hand over her mouth. "Momma had the same prescription once. But we soon found out it was bad for her. That was years ago. I threw hers away."

"You can't tell anyone you used his prescription," I said, "ever. They'll think he was part of it."

"But why?"

"So you'd marry him. So he'd inherit . . . well, you can imagine what Aunt Margaret would say. She'd take it out on him. He's going to be left to deal with all this."

"I won't tell," she said.

"You shouldn't have involved him."

"I won't tell."

I felt as if I were chastising my own daughter for a breach of etiquette or unclean act, as if Aunt Edna had put a dirty binky back in her little sister's mouth.

□   □   □

It doesn't seem to matter how old I get, my father always wakes up earlier than I do. We sat in the kitchen, looking into our coffee cups, much as we'd done twenty years earlier when I'd come home from college. We silently waited for the rest of the world to wake up. I was uncomfortable keeping things from him and never felt more of an accomplice after the fact than I did that morning. I had no compulsion to break the news about his sister and mother to him. I only wished I knew as little as he did. I wanted to enjoy the wedding in ignorance, too.

I said, "I used to wish I'd never found out about Sam. But now I'm glad I did. It's changed me somehow for the better. I didn't know I was vulnerable but I was."

"It's good to know you're vulnerable?" he asked.

"Yes," I said. "It makes you appreciate things, everybody I mean, more. Even yourself. I don't think I liked who I was for a long time."

"Well, that's a sad thing to say. I've always liked you."

"Well, you always will."

"So you see, you're not vulnerable where I'm concerned."

"Sure I am. I'm going to lose you some day."

He paused, crossed his arms, and stared at me. "What thoughts, Sarah."

"Well, I am. Daddy, what's the worst thing that could ever happen to you?"

"I don't understand."

"I don't mean to you, physically. I mean emotionally."

"Jesus, Sarah Rabbit."

"Really."

"I suppose if I were to lose your mother or you or Mike. As old as we are, your mother and I still worry about you and your brother every day."

"That's it for me, too: if Susan or Michelle were lost, I don't know what I'd do."

"Why dwell on it, Sarah? You can't lessen the pain by anticipating it, honey."

"Do you remember when I used to draw, Dad? I mean before the Christmas ornaments, when I was in school."

"Sure I do."

"I think somehow I got sidetracked. I want to draw again."

"Getting sidetracked is what's called getting a living: food, water, and diapers. Getting sidetracked isn't dishonorable."

"I know that. But for me, the honorable thing to do now is to go back to work trying to be an artist."

"What does Sam think?"

"What does he have to do with it?"

"Oh. OK. How are you going to feed yourself?"

"I don't know. Isn't it more important to work that out second rather than first? I've got some money saved. The girls are both going to state schools and their tuition is far less than Sam and I ever thought it would be. They both work."

"What are you going to do, Sarah? After the wedding?"

"What do you mean?"

"Are you going home with Sam or with me and your mother?"

"Neither."

"Then what?"

"I'm staying here."

"Don't you think that's a little selfish? Edna has had you all this time. Why not give her and James some space of their own?"

"She's asked me to stay, Daddy."

"You should get a place of your own, Sarah. Sam is alone. You should be, too, until this thing is settled."

"But what if it's not settled? What if it's unsettleable?"

"You still shouldn't take advantage of your aunt's hospitality. She had a life of her own before you came. She's about to have a new life with James. It's their life, not yours."

"Daddy, I'm not staying for my sake. I mean, I am, but mainly I'm staying for Aunt Edna. I'm not supposed to tell but here I go again. She's sick, Daddy. She wants a happy wedding so you can't talk to her about this till afterwards, please."

"About what?"

"She has cancer. She's had it for some time and she's not going to beat it. It's in her pancreas and there's nothing they can do. I'm going to stay until it's done. It might only be a matter of weeks."

My father looked at me silently for some time, processing all this information as if he'd been given a complicated proof. Finally, he said, "I'm sorry for backing you into a corner."

"It's all too sad," I said.

"That's what killed our father," he said listlessly. "I won't say anything till she comes to me with it, Sarah. I'm just glad Mom didn't have to watch her go through this the way she had to with Dad. It's not going to be easy for you, you know. She'll deteriorate rapidly from here on out. I couldn't believe how quickly Dad fell away. Your aunt helped when he was dying. At least she knows what she's in for. That's probably the hardest part for her. Poor old James. Thank God he's blind."

□ □ □

The wedding was at ten and by nine everyone had arrived except Sam and the girls and Brother and Sister Roberts. Darcy and Mike, Thelia and Billy, my mother and father, JoAnn, James, and two of his friends who dated all the way back to his schooldays sat in the rows of chairs turned pews in the living room. Aunt Edna was firmly lodged in her bedroom and wouldn't let me attend her. I'd asked about a wedding dress weeks before and she'd said she was prepared, that she had a new outfit she'd bought in the spring and never worn.

"Is it white?" I asked.

"Yes."

"Can I see it?"

"No."

"Why not?"

"It's a surprise."

"It's supposed to be a surprise only for James, not for everyone else."

"It's what I want to wear."

"Do you have matching shoes?"

"Yes."

"Do you have something old and something blue?"

"I'm going to wear Momma's sapphire ring."

"Can't I see the dress, please?"

"No."

"Cripes, Aunt Edna!"

And so it had gone. I'd even sneaked into her room before we went to Scotland, poked through her closet, but she'd hidden the dress, or it was off being altered.

I knocked on her door several times the morning of the wedding, asking if she wanted my help with her corsage, if she wanted any baby's breath in her hair, if I might help with a zipper. This last brought the response that she'd been dressing herself for sixty years and she thought she could handle it today, too. So I went back to my chair next to JoAnn.

"Aunt Edna doesn't look very good," JoAnn leaned in and whispered. "Has she been taking her ginseng?"

"Yes, JoAnn."

"I can't believe she's getting married before I am."

James's two old blind friends both turned our way.

"You're whispering very loudly, JoAnn," I whispered to her. She'd done it to me again, forced me into a whisper.

"It didn't take her very long," she sissed. "I mean, she didn't mourn Grandma very long before she decided to get married. I think it's a good thing, don't you?"

"You don't think it's a good thing. You think it's exactly the opposite and you're hoping I'll say so first."

"That's not true, Sarah." She said this into her armpit, as if she were trying to blow her deodorant dry.

"She misses Grandma terribly. She loved her more than she loves anyone else in this room, including you and me and maybe even

James. She could have put her in a nursing home years ago and had a life. And that's the last thing I'm whispering to you."

I sat up straight in my chair. JoAnn fumbled in her purse. Darcy turned around and asked me if I'd seen some goddamn movie and while I was answering her, JoAnn grabbed the pressure point on my wrist. My hand popped open and she put into my palm, I kid you not, six horse-sized pills. Two were amber gel capsules, two looked like compressed hay bales, and the last two, green and orange, were simply thrown in for color. My immediate urge was to squeeze open her mouth and pitch them down her own throat. Instead, I dumped them back into the maw of her purse and then I broke my word: I whispered to her again.

She didn't whisper back. She said aloud, "Did you hear that, Darcy?" Darcy said, "No, I didn't. What'd she say? Why are y'all whispering?" Neither of us responded.

Sam and the girls came through the door then and I got up from the thing I'd said. I'd told JoAnn there was no pill on earth that was going to make me a virgin or make her not one. We've spoken again since then and things are better now but I was pretty pissed off. I got Sam a cup of coffee out of habit. He thanked me and then went and sat right between James's two friends, shook their hands, and was soon in deep conversation. I'd been too afraid to do that, as much as I wanted to. He did it with a natural ease that made me envious. He probably could have talked a dozen women into bed with him over the last twenty years. Maybe the fact that there was only one was a tribute to me. Hmph.

Mike asked me if Brother Roberts knew that Aunt Edna's fiancé was a black man. "I hope he doesn't know," he said.

"He told Aunt Edna on the phone that he remembered James from the funeral. She's not sure if he does or not."

"Do you think he's ever done an interracial wedding?"

"I don't know. There were never any blacks in the congregation when I went to his church twenty-five years ago, and he's been retired since then. Ask Mom and Dad."

Amazing, how this still worked with Mike. He trotted right over to them.

When Brother Roberts arrived, James met him at the door like an old friend. His toupee was flatter than I'd last seen it, as if he'd slept in it for a month. But one thing about Brother Roberts: he always kept his hands out in front of him. He believed what he said and had nothing to hide. Sister stood behind him silently, wearing the same pink dress she'd worn to Grandma's funeral. She smiled an unwavering smile and would occasionally touch the corners of her mouth with her white-gloved hand to wipe away spittle. I heard her ask James when she would sing, and I thought, the poor thing thinks she's at another funeral. But I was wrong.

James called me to his side and said, "Sarah, I think we're ready now. If you could get everybody in their seats, and place the good pastor and his wife in front of the TV, and put me where I'm supposed to go, I suppose then you can tell the bride we're ready."

"Where is she?" Sister Roberts asked.

"Oh, she's in hiding," I told her.

"That's right," she said. "We don't want the groom to catch sight of her before the ceremony." James and I stood expectantly for a moment, waiting for her to laugh after her own joke, but she never did.

I guided everyone to their places and then went and knocked on Aunt Edna's door. She opened it a crack, not far enough that I could see.

"We're ready. Brother Roberts is here and everyone's in place."

"OK. Go sit down. I'll be out in a minute." She closed the door.

I took my chair next to Sam. "I like weddings," he said and clasped his hands.

It seemed like Aunt Edna kept us all waiting far too long. The room grew so silent I could hear the fans on the air conditioners turning and beyond the fans a bird chirping outside. People shifted in their chairs and the glue joints cracked like the shell of a bug breaking underfoot. The simple passage of time, any time, is tension-filled. Finally, Aunt Edna stepped out of her bedroom and came out of the hallway into the assembled company. She wore a crisp white cafeteria uniform with freshly bleached sneakers. The only addition I could see to her workaday outfit was a pair of white hose and her four ten-year service pins. I'd seen this outfit in her closet. She had half a dozen of them, white polyester short-sleeved, knee-length dresses with big plastic buttons down the front for closure. The only thing missing from her lunchroom attire was the hair net. James and his two friends couldn't see her, of course, but the rest of us, with our accumulated gasps of surprise, let him know she'd arrived. He smiled broadly and bobbed in anticipation. She walked to his side and took his hand. Daddy stood up and sat down.

"Hello, Edna," he said.

"Hello, James."

"You look beautiful," he said.

"Thank you. You are a handsome man."

"I know," he said. "I know."

"We'll be married now, Brother Roberts," she said, and they turned slightly toward him, as if they were waiting for the lightest of kisses to their cheeks.

Brother Roberts stood with an open Bible, his hand upon the pages, yet never referred to it.

"Before we begin, we'll begin with a song."

Aunt Edna looked mildly perturbed, as if this wasn't something they'd discussed.

"Edna," Brother Roberts said, almost wickedly, "James wrote a song for you while you were lately away and passed it along to Sister Roberts who has added music to his lyrics. It's their gift to you today."

Sister Roberts put one hand on the console TV to steady herself, and then sang, in her consistently quavering voice:

> Sweet Little Cafe
> Wonder what she's gonna say
> When I see her today
> Sweet Little Cafe
>
> When she is home
> By herself all alone
> She calls me on the phone
> Sweet Little Cafe
>
> She's got that certain something in her style
> She's got a bit of heaven in her smile
>
> She promised me
> That she'd say yessirree

That's good enough for me
Sweet Little Cafe

I'll follow you
Through everything you do
I'll cane your chairs too
Sweet Little Cafe

Well, by the second stanza Aunt Edna was in his arms, and my father and I were dog-weeping and even Sam had tears in his eyes. All the other guests were smiling. The blind were tapping their feet. James had written this before he'd known about Aunt Edna's illness, of course. They were a trembling entwined mass of bowed heads and drooping shoulders, as if they'd melted together in a hot sun. Their knees seemed unstable and I don't think they could have stood alone. My mother opened her purse and started passing out Kleenex, even rising to give one each to James and Aunt Edna when they came to a sustainable stasis. Sister Roberts seemed pleased that she'd brought the room to a state of quivering jelly. She took a seat in the first row and tucked one hand under the other in her lap, as if she were putting a ten-dollar bill in a birthday card. Meanwhile, my mother, my daughters, and everyone else who didn't know Aunt Edna was dying looked at those of us who did with the fixed gazes of people seeing their first epileptic fit. Brother Roberts kept smoothing the same two pages of his Bible with his palm. Finally, before Aunt Edna would turn back toward the preacher she looked at Sam and my father, compared them with me and James, and she knew that I'd told. The upper lids of her eyes lowered and her lips compressed and stretched into a thin strand of barbed wire stretching across a bleak horizon. I stopped crying right away.

"What are we here for?" Brother Roberts asked, and I thought, Ha, your usual crowd isn't here.

But soon enough, James's friends responded. "We're here for a wedding," one of them said.

And the other added, "That's right," before Brother Roberts could affirm the answer himself.

"And what is a wedding?" Brother Roberts trumped.

"It's a blessed union," one said.

"That's right," said the other.

A general tumult of head bobbing.

It was plain to Brother Roberts that he was going to have to come up with a tougher one. "What does Paul teach us in his first epistle to the Corinthians?" He patted the frail pages. He waited. He raised his eyebrows in expectation. At last he said quietly, in a serene acceptance of exasperation, "'Let the husband render unto the wife due benevolence; and likewise also the wife unto the husband. The wife hath not power of her own body, but the husband; and likewise also the husband hath not power of his own body, but the wife.'" Here he repeated, "'Likewise also, likewise also,'" with some gravity. "We belong to each other, husband and wife. Paul was a single man and he counseled that if we cannot abide our loneliness then we should marry, 'for it is better to marry than to burn.' What's that all about, 'to burn'? To burn because we've committed sin or to burn with lust or is it to burn because we won't acknowledge desire? Paul tells us that a husband and wife can save each other, even if one of them is an unbeliever. Amazing, isn't it? Marriage is that powerful. 'If any brother hath a wife that believeth not, and she be pleased to dwell with him, let him not put her away. And the woman which hath a husband that believeth not, and if he be pleased to dwell with her, let her leave him not. For the unbelieving wife is sanctified by the husband.' So marriage is a wondrous and powerful gift we give each other. I'm so pleased that James and Edna have decided to sanctify one another, such is their love. It is better to marry than to burn."

From there on out the ceremony was the usual give and take of vows, rings, and kisses. Both my girls yelped a bright cheer at the kiss, and Sam patted my fat knee.

Later, I confronted Aunt Edna about her dress. "It was brand-new," she explained. "I'd bought it before I decided to retire. I couldn't return it because I'd had it altered. Military people wear their uniforms to be married. I'm just as proud of mine."

I sat back on my heels and narrowed my field of vision till only her eyes were in it. She braced herself. "I think it was perfect," I said. "I'm glad you didn't let me influence you, and I'm glad you included me in the surprise."

"You told your daddy and Sam, didn't you? Men don't cry at weddings."

"I had to, Aunt Edna. They were both giving me hell about staying here after your wedding."

"It's OK. Funeral tears look pretty similar to wedding tears. I'd like to bottle Sister Roberts's voice and sell it as a depressant."

"What about James writing you a song?"

"I didn't know anything about it. I thought I was going to be charged for something extra I hadn't ordered."

"When do you want to sit everybody down?"

"After Brother Roberts leaves. Let everyone have their lunch and then we'll talk. I know your dad and everyone else need to start back home."

It was only ten-thirty in the morning but she was already exhausted.

"Your hair is beautiful," I said.

"I think hair is such an improvement over bald, especially in an elderly woman. I worked on it so long this morning that my arms got tired. When I get worse I want you to cut it all off. It's easier that way. I always kept Momma's short. I wonder if you'd take James and me downtown tonight. I think I'll be too tired to drive."

"Of course," I said. Their honeymoon was a night at the Worthington. At that very moment Susan and Michelle were outside decorating Aunt Edna's car. They tied a pair of old shoes and a couple of soup cans to the bumper, and wrote, "Just Married" on the windshield. On the driver's-side window they drew a large square using white shoe polish. There was an arrow pointing to the square with the inscription, "Babe in a Box." The box on James's side of the car said he was a "Hunk in a Box." As it happened I turned out to be the "Babe" and Aunt Edna the "Hunk." James sat in back on the way to the hotel. The drive back home that evening was somewhat strange, as I felt I'd just been married to myself. From the outside I was both babe and hunk.

"What about that Brother Roberts?" Aunt Edna said. "I think he's mellowing with age. Do you think James's faith will carry me across?"

"Isn't it a pretty thought," I said. "I mean, to think that faith and love are the same thing and that as long as one spouse is constant the other . . ." but I couldn't carry the idea through to any logical conclusion.

After James's friends had pressed a hundred-dollar bill into Brother Roberts's palm, we all sat down to lunch.

"Sit me down in that ladder-back with the cane seat, Sarah," James said. "You're gonna have to help Del and Stony, too. Both of them fellas are blind as bats. I don't know why blind folks just don't stay home. Always tripping over your nice things."

But Stony and Del were already on their way to the table, guided by Thelia and Billy.

"You're the one always tripping over things," Stony said: "I don't have four stitches in the side of my head."

"That was a dog that made me stumble. I'd have caught myself, too, if I hadn't actually stepped on the dog with my other foot when I fell."

"That dog covered a lot of ground, didn't he, Stony?" Del said.

"When was this?" I asked.

"1951," James said.

"He's been riding that dog ever since," Stony said. "It's a very unstable world for old James."

"I never fell out a window," James countered.

"That window was left open," Stony said. "Anybody could have fallen out of it. Everybody knows that."

"Billy," James said, "did I ever tell you the time Del was put in an elevator down at Leonard's Department Store?"

"Yes."

"Well, here it comes again. His brother put him in an elevator by himself so he could ride the new escalators. He thought they'd be too tricky for Del. When his brother got over to the elevator to pick Del up, he was standing in there having a conversation with nobody."

"I'm telling you there was somebody in that elevator," Del said.

"There was a vent in that elevator that was sighing every minute or so. Ol' Del was wooing that vent."

"That isn't so."

"Thought it was in love with him," James said.

"I got more response from it than I ever did from my wife," Del said and smiled. "When you're blind you never know if you're alone. I closed the door of the bathroom once, pulled my pants down, and the awfullest lot of giggling breaks out. My little sister had three of her friends in there and all of them standing in the bathtub."

"James," my father asked, "has Edna ever told you about the time she almost burned down the north side of Fort Worth?"

"No, she has not."

"Well, her and Webby Stickels . . ."

"Webby who?"

"Webby Stickels. That was Edna's first boyfriend. He had some extra skin between his thumb and index finger . . ."

"Oh, Buddy, don't tell that story," Aunt Edna snapped.

"Too late now," Daddy said.

"I'm not her first boyfriend?" James said.

"Edna and Webby both got bad grades on a math test and rather than bring them home to their parents they decided to burn them. The wind was blowing that afternoon so they wadded up the tests and put them inside a stack of old tires out in the alley here. They figured they'd burn in there and wouldn't blow away. Well, our daddy had been pouring his used oil in them old tires for years. Man, you should have seen the smoke. Fire crept out from underneath the tires and ran through all the high grass in the alley, burned the backside of everybody's fence, and a lot of trash before the fire truck came and put it all out. Ol' Webby confessed right away but my little sister held her ground and to this day won't admit her test was in that fire, too."

Aunt Edna sat with her arms crossed.

"What happened to Webby?" James asked.

"Oh," Aunt Edna said, "he had that extra cut out a year or two later and I never saw him much after that."

"What was his real name, Edna?" Daddy asked.

"Charles," Aunt Edna said. "Momma whipped me for three days after that fire. She said it wasn't for the fire but for the lie. That spring the alley was so clean and green, new grass growing up. After the fire the whole neighborhood got back there and cleaned up. There were so many things the fire had uncovered: old bottles half-buried, car parts, the bones of a dead cat."

"Daddy tried to take the blame, didn't he, Edna?"

"He said it was his fault because he'd poured all that oil in those tires and onto the ground. He never liked to see us whipped."

"Momma did all the whipping in our family," Daddy said.

"I'd have been a heathen renegade if she hadn't," Aunt Edna said. "I think she whipped me so much because I was an accident."

"You weren't an accident," Daddy said.

"I was too. They weren't planning on any more children. Who'd want more after Margaret and you? They'd already given away the cribs and the strollers and the high chair. Everything up in the attic was mine, bought new for me."

"Well, you were always Dad's favorite and ended up being Mom's."

"No, that's not true, Buddy. She loved you best. And I didn't burn my test because I got a bad grade. Webby burned his and I threw mine in, too, because I was his girl."

"What did you get?" Daddy asked.

"An A minus."

"You burned an A minus?" James asked, incredulous.

"The A minus was already in my head, and burning it made Webby less lonely. Boy, those tires made a black smoke."

And so it went for a couple of hours, mostly between James and his friends, who seemed to have an endless supply of tripping stories. Stony and Del left after lunch. The rest of us lingered over the crusting remnants of food. At last Aunt Edna said, "Well, I love you all, but I've got some bad news." James sat there silently with his head bowed, and I sat between my girls holding each one's hand. Thelia listened with her hand over her mouth, but I think she was only concealing the fact that she already knew.

When Aunt Edna finished, Daddy asked, "What can we do, little sister?"

"Well, I wish there was something you could do. I know it would make you feel better if there was something you could do. James and Sarah are here. I'm lucky to have them. There's nothing in the world I need. I was thinking maybe you could come down next weekend and help me with my paperwork, Buddy. I want to make sure all that's settled before I get too sick."

"There's no other doctors, somebody you could see?" my mom asked.

"I'm tired of seeing doctors. And I'm tired of medicine. Everyone's done their best. It's all right to die when you're tired. I've had a real good life and I'm not sorry one bit but for the time I'll lose with James."

An hour later everyone was gone, with promises to return the next weekend. Michelle told me she'd quit her job and come help me and I told her not now, maybe later. Thelia spent some time with her father alone in the bedroom and came out alone, wiping her eyes. Billy just seemed bewildered by it all. While his mother was in talking to James he asked me, "Does this mean Grandpa will come home?"

"I don't know," I said. "I haven't talked to him about that."

"He won't live here by himself. He likes company."

□ □ □

I took Aunt Edna and James down to the Worthington in the early afternoon. Aunt Edna wanted a nap before they went down to dinner that night, and she figured she'd get to wake up twice in a fancy hotel for the price of one night. I picked them up again the next morning after breakfast.

"We could see the Blackstone Hotel from our window, Sarah. Mr. John F. Kennedy spent the last night of his life there. I hope he had a good night's sleep in Fort Worth," James said. The Worthington lays out a pretty fine buffet on Sunday mornings, and James said he ate some of everything. "The man made an omelet while I stood there and waited on it," he said. "It didn't seem like much of an improvement over having a waitress bring it to me. Edna said everything looked grand, but it just seemed like a lot of shuffling to me, moving from one place to another to fill out your plate. Coffee was good though. I had three cups of that coffee, and one little glass of every kind of juice. I'm a good juice drinker."

My Aunt Edna loved him so. She just gawked at him and smiled, waiting for each word to balloon from his mouth, become bulbous and transparent, and then pop. Watching her with James was little different from watching Susan with Scott: it filled me with a vaguely nauseous envy of joy.

□ □ □

Aunt Edna's first week of marriage was the last she spent outside her home. We went to see her doctor twice and I went back a third time to be trained to do injections. Aunt Edna would need them for pain during the last stages. She spent an hour with a lawyer preparing her will.

James didn't accompany us and she asked me to wait in the lounge. We visited her credit union and bank where she closed one account and opened another. I had to sign a signature card, which would give me the ability to pay her bills.

At the end of the week, we all went to the Kimbell to see an exhibition that opened while Aunt Edna and I were in Scotland. *Paper to Stone, Stone to Oil: Three Centuries of Drawing, Sculpture, and Sculptors' Drawings* was a fascinating collection of sculptors' preliminary works, the sculptures themselves, and other artists' renderings of these same sculptures. Here was a study of how the two-dimensional informed the three-, and vice versa. The exhibition began with several sixteenth- and seventeenth-century European academy charcoals of classical statuary. Within moments we were standing beside the statues or casts themselves and were able to judge the early classroom work of several painters who'd later become quite famous. We all walked slowly through the galleries, listening to our headphones. Aunt Edna had James's elbow firmly in hand, keeping him away from the many plinths and pedestals. We moved on to the preparatory drawings of Bernini and Rodin, Degas and Calder, their respective sculptures, and finally to sketches and paintings by more modern artists of these earlier works. A bright, multicolored Calder was suspended in the last gallery. Hung on the walls around it, as if the mobile had been put into a kaleidoscope, were twenty paintings of this same mobile from different angles by art students at Texas Christian University.

But I have to say I didn't grant much attention to the art. Before we'd left the first gallery a guard approached James and asked quite bluntly, "Sir, are you vision-impaired?"

I think James thought, at first, that the question came from his headset. "What's that?" he asked, taking the phones from his ears.

"All the sculptures that have the raised blue dot on their pedestals may be touched," the docent explained.

"Oh, thank you," Aunt Edna said. "We didn't know."

The man smiled and returned to his station beneath a doorway connecting two galleries. Museum guards are always prepared for earthquakes. If the earth is struck by a planet-wide quake it will be populated afterwards by an inordinate amount of patient, art-loving vigilants.

"They want him to touch the statues," Aunt Edna told me.

"Don't let me knock them off, Edna," James said. "I know this stuff is expensive."

"Do you want to touch them?" Aunt Edna asked.

"Of course, I do. I could listen to this tape recording in my own bathroom for all I'm getting out of it."

"All right, all right."

We approached a small Roman copy of a Greek torso very slowly, still unsure of ourselves, so unaccustomed were we to touching museum displays. The act of reaching out seemed taboo. I was afraid he might jump up and run away, if the poor fellow had had legs. I suppose our timid hands might seem reverential from a distance. But it was only Aunt Edna and I who were awkward. James was gentle but inquisitive, as if he were looking for change in between the cushions of someone else's couch.

"What stone is this?" he asked.

"Marble," I said.

"It's been somewhere cold," he said. "This man's lost his ends."

"My body used to be like this, Edna, young and solid. I wish you'd known me then. Of course I wasn't as smart then as I am now. Let's go to the next one."

And so we proceeded from sculpture to sculpture, from entwined lovers, to a Degas dancer, to a small Egyptian sphinx, to a colossal Greek foot, to more modern vegetable forms. James was having a wonderful time, his hands remaking the sculptures just as later artists did by drawing and painting them. But halfway through the exhibition Aunt Edna said, "I can't find a chair."

"They could have done this same exhibition with chairs, couldn't they?" I said.

And she said, "No, no. I just want to sit down. I'm tired."

I found her a bench in the sunlit inner courtyard. We sat beneath Bourdelle's *Penelope*.

"What's wrong with her?" James asked.

"Are you OK, Aunt Edna?"

"I'm just so tired."

"Do you want to go home?"

"No. I want to see the rest. But I'm not going to be able to, am I?"

"I don't know. Do you feel that bad?"

"I need a wheelchair, Sarah. Maybe they have one."

"OK, I'll go ask."

So that's how we finished the exhibition, how we finished Aunt Edna's last afternoon outside her house. While I pushed the chair, James walked alongside her holding her hand. We'd move from work to work whenever Aunt Edna would say, "OK." James would reach out and survey the sculptures with one hand instead of two, unwilling to let go his grip on the crumbling stone of my aunt.

□ □ □

She took to her bed that day and from then on was out of it for only a few hours at a time. She'd go and sit in the recliner and watch TV for a while, or dabble with some watercolors, but was distracted by pain and discomfort, by the medication and the encroaching disease.

Mom and Dad returned for the weekend and were shocked by her decline, even though they'd seen it all before with his father. Aunt Edna sat with Dad for an hour going over some of her paperwork. She wanted him to be the executor of her estate. They sat at her kitchen table with their backs to us. As she'd speak he'd nod quietly in assent and make a note in a small binder. Dad called Aunt Margaret that weekend and told her how sick their sister was. He told her to come see Aunt Edna not for Edna's sake but for her own.

My parents stayed through Tuesday morning because Aunt Edna asked them to. She told Dad she didn't know what kind of condition she'd be in when he returned on Saturday and that there was something that needed to be done. She wouldn't tell him what.

Aunt Edna had pretty much lost all interest in food because it upset her stomach so, but she would eat applesauce and actually asked for banana pudding. On Monday night she got out of bed to eat her own dinner and fix James's. I offered to make it but she quite firmly put me in my place this one last time by squeezing my wrist and saying, "It pleases me to do for him. Tell him to get in here; I want him to watch me cook his dinner."

"Yes, ma'am."

I was afraid to leave the kitchen for fear she'd lose her grip on the stove. But I brought James back and sat him down. She asked him, "What's your favorite food in the world, James Laurent?"

"You," he said.

"James."

"You know what it is."

"Do you want an egg sandwich tonight?"

"I'd eat one three times a day," he said. "Don't have to chase it around a plate. Pick it up once. Three eggs, break the yolks, salt and plenty of pepper, white bread."

Aunt Edna bent over and took her cast-iron skillet from the oven, where she kept it at hand. Mom and Dad came in then and sat down, and we watched and listened to her heat the pan, melt the butter, break open the three eggs, and fry them. She ladled them onto a slice of Mrs. Baird's bread, doused them with salt and pepper and covered them with a second slice. Then she carried the plate to James and sat down next to him with her plastic cup of applesauce.

James picked up the sandwich and said, "See, that's the last time I'll have to find it. Some people add bacon to their egg sandwich and that makes the kitchen smell good but then it's not an egg sandwich anymore. You add more to it and it gets less. Thank you for making this egg sandwich for me, Edna."

She took a half spoonful of sauce and watched him eat. It was such an intimate scene, James eating and her watching, that I felt ashamed to look. It was something I had no right to witness. My parents got up first and left, and so I followed them, still in training. It was the last meal she cooked for him, the last thing she cooked for anybody, after doing it for thousands for forty years or so. Everyone now laments the loss of the artist, but those of us who knew her miss the cook more.

□ □ □

On Tuesday morning, at eight, a police car pulled up outside the house. Aunt Edna had called the Fort Worth Crimewatch number that runs across the bottom of the TV screen during certain news stories. When the police arrived, a detective and a uniformed officer, she'd just been through the exertions of getting up and going to the bathroom and was still breathing hard even though she was lying in bed. I answered the door. The detective asked for Aunt Edna and I took him into her bedroom. My parents and James and the uniformed officer followed. Introductions were made around the room. My parents and James were clearly at a loss.

"What's going on?" my father asked.

"I asked them to come see me, Buddy. I've done something I had to do even though I knew it was against the law. No one knows about it but me [this was a lie for my sake]. You and Margaret both, and you, too, James, have a right to know what I've done and why I did it. And the police are here because I didn't want you to ever feel you were hiding something. It's wrong to ask people to do that. I get more confused every day so I wanted to do this now, while what I did still makes sense to me."

"Are you ill, Mrs. Laurent?" the detective asked.

"Yes," she said. "I have pancreatic cancer."

"May I sit in this chair to take your statement?"

"Yes, sir."

He took a clipboard and a small tape recorder from his briefcase.

My father squatted at Aunt Edna's bedside, "Why don't we see a lawyer first, sister? Get some legal advice."

"I don't need any legal advice, Buddy. I don't need a lawyer." She turned to the detective. "This is what I did: When I found out I had the cancer two months or so ago, I was still caring for my mother, Mrs. Elizabeth March Hutton. I'd been caring for her for twenty years. She was an invalid. She was eighty-nine years old. It came to my mind that she would be lost in this world without me. She was estranged from her other children. I had no children. Her life was almost at an end. Her most fervent prayer was that she'd die before any of her children did. She thought this pain would be more painful than dying herself. I didn't know where she'd go after I was gone. She'd had personal care from a loved one for so long that a nursing home would have been a slow and lonely death. I decided not to let her suffer through my death and her death, too. I felt as if she were my child as well as my mother and that I was ultimately responsible for everything she did and would suffer. And so I put her to sleep. I gave her medication and she died in her sleep. That was on May 18. She died in her sleep without pain and I did it. I have since been on a trip to Scotland and married Mr. James Laurent here. I know that makes me look bad but I stand by my actions and am unrepentant, though I have assailed myself with every argument I can come up with. It was a decision I made for us as a couple, my mother and me. I am prepared to answer any questions and acquiesce to any judgments. I only hope that my brother and sister can forgive me, that my husband will forgive me, even though I'll tell you all right now I'll never be sorry for what I've done. We lived in our own little world and in that world I did the right thing. There's no present and future pain for her. That's all I have to say."

My father left the room, followed by my mother. James sat silently, his hands on his knees. The detective looked at me because he must have felt I was staring at him. He spoke to Aunt Edna, "You'll have to excuse me, ma'am. Our department usually receives tips from informants. We offer a thousand-dollar reward for tips that lead to convictions. This is a little bit out of our normal line of work. May I use your telephone?"

"Yes," Aunt Edna whispered.

The uniformed officer followed the detective into the living room. James and I sat with Aunt Edna. She smoothed out the sheets over her stomach and legs.

James said, "Why'd you have to tell these men this thing? Wouldn't confessing to me have been enough? Why'd you have to hurt everybody? Why'd you have to be so selfish to confess, to bring all this attention to yourself?"

"I didn't want to die with it, James. I didn't want you to live with it alone. These policemen have protected me all my life and I did something behind their backs and now I'm making it right."

"You did what was right two months ago. This was wrong. They're going to take you from me. I've got so little of you left and they're going to take . . ." His voice dissolved and he put his hands over his mouth, the way I'd put my hands over my eyes. A single sob escaped before he brought himself together enough to speak again. "I oughtn't to cry in front of white people," he said.

"What?" I asked. "James?"

"I don't like crying in front of white people. I've done it too much lately. When I was a boy my daddy dropped me off at the school for the blind. He was going to leave me there with all them strange people and noises. My teachers were black but the principal was an old white man. I started to cry and Daddy bent down and popped me and told me I was never to cry in front of white folks, that I was to be prouder than that."

But James couldn't help himself and covered his mouth with his broad, callused hands again. His pupils swung like tree branches in a storm.

"I'm sorry, honey," Aunt Edna said. "I'm sorry."

He stood up, let his hands flail in darkness. "I know you married me out of pity, to give me this damned old house. Well, I won't have it. All I wanted was you." His knuckles were slamming against the chair and the wall behind him. I took hold of him bodily.

"Stop," I said.

"Get me out of here," he yelled.

Together we left the room. Aunt Edna's face was grief-torn, contorted and pale.

All the way to the back porch he was whispering to me, saying over and over, "They're gonna take her, they're gonna take her."

The concrete was still cool, but the day was warming in waves of heat. Vegetation shimmered in the rising air. The morning dogs were quieting one by one and even the insects seemed to be in a frantic search for some place to hide from the sun. It didn't seem fair that it should be so mercilessly hot, day after day. Our heat wasn't the heavy sog of the indolent South but the heat of an active, searing force. It used up all the oxygen in the near combustion of grass and bark. The sun made all colors reflect light, even the dark undersides of dead leaves, the black holes of squirrel dens. The house behind us and the yard beyond expanded in cracks of rasping release, searching for a way out of themselves.

James sat on the stone stoop, his own face blown dry. He asked me, "Do you think she did this thing because of me?"

"No," I said. "And even if she did, you were the third reason. She was second and Grandma was first." I was my aunt's disciple but all I wanted to do at that moment was set this person I worshipped on a pedestal so I could throw rocks at her. James was hurting so badly. "She didn't give Grandma the chance to reciprocate," I said. "She might have wanted to take care of her in her illness. She might have wanted a daughter again at last. Maybe it would have saved her opinion of herself at the end of her life."

"That's a nice thought, Sarah. But I knew your Grandma, too, remember? She was a relentlessly sad old lady. She spent her days manipulating your sweet aunt. She was like a two-year-old gone wild in rage and jealousy and suspicion and hunger. She sucked up Edna's life. There was hardly room for anyone else in it. Believe me, I tried. People didn't visit this house because there wasn't room inside it for more than two."

"But she didn't give any of the rest of us the chance to take care of Grandma."

"She knew you wouldn't. Who'd ask somebody to take care of a child like that?"

"James, when she was in Scotland, when we were in Scotland spreading the ashes, she did it with her hands, and before she finished, she put her fingers in her mouth. There was ash on them and they came out clean."

"She loved her momma," he said. "She loved every moment of that bitterness. I can't explain it. She can't either. I've asked her."

"It wasn't right, though," I said. "Grandma had a right to her pain, as much as any of us."

"That's sweet, Sarah. That's pretty. That's why they're going to take her away. There's how many days left? And we're going to lose those. Would you allow your child to suffer?"

"What?"

"If one of your girls was going to exist only in misery and pain, even if it was only emotional, would you let that slide by?"

"I'd have to."

"Would you?"

"I'm going to go back inside. That policeman just hung up the phone."

"Take me," he said.

My father was speaking to the detective. He said, "I'm sorry. We're all a little stunned. We thought my mother died a natural death."

"Do you think your sister is a danger to anyone else, or that she might hurt herself?"

"No, sir." Then my father said a strange thing. He said, "I don't think she meant to hurt anyone."

The detective tilted his head slightly. "How ill is she?"

"She won't live another two weeks," Daddy said. "What happens now?"

"They're going to send out a homicide detective and he'll work up the case. I'd like to get everyone's name, address, and their relation to Mrs. Laurent before I leave. Homicide should be out sometime this morning or in the early afternoon. There was a shooting at a convenient store this morning and they're all over there right now."

"Can you tell us what will happen?" my father asked.

"Homicide will do an investigation," he said.

"But there's nothing to investigate. My mother's body was cremated and her ashes spread in Scotland, all over Scotland. My sister lived here alone with my mother. You know as much about this as the rest of us."

"They'll do the investigation. They'll interview Mrs. Laurent in depth and will probably want a statement from each of you."

"But she's confessed. I'd like to know if she's going to be arrested."

"Homicide will send the results of their investigation to the district attorney's office. The D.A. will decide whether to issue a warrant and arrest her or forward the case to the Grand Jury. The Grand Jury will either indict or no bill the case."

"How long would that take?"

"Perhaps a month or more, depending on their caseload."

"She'll be gone by then," my father said.

"I think she's figured that out," the detective said, and once again opened his notebook.

My father put his hands in his pockets and walked away.

This was the first of many times that Aunt Edna was accused of being calculating and manipulative. One columnist even went so far as to compare her case to the somewhat more common murder/suicides that end troubled romances. Although her death wasn't self-inflicted, it was imminent. By committing her crime shortly before her death she knew she'd escape punishment. That was why she waited till she was so close to losing her life, the papers asserted: she would get away with murder. Our trip to Scotland was described as a "vacation." Her marriage to James was "bizarre," the last act of a "tortured mind." All of this and more was to come. In the meantime, the policemen left and another set arrived.

Aunt Edna spent most of the day alone in bed. She was questioned first and then the rest of us, one by one. Every time I'd go in to see her she'd ask how James was.

"He's a mess," I told her. "Thelia is coming over to see to him after she's found someone to watch Billy."

"Doesn't James want to see me?"

"They're questioning him now, Aunt Edna. They even asked me if I didn't think all this was planned so you and James would inherit the house, so that y'all could be together."

"Nonsense," she said. "He'll be all right. James is solid."

"You've made him unsolid."

"I didn't plan anything, Sarah. Everything happened one day at a time like it always does. I didn't go looking for someone to kill any more than Sam went looking for an affair. One day the reason is just there."

Her voice was weak and ragged, like the slow dry turning of a wire and screen flour sifter.

"Look, you can't expect James to be as strong as you. Your loss came two months ago. His loss is approaching. Your grief will last only for the time between Grandma's death and your own. His will go on and on."

"I know it was selfish to love him. I tried for a long time not to, but I couldn't help it. I know it's the worst thing I've ever done. Sarah, I don't want him to suffer."

"I know," I said.

"Whenever he comes in here, he can hardly speak he's so worked up. I don't want him to suffer."

"I know."

"Any longer than he has to. There'll come a time when I'm no longer here but my body will linger and James will linger, too, suffering. He doesn't need to."

"We'll see when the time comes," I said.

"I don't want James to suffer."

"It's too late," I said.

"Any longer than he has to."

"OK."

□   □   □

James finally went back in to see her late in the afternoon and spent an hour with her alone. He came back out for dinner, and Thelia offered to take him home but he refused.

"This is where I live for now," he told her.

My parents went home to Saint Louis for a couple of days so Dad could attend to a few things at work. I worried about them all night, as he'd insisted on going home that evening. It was a long drive north in the dark. I kept waking up and figuring out where they were on I-35. About the fifth time this happened I realized how quiet the house was. The groans and pops of the walls had ceased. It was as cool as it was going to get that night, the mid-eighties. The fan of the air conditioner seemed to muffle everything else. James was in bed with Aunt Edna. He was a flopper. He'd toss himself from side to side all through the night, and the old springs on Aunt Edna's bed would creak and gurgle. I listened for a long time late that night but never heard James roll. It was irritating that he wouldn't simply turn over and let me go back to sleep. And then, in this oppressive silence, I crept back to the detective's questions about whether Aunt Edna might hurt herself, or if she might be a danger to someone else. If she'd calm the sufferings of her own mother, why wouldn't she assuage her own, or even James's in the same way? Mightn't even James, in his present state, suggest it, ask for it? I pulled the sheet off my legs and sat up. The silence was stifling. I was sure I was the only living being in that house. What an idiot I was not to have thought of these possibilities sooner. I was always arriving at conclusions only after they were obvious. I stood up and wavered in the darkness, waiting to let my feet get their bearings. The closest street lamp was half a block away. I could just make out my open door. It's narrow rectangle was only one degree lighter than the darkness itself, a gradation of shading I've never been able to obtain with paint or charcoal. I stepped quietly down the hall and into their room. I stood there, holding the casement so as not to lose my balance in the dark. All was quiet. Surely I ought to hear their breathing. I nearly fell over when James said, "Who's that?"

"It's me," I whispered hoarsely.

"Everything's all right, Sarah. She's sleeping now."

"OK," I said and then, "Jesus, you scared me half to death."

"Fat people walk heavy," he said. "Go back to bed."

"OK." Still, my heart was pounding as I slid under the sheets. I got up again and turned on a small lamp to alleviate that consuming darkness and the little black corner it had backed me into. And there I lay for another two hours under a single sheet, staring at one of Aunt Edna's paintings and the very chair beneath it, wondering once again which came first, the statue or the study, suspicion or knowledge, and which would be my final resting place when all this was over with.

□ □ □

If my father was angry with Aunt Edna he never let on. After that first brief exit from her bedside, he treated her as if her revelation were nothing more than a confession of the obvious, as though she'd told us she'd once stolen a pack of gum or had once masturbated. I've asked him twice how he feels and all he'll say is that Aunt Edna was responsible for Grandma. He and Aunt Margaret left their mother to her. He wouldn't second-guess her. "But I do feel guilty," he added. "If I'd been around more my little sister wouldn't have faced that awful decision alone." So my father carries this guilt of absence over the deaths of both his parents. He wouldn't condemn Aunt Edna. Over the next week he called the district attorney several times to make sure he understood the circumstances of his mother's death and how he, as her son, desired that no action be taken against his sister. The D.A. asked for a letter from Aunt Edna's doctor stating her diagnosis and the probable outcome. That letter was all the time we needed. The doctor, through kindness or procrastination, took two days to write it and then mailed it to the wrong office. The D.A. was in no hurry either. He sent the case to the Grand Jury two days before Aunt Edna died, and the Grand Jury, upon her death, simply dropped the case. So Aunt Edna has no criminal record. What did crawl out of a hole as a result of all these phone calls and procedures and police reports was a single reporter from the *Star-Telegram*.

□ □ □

Daddy picked up Aunt Margaret at DFW a couple of days later and on the drive to the house told her about the killing. She thought she was coming home only to see a dying sister. By this time Aunt Edna was completely bedridden. She'd cooked her last meal, painted her last chair. She drank from a straw and urinated into a bedpan. Her feet were swelling and beginning to turn purple. Her hands seemed huge on her wrists. First her eyes and then her skin took on the hue of dried squash, her body a gourd hung on a fence. James and I massaged her back whenever she asked and ceaselessly offered food and water. "Is there anything you want, Aunt Edna?" I asked countless times, till she stopped answering and waved me away. We rented a hospital bed and Daddy picked her up while I broke down her old bed and rolled the new one under her. Her back hurt the most. The cancer seemed to put pressure on her spine. For now she was on pain pills but in the refrigerator, for later, were several vials of morphine. The doctor said when she asked for it, I could give Aunt Edna a shot a day.

My Aunt Margaret, I want to say the best thing about her that I can: she left almost as soon as she arrived. Uncle Alf and JoAnn remained in Phoenix, I think, under house arrest. She didn't recognize James as Aunt Edna's husband. She didn't eat a single meal with us. She never removed the strap of her purse from her shoulder. When Daddy brought her in to see Aunt Edna, her usual language left her. She stood erect and motionless, her eyes dead insects between the window and screen. Aunt Edna's bed was tilted up somewhat so she wouldn't have to crane her neck to see.

"Hello, Sister," Aunt Edna said. Her lips were yellow and wet, and her own eyes were already washing out, becoming flaccid and unaware, so different from the eyes that had guided the brush.

"Why?" Aunt Margaret asked.

"I don't know anymore, Sister. I'm sorry."

"What's to be done?"

"I've only got to die now," Aunt Edna said.

"Do you want me to forgive you?"

"If you want to, Sister."

"You haven't called me Sister since we were children."

"I feel like a child again. Then I feel old. Then like a child."

"Momma could have been here kissing you good-bye right now."

"Aunt Margaret," I said softly.

But it was too late. Aunt Edna's chin fell to her thin nightgown and she was weeping, having no strength nor breath enough to weep, yet her eyes still watering and her head dipping in repeated motions of loss and loss and loss.

Aunt Margaret turned and left the room.

James asked the room loudly, "Who was that come calling from hell?" He struggled up from his chair and together we tended to Aunt Edna as best we could. For several nights in a row, James slept in an armchair at the foot of the bed, his ear turned toward her. It was strange, walking into their room with a pill or a cup of water and seeing him staring into the corner, concentrating on her every breath. He became, at last, almost as depleted as Aunt Edna. He slept little, ate less and less as she did. I knew how he felt. When you're feeding someone with a baby spoon and after three bites they've had enough, your own hunger drops in empathy. Afterwards, away, I ate almost desperately, ravenously, affirming my fear of death.

I didn't know about it at the time, but after Aunt Margaret left the bedroom she asked my father what they would do about the house when Aunt Edna was gone. He told her he assumed that wouldn't be their problem. Their mother had left the house to Edna, and everything that was Edna's, according to Texas law, would belong to James. She asked if the marriage couldn't be annulled. "It's our house," she said. "We grew up here. It shouldn't even be Edna's because she shouldn't have inherited it. Momma shouldn't be dead. As far as I'm concerned it's still Momma's." My father held up his hands and told her he wasn't going to talk about it. He'd talk about it later. She said, "Well, then, take me back to the airport."

"Now?"

"Yes."

And he did. Margaret never saw her sister again and didn't come to the funeral. I suppose, to some extent, it's unfair of me to be so outraged at legitimate outrage. I didn't lose my mother by my sister's hand.

□ □ □

Other visitors that last week were Mrs. Rodriguez from next door. She brought James and me lunch several times, but only once went in to see Aunt Edna, crossing herself as she left the room. Two of my aunt's coworkers from the school cafeteria came by and held her hand for almost an hour each. James asked Brother Roberts to drop in and he did, laying his old, water-stained Bible on Aunt Edna's bed, but curiously, holding only James's hand.

"Who is God?" Brother Roberts asked.

James answered, "God is the best man I can be."

Brother Roberts never paused. "God's the fella that's not going to let y'all be apart, wherever the two of you go."

"That's right," James said.

At that point Brother Roberts didn't know about Aunt Edna's involvement in Grandma's death. But he, and everyone else in Texas, did the next day. The *Star-Telegram* called that evening, asking for an interview. I told them no. The story was in the next morning's paper. The headline read DEATHBED CONFESSION. At five o'clock in the afternoon there was a live news broadcast from a truck parked in front of the house. All they had was the police report, but that was enough, along with pictures of the house with the shades down. Reporters kept calling and ringing the doorbell until I took the phone off the hook and pulled the fuse on the bell. Our mail went missing for three days in a row. The lead in the evening news was invariably, "There's a confessed killer dying inside this innocuous home on this quiet street in north Fort Worth. She committed the perfect crime and will go to her death unpunished." There were, by week's end, interviews with the district attorney, Grandma's doctor, some of Aunt Edna's coworkers, and of all people, that plot-selling undertaker. *Time* magazine had a little bottom-of-the-page, news-disguised exposé.

Aunt Edna was unaware of everything outside the house and unaware of almost everything in her bedroom. She wasn't interested in TV. I carried in several of her art books but they were too heavy to rest on her lap, so I'd hold them open and turn the pages, much as she must have done with *Scotland from Above* for Grandma. The first plate or two would hold her interest but then her eyes would glass over and sooner or later she'd look at her hand or pull at her nightgown. I fed her pudding and baby food and sips of apple juice and water. She'd take a bite or two, then hold her lips tightly compressed.

"Have a little more, Aunt Edna."

She'd frown and shake her head, close her eyes.

Her doctor came by the house. He never mentioned the news stories. He said we could take her to the hospital and have her blood cleaned but that it would only delay the inevitable by a couple of days. He gave her a shot of morphine, showing me how once again.

Two days later she stopped speaking and eating. She lay still in her bed except for an occasional stroke of her hand across a transparent canvas. She didn't manufacture a God in her last weeks, or recall some old faith, but moved from one memory of painting to another. I'd gone to two shots a day. Each time we touched her, she moaned in pain. Her muscles ached with dehydration. She was slowly dying of thirst.

I was more worried about James at this point than my aunt. He'd sit and talk to her, begging her to say something back or just squeeze his hand. Several times Daddy had to help him from the room because his body couldn't hold direction.

Aunt Edna's breath began to catch and rattle and for two days I thought she'd die within the hour. The sound was almost too much for James. He'd put his hands over his ears and bow over and ask, "Why do You make her suffer?" He whispered to her, "Go on now. I'm all right now."

But he lied. When he wasn't with her, he paced the house, counting the steps, turning at the exact same place each time. I thought he'd wear through the oak to the earth and then go on through that. I'd find him exhausted, leaning up against a window or the bookshelf, as if it were the view or the story that was too much to bear. Then I'd try to make him eat something or go to bed. I think he thought the only way to ease his pain was to die before she did. If she wasn't going to die, then he would.

I did what she'd asked. At least I think she asked it. While James and Daddy were out of the room, I gave her more morphine than the alleviation of pain required. She died in the evening, at seven-fifteen. Daddy was sitting on the back-porch stoop. I was in the kitchen. James was with her. He called out to us, so he wouldn't be alone.

□ □ □

So there are two murderers in the family now, me and Aunt Edna, though I've kept my secret longer. It has taken me a year to write about only three months of my life, to come to legible terms with it. I realize now that I'll always be behind, falling further behind, and that there's no hope of catching up by the time I die. There are too many things to examine in a given day to reach any full understanding before the next morning.

□ □ □

We had Do Not Resuscitate orders and so the paramedics simply confirmed the death and made a short report. It was the staff of the crematorium who took Aunt Edna's body away from the house. How empty the house felt when she was gone, like the slipcase of a lost book. The house seemed that unnecessary. James left ten minutes after the body was gone. He went home to Thelia and Billy. When we pulled up in the car, they came outside quietly and both of them found places under his arms.

Daddy and I cleaned the house. We returned the hospital bed and threw away that fat ring that raised the toilet seat, the plastic juice bottles, the bedpans. We took the leftover cans of Ensure and the baby food to the local food bank. Daddy, as executor, met with Aunt Edna's lawyer and began the long process of closing down a person's life in paper.

Once again we moved all the chairs out into the vacant lot for a memorial service. I retrieved Aunt Edna's ashes in the box she painted for her mother.

□ □ □

For a time, following my aunt's funeral, I remained in her home and spent hours moving from chair to chair. For hours I would examine the shadow of the chair I'd just left. What a wonderful deep blue shadow a chair makes. Aunt Edna left the house to Daddy and Aunt Margaret, with the provision that James or I could live there as long as we liked. The furnishings were to be parceled out as my father saw fit. All her nieces and nephews received gifts of several thousand dollars. To James she left a surviving spouse's pension. And finally, she left her "lunch money," as she termed it in the will, to my daughters and to Billy for college tuition. By the time they all graduate, she'll have returned every dime to a school. To me she left her art supplies and all her paintings. When I heard this I walked out into the middle of the street and stood in the dust of her leaving. I did not know what to do with this inheritance, all the knowledge, the sketches, the half-used tubes of paint, the quick renderings, and the finished paintings. There was too much. I knew too much.

If my aunt had been anybody else, the fact that she married a blind black man late in her life would have been the most noteworthy event of her life, but that event was surpassed in significance by her last moments with her mother, and once again by her paintings.

One of the reasons E. B. White left New York City for a Maine farm was because he had too many chairs, one hundred and fifteen of them in all. He was chased out of New York by chairs. Chairs chased me out of Aunt Edna's house as well. One day, a month after her death, I picked up a sheaf of drawings and two of her paintings and carried them to the Pickett Gallery on West Seventh Street. Jeremy Pickett dealt in contemporary art and sculpture. I showed him the oils, the watercolors, the charcoals. From the first, he was interested, spoke to me as if I were the artist. I corrected him immediately.

"Is she represented by any other galleries currently?" he asked.

"No."

"Where has she shown?"

"Nowhere."

"Never?"

"No."

"How long has your aunt been painting?"

"Maybe thirty years."

"So there's more than these?"

"There's everything."

"Of this quality?"

"These were by the door as I went out."

"Are you going to represent your aunt?"

"I suppose," I said. "She can't. She died several weeks ago."

"Are the paintings yours now?"

"Yes."

"If I locked up now, could we go see the rest?"

"You don't want these?"

"I might want everything," he said and smiled.

He followed me back to the house that day and spent several hours going over the paintings. There were racks of them in the attic, and literally thousands of drawings and watercolors. Referring to the chairs, I said, "Insistent, wasn't she?"

"Poussin said of painting, 'It is necessary that the subject be in itself noble, and that it give scope for revealing the painter's mind and industry.' I don't know what he'd think of chairs but I think your aunt succeeded with her choice of subject."

He left the house that day with a promise to make a few calls and let me know how the collection might best be handled. In the meantime he asked that I pull everything out of the attic, appalled by this choice for art storage. He reminded me of Jonathan, and I trusted him immediately. But he wasn't even back at the gallery before he rang me on his cell phone.

"Sarah," he asked, "your aunt Edna, was she in the news lately?"

"Yes," I answered.

"It didn't strike me until just now. All right."

I thought that would be the last I'd hear from him, but the next day he came by with a contract that guaranteed him a flat 40 percent of any sale. It seemed reasonable and I signed it. That evening he called and asked if I could receive a guest, if I would lay out, make accessible, all of Aunt Edna's work.

"All at once?" I asked. "Which ones?"

"All of it. We'll come by in the late morning, about ten?"

"OK," I said, hoping this wasn't going to happen three or four times a week. I had thought it would all be displayed at his gallery.

I got up early and began to lean the canvases against chairs, one against the knees and one in the seat. I spread them on beds and on the kitchen and bathroom counters. I went out the back door, down the steps, and into the trees with paintings. When Jeremy arrived I was still mopping sweat from my brow. Our guest was none other than Benjamin Coates, the scion of Fort Worth real estate and east Texas oil fortunes. He and Jeremy walked from room to room, occasionally picking up a painting and examining it closely. After an hour Mr. Coates shook my hand, complimented Aunt Edna, and said to Jeremy, "I'm interested."

Mr. Coates left in his own car.

"Which one is he interested in?" I asked Jeremy.

"All of them. Everything," he said, beaming. "I knew he would be. I told him that's the only way we'd sell for now."

I was stunned. All I could think to say was, "I have to send one drawing to Scotland."

The negotiations took less than a week. Mr. Coates promised to keep the collection intact for a minimum of ten years. My father, James, and I could each select one painting to withhold. Mr. Coates would also retain any of Aunt Edna's chairs found to be represented in her work. He intended, but was not bound, to loan the art to local museums. The price was 1.17 million dollars.

What Mr. Coates bought, beyond the art and the chairs, was an amazing amount of attention. Once again Aunt Edna made headlines. Within four months the collection was a special exhibition at the Fort Worth Museum of Modern Art. By the end of the first year of Mr. Coates's ownership, he'd built a beautiful small museum for Aunt Edna in the arts district of Fort Worth, a block removed from the Kimbell and Amon Carter museums. The chairs sit below paintings of themselves much as they did in Aunt Edna's house. A catalog of the collection was published and quite frequently, paintings and chairs are loaned out to other museums. I am a part-time assistant curator. This work began as a request from Mr. Coates for an essay on Aunt Edna's last few months. He's getting more than he asked for.

Ruskin said that we draw to make "records of such things as cannot be described in words" or "to preserve something like a true image of beautiful things that pass away, or which you must yourself leave." I've found that my aunt Edna cannot be described in words. She left a way to know her in her work, and she left me a way to find myself in concave cakes of color, wrinkled aluminum tubes, and the hair of dead animals. Aunt Edna came back from Scotland with dozens of photographs of chairs. These are the chairs she'll never paint. I've begun to paint them for her. Perhaps it will only be a phase of my career, my blue chair period. Perhaps I will become a painter of chairs. I would like to merge my life gracefully with hers, without noticeable line, the brush strokes changing so imperceptibly that it will seem a natural transition from her life to mine, an artistic breakthrough that afterwards seems inevitable and well-deserved.

Sometimes I long for a chair like I long for sleep. Just let me sit down. It seems like both luxury and right.

In Aunt Edna's museum, whispers still fall softly against her paintings. They lodge in the curve of brush strokes and reside there like dust. It will be centuries before some conservator removes this residue of gossip and speculation. I walk through the museum and think about spraying the paintings with the juice of boiled green beans.

There are those who argue that the reason Aunt Edna confessed to the police at last was to ensure her own immortality, that she knew I'd take her paintings to the galleries. People say her ego was monstrous: to consider her own life so important that her mother couldn't go on living without her. I return to that table in Plockton, my dying aunt painting on a napkin with water, producing only wetness and wrinkle. It was the painting she loved; it was her life she loved; it was her mother she loved.

□ □ □

At the funeral, Brother Roberts showed up without his toupee. He'd lost it. Couldn't remember where he'd last put it down. James sat in the front row, nodding to every word. I sat next to him, Thelia on the other side.

Brother Roberts said, "James here, this mourning husband, can't see us but he knows we exist. We can't see God but He's here, too."

James smiled into his lap and whispered, "I am twice removed from God."

The muscle relaxers slowed Grandma all the way down to death. Morphine, an opiate, carried Aunt Edna away as if she were ashes in a stream. All clouds seem cinereous now. Sometimes I think I wouldn't have told any of these things if I thought there was a God in heaven or that Aunt Edna would be embarrassed. The last thing Brother Roberts said: "Lord, we wanted more of her." I try to picture him skating on Duddingston Loch.

I've asked James recently if he felt she betrayed him. "No," he said slowly. "People focus on the wrong things. I'm more blind than I am black. She was more kind than she was white. We were a good couple. Turn your wipers down a notch, Sarah. It ain't raining that hard." He says he's decided at last to become "a man of loose habits and questionable morals." He says this and laughs, as if he sees a way. "I think I'm going to retire. I'm tired of mending chairs. It's my turn to sit down for a while." He has begun to leave by the door he came in. Thelia tells me he's taken to using the bathroom outdoors, in their backyard. She says he told her that man wasn't meant to pee in a pool of water. He never heard of a dog peeing in the water. So he pees on the ground, where it's quiet.

I've told Sam that the first requirement in returning home is going away. He tells me he has grown accustomed to waiting, lives in waiting almost as happily as he can imagine a happy life. My daughters have grown sullen over our separation and blame me now more than Sam. When I tell them I want to scatter parts of myself all around the world, they say I've already done that to our family.

I train docents for Aunt Edna's museum. I tell them it's not what the matter is, but that it matters. I tell them to let only the blind touch the paintings.

Just before Aunt Edna passed away, I asked her where she'd like to be buried. She looked at me, faintly surprised, and smiled. It was the last time she smiled in my presence. Smiling, she asked, "Darling Sarah, where in the world would you like to go?"

"To Italy," I said.

"Then, me too."

Her ashes are scattered across Italy: in Florence, Venice, and Rome. Sam and I took her there. I am in Italy alone now. I watch the children walk to school and occasionally shake the pocket-worn silver on my wrist at them. Here, my wounded dimes are now foreign coins. I have become large, an expert in olives. A chair, at last, is simply a stable platform for repose.

Acknowledgments

□ □ □

Many people helped build this book. Wade Wilson sent along information on chair painters. Mr. Bob White of White's Funeral Homes, Weatherford, Texas, took time to speak to me about mortuary practice and law. Isabelle Tokumaru, a conservator at the Kimbell Art Museum, had wonderful advice on painting technique and was an insightful reader of the manuscript. Many artist friends shared their stories of painting chairs or visiting famous chair paintings. Anne Helmreich knew about Pittsburgh chairs and parking spaces. Jenny Conn walked her Fort Worth neighborhood in the early mornings and took pictures of chairs left in the yards. Elaine Markson, my patient agent, sold the manuscript to not one, but two publishers. Marah Stets, of Scribners, and Anne Czarniecki, of Graywolf, were both wonderful editors. My grandfather, Thomas Ely Dennis, wrote "Sweet Little Cafe" for my grandmother, Virginia Frances, in the 1930s. I miss the people and landscape of Scotland every day I'm not there. And finally, the characters of many of my books end up leaving Fort Worth, Texas. They're out of their minds. I'm staying put.

Suggested Topics for Discussion

○ ○ ○

1. In the opening chapter, the revelation of Sam's affair radically shifts the way Sarah views her husband, their marriage, and her plans for the future. After traveling to Scotland with Aunt Edna, have Sarah's feelings concerning the affair changed? Will she leave Sam, or will they work through their marital problems?

2. Sarah says she loves Aunt Edna and regrets not seeing her sooner. What do you make of Sarah's decision to stay with Edna? Is it motivated by love? Is it an act of revenge? A form of self-protection? Avoidance?

3. Sarah's parents, Aunt Edna, and James all provide Sarah with advice about her marriage. All three seem to suggest that Sarah should give Sam another chance, or at least give him an opportunity to explain his actions. What do you think about their opinions? Does Sarah take them to heart?

4. In Plockton, Aunt Edna puts her fingers in her mouth and sucks them clean of her mother's remaining ashes after she scatters them. What do you make of this action? What does it mean?

5. What do you think Aunt Edna is trying to say when she compares Bean Highe, the washerwoman, to Sarah?

6. Did your opinion of Aunt Edna change after she revealed how her mother died? Why or why not?

7. When Sarah goes to Jonathan's house to talk about Aunt Edna, her cancer, and the future of all her paintings, she asks Jonathan to draw her. Why? Does she have anything to feel ashamed about?

8. Do you agree with Aunt Edna's belief that it was right to hide her pancreatic cancer and the true nature of her mother's death from James until after their wedding?

9. Do you think Sarah's actions were justified when she did what Aunt Edna asked? What do you think motivated her decision to follow Aunt Edna's instructions?

ABOUT THE AUTHOR

Joe Coomer lives in Texas and Maine. He's fond of worn chairs and the artists who paint them. He feels there is still a great deal to be done in this field, and happily reports that in both Texas and Maine, chairs seem to be waiting patiently. Arise you artists, he calls, and turn to the warm support behind you. Is it not of noble stile? Your subject awaits. He likes dogs as well, and as a painting subject, they will also sit a spell.

This book is made possible through a partnership with the College of Saint Benedict, and honors the legacy of S. Mariella Gable, a distinguished teacher at the College.

Other titles in the series include:

Loverboy by Victoria Redel
The House on Eccles Road by Judith Kitchen
The Weatherman by Clint McCown
Collected Poems by Jane Kenyon
Variations on the Theme of an African Dictatorship by Nuruddin Farah:
    Sweet and Sour Milk
    Sardines
    Close Sesame
Duende by Tracy K. Smith
All of It Singing: New and Selected Poems by Linda Gregg

One Vacant Chair has been typeset using Trump Mediäval, a type-face designed by Georg Trump and first issued in 1954 by the Weber Foundry, Stuttgart, Germany. Book design by Wendy Holdman. Composition by BookMobile Design and Publishing Services, Minneapolis, Minnesota. Manufactured at Friesens on acid-free paper.